River Dragon

A Hidden Secret. An Ancient Prophecy. A Queen's Ordeal.

River Dragon
A Hidden Secret. An Ancient Prophecy. A Queen's Ordeal.

Rising Sun Press Works
P.O. Box 81, Grand Isle, ME 04746
www.riverasun.com

Library of Congress Control Number:
2024901890

ISBN (paperback) 978-1-948016-23-0
(hardback) 978-1-948016-19-3
(ebook) 978-1-948016-22-3
Sun, Rivera 1982-
River Dragon

Cover art and design by Rivera Sun

Reader Praise For *River Dragon*
Book 5 of the Ari Ara Series

"The characters are so alive that they get under your skin (and into your heart) like real friends and mentors. - **Anne Walter**

"Best storyteller in a generation! AND she makes nonviolent resolutions to complex problems seem exciting, realistic and deeply satisfying." - **Lisa Marshall**

"This latest is really popular in the YA world in my town. All I have to do is give the parents one Ari Ara book ... and it won't be long before they want more! (I suspect the parents are reading *River Dragon* just as eagerly as their children!)" - **Tom Hastings, Portland State University**

"*River Dragon* was my favorite book in the Ari Ara Series. The twists and turns made it a page turner." - **Darlene Goetzman**

"This book is a treasure for readers of all ages, but it's especially meaningful for our young people who may not yet see the power of peace over conflict. It's a remarkable guide to navigating life through nonviolent action." - **Heart Phoenix, River Phoenix Center For Peacebuilding**

"To read *River Dragon* is to enter a richly imagined world. It is to journey alongside a fifteen-year-old Ari Ara, fierce in her dedication to the nonviolent Way Between as she undergoes 'The Ordeal of Queens' in a world so much like ours in its 'pointless, painful devotion to war.' How she manages these ordeals, discovering herself and what she can offer her world, is beautifully narrated in this latest addition to the Ari Ara Series." **- Andrew Moss**

"The most important book I know. All the magic of *Narnia* and *Harry Potter* with a vivid, fun, and relatable embodiment of the deepest values needed right now." - **Anna Beale**

"I absolutely adore the Ari Ara Series. I think everyone should read these books! It's not only a fun epic adventure series but the nonviolent way between approach is inspiring. It is truly a creative masterpiece." **- Melissa Pember Karapanos**

"I laughed, cried and was thrilled by Ari Ara's courage and capacity to practice peace despite all odds. I am sharing this series as far and wide as possible." **- Madonna Quixley, Let's Talk Peace Ballarat, Australia**

"My family has enjoyed the whole Ari Ara Series immensely ... we've already started reading it all over again!"
- Karisha Longaker

"Peace for our children's children."
- Jeff Lott, Peace Week Delaware

"The perfect series to share with my children." **- Dr. Nick Meyer**

"Such a captivating series. It offers so much to learn about peaceful negotiation!" **- Carol Ranellone**

"It's not only engaging for young people, it's also inspiring for adults, including long time activists."
- Jan Slakov, Conscious Canada

"There is nothing like the Ari Ara Series in our current cultural landscape ... the kind of complexity, compassion and commitment to do no harm is the story that the human soul needs for our next level of development." **- Laurie Marshall, Unity Through Creativity Foundation**

"In a world oversaturated with violence, Ari Ara's adventures inspire young readers to challenge the status quo and build a more peaceful world." **- Patrick Hiller, father, Peace and Conflict Studies scholar**

For Cindy Reinhardt

Other Works
by Rivera Sun

Novels, Books & Poetry

The Ari Ara Series:
The Way Between
The Lost Heir
Desert Song
The Crown of Light
The Adventures of Alaren

The Dandelion Collection:
The Dandelion Insurrection
The Roots of Resistance
Winds of Change
The Dandelion Insurrection Study Guide
Rise & Resist

Other:
Billionaire Buddha
Steam Drills, Treadmills, and Shooting Stars
Rebel Song
Skylandia: Farm Poetry From Maine
Freedom Stories: volume one
The Imagine-a-nation of Lala Child

A Community Published Book Supported By:

David G. Schwartz and Alta H. Schwartz
Anna Beale
A'Marie B Thomas-Brown, Yes2Breadth
Alan Cohen
Andrew Moss
Anne Walter and Joe Grant
Heart Phoenix & Jeffrey Weisberg,
River Phoenix Center for Peacebuilding
ashley olson
Barbarians Dragonheart, Behavior Medicine Associates
Brigit McCallum
In memory of Avery Mikel
Xikuey Otzelotl
Romaldo and Carol Ranellone
Caroline Corum
Al Lawler Jubilee Partners Comer GA
Cindy Reinhardt
Beth Kopicki
Darlene Goetzman
David Hart
Debra Fant
Chili Palmer Finn
Aila and Amalea de Lorimier
Genevieve Emerson
Gerry Yokota
Hadley C
Luca Matthies
Jaimie Ritchie, Aikido Practitioner
Jan Slakov (Conscience Canada board member)
Jayanne Sindt

Jeff Lott/Peace Week Delaware
Joni Caldwell
Jennifer Atlee
Julian and Joann Terranova
John Raby
Karisha Longaker
Kathleen Temple
Laurie Marshall, Unity through Creativity Foundation
Leah Boyd
Leslie A. Donovan
Lisa J. Marshall
Lorraine & George Cook
"Lou" Laurie Engelhardt
Madonna Quixley, Let's Talk Peace Ballarat
Uma Schink
Maigan & Aeon Underwood
Maja Bengtson
Marada Cook
Marcella Makinen
Margaret Sharp
Marirose NightSong
Markus Seischab
'Dr. Mark' Stemen
Mary Ellen Quinn
Megan Toben
Melissa Pember Karapanos
Michael Harrington
Natalina
Natasha Léger, Executive Director,
Citizens for a Healthy Community
Dr. Nick Meyer
Oliver Hiller

Babu and Seneca
Sarah Morgan Bunting
Rebecca Zook
Rick Brown
Sam Trenka
Scott Springer, The Bay School
Prof. Sean Duffy, Albert Schweitzer Institute,
Quinnipiac University
Shawnee Baldwin, Acacia Zawadi: Seeds for Change Fund
AJNA NAYELI
Theresa McCarthy Flynn, OFS
T. Potter
Veralyn Kentin
Heather Carver
Vickie Aldrich
Virginia Dixon
Xenia Fox

&

Tom Hastings
in memory of
Rev James Lawson
who inspired so many of us to learn more nonviolence

River Dragon

by

Rivera Sun

Table of Contents

Chapter 1	Heir Apparent	pg. 3
Chapter 2	The Great Lady	pg. 15
Chapter 3	Nightmares	pg. 29
Chapter 4	Swords & Shields	pg. 39
Chapter 5	The Book of Queens	pg. 49
Chapter 6	Alinore's Journal	pg. 65
Chapter 7	The Gateway Abbey	pg. 79
Chapter 8	The Orphans Hall	pg. 93
Chapter 9	Triumph & Suspicion	pg. 99
Chapter 10	When I Am Queen	pg. 107
Chapter 11	For Love's Sake	pg. 115
Chapter 12	Marin's Mountain	pg. 123
Chapter 13	Two Dead Sisters	pg. 135
Chapter 14	The Brackenmarsh	pg. 147
Chapter 15	The Water Maze	pg. 161
Chapter 16	Fanten Dreams	pg. 179
Chapter 17	Seeker's Station	pg. 187
Chapter 18	The Ruse	pg. 195
Chapter 19	Two Roads	pg. 207
Chapter 20	The Citadel of the Sisterlands	pg. 221
Chapter 21	The Pledge	pg. 239
Chapter 22	The Sanctuary	pg. 253
Chapter 23	Prophecy's Daughter	pg. 257
Chapter 24	The Fanten Grandmother's Secrets	pg. 261
Chapter 25	River Dragon	pg. 277
Chapter 26	Nshoka Shulen	pg. 285
Author's Note		pg. 301
Acknowledgments		pg. 305
About the Author		pg. 307
Other Books By Rivera Sun		pg. 308

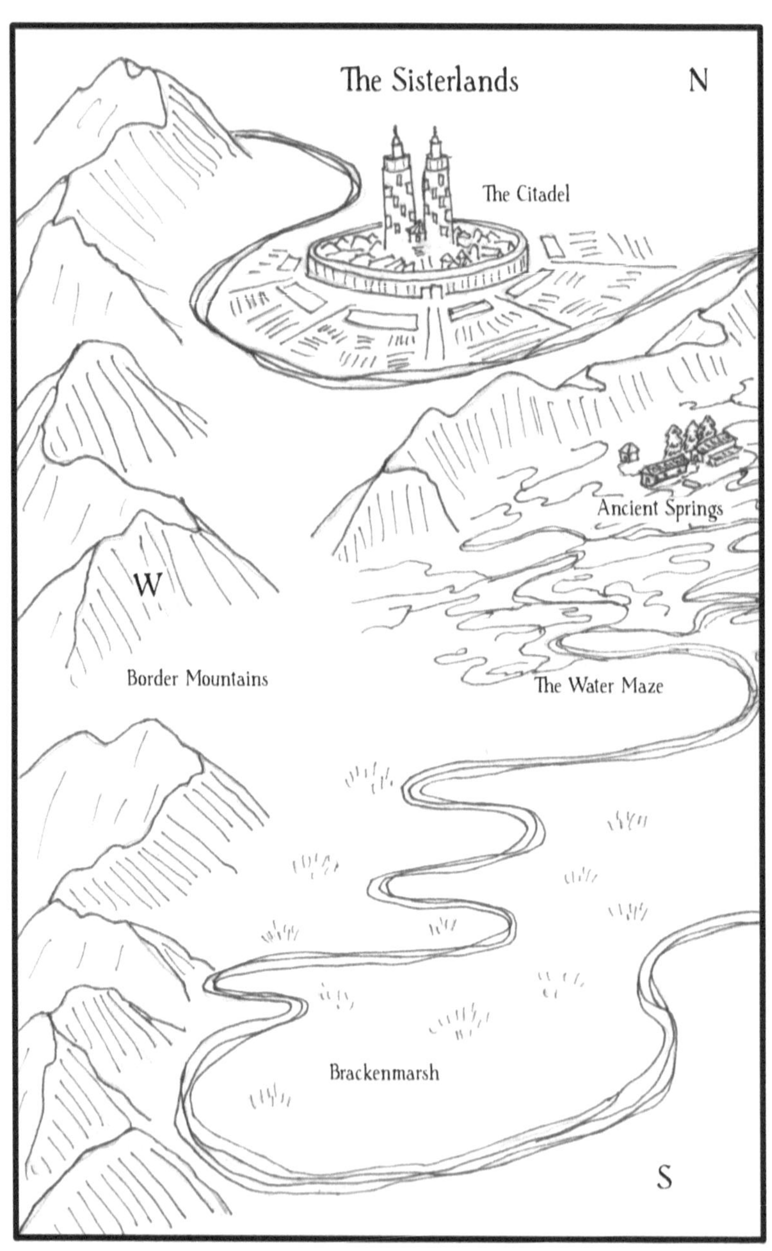
The Sisterlands
N
The Citadel
Ancient Springs
W
Border Mountains
The Water Maze
Brackenmarsh
S

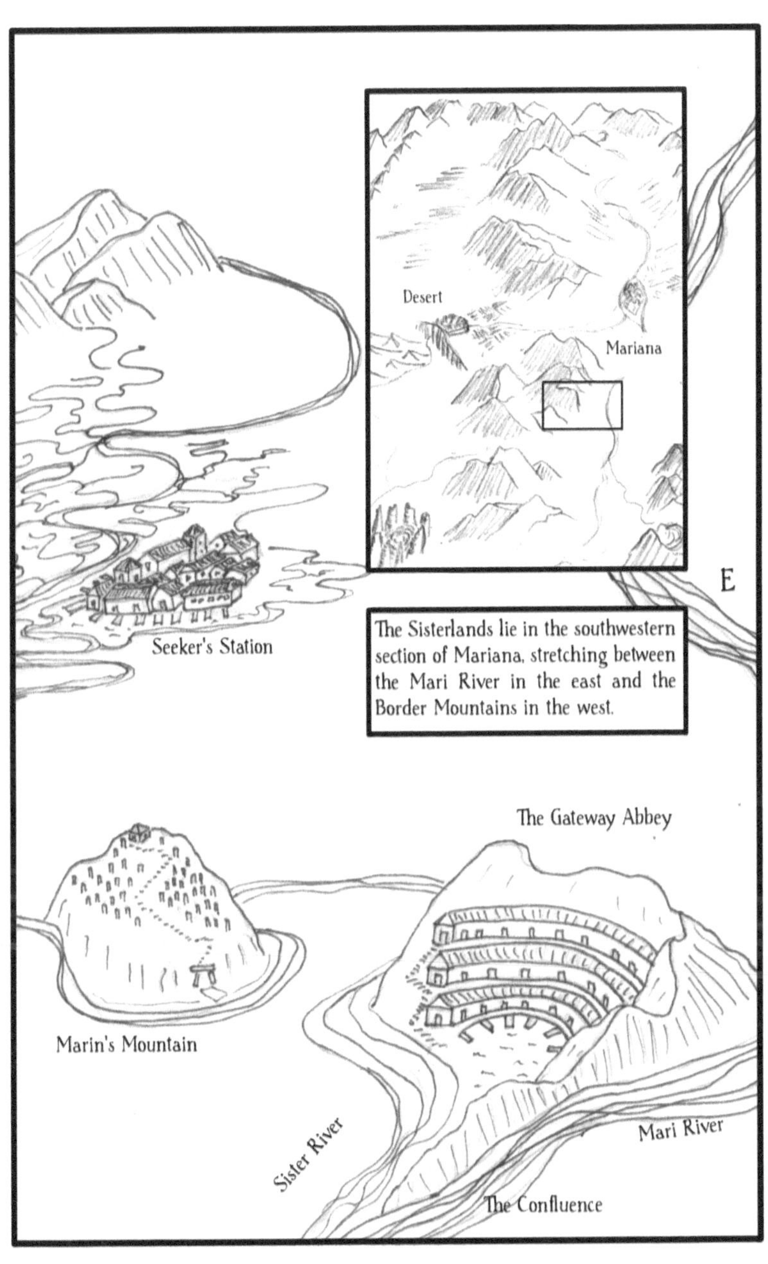
Desert
Mariana
E
Seeker's Station
The Sisterlands lie in the southwestern section of Mariana, stretching between the Mari River in the east and the Border Mountains in the west.
The Gateway Abbey
Marin's Mountain
Sister River
Mari River
The Confluence

The Prophecy of the Lost Heir

One will come, a child born of two lineages, mother dead, father distant. Lost at birth, appearing half-grown, this child shall inherit two thrones, one in the desert, the other on the water. Uniter, Divider, Liberator, Destroyer; floods follow in this one's footsteps, famine stalks the heels of the heir. Upheaval and conflict surround this child, a war breaker, change maker. By the Mark of Peace, the lost one is found. Then the once broken becomes whole; the once wounded, healed; and the once forgotten remembered again.

CHAPTER ONE

. . . . .

Heir Apparent

Gritting her teeth, Ari Ara waved to the crowd, a fixed smile plastered on her face. The horse fidgeted beneath her, sensing her discomfort and distraction. Her fitted jacket was so stiff that she could hardly move.

Designed to prevent slouching, Ari Ara thought in annoyance, *and any other motion unbefitting to a royal heir.*

Solid as a suit of armor - and just as uncomfortable - the jacket held her ramrod straight as she rode through the tight-packed streets. Thickly embroidered patterns of river dragons - the symbol of the royal house of Marin - curled around the cuffs, arms, collar, and panels of the jacket. The heavy fabric weighed more than the thin strands of silvermail beneath it. She'd argued against wearing the woven metal garment, but lost. The silvermail protected her from assassins' arrows. As the double royal heir to two thrones, her life was not merely her own. Her discomfort with the weight of security was a small price to pay for the stability of the world.

It's worth it, she told herself. *When I'm queen, I'll make it possible to ride through the streets without armor.* She grinned, thinking of all the changes she longed to make when she wore the crown. Build peace. Retire the army. Use the money to build schools. Train children to solve conflicts, not fight them. Teach everyone how to make peace not only possible, but inevitable.

Since the Great Lady of Mariana had summoned her to return home, Ari Ara had imagined this day a thousand times. She hadn't expected her arms to ache from hours of waving, however, nor for her legs to shake with cramps, nor her back to scream from riding a slow-plodding horse, nor for her cheek muscles to twitch from constant smiling. She tried not to squirm as the procession inched through the enthusiastic throng of people packed into the streets of Stoneport. At this rate, it would take them a week to reach the river dock where her aunt, the Great Lady Brinelle, waited to welcome the long-exiled heir and take her down the river to Mariana Capital.

Thank the ancestors we didn't try to ride all the way there, Ari Ara thought.

She'd rolled her eyes when Shulen – her gray-haired mentor - had insisted that they travel from the Spires to the Stonelands discretely. He'd served as Captain of the Guard under two queens and saw assassins hiding behind every bush. But she'd overlooked the tedium of wading through teeming masses of people. Never mind flung daggers or poison-tipped arrows. It was more likely that cheering students would crush her with adulation. It had taken them hours to cross the city.

Every fishmonger, farrier, and farmer wanted to see the fifteen-year-old daughter of Queen Alinore of Mariana and Tahkan Shirar, the Harraken Desert King. Schoolchildren and scullery lads scaled the pillars of buildings to see the fabled Lost Heir who had been found at age eleven, hidden in the High Mountains.

Street urchins and shopgirls scurried into the streets to catch a glimpse of a legend-in-the-making as she returned to her mother's lands after being exiled. Porters and potters packed the sidewalks, gawking at the child of their mortal enemies, the Harraken. Merchants and milliners jostled for a view of the girl who evoked hope and hate simply by being alive. Dockworkers and river sailors debated whether she'd defend the nation or betray them to the desert demons. Cooks and housekeepers argued about her outspoken dedication to peace. Warriors wondered what the Heir To Two Thrones heralded for their future.

Ari Ara resisted the urge to loosen her collar. The day's warmth made trickles of sweat run beneath the frothy cascade of shirt frills that fell like lily blossoms down her front. Her copper hair blazed in its braided crown and only the bronzed skin of her father's desert-dwelling people kept her from burning red as a hot coal.

Ahead of her, Minli of Monk's Hand swiveled on his horse's back to toss her a bolstering grin. His golden stallion stood with infinite patience, head high, swishing his white tail as proudly as if he bore the royal heir. The desert horse had once belonged to Ari Ara, but had traded loyalties the instant he met the one-legged Minli. Ari Ara couldn't blame the horse. She, too, held a ferocious loyalty to the fifteen-year-old boy. Minli was her best friend, her oldest friend. Under the tousled bird's nest of brown curls lay one of the best minds of their generation. Clever, studious, and quick-witted, Minli had hauled Ari Ara out of trouble more times than she could count.

Unbound by the same expectations of stiff dignity as she, Minli fanned the front of his white tunic against the heat. The black symbol of the Mark of Peace inked on the back puckered and billowed. The circle rippled, the two halves of river waves and sand dunes shifted as if wind-stirred. Ari Ara twitched her shoulders where, hidden under her clothes, the same black circle had been emblazoned on her skin, the sign that she was the heir. Ari Ara's eyes swept up to the flags that surrounded her procession, all bearing the same symbol, all borne by members of the Peace Force.

They carried no weapons. They fought no battles. They waged no wars.

They were followers of the Way Between, the ancient non-martial art of working for peace. They stopped fights and forged friendships. They resolved conflicts and aided reconciliation. They strove for a peace rooted in justice and had traversed the Border Mountains all year, quenching the smoldering embers of hatred that so often sparked the fires of violence into the inferno of war.

As soon as Ari Ara had been summoned to return to Mariana, twenty of the Peace Force members had gathered at her side. From their outposts in villages and mountain towns, they journeyed long and hard to assemble in a show of support. Commoners and nobles, riverlands residents and desert dwellers, elders and parents and youth, professors and carpenters: the Peace Force embraced them all. Ari Ara's smile shone as she gazed proudly at her friends. Each one had vied for a place in her honor guard.

We wouldn't miss this for all the coin in Mariana Capital, they'd written, sending word on the wings of messenger hawks. *It's a moment that will go down in history.*

Ari Ara wished her father was here. But the Marianan nobles had specifically - and strongly - insisted on disinviting the infamous Desert King from joining the returning procession. Tahkan Shirar had ridden off into the desert wilds in a storm of fury. No amount of diplomatic efforts had been able to smooth the matter over. Not yet. Tahkan would not forgive this insult easily. He seethed with pride and clung to honor. The copper-haired man hissed with ferocious temper and fierce protectiveness of his people.

I am going into the mountains, he wrote to Ari Ara, *where I can fling lightning bolts into boulders instead of at the heads of riverlands idiots.*

Given the glowering looks shot at the Harraken members of the Peace Force, the Desert King's absence was possibly for the best. Scars cut by millennia of wars would not be healed overnight. It had to be taken one step at a time.

Like this procession, she thought, sighing and craning ahead to see what delayed them.

The Peace Force members were slowly opening a path through the crowd, parting the dense pack of people with infinite patience. With easeful words and small chuckles, they formed the flanks of a gentle plow, opening a furrow for the procession to follow. As she inched forward, Ari Ara nodded at a beaming stone carver and winked at a solemn-eyed child sucking her thumb beside her mother. She caught the eye of a pack of students clinging to the shoulders of a tall statue and smiled. One of them clutched his heart as if shot by love's arrow and toppled backwards into his friends' surprised arms. Ari Ara stifled a giggle.

"Are you *flirting* with him?"

She pivoted toward the incredulous voice at her elbow. Finn Paikason's black eyebrows pulled into a scowl. He craned over her horse's neck to stare at the students. Rangy as a yearling elk, sturdy as a mountain goat, the youth drew as many askance glances as the desert dwellers. The Paika of the Border Mountains were loyal to none and sometimes enemies to all. The rumor that the heir to two nations had lost her heart to one rankled many. But Ari Ara didn't care. She loved the stormy-eyed, wild-built boy – as he well knew!

"He's flirting with me," she retorted, rolling her eyes at Finn. "There's a difference."

"Not that I blame him," Finn added, finally grinning. "You look amazing."

She turned to him with a blazing sunbeam of a smile. Finn remembered all over again why he'd fallen in love with her . . . and why he chose to be at her side through all of this. Ari Ara de Marin en Shirar was the most remarkable person he'd ever met. She had trusted him when no one else did, listened when all other ears – and minds – were closed, and saved the clans of his family from death when few others thought them worthy of aid. She'd braved dangers with him and matched him in the Paika's wild dances. He owed her. He loved her. And he'd ride alongside her as far as he could.

"You look every inch the heir," he assured her, casting an appreciative glance up and down her fancy clothes. "All that scrubbing paid off."

She made a face at him. Ari Ara had entered the inn last night dusty from the road, hair wild with the wind, the knees of her trousers streaked with grass stains, and her boots scuffed dull with crosshatched wear. She left this morning afraid to sneeze, not a hair out of place, the finest garments catching the light, coiffed beyond even her own recognition. The fleet of servants sent by her aunt, the Great Lady Brinelle, had taken one dismayed look at her and thrown her into the bathtub for a scorching soak. They washed her hair so many times, she suspected them of attempting to rinse out the telltale red of her father's people. They scrubbed her from the tips of her toes to the edges of her ears. Ari Ara grumpily thought they were trying to rub out all signs of her madcap adventures, leaving only a bland, well-behaved, fifteen-year-old heir.

She doubted their strategy would work.

Reading something of her thoughts in her expression, Finn dropped the reins of his shaggy mountain pony and reached up to squeeze her knee.

"Hey. You're beautiful even when you're covered in thistle-burrs and plastered with mud. These people don't know what they're missing."

Ari Ara blushed in delight and gave Finn a tender look. Minli - with all the exasperation of a best friend - called it her love-struck, doe-eyed stare. She couldn't help it. Finn was lithe of limb with a rugged, rough-and-tumble grace that was more mountain goat than courtly dancer. A tangle of dark curls topped his acorn-shaped face. Stormy eyes shone with a touch of perpetual mischief. Ari Ara thought she could drink in the sight of him all day, like a long draught of a sparklingly clear mountain stream.

He caught her eye and winked. Then, for a split second, he contorted his features into a perfect mimicry of the statue behind him. Ari Ara snorted with laughter. Her gloved hand flew to her lips to hide her guffaw. Her shoulders hunched with mirth. Finn imitated another statue - and there were plenty to choose from.

Stoneport was a raucous, clattering sprawl of a city. In a precise grid, the smooth-laid streets led to the bank of the vast Mari River where numerous docks and jetties jutted into the water. The city served as the shipping hub for the sculptors and stone masons, quarriers and miners of the bustling stoneworkers' guild. Every inch of the city bore intricate stone carvings on the trims, facades, and portals of the buildings. Statues of battle heroes and famous warriors lined the road. Busts of ancestors crowded the rooflines of their descendants' family homes. Plazas contained riotous fountains churned by an ingenious underground system of waterworks driven by the river's current. Ari Ara longed to twist and turn, marveling at it all, but she was under strict instructions not to gawp like dying fish.

As they crept forward through the crowded streets, Finn coughed under his breath, caught her eye, and whipped out a perfect imitation of the goggle-eyed, ferocious warrior behind him.

Ari Ara burst into giggles.

She had scarcely composed herself when he dropped his mouth downward and eyes skyward copying the pathos of the grieving war widow statue on the corner.

Shulen kicked his horse between them and ordered Finn to fall back.

"We were just having – " Ari Ara started to protest.

"Fun is not the point of this procession," Shulen scolded, anticipating the end of her sentence. "Do not dishonor the people of the Stonelands with mockery."

Finn reined in his shaggy pony and dropped back to the rear. Ari Ara craned around.

"Eyes front," Shulen ordered. "Sit up straight. Try to act like the royal heir that you are."

He signaled over his shoulder and Emir Miresh – a dark-haired, warrior-trained youth just a few years older than Ari Ara - drew up on her righthand side. Flanked by the stern pair, Ari Ara resigned herself to a much more tedious ride through the city. They turned off the broad avenue to the central port, following the quay-side docks to meet the Great Lady. The crowd thinned, giving way to the bustle of oxen teams pulling crated statues and winches hauling granite blocks onto barges. The river sailors paused their labors as the Lost Heir passed, leaning muscular arms on ship rails or waving from the rigging. On the landward side, the clerks of shipping companies jostled in the windows, vying to catch a glimpse of Ari Ara. As word spread, the midday taverns emptied. People filed into the street and pressed their backs up against the buildings to let the riders pass. Emir and Shulen scanned the narrow corridor cautiously. There wasn't much room to maneuver.

Ahead of them, the sound of chanting arose. Ari Ara peered

over her horse's head, looking toward the intersection. A cluster of blue-garbed sisters, spiritual counterparts to the monks, huddled on the corner, eyes closed, swaying side to side as their lips moved over the words. They held their hands up, one arm crossed over the other, fists balled to block bad spirits or omens. Ari Ara furrowed her brows, straining to catch the words. The streets snarled with competing sounds - voices, bellowing mules, ratcheting winches - but she recognized the chant. She scowled. It was a warding prayer, a protection against evil. The monks where she'd grown up had used it once when a beast dug up a baby's grave in the village. Ari Ara swiveled left and right in her saddle, looking for what they were chanting at.

Behind her was a wall. A plain brick wall at the back of a warehouse. She craned around again. As the riders clopped down the length of the cobbled street, the sisters pivoted, tracking them. One caught her eye and glared. Then the woman deliberately turned her head to the side and spat. Ari Ara's mouth fell open in shock. They were chanting against *her.*

A rattle of words burst from the lips of the blue-robed woman, rising over the chanting:

"One will come who heralds ill, prophesized, foretold, feared. Death follows in her footsteps, war-breaker, change-maker. Chaos and upheaval chase her. Famines, floods, misfortune stalk her."

Ari Ara gaped, recognizing some of the familiar words of the Prophecy of the Lost Heir - the one that foretold her existence. The phrases had been severed from context, mashed together with baseless claims, and twisted into a litany of doom.

"Shulen," she muttered, annoyed.

"I hear them."

The warrior's reply came low and calm. Too calm. In his quiet, Ari Ara recognized the taut carefulness of high alert. He shifted to move his horse between her and the chanters, but before he could interposition himself, a round, hard object hurtled through the air. Ari Ara ducked low, flattening against the horse's mane.

Something smashed against the bricks, a crunching splat followed by a gagging stench. A trail of slimy yellow oozed down the wall.

"Eggs – they're just eggs!" Ari Ara cried out, nearly laughing in relief, moving swiftly to forestall Shulen's instinctive reaction to a threat.

She ducked as another rotten egg whipped past her head. A third flew toward her as she straightened. Without thinking, she reached out for the egg. Her focus tightened. The world slowed. She dropped into the ancient practice of the Way Between. Neither fight nor flight, the non-martial art drew upon the teeming field of all other possible reactions. With four years of daily training under her belt, the graceful motions hummed in her bones and sang through her blood. Time elongated under the intense stare of her sharpened attention. Her breath sounded loud in her ears. The shouts turned muffled and dull. Delicately, she touched the edge of the egg's shell, not catching it – anything that forceful would smash it – but merely redirecting its path. She gently tugged the egg into a long arc, rolling it through her fingers and palm, rotating her arm over her head in a circle, spiraling the egg around and sending it back –

Splat!

Slimy, yellow yolk and clear whites smashed on the blue robe of one of the sisters. Her snarling face shattered into a shocked gasp. Heads swiveled. The chanting faltered. Shulen swore under his breath. In the moment before shock switched to fury, he signaled to the Peace Force to open the street and form a barrier between the sisters and the heir. Then he grabbed the reins of Ari Ara's horse, kicked his own mount into motion, and led the riders out of the intersection. He cantered in silence down the last blocks, ignoring Ari Ara's demand to go back and apologize, or talk to the women, or at least explain to everyone that they'd got the Prophecy of the Lost Heir wrong. It wasn't *all* gloom and doom.

"Not now, Ari Ara," he growled. "Let the Peace Force handle this."

His voice was so taut with worry that she reluctantly nudged her horse forward and rode on.

CHAPTER TWO

. . . . .

The Great Lady

The Great Lady Brinelle was pacing the docks when they arrived. A formidable woman, her tailored skirts slapped around her as she strode. Though the sprawling river docks of the Stonelands bustled with the cries of dockworkers, the rattle and ratchet of heavy lifts, and the thunking knocks of wooden ships on piers, the stretch of granite dock nearest to the Great Lady stood empty.

They're all afraid to come closer, Ari Ara thought, noting the crackling intensity that emanated from her aunt. The granite itself seemed to quiver under the forcefulness of the Great Lady's pacing.

The moment she spotted them, Brinelle froze and her stillness was worse. The maelstrom of her agitation tightened into straight-spined steeliness. Ari Ara - who always approached her aunt with a mix of affection and apprehension - crossed the last horse lengths with a queasy sensation in her gut.

"Welcome, niece," Brinelle said grandly, as if she wanted to prove her faith in Ari Ara's bloodlines, as if a vast crowd had assembled, or . . . as if spies hid in the damp air of the river bank.

With guarded and measured motions, the Great Lady embraced her. Each gesture was calculated for diplomacy and for their repetition – and distortion – through the rippling rumor river that would carry them out of context. Later, Brinelle would embrace her niece with a broad smile creasing her strong features. Three years had raced past in an endless stream of meetings, turmoil, scandals, and the usual nonsense of political feuding between nobles. Brinelle had weathered it unflappably, emerging from the barrage with a few more grey hairs at her temple and a score of invisible scars that added a deeper cut to the furrow-lines of her frown. She had served as Regent of Mariana for fifteen arduous years. Strife had imbued her gristle-and-marrow soul with toughness.

Her brown eyes raked the girl in a swift glance of examination. Three years was an eternity at that age. The last time Brinelle had seen Ari Ara, the top of her head had scarcely reached Shulen's chest. Now, the girl's chin crested the old warrior's shoulder as she stuck it up, steeling herself under her aunt's scrutiny.

"It gives the House of Marin great pleasure to welcome you back to your homelands after so many years away."

"Er, thank you?" Ari Ara replied awkwardly. She'd had a speech prepared for this moment, but the incident with the egg had driven it out of her head. She attempted a small bow, realized it was supposed to be a curtsy, grimaced, switched midway, and managed to botch that, too.

Brinelle buried her chuckle under a cough and made a mental note to reinstate the girl's etiquette tutorials as soon as possible. At fifteen, Ari Ara was no more ready for Marianan high society than she had been at twelve. Beside her, Minli of Monk's Hand Monastery folded into a graceful bow, one fist curled under his cupped palm, crutch tucked smoothly beneath his arm, nary a hitch in his balanced posture as he rose. Brinelle was impressed, but unsurprised. The boy was studious and intelligent; he anchored Ari Ara's impetuousness. His sharp wits had come to the girl's rescue more than once. Brinelle planned to train him as an ambassador or minister's aide. Ari Ara would need his cleverness at her side in some official capacity. Their lives were not their own, little though they realized. She held them all like game pieces on the vast board of the world.

"Lady Aunt," Ari Ara said, "*this* is Finn Paikason."

The Great Lady made a noncommittal *humph*. One eyebrow lifted as her cool gaze took in the youth. Finn had dressed in his finest clothes with intricate embroidered whorls and hatches matching the orange-red of his fox cap. Finn stood a head taller than Ari Ara, verging on the last growth spurt before he reached his man's height, his shoulders slightly too broad for his chest. He had the look of a charmer, which Brinelle distrusted in anyone let alone a Paika. To the Marianan regent's sensibilities, he was a feral creature hauled down from the mountains. She half-expected him to snarl and bare his teeth at her.

And she wasn't entirely wrong.

Sensing her disdain, Finn's dark eyes glowered. A surly resentment built in his throat, blocking off the greeting he had rehearsed. The two turned away from each other without a further word, leaving Ari Ara gaping at their bristling animosity. She opened her mouth to protest, but the Great Lady moved onward, turning to Shulen and wading through the necessary tedium of the formal welcome home.

By the time they finished, the rest of the Peace Force members had reached the quayside. Ari Ara's once-gleaming honor guard wiped spittle off their faces and straightened their disheveled tunics. Several bore the stench of rotten eggs. Many were red-faced with the effort of controlling their tempers and mastering their responses in order to diffuse the situation.

Minli moved among them, listening to their reports from the intersection. A brawl had almost erupted between the venomous sect of the heir-hating sisters and the most fervent worshippers of the Lost Heir. Standing between the two groups, the Peace Force dealt with the blustering ringleaders of each faction and talked them back from the precipice of violence. As they did, they formed two lines in their white tunics, inching the groups apart until everyone had stepped onto opposite sides of the streets. Tempers cooled. The crowd of onlookers dispersed. The Peace Force ensured that a fight would not launch, then moved on. Their task today was not to solve the world's problems, merely to prevent violence from marring the return of the heir.

The Great Lady offered them formal words of welcome, then frowned. She snapped her fingers and her aide stepped up to her elbow. The bland man had a knack for sliding along invisibly - a useful skill in service of the royal house.

"Arrange land-route passage for the horses and the Peace Force. They will not all fit on our ship."

Shulen's iron filament eyebrows touched over his creased forehead.

"Surely there's plenty of room on the royal barge?" he objected.

"We are not taking the royal barge," Brinelle answered, striding down the length of the granite dock toward a ship moored at the end.

"*That's* the ship we're taking?" Shulen exclaimed, a note of utter disbelief - and a small tone of dismay - in his voice.

The vessel's sides were black with age and pine pitch tar. Her blue sails had faded to a streaky grey. Her hull was pitted with dings and gashes. The gold lettering on the stern boldly declared the ship's name to be the *Fair Defiance*.

Ari Ara liked the look of the vessel. Battered and weathered though she was, the Fair Defiance tugged at her moorings, eager to obey the siren song of the current. Her prow leaned downstream, yearning. A monstrous carving curled around the bowsprit, half human, half scaly fish, wrought with exquisite details from the tumble of mussel shells in its hair to the fanned gills at its throat to the pointed teeth barred in a wild and wicked grin. The ship stretched longer than a sloop, smaller than a trade vessel, sleeker than a barge, and nimbler than the typical noble's pleasure boat.

Shulen, however, was not pleased.

"A queen-to-be does not slink into her own capital on a battered ship," Shulen reminded the Great Lady huffily, insulted on Ari Ara's behalf. He'd served two queens before her and knew protocol as well as the tutors. Ari Ara should enter the capital city amidst the fanfare of horns and showers of flower petals.

"I have my reasons," Brinelle said sharply, accompanying her cryptic comment with a haughty flick of her hand. "We must travel swiftly – more quickly than in the cumbersome barge – if we are to arrive tomorrow night."

Shulen's frown deepened.

"A night arrival?" he questioned, affronted at the thought of entering the city under the cloak of secrecy. "What's the meaning of this? What's going on?"

Brinelle paused and spun back to him, lowering her voice.

"There have been ... developments. We must take precautions."

Shulen's hackles rose.

"What – "

The regent cut him off with a sweep of hand, commanding his silence.

"Not here. Not now."

She strode aboard and signaled to the waiting crew. The aide hustled his underlings into action. The river sailors leapt into motion, readying the vessel for departure. A horse tender approached to lead the horses away. A team of stable hands would bring them by road to the House of Marin's stables near Mariana Capitol. Minli's desert stallion snapped at him, but the others followed along placidly enough. Travel bags, panniers, and sacks were tossed from shore to ship.

Ari Ara greeted the captain's salute with a grin and a handshake - the woman was as weathered as her vessel and undoubtedly had a story for every scar and scrape. Her words of welcome, however, drowned in the scuffle of voices behind them.

"Yeah, I'm part of the Peace Force, but I'm also - "

"I know," the Great Lady cut Finn off coolly, eyeing him with stern disdain. "You will still travel by road with the others."

Finn teetered on the dock edge by the gangplank, blocked by one of the Great Lady's guards. Ari Ara whirled and came to his rescue.

"He goes where I go," she told her aunt, lifting her chin defiantly.

"Nonsense," Brinelle scoffed. "He's a Paika. You're the heir. No matter how . . . infatuated you are, you two cannot be joined at the hip."

Finn Paikason glowered, his pride stung for the ten thousandth time in his sixteen years of life. His clans bore the brunt of the two nations' animosity. Dwelling in the Border Mountains, constantly caught in the crosshairs of war, vulnerable to the attacks of far larger armies, the Paika had endured and survived without the luxury of loyalty. They worked for the highest bidders, switched allegiances as the winds of victory shifted, and turned sides at the brink of defeat. As far as the Marianans cared, he was a good-for-nothing Paika descended from a long line of treacherous, backstabbing traitors who'd been disloyal to everyone in every war in every epoch of history. Even if Finn had been temperamentally suited to being a royal partner - which he wasn't - the people would never accept him.

In his prickly defiance, Finn reminded Brinelle strongly of Ari Ara when she'd first come down from the High Mountains. The Great Lady felt weary at the thought of housebreaking *two* of them. It would be best to separate the pair and let this infatuation fizzle out like a cold spark.

"He will go by road," she repeated, her tone signaling the end of the discussion.

"Minli's coming on the ship," Ari Ara pointed out, gesturing to where the one-legged boy stood by the mainsail, listening along with Shulen and Emir.

"Minli of Monk's Hand is renowned throughout two nations for his good sense and discretion," Brinelle reminded her sharply. "This boy - "

"Finn," she cut in, exasperated. "His name is Finn. You know that."

All winter long, Ari Ara had written her aunt repeatedly about the boy she loved. She'd extolled Finn's strong qualities, talked about his loyalty, his clan's culture, the service he'd rendered Mariana, his participation in the peace efforts.

"- is a Paika," Brinelle went on, "and everyone knows - "

"Paika can't be trusted."

Finn muttered the words on the same breath as the Great Lady. Ari Ara's heart wrenched. She drew breath to renew her arguments.

"Never mind," Finn growled with a shrug of his bony shoulders. "I didn't expect anything else."

"Let him on," Minli called out, tucking his crutch under his arm and coming over. "Finn can bunk with me. He was sent as a

Paika emissary, after all. They'll be insulted if we leave him behind."

Finn shot Minli a grateful look for his tact. Brinelle scowled. Ari Ara pleaded with silent eyes. At last, the Great Lady sighed and threw up her hands.

"Fine. We shall deal with this later. For now, he travels with Minli."

Irate as a bee-stung bull, the formidable regent snapped out orders to depart. Captain and crew cast off the heavy ropes that bound the ship to the stone moorings of the granite quay. Like a hound unleashed, the Fair Defiance surged into the river's yearning embrace. The sailors loosed the sails. The captain's orders sang out in the lyrical lilt of river sailors' jargon.

Once they reached the center of the wide Mari River, far from earshot of the shore, the Great Lady summoned Ari Ara and Shulen to a conference in her quarters. Despite the rugged appearance of the Fair Defiance, the ship clearly served the House of Marin regularly. The captain's quarters beneath the aft deck had been partitioned into two berths, one for the captain, the other for high-ranking guests. Brinelle's trunk stood in the corner next to a generous bunk. A second bed for Ari Ara was tucked beneath the sloping side curves of the ship. A red curtain could be drawn around the sleeping area for some privacy. A wide window in the ship's stern let in light through panes of crosshatched glass. A heavy desk stood bolted to the floor. A cabinet shelf full of books, scrolls, parchment, inks, and maps lined the inside wall that divided the two quarters.

As soon as the cabin door swung shut, Ari Ara wheeled on Brinelle and renewed her protests on Finn's behalf.

"How can you be so rude to him?"

"There are more important things at stake than your crush on that boy, Ari Ara," her aunt snapped testily, "even if it is one of the most ill-conceived notions you've come up with yet."

"Love isn't a notion!"

"Enough!"

The Great Lady's voice thundered. They didn't have time for this foolishness. Even now, the capital city turned against the returning heir. Each second of delay squandered crucial time in Brinelle's endless battle on Ari Ara's behalf. For four years, ever since the Mark of Peace had revealed this headstrong girl to be the heir, the Great Lady had fought for her acceptance among the suspicious and fractious Marianans. While Ari Ara had many supporters, her detractors were equally fierce, strongly motivated, and hard at work undermining her popularity among the common people. Some - like the disgruntled nobles from the House of Thorn - were hardly a surprise; they'd tried to sabotage Ari Ara from the beginning. No, it was the unexpected factions that had Brinelle worried.

"My spies discovered that some of the Sisters have been spreading lies and rumors about Ari Ara, especially among the warriors," she confessed to Shulen, rubbing her temples at the headache of dealing with the religious order.

"That explains the egg," Ari Ara muttered under her breath.

"What?"

Brinelle pinned her with a look as sharp as her hearing.

"It was nothing," Ari Ara said hastily. "There were some sisters chanting about the prophecy."

The Great Lady's lips tightened. The prophecy warned of disasters following the arrival of the child of two nations who bore the Mark of Peace. A sect of the Sisters interpreted it as a portent of doom.

"They threw rotten eggs at us," Shulen reported stiffly.

"How dare they!" Brinelle exclaimed, indignant.

"Oh, for ancestors' sake," Ari Ara groaned. "It wasn't that big a deal."

"Not until you threw the egg back," Shulen commented in a sour tone.

The Great Lady whirled on her.

"What were you thinking?!" she burst out, appalled. She leapt from her chair and paced the confines of the ship's quarters in agitation.

"I didn't - I wasn't," Ari Ara stammered.

"Clearly."

Brinelle snorted, her tone half-exasperated, half-worried.

"I didn't *mean* to hit her on the chest," Ari Ara burst out. "It just happened. I just - "

But whatever rationale had whipped through her mind in the moment wilted under her aunt's withering glare of reproval. In hindsight, Ari Ara realized how stupid it was to hurl the egg back at her detractors. Nor was Brinelle alone in her view.

"You could have sent that egg in any direction," Shulen scolded, his deep disappointment evident in his voice. "Instead, you made matters worse."

"They threw the egg in the first place! Why are you being hard on me?!" Ari Ara grumbled, crossing her arms over her chest and slouching in her chair.

"Because you want a better world than this. You have a higher standard to maintain," Shulen told her.

"And you're the heir," Brinelle pointed out, shaking her head. "You'll need to do better than this when you're queen."

"If I'm ever queen," Ari Ara sighed.

"*When*," her aunt corrected sternly. The girl had to take it seriously. The day of her coronation loomed closer with the turn of each season. "You'll need to know the proper behavior for instances like this."

"I'll just ask Minli to sort it out," Ari Ara muttered.

Brinelle stifled her sigh. *That* seemed all too believable. More than once, she'd thought how much easier it would be if Minli, with his clever mind and quick-witted responses, had been the Lost Heir. The boy was a born statesman, patient and slow to temper, sensitive to the pride or concerns of others, swift to find solutions that worked for everyone. Gentle, receptive, thoughtful, considered, measured.

The opposite of Ari Ara.

Brinelle kneaded her temples again.

Headstrong. Stubborn. Impetuous. These were the qualities that leapt to mind when she thought of the girl. True, her passion for justice was unparalleled, but she had no patience for the long arc of change. She cared deeply for peace, but often lacked the temperament to bring it about. Brinelle could not count the number of times the girl had waded into the fray of a conflict and relied on Minli to get her through it. Ari Ara was a catalyst, an explosion, a streak of lightning in the dark sky. She revealed the problems, broke the silence, uncovered the rotting stench of injustice. The world needed people like her . . . though not necessarily on the throne.

Much as she wished, for Ari Ara's sake, that the girl's life could be one long string of adventures galloping across the desert or trekking over mountains, they had both known the day would come when Ari Ara would have to rein in her wild temperament to take up the duties of her blood.

"Your actions now have long-reaching consequences," she warned her niece, drawing breath for a lengthy lecture.

"As if they didn't before," Ari Ara groaned, rolling her eyes at the upheavals that had trailed in her wake.

"This incident with the egg – "

"I'm sorry, alright? It was a stupid thing to do," Ari Ara admitted, slouching even lower in the chair.

"Don't interrupt," Brinelle chided. "Sit up straight and listen for once."

There was trouble in the capital, she explained, trying to strike the right note between caution and alarm. That sect of doom-mongering sisters had been flooding the rumor mill with dire predictions. Their grumbling fear that Ari Ara's reign would end in catastrophe had triggered unrest across the island city. Brawls had broken out between university students and noble youths. The Watch had been forced to wade into the fray. There'd been countless scuffles between the street urchins – undyingly loyal supporters of the fabled Lost Heir – and the Orelands faction who despised Ari Ara. There'd been a petition submitted to the Assembly of Nobles to have her exiled again. Demonstrators marched through the streets in support of her. Protests erupted in the square against her.

The Great Lady's face showed a momentary fatigue. She had battled many foes and factions throughout her years as regent. Some quickened her pulse for the fight. But this? This cut to her soul. Brinelle did not like to quarrel with the Sisters. They were the intermediaries of the ancestor spirits; she preferred to have as little to do with that realm as possible. As Great Lady, she fulfilled her ritual obligations, sat vigil at the solstices, presided over certain ceremonies . . . but she did not care to meddle with the unseen. She and the Sisters had always had an easy alliance. They dealt with the spirits. She dealt with the nation. Their purviews crossed – yet rarely clashed – in the loyalties of the warriors. The House of Marin commanded them, but the Sisters trained and raised them. Battling at the sword's edge of life and death, such fighters put faith in the Sisters' guidance from the ancestor spirits. Brinelle's authority in the present could not compete with the weight of the past.

"Something's brewing," she worried. "I can feel it in my bones.

I don't know what, but – "

"You're being cautious," Shulen finished her sentence with dawning comprehension. Factions had tried to kill Ari Ara before – and undoubtedly would again, given half a chance. That ruled out a grand procession into the teeming crowds of Mariana Capital.

"So, what do we do?" Ari Ara asked, bolting to her feet, eager to tackle the challenge.

"*You* will do nothing," Brinelle told her firmly. "You will let your advisors and guardians deal with this matter. You, as heir, will treat the Sisters with utmost respect and diplomacy."

Ari Ara scrunched her nose, thinking of the egg. Too late for that.

CHAPTER THREE

. . . . .

Nightmares

"Could you just go ask him again?"

Ari Ara tried to keep the pleading note out of her voice. Night had fallen like a cloak, settling the shoreline into dark folds and lurking shapes. Candlelit windows gleamed on the riverbanks, revealing glimpses of people's lives. Late dinners and wild parties. Old couples knitting and spinsters reading. A squinting scribe bent over his parchment. A young mother humming as she patched the worn-out knees of her child's clothes. Minli and Ari Ara sat on the lattice lid of the bulkhead over the prow hold, pointing out the unexpected sights – like a woman waltzing with her cat – and discussing what to do about Finn.

Shulen stood guard two paces away, trying not to eavesdrop on the angst-ridden conversation. The ship's crew slipped about their tasks, sure-footed as cats. Under the middeck lanterns, a pair of seamstresses gossiped in hushed voices as they repaired the tight jacket that Ari Ara had ripped off as soon as they left port. Even with goosebumps lifting on her arms, Ari Ara refused to put it back on, preferring to shiver in her white blouse. She'd yanked open the buttons of the frothy frontispiece, complaining that Marianan fashion was already trying to drown her.

"Just go to Finn's berth and tell him to talk to me," Ari Ara urged Minli for the tenth time in as many minutes.

Minli folded his arms across his chest and refused. He'd spent all afternoon trying to clear the storm clouds of Finn's anger at the Great Lady's scornful dismissal.

"No. *You* go talk to him."

"He won't even look at me. I feel like an idiot just standing there shouting at his back."

Minli rolled his eyes. They'd been having some version of this talk for a month. Ever since the summons came, Minli had patched up countless spats and endless tiffs between them. He didn't know how many times he could hold together the fraying strands of their relationship. Finn adored Ari Ara ... except for the unavoidable reality of her royal blood. The Paika youth detested cities, resented Marianans, and deep-down shook with nerves over the thought of Ari Ara *actually* becoming queen.

"What would that make me?" he complained to Minli when she wasn't within earshot. "A royal boyfriend?"

He scoffed at the notion. Minli studied him, dubiously agreeing that Finn Paikason made as unlikely a royal consort as he could imagine. He was a Paika, a son of jagged peaks and ice-cold streams, deep forests and wild winds. Finn loved Ari Ara, but she was not his only love. The further they traveled from his homelands, his clan, and the traditions of his people, the unhappier Finn grew. His heart pulled him between both his loves, and when it broke, Minli wasn't sure which way Finn would split.

It had been a very long month.

"Come on, Minli," Ari Ara cajoled, throwing an arm over his shoulder and jollying him slightly. "You're so much better at this stuff than me."

Minli snorted.

"All the more reason for you to practice inner *azar,*" he told her.

The Old Tongue word for the Way Between rang like a bell in the darkness. *Azar* did not fight back with punches and swords – that was *attar,* the Warrior's Way – it responded with compassion and courage. *Azar* did not back down or run away – that was *anar,* the Gentle Way – it drew a line in the sand and refused to cooperate with the abuse or injustice. Creative and clever, *azar* flowed through obstacles like water around stones. It halted violence. It found solutions. It brought peace and worked for justice for all, not just those with the biggest muscles. There were thousands of ways to express *azar* from listening deeply to speaking honestly; from calming someone's anger to blocking an attacker's blows. The Way Between could be used to stop a war, halt a fight, or patch up an argument with your friend . . . but only if you studied and practiced it.

Both Ari Ara and Minli had trained in it for years. And while Ari Ara excelled at the outer forms – diving, rolling, turning aside punches, stopping the momentum of violence – Minli was much better at inner *azar.* He had the temperament for thoughtful listening, handling strong emotions, staying level-headed, finding solutions to conflicts, and resolving differences. They needed all of these skills to wage peace, so Ari Ara persisted in her efforts with inner *azar.*

Her true love, however, was the physical motions of outer *azar.* Each morning she rose at dawn and gladly hurled her limbs over, under, around, and through the exercises. She ran circles around everyone but Shulen. But, as the old warrior had taught them, those movements were the least of the skills encompassed within the ancient non-martial art.

"The Way Between can turn aside an assailant," Shulen had told them, "but it is far better to prevent such simmering animosity from boiling over into violence. *That* is how a wise person uses it."

Ari Ara was far from wise and didn't mind admitting it. Under the soft curtain of night, Minli and Ari Ara discussed how to handle the argument with Finn. As they had done in countless training exercises in the Border Mountains, they talked through the scenarios of how this fraught conversation might unfold. True, the trainings had been designed for fostering peace among former enemies, but the skills translated to lovers' quarrels, too. Minli made her listen to the uncomfortable truths that Finn was likely burdened with. He tossed bitter comments at her to see if she could weather them without being baited into returning verbal arrows. He let her try out her remarks and responded in the half dozen ways that Finn might. He helped her wrestle with her own insecurities and fears so it wouldn't compound the problem with Finn.

Listening silently, Shulen's heart surged with pride for these two apprentices of his. If all people could guide each other as these friends did, their world would never know the horror of another war. A nation that came to shouts and blows over personal disputes had little ability to handle its political conflicts with another country. He'd seen nobles charge into war because an opposing commander insulted their horse. Countless lives had been lost because rulers couldn't resolve their differences at the negotiating table – and sometimes wouldn't even try. He himself had unleashed carnage in a futile attempt to use revenge to ease his unspeakable grief after the murder of his wife and child. If he had had a friend like Minli, the course of history would have been altered. If the Great Lady Brinelle had been advised by someone utterly committed to the Way Between, then the War of Retribution after the death of Queen Alinore would never have transpired. Shulen listened to the future queen of Mariana accept the wisdom of her friend and felt hope for them all.

"Now, just go talk to Finn," Minli urged once they'd exhausted all their exercises.

Ari Ara hesitated.

"Maybe I'll just sleep on it," she wavered.

"Better deal with it now," he countered, "or you'll have nightmares over it."

Ari Ara let out a groan. Shulen and Minli exchanged silent glances. Ari Ara's nightmares had started as soon as the summons had arrived. She woke from them gasping and crying out, tangled in the covers. As they had traveled to Stoneport, Ari Ara had told both her best friend and mentor about the terrors that plagued her slumber.

Avalanches of paperwork. Squeezing prisons of corset dresses. The droning voices of officials drilling into her skull. Falling from the heights of the House of Marin. Drowning in the Mari River. Statues that attacked her. Most of the bad dreams were simply the usual patterns of nerves, the fear of failing, rehashes of the pressures that weighed on her. A few relived the dangers she'd survived the last time she was in Mariana: dodging an assassin's dagger, being threatened with imprisonment for being an imposter, trying to win a duel to the death.

Shulen taught her meditations to use as she drifted into slumber and offered her an herbal tea to help her sleep more soundly. Nothing worked.

"These aren't ordinary dreams," she'd muttered once, red-eyed with exhaustion. "They're testing me."

She refused to elaborate further, leaving him in the dark, spiraling through endless questions about her comment. He gnawed on his worry like a dog's bone. Until the age of eleven, Ari Ara had been raised by the elusive Fanten in the High

Mountains, a culture shrouded in secrets and mystery. For them, the dreamrealm seethed with significance. A third of one's life took place in slumber, even more for the Fanten who slept the deep sleep through the winter. Their culture *walked* through dreams, studied, learned, explored, and communicated across a vast, ever-shifting realm of dreaming. Fanten dreams ran truer than waking life, but Ari Ara was not of their blood. Unless something of their abilities had rubbed off on her as a child through herbs or medicine or upbringing, she should not be dreaming as they did. The nightmares were simply unusual in their intensity. It was the only explanation.

Night after night, Shulen stood guard, anxiously watching as she writhed, twisting and turning in the torment of her dreams. For all his skills at battling enemies, he could not help her in the dreamrealm. He listened to her low mutterings, watched her limbs thrash, stood by helplessly as she struggled. Night after night, he shook her awake, calling her name as her eyes stared wildly at nothing, still gripped by the specter of her dreams.

Shulen inhaled a sharp, deep breath of the river-scented night, wincing over the stench of the brackish shallows and the inevitable city-odors along the congested stretch. He overheard snatches of Ari Ara's whispered confession of her latest nightmare to Minli, something about fending off the Mari River dragon, the symbol of the royal house. Ari Ara shuddered as she recollected its scaly, coiling clutches.

Shulen's anger flared. Her father should be here to comfort her. Tahkan Shirar could sing the lightning down from the sky. Surely he knew a lullaby to ease his daughter's slumber. If he truly cared about his child, Tahkan would be at her side. Shulen resented the man's absence . . . even if he understood it.

Tahkan Shirar was not sulking over diplomatic insults.

On the wings of a messenger hawk, the Desert King had sent

a note to Shulen:

I've headed south. There's a song there, a secret I need to hear.

A new whisper of evidence had reached his ears, a tendril-thin hint of truth, a clue to the long-elusive answer about who had attacked Queen Alinore, his wife and Ari Ara's mother, over fifteen years ago. The mystery of the assailants haunted everyone. Wars had been fought and lost over it. The future shivered in its uncertainty. If they had attacked once, what was to stop them from striking again? Until the threat was known, Ari Ara would never be safe from these shadowed factions. Tahkan had vowed in the binding language of *harrak-tala*, the Desert Speech, that he would uncover the truth.

He asked Shulen to keep the purpose of his journey quiet.

Let everyone think I am still sulking over that diplomatic insult. Burn this message. Tell no one, not even Ari Ara.

The identity of the attackers was the most dangerous and closely-guarded secret in the world. The news that Tahkan Shirar had renewed his search would put the two nations in an uproar. Through the weeks of their journey into Mariana, Shulen had watched the skies for messenger hawks, anxiously waiting for Tahkan's veiled, sparse updates:

Onto something.

Closer.

Nearly there.

It was maddening. Tantalizing. Never enough.

Shulen, too, had lost a wife and child on that day. While he battled the attackers, buying time for Queen Alinore to reach safety, his own family had been slaughtered. He wanted answers – and Tahkan's messages rarely satisfied him. The most recent letter had irritated him so fiercely that he crumbled it in his fist and threw it into the hearth fire.

Keep your eyes on that Paika boy. Don't leave the two of them alone.

Tahkan Shirar and Finn Paikason had taken an instant dislike to one another. Their icy attitudes rivaled the winter storms outside the Paika's houses during the Desert King's late winter visit. It would have been comical if it wasn't so fractious. Ari Ara had spent all of her father's stay soothing the ruffled feathers of one, then settling the bristling hairs of the other. Minli told her it was excellent practice in the Way Between. She wasn't amused.

She'd been so stressed over Finn and her father's friction that Shulen decided not to mention the Desert King's overprotective message.

Tahkan is worrying over nothing, Shulen grumbled in silent displeasure. Ari Ara's infatuation with Finn Paikason should be the least of her father's concerns . . . even if it was causing his daughter heartache at present.

Around him, the Fair Defiance muttered under the breath of wind, mumbling in the creak of boards and the moan of wood. Shulen married his footfalls to the sounds as he discretely trailed after Ari Ara as she sought out Finn. She heard him anyway – her senses were sharp as the Fanten's – and shot him a glance of nerves and annoyance. Shulen ignored it. From now until her last breath, he or another member of the Guard would stay close as a shadow, protecting the royal heir from kidnapping and assassination. Ari Ara had to get accustomed to this inconvenience. One of his pressing duties was to retrain the Guard in the Way Between. He and Emir Miresh could not maintain a full rotation alone . . . and Ari Ara insisted that her protectors not be killers.

"Otherwise," she pointed out, "we're as bad as the people we're defending against."

Shulen positioned himself at the end of the corridor, close enough to cross the distance to Finn's cabin in two bounds, but far enough away to give Ari Ara a semblance of privacy. He pretended not to see her hesitancy and uncertainty as she shuffled her feet in the dim light belowdecks. Ari Ara lifted her knuckles to rap on the door.

Silence.

Her hand halted just above the wood, frozen as her courage faltered. Shulen's heart skipped a beat. He struggled to stay silent, to refrain from intervening. It was not his place. He was her mentor, not her father. If she asked for his advice, he'd give it. He had done so with her mother and grandmother, standing guard over two generations of queens. Duty came first. His role was simply to protect her.

This one is different. She is different. Shulen admitted to himself. He had been dedicated, almost devoted to his duty in service of Queens Alinore and Elsinore. He would have laid down his life for them and nearly had. But his respect for them was a pale shadow to his love for Ari Ara. She was like a daughter to him.

Almost.

The hard knock of her knuckles on the door broke his thoughts. Finn's muffled voice called out a begrudging permission to enter. Shulen shifted closer as Ari Ara slipped inside. He could keep her safe from assassins . . . but she would have to brave nightmares and heartaches on her own.

CHAPTER FOUR

. . . . .

Swords & Shields

The journey south sped past swiftly. By the following night, the shoreline was jammed with the swelling sprawl of Mariana Capital. When the island city's lanterns and lit windows gleamed like a low constellation of stars, Ari Ara, Brinelle, and the others gathered abovedeck. Each stood quietly, holding their churning emotions close to their chest, no two reactions the same. The river bore the vessel swiftly, inexorably, toward the looming threshold of change. Ari Ara wavered between eagerly leaning into the downstream charge of the ship and nervously bracing her heels into the wooden deck as if that could halt their rushing pace. The heavy folds of her gold and blue overcoat were not the only things weighing on her. She couldn't wait to pull the pins out of her hair; it was ridiculous to use that many at any hour, let alone in the middle of the night. No one was even going to meet them at the North Bank. Who would even see the result of all this fuss?

In the moonlight, the city loomed like a crouched beast wallowing in the shallows. On the north end of the river island, a wide levy formed a wall against the spring floodwaters. A landing dock sat at its feet. A flight of stairs zigzagged up its thickness. The ship pivoted slowly, carefully, and the river's pull drew it snugly up against the wooden buffers hooked to the stone pier. The crew threw heavy ropes over the pilings.

"It's straight to bed with you," Brinelle warned Ari Ara. "I'll grant you one rest day and then your studies and duties will commence."

Ari Ara's groan collided with a yawn. Her aunt rattled on, detailing her expectations for the formal return of the heir. She would put the girl through intensive preparation and rigorous training. Ari Ara would shadow her aunt in council meetings, learn how to decipher legal documents and write formal decrees. They had to make up for years of lost time – and the nobles would be watching her like vultures, hovering overhead, waiting for her to make a mistake.

"Cover your mouth when you yawn. You look like a roaring sand lion."

Ari Ara personally thought there were worse comparisons, but she did as her aunt asked.

"The antics you got into as a twelve-year-old cannot be repeated," Brinelle warned her. "You are growing fast and must behave like it."

Ari Ara stifled a sigh and sidled toward Minli. Brinelle shot a pointed look at Shulen. *This* was precisely what she needed to grow out of. The next couple of months would be like walking over glass.

"She is going to have to be on her best behavior, Shulen," Brinelle murmured softly, leaning toward him so Ari Ara wouldn't overhear, already anticipating failure. "I cannot stress enough how fragile her position remains. The nobles' vote to confirm her swung by just one flip – half of them still dislike her with varying degrees of intensity."

"My job is to keep her safe," Shulen reminded the Great Lady. "Yours is to prepare her for her responsibilities."

"Ah, but she listens to you, not me."

"Is that what you think?" Shulen asked with a wry chuckle.

Brinelle's smile flashed briefly.

"You're more a father figure to her than Tahkan. What on earth is he thinking, taking off in a huff?"

Shulen diplomatically held his tongue.

"When I get ahold of him," Brinelle started to grumble. Then she broke off.

Thud-Thud.

A heavy, low drum beat sounded. The sound banged against the thick north wall, lifted from an unseen force in the warriors' training yards next to the House of Marin. Brinelle paled, recognizing the sound of the percussion of thousands of warriors slamming the hilts of their swords against the steel-studded wood of their shields. Were the warriors raising an alarm?

Brinelle's eyes widened at a sudden thought. Then, her gaze narrowed, furious.

It couldn't be . . .

"Shulen," she murmured.

"Look," he answered, pointing to the dock.

Two figures slid out from the pooling shadows of the stairwell. Black cloaks fell from their shoulders. White robes captured the gleam of moonlight. A swish of fabric swept the stone dock, whispering to the murmuring current. One woman moved with the soft grace of light, gentle in demeanor. The second woman's strong limbs cut through the night in sword-slashes of firm gestures. Ari Ara recognized them both.

"What are the Twins of the Sisterlands doing here?" Ari Ara asked, her high young voice suddenly loud.

Brinelle hushed her. The pair led the women's order; the Warrior Sister overseeing the training of fighters, the Mother Sister tending the orphans.

"Ari Ara of the High Mountains."

The Twins spoke together, one voice steely and hard, the other soft as thistledown.

"The ancestor spirits call your name."

"No!" Brinelle's sharp intake of breath punctuated the ritual invocation. She gripped Ari Ara's shoulder as if the gesture could halt the Twins' next words.

"The fate of nations follows in your footsteps."

Shulen stiffened with disbelief.

"The time has come to weigh your character."

Ari Ara cast a wild, confused glance at her aunt, hoping for a hint. Nothing.

"And see if it balances on the scales of power."

A spark hissed in the silver light.

"We call you to the Ordeal of Queens."

A second spark crackled and died. The third caught. Twin balls of flame swung from long chains, back and forth, mesmerizing, once, twice, thrice. Then the flames leapt, growling and hissing into the air, arcing in a wide circle around the Twins. The spinning fires kept the heir and her companions from disembarking from the ship. The sisters had blocked the staircase and denied them access to the House of Marin and the city beyond.

"You will come south to the Sisterlands. This city is barred against you until you pass through the trials of the ancestor spirits."

"I order you to stand aside," the Great Lady of Mariana

commanded. "This is neither the time nor the place for this foolishness."

"You dare question the will of the ancestors?" the Warrior Sister challenged her in a voice that rasped like steel over steel.

"They have called Ari Ara, not us," the Mother Sister intoned with the ringing resonance of a bell.

"You conniving – "

"Watch your words, Brinelle de Marin!" the Warrior Sister barked, her voice severe with disapproval. "The ancestors are listening."

"So?" Brinelle shot back, undaunted. "Let them bear witness to your false invocation of their names. Stand aside or I shall have you removed."

"By whom, exactly?"

There was no mistaking the triumphant gleam in the Warrior Sister's eyes. On the heights of the stone wall, a roar of flame sounded. Sisters in blue robes so pale they seemed like pools of fallen moonlight rose from their hidden crouches, casting off the mask of black cloaks. They spun their chains of fire round, circle upon circle blazing bright in the moonlight.

Thud-Thud. Thud-Thud.

Thousands of warriors struck sword against shield, summoned by the Twins of the Sisterlands. They drummed with ferocity and strength, compelled by a sense of righteousness, responding to the ancestor spirits' call to initiate the heir.

Brinelle went white. *She* was the head of the Marianan army, but they were beyond her command now.

"This . . . this is mutiny," she spluttered, clearly unnerved.

"No, Great Lady," the Warrior Sister corrected her, "this is tradition. Your warriors stand by the ancestors. Not even you can stand against them."

The Great Lady gaped at them in shocked fury. She slammed

her fist down on the ship's rail. This insubordination of the Sisterhood would not – could not – be tolerated! They had barred the city against the girl! It was a slap in the face of the Great Lady – everyone knew she intended to return to Mariana Capital with the girl. In her fifteen years ruling, Brinelle had never been so close to losing her iron grip on power. How had she not anticipated this scheme? She could kick herself for not seeing this move coming.

Despite everyone else's dismay, a thrilled tingle ran through Ari Ara. Whatever was happening was certainly more interesting than stuffy tutors and protocol lessons.

She edged over to where Finn and Minli stood huddled together near the prow.

"So," Ari Ara asked, clearing her throat, "what's this ordeal thingy?"

Minli and Finn stared at her with matching looks of disbelief.

"How can you not know about the Ordeal of Queens?" Finn asked. Even *he* knew about the spiritual test of an aspiring monarch.

Ari Ara shrugged impatiently. She could recite the reasons for the gaps in her education. People had certainly mentioned them often enough: she'd grown up unschooled in the High Mountains, raised by the Fanten, and sent out to tend sheep until she was eleven. The list of things she should know – but didn't – could fill volumes. That's why she had Minli. Didn't everyone need a friend who had memorized half the library?

"Are you going to tell me or not?" she asked Minli.

"It's a series of challenges you'll have to do before you're allowed to ascend the throne," he explained. "They prove – or disprove – your worthiness in the eyes of the ancestors. The Sisters conduct them in their territory to the south. The spirits are somehow involved."

"And?" she prompted when he fell silent.

Minli shrugged.

"That's all I know – the whole thing is shrouded in mystery and secrecy."

"So, that's it? A test? Why is my aunt so upset?" she asked, gesturing to the hushed argument raging between Brinelle and Shulen. What was all the fuss about if she had to do this ordeal at some point, anyway?

"You're only fifteen," Minli said.

"And woefully unprepared," the Great Lady said, striding over and charging into the conversation. "Heirs have failed - or worse, died. The Sisters should not have invoked the Ordeal of Queens so soon, and certainly not without consulting me."

Then there was the question of timing. Why now? What were they playing at? Roka and Sorra Maro, twins by birth as well as position, had ruled the Sisterhood for decades. In all that time, they had rarely contradicted the will of the House of Marin. Brinelle sighed the weary sigh of a warrior who has battled for days and must somehow rise to another. It had not been easy to repeal Ari Ara's exile and gain the nobles' confirmation of her claim to the throne. The vote had passed by the slimmest of margins. The Warrior Sister had flipped her vote in support of the girl . . . and now Brinelle knew why. Roka Maro simply wished to discredit Ari Ara through the guise of the ancestor spirits. Undoubtedly, she planned to sabotage the ordeal every step of the way. By calling the ceremony so soon, they could ensure that Ari Ara would fail.

"Take our ship to the south docks," the Great Lady hissed to the captain. "It's the Twins that will leave this city, not us."

The captain drew breath to give the order, but Shulen spoke.

"Wait. Don't do that."

The Great Lady spun on him, livid.

"You dare question my orders?"

"You cannot possibly challenge the Sisters. Not over this," Shulen told her quietly.

"I will throw them out of the capital by their robes."

"Oh?" Shulen asked her sharply. "You and what army? Pull yourself together, Brinelle."

"I could say the same to you, Nshoka Shulen."

Their use of first names shocked Ari Ara almost as much as the thudding drumbeats of the swords and shields. She had never heard anyone call Shulen by his childhood name. Nor would the duty-bound man ordinarily abandon the Great Lady's titles and honorifics. The night had turned inside out. The structures of the world had upended.

"They are forcing our hand," Brinelle grumbled, glaring at the Twins. The Sisters waited, impassive and opaque with mystery, fire whirling, expressions masked by the swirl of smoke and shadow. It was a clever trap. Brinelle could see no way out, not with the warriors participating in the invocation of the sacred ritual.

"Then they will regret it," Shulen said quietly. He had faith in Ari Ara. If she passed the ordeal, it would silence her detractors and grant her an unquestionable right to rule.

Thud-Thud. Thud-Thud.

Ari Ara's heart boomed louder than the thousand swords of Mariana's warriors. The whirl of the fire dizzied her. The acrid smoke stung her eyes. Everyone argued around her.

"It is too soon."

"We can prepare her."

"It is dangerous."

"She will have us by her side."

"What if she fails?"

"What if she succeeds?"

Ari Ara cut into the endless spiral of words.

"I have to do it, right?"

Both Shulen and Brinelle nodded.

"Then there's really just one question," Ari Ara pointed out. She lifted her chin and set her hands on her hips, defiant. A spark of excitement gleamed in her stinging eyes. Her hair blazed in the firelight.

"What are we waiting for?"

Brinelle blinked. Shulen smiled. The captain gave orders to cast off. The sailors loosened the mooring ropes and flung them aboard. With long oars, they heaved the ship away from the dock and unfurled the mainsail to fight the downstream current long enough to circle around the river island.

"This is not over," Ari Ara told the Twins of the Sisterlands as the ship pulled away from shore.

"No," the Warrior Sister agreed, her toothy smile sharp in the night. "This is only the beginning."

CHAPTER FIVE

. . . . .

The Book of Queens

"Tell me about the Ordeal of Queens," Ari Ara declared, pacing across the tight confines of their quarters. "What is it like? What will they test me on?"

"Patience, for one thing," Brinelle told her archly, setting her butter knife down between the tines of her fork, patting her mouth with her napkin, and signaling for a servant to clear the breakfast dishes away.

Ari Ara rolled her eyes. She'd been patient – for hours and hours, waiting for Brinelle to wake up. Ari Ara had hardly slept and when she did, her dreams ran in tangled vines of imagery – ancestor statues chasing her, standing at attention before an army, her mother weeping over her. She didn't bother to ponder their meaning. She had simply leapt from her blankets before dawn and put herself through a challenging sequence of moves in the Way Between. Nothing settled her unease better than a sweaty, rough-and-tumble practice.

Then she'd ignored everyone's squawking protests and jumped into the river to rinse off. Dripping, happy, and clean, she squelched back to her quarters where the dressiers had clucked over her like a pair of disapproving hens. Ari Ara wolfed down her breakfast while they fussed over her tangled hair. She shoved on the clothes they laid out, silently thanking the ancestors that it was just a comfortable shirt tucked into a loose-fitting pair of trousers. Someone must have had a word with them about allowing the heir to breathe and move. Ari Ara suspected Shulen – it was a matter of security, after all.

After breakfast, she waited restlessly for her aunt to rise, bathe, dress, eat, attend to urgent matters, send out several messenger hawks, and finally answer her questions.

The sun blazed beyond the crosshatch panes of the ship's stern window. Overnight, the curling bends of the Mari River had carried them far from the capital city. The congested sprawl of docks and warehouses had given way to river ports and millhouses. Farmlands spread throughout the fertile floodplain. Houses and towns stood back, respectfully giving the Mari River wide berth in her eons-long wandering betwixt snowmelt and floodwaters, rain surges and sandbars. They would follow the Mari's vast current south for a week before turning the prow of the Fair Defiance into the mouth of the Sister River.

At last, the Great Lady began, lifting a hand to forestall Ari Ara's interruptions.

"Every monarch of Mariana has undergone – and passed – the Ordeal of Queens and Kings. It is a two-fold test. On the one hand, it reveals the strength of an aspiring ruler's character, for better or worse. Are they generous? Wise? Determined? On the other hand, it shows whether or not the monarch has the approval of the ancestors. At each step of the ordeal, the spirits will be watching and weighing your worth. It is they who will determine if you deserve the mandate to ascend the throne."

"How will we know what the spirits decide?" Ari Ara asked.

"The Sisters," Brinelle answered, still sour over their antics.

As intermediaries, the most renowned and respected of the spiritual women would listen for the instructions of the ancestors. From this guidance, hermit sisters and abbesses alike would set tests for Ari Ara. Sailing up the Sister River - a tributary of the vast Mari - Ari Ara would stop at shrines, temples, and abbeys to undergo trials. The Ordeal of Queens would start at the Gateway Abbey where the two rivers met. From there, they would proceed upriver to the sacred shrine atop Marin's Mountain and continue for several weeks until they reached the Citadel of the Sisterlands. In this walled city, the Sisters would weigh the results of her tests during the ordeal. The ancestor spirits would be consulted. Her triumphs and failures would be measured and her fate decided.

"The conclusion of your Ordeal of Queens will coincide with the Summer Trials," Brinelle explained, mentioning the annual competitions of the warriors. The Sisterlands' Summer Trials were famous, second only to the Spring Trials held in Mariana Capital. "You will be expected to preside over the trials while the decision on your ordeal is being made."

If she passed, the Sisters would accept her blood oath - a small nick across the palm - in the Sanctuary of the Citadel. And that was that. No one could ever again question her right to rule, not warrior, not sister, not noble or commoner.

If she passed, that is. Brinelle spent the better part of the next hour hammering in the point that many aspiring queens and kings never made it to the final convocation of the Sisters. Stories abounded of heirs rejected early on, crippled, sickened, or killed. Or they gave up and turned back. Or surrendered their attempt in deference to the demonstrated will of the ancestor spirits.

"Alright, I get it," Ari Ara cut in. "Work hard or I'm doomed. But *what* exactly are the tests? What will they be like?"

Her aunt shook her head. No one knew precisely. The specific challenges were never repeated twice. Nor were the accounts written down or spoken about by the monarchs. Sworn to secrecy, the ritual was more mysterious than the spirits themselves.

"How am I supposed to prepare then?" Ari Ara groaned.

"We may not know *how* you will be tested," the Great Lady answered, "but we know *what* you will be tested on: the virtues of a queen."

"What are those?" Ari Ara asked, a twinge of nervousness running through her. She didn't feel particularly virtuous . . . or queenly.

"The Ordeal will test you on many qualities. Courage - which you have plenty of. Charity and compassion. Patience - not your strong suit. Restraint and decisiveness. Humility and pride."

Ari Ara's mind reeled.

"Wait! How will I know which one they're looking for?"

"You won't."

The answer was not reassuring. Nor was the rest of her Lady Aunt's lecture. The list of qualities under scrutiny could fill a room. It was impossible to keep them all straight. The ordeal would look at her loyalty, dedication, willingness to make sacrifices, moral character, integrity, honor, dignity, receptiveness, clarity, articulateness, wisdom, valor, confidence, and more.

"This," Brinelle intoned, sliding a heavy volume across the desk to her, "will be your best preparation for the unknown. Your mother memorized this volume, studying it from girlhood onward."

Ari Ara shot an unenthusiastic glance at the thick book. There was no way she could even read it all, let alone memorize it.

"Start at the first chapter and *apply* yourself," Brinelle ordered her with a warning tone, knowing the girl's reluctance toward studying. "I will return in several hours to test you on the content."

Then she swept out of the cabin to attend to the hundred

other tasks this unexpected detour demanded of her. A dozen messenger hawks had to be sent and a dozen more found in the next town. The Great Lady had supporters to rally and allies to cautiously alert. Her spies needed to be deployed to ferret out the hidden motives behind the timing of this ordeal. She must unearth the ringleaders who had tugged this spider's web of political intrigue into motion. She had to shore up the commanders' fealty to the House of Marin and ever-so-carefully erode the blind allegiance to the Sisters.

On top of that, she'd been up half the night arguing with Shulen over matters of security. The infuriating man wished to send for the Peace Force to provide protection for Ari Ara. Brinelle was appalled – a contingent of fully armed, fully trained members of the Guard were already on duty – but Shulen had led the Guard for decades. He, more than most, knew what the duties entailed. The old warrior felt Ari Ara could be better protected with the Way Between than with the threat of violence.

Brinelle rubbed her temples, the vise of a headache gripping her as she wrestled with the drawbacks. The Marianan heir apparent could *not* enter the Sisterlands with Harraken Peace Force members at her side. The mortal enemies of their nation could not be part of the high ritual of the Ordeal of Queens. Bad enough that Tahkan Shirar, as her father, had to be issued a formal (and controversial) invitation. Protests over the possible arrival of the Desert King were undoubtedly already erupting in Mariana Capital. In the Great Lady's opinion, they needed to add more armed guards to their security, not fewer.

But, in the end, she and Shulen worked out an uneasy compromise: no more sword-bearing guards and the Peace Force would meet them at the end of the Ordeal of Queens. Immense crowds would gather for the Summer Trials, anticipating the historic announcement about the royal heir. The Peace Force's presence could be useful then. No matter which way the decision went, Ari Ara could use supporters in the crowd.

One thought led to another and Brinelle made a mental note to summon all of the nobles who held Ari Ara in high esteem. She would need another set of messenger hawks at this rate. The Great Lady had much to accomplish while the heir studied.

Under the age-darkened wooden beams of the ship's quarters, Ari Ara flipped open the cover of the book and willed her eyes to focus on the words. It was an old text, the symbols embellished with countless flourishes. She sighed. She'd rather scrub river slime off the decks than try to decipher this. She resigned herself to an arduous couple of hours.

A queen must be friendly and welcoming.

A queen must be gentle and wise.

A queen must be vigilant and alert.

A queen must be consoling and kind.

After an hour of this litany, Ari Ara flipped to the end of the chapter, hoping the book grew more interesting. It didn't. It went on ... and on ... and on. Was there anything a queen shouldn't be? Shallow and silly? Vain and self-centered? Half of the rules contradicted the others.

A queen must be cautious and bold.

A queen must be modest and proud.

A queen must be generous and frugal.

Ari Ara wondered if there was another book for kings. If so, was the list any different? Were all heirs tested in the same virtues? Or did it depend on gender, age, and experience? From Brinelle's dire warnings, she knew that some aspiring kings had been young, like her, but others were already grey-haired grandfathers when they attempted to take the throne. Did the ancestors weigh the potential ruler on the strengths demanded by the times? Some had been scholars and diplomats, but most Marianan rulers had also been warriors and battle strategists. Would the ancestors judge her badly for her love of peace?

She rubbed her eyes and stared out the crosshatch windows. The morning had crawled by while she studied. The dense river ports had given way to smaller villages. Fish weirs dotted the reeds in the shallows. Large swaths of water-loving grains swayed on the flatlands, nourished with rich minerals from the annual floods. On a brilliant blue day such as this, entire villages poured into the wetland fields to stand ankle deep in the muddy silt, planting slender stalks of seedlings. Along the raised berms between the fields, a group of children ran and shrieked with laughter as they tugged at the strings of a kite.

Tap. Tap. Tap.

A persistent sound at the windows broke her reverie. She frowned as her eyes struggled to focus on the glass.

Tap. Tap-tap.

Ari Ara rose, scanning for a bird or a borer beetle or something that could make such a distracting tapping noise. She saw nothing. Baffled, she opened the window and stuck her head out. A tiny, hard object smacked her head.

"Ouch!"

"Whoops! Sorry."

Finn's voice hissed out a laughter-lined apology from above her. She craned upwards. He was hanging over the rail on the upper deck, grinning.

"You've had your head in that book all day," he pointed out, tossing a toasted hazelnut at her. "Take a break."

Ari Ara caught the nut and popped it in her mouth.

"Can't," she answered as she ate. Her hand flew up to cover her mouth. A queen didn't eat like a cud-chewing cow, after all. "It's not a long journey to the Sister River. I've got a lot to learn before then."

Finn flung another hazelnut toward her, half in jest, half in annoyance. At this rate, they'd never spend any time together. Maybe he *should* just go back home.

"Too bad," he told her with a shrug. "I thought of a game you'd like. It involves the Way Between."

A gleam of mischief shone in his eyes.

"What's this game?" she asked, enjoying the way the sunlight stranded through his curls.

"Search for the Lost Heir."

Ari Ara burst out laughing. All the orphans knew that game, hiding while a seeker tried to find them. She'd played with the children at the monastery back before anyone - including her - even suspected she was the heir.

"Ah, but in this version," Finn cajoled, the corner of his smile folding, "you, the real Lost Heir, use the Way Between to explore the ship before the Great Lady - "

" - or Shulen - "

"Right, or Shulen, catches us and sends you back to that boring old book."

It was a boring book, Ari Ara agreed. She waffled. Then shook her head.

"Brinelle will yell at me," she warned, even as her resolve wavered.

"Not if you win," Finn said with a wink.

Ari Ara's laughter pealed. A grin slipped across her face. She slung her leg through the window frame. She'd be back before anyone noticed. Tucking her feet on the sill, clinging to the inside of the frame with one hand, she stretched upwards. Finn hooked his leg over the thick rail and around the vertical rungs. Leaning precariously, he clasped Ari Ara's outstretched hand and heaved her up. Scrambling her feet up, Ari Ara pulled herself onto the top deck and crouched next to Finn. The captain stood by the round wheel, eyes fixed on the watercourse ahead. Finn pointed to the rowboat. Waiting until the captain squinted into the western sun, they crept behind its bulk. From there, they darted down the short flight of stairs to the main deck and hid in back of a stack of barrels.

"The first challenge is to cross to the stairs to the lower decks," Finn told her in a whisper.

She peered through the narrow gap between the barrels. Across the bustling deck, the bulkhead to the lower decks had been propped open in the fair weather. A dozen crew members and passengers moved about their tasks. Finn could saunter past them whistling, but if they spotted Ari Ara, she'd be sent straight back to her studies. She rolled her shoulders and took a deep breath, settling into the taut focus of the Fanten when they did not wish to be seen. Her eyes studied the motions of the deck, the rhythm of gestures, the patterns of motions, the map of footsteps through errands and chores. With the soft tension of a stalking cat, Ari Ara dropped into the Way Between. She waited one breath. Two. Her eyes flicked east. A flock of marsh geese rose from the bank. Their raucous honking drew gazes. Ari Ara slipped out from behind the barrel.

Scarcely daring to breathe, Finn watched her turn, light as wind, delicate as snow, as unstoppable as water. She took three steps while everyone's eyes tracked the flight of the brilliant, green-chested geese. She revolved around the back of a sailor as he turned back to his task. She slipped backward between a pair of her aunt's servants as they parted ways. The mainsail mast blocked her from the view of the boatswain. The *whoomph* of the sail catching wind hid her from the cabin boy's gaze in the crow's nest. A crew member bent to coil rope; she darted behind her. Ari Ara moved between the backs of heads, distracted eyes, and turned gazes. She slid through the hidden space that threaded between tasks and duties, habits and gestures, circumstances and the unexpected.

With a triumphant grin, she reached the bulkhead and dropped down into the shadowed hold, tossing a wink at Finn over her shoulder. He followed with Paika stealth, determined to match her feat. He was within arm's reach of his destination when the cook's apprentice greeted him with a friendly halloo. Finn sighed and abandoned the effort. He waved to the lad, then climbed down the ladder.

"I've never seen anyone move like that," he murmured to Ari Ara as they crept behind the stacked crates in the main cargo hold.

"You've never seen the Fanten, then," she answered, dismissing her skill as clumsy by comparison.

"No, and if that was any indication of their skill, I never will," he replied. "Come on."

He showed her the passenger berths that lined the hull of the boat, then the crew's shared quarters strung with hammocks. The galley was crammed into a closet-sized room scarcely big enough to fit both the red-faced cook and the harried scullery lad. Creeping through the narrow corridors, they climbed down a steep ladder-like staircase into the bottom hold of the ship. The sharp scent of pine tar and dampness clung to the still air. Crates loomed like crouching beasts. Wine sloshed in wooden casks. Boxes of packed straw held an assortment of merchant wares to supply the Fair Defiance's passengers. Ari Ara and Finn were nearly caught when a crew member came looking for a spare coil of rope. Ari Ara shimmied onto the top of a stack of crates and squeezed under the low ceiling. Finn flattened behind the wine casks. The sailor heard the scuffle and paused to peer into the shadows.

"Knew there were rats down 'ere," she muttered.

Ari Ara tried not to laugh.

By the time they'd explored every inch of the ship, the midafternoon sun blazed past the sky's pinnacle. Ari Ara's hair was a wild mess of tangles and curls. Stains spotted her shirt and a smudge smeared across her right cheek. Finn had cobwebs plastered to his back and a grey layer of grime streaked down his chest.

"Betcha can't cross the deck unseen twice," Finn dared her.

"That's a bet you'll lose," she countered.

They headed for the bulkhead up, but as soon as they turned the corner into the corridor of passenger berths, they nearly collided with Shulen. Fortunately, he opened the door to his quarters and blocked them from view. Ari Ara yanked the latch to a narrow broom closet and shoved Finn inside, squeezing in on his heels. Stifling their giggles, Ari Ara held a finger to Finn's lips until Shulen's footsteps faded down the hall.

Bursting out, they sprinted in the opposite direction, swung around the corner . . . and smacked into Brinelle. Ari Ara's feet skidded on the slick floorboards. Finn overreached as he grabbed for her. They toppled to the ground in a tangle of limbs and laughter.

"That's quite enough of that!"

Brinelle's scolding tone cracked through the corridor. The bell of her skirts swung as she strode toward them. With matching sighs, Ari Ara and Finn broke apart and rose to standing. Brinelle held a stack of letters in one hand, tapping them impatiently against her palm.

"Discretion in all matters . . . " the Great Lady prompted pointedly, quoting from *The Book of Queens.*

Ari Ara shuffled her feet, trying to dig up the concluding line.

" . . . is the virtue of a wise queen?" Finn guessed with a shrug.

Brinelle glared him into silence.

"Continue from there," she commanded her niece. "You will

not have anyone's aid during the ordeal."

But Ari Ara drew an utter blank. She babbled out a jumble of verses – some of which never appeared in the book – and Brinelle dragged her back to her quarters to study.

"Honestly, Ari Ara! A *queen devotes herself to mischief?* Perhaps you do, but that is *not* a quality the nation needs in its monarch. You must take these studies seriously. I cannot be your taskmaster all the time. I've far too much to do."

Brinelle gestured to the pile of paperwork on her desk. She had deputized her immense staff to handle as many of her regular duties as possible, but the unavoidable weight of governance required attention. The running of a nation did not halt in her absence from the capital. It barreled onwards with the usual onslaught of trade disputes, border tensions, judicial rulings, nobles' squabbles, and bureaucratic headaches. Legal documents had to be signed. New bills revised. Petitions from the stonemasons' guild had to be answered. If Ari Ara thought her studies were burdensome *now*, she would doubly dislike them when she was queen.

Someday, Brinelle thought, as she nudged the lanky fifteen-year-old toward the desk, *all these tasks would be hers.*

Ancestors help them all.

The Great Lady pointed sternly to *The Book of Queens*. Ari Ara stared at it moodily. She did take the ordeal seriously. She wanted to be a good leader . . . she just wished it wasn't quite so tedious.

"I'm sorry," she told her aunt. "I just hardly get to see Finn at all, and he's already feeling unwelcome, so . . ."

She fell off, shrugging.

Brinelle set her paperwork down on the desk.

"I don't hate him, you know."

The Great Lady's voice was gentle, tinged with a rueful sigh. She settled into her chair and gestured for Ari Ara to sit. The girl ignored the invitation and paced the room like a restless tiger.

"In a way, I even admire him," Brinelle said, tapping her fingers on the wooden desk. "Both of you are being very . . . brave."

Foolhardy, Brinelle's cynical mind grumbled. But she didn't want to fight with her niece. She had to find the Way Between their differences. Ari Ara needed her support, and the nation needed an heir. Brinelle couldn't remain regent forever. The political turmoil had strained the nation to a breaking point. She didn't know how much more tension their frayed bonds of history and culture could withstand. A firm heir, anointed by the ancestors, was her best hope of reuniting the splintering factions under the blue banner that had carried them through thousands of years.

"Look at me," Brinelle urged, a tone of invitation replacing her usual commands. "You are neither the first, nor likely the last, person in our family to have a star-crossed love. A Paika boy is nothing compared to your mother falling in love with the Desert King."

A snort of surprised laughter burst from Ari Ara. Brinelle held her breath - and her tongue - waiting to see if the girl would unwind her tight-wound defenses and listen.

"Yeah, see? It could be a lot worse," Ari Ara said in a muffled, grudging tone as she tossed her limbs into the chair across from her aunt.

"Indeed."

Ari Ara had no idea of the intensity of shock and the firestorm of condemnation that had raged when Alinore announced her betrothal to the leader of their ancient enemies. It was interpreted as a betrayal, sheer treason, utter affrontery. The calls for the queen's abdication had boomed louder than the great gongs of the monasteries. Brinelle had not realized her cousin's strength until she withstood the ferocity of hate that slammed into her in that moment. Alinore did not abdicate. She did not break off her engagement. She drew upon the power of her lineage and held fast. Alinore convinced her people, the nobles, the warriors, everyone, that her marriage to Tahkan Shirar would usher in an era of peace and prosperity, an end to the seemingly endless cycle of war and violence, widows and orphans. And, for the most part, the queen had been correct. Trade flourished. Arts and culture lofted to new heights. Children grew under the loving care of their living parents.

All of that ended with Alinore's death. Not until Ari Ara was discovered in the High Mountains did that fleeting hope rekindle in the hearts of people. Before she stepped down as regent, Brinelle wished to ensure her cousin's child could continue that legacy.

"I have a gift for you," she told Ari Ara. "It was your mother's."

She rose to fetch a small bundle wrapped in a weather-proofed cloth. She had sent for it from the capital last night, her final task before exhaustion claimed her. Galloping horse couriers delivered it, switching out steeds at the copious way stations along the river route until they overtook the Fair Defiance and rowed the package over in a dinghy.

The time had come.

Ari Ara's curiosity burned. Wistful yearning lit up her face. A pang twinged in her aunt's heart as she spotted the telltale shine of emotion in the girl's eyes. It was not her wish to cause her niece heartache.

Better me than the unfeeling world, Brinelle thought. The world would not be so kind.

The Great Lady pulled a small worn book out from its wrappings and placed it in Ari Ara's hands. The leather cover was soft with age and wear. The edges of the pages yellowed and curled.

No title or words marked the front. A red ribbon held it bound shut.

"Alinore kept a journal. We retrieved it from the High Mountains along with her body. I thought to give it to you years ago when you first came to the capital, but . . ."

Brinelle trailed off. Ari Ara had been so small, so young, so wild. At twelve, she could barely read, nor could she sit still long enough to truly listen to her mother's words. And, if Brinelle was honest, she had been waiting to see if Ari Ara truly was Alinore's daughter. By the time it became obvious - to her, anyway - it was too late. Ari Ara had been exiled. Brinelle couldn't bear the thought of the fragile book risking storms and floods, mud and dust, falling into the wrong hands or catching fire. She had loved her cousin dearly, missed her daily, and had reread the journal multiple times over the past years.

To her surprise, however, Ari Ara set it down, reluctantly.

"I'll . . . I'll wait to read it until after I finish studying."

Brinelle's eyebrows lifted, quietly impressed by the maturity of the girl's decision. She could see the intense longing in Ari Ara's eyes, though, and took pity on her.

"You can return to *The Book of Queens* tomorrow. The journal is as much a preparation for being queen as anything," she declared in a thoughtful tone. "You'll even find a small entry on your mother's ordeal. Nothing specific, I'm afraid."

Ari Ara dove for the journal, cradling it in her arms with an awed look. Brinelle realized with a thump of heart that *this* was the perfect time for Ari Ara to read it.

As she crossed the threshold into being a young woman.

As she prepared to take the throne.

As she discovered the true costs of love.

CHAPTER SIX

. . . . .

Alinore's Journal

Thank the ancestors for this journal. I can scribble during long boring meetings and everyone just thinks I'm taking notes.

Lying on her stomach on the bed tucked beneath the ship's ribs, Ari Ara's laughter pealed, bell-like. She had not expected her mother to be so funny. Yet, young Alinore filled the pages of her journal with wry commentary and shockingly honest opinions on everything from the fashions of her teenage years *(more feathers than a chicken)* to the state of the nation *(content as a pig in mud)*.

At first, too wound up to focus, Ari Ara had simply flipped through the pages, mouth agape. In the early entries, the words inked onto the paper scrawled, impetuous and hasty, as Alinore rushed to jot down her thoughts. Later, the handwriting turned intricate and well-formed, as if she savored each word with long pauses for thought. The journal began on Alinore's sixteenth birthday. She was not pleased with the gift of a blank book to write in. What she really wanted was a new horse, a certain war stallion her mother refused to let her ride.

For ancestors' sake! Brinelle has one. If I'm to be trusted with the nation in a few years' time, why won't they trust me with a decent horse? I love Mittens, but she wouldn't leap a ditch if her tail was on fire. What I'd really give my left ear for is a desert horse. They're magnificent. But my protocol tutor says I'll start a scandal if I ride one. Still, maybe I can convince the desert ambassador to let me try his mare as an act of diplomacy. Worth a try.

Ari Ara's heart flipped inside out as she read. She'd imagined Alinore too many times to count, but always older, as a mother, not so close to her own age. There was little hint of the wise, peace-loving, young woman everyone described with misty-eyed reverence. At sixteen, Alinore fretted about her skin *(blotchy one day, pale as old milk the next, and red as a beet if I get any sun)* and anguished over her studies *(I am such a dunce at mathematics – thank the ancestors I can hire scholars for that stuff when I'm queen)*. She scribbled down the snarky remarks she stifled at official functions. *(Pulchritude is such an ugly word for 'beauty'. Why would Lady Y name her daughter that?)* She included nicknames for the most annoying ministers. *(Old Podgy – Podigrius. I really must stop calling him that in my head or it will slip out in a meeting!)* She and Brinelle were close as sisters. *(I wish she'd stop calling me 'Nore every time I call her Brinny. Sounds like snoring – which I do* not *do, even if she claims to have heard me from across the hall.)*

The ship rocked slightly over the wind-lapped waves, gliding down the river. Dusk clung to the window. Brinelle had returned, shuffling papers about, eyes pointedly fixed on her work. Trays of dinner food had been delivered and placed on the end of the desk. Ari Ara collected one and slid it onto her bunk. She lit a lamp and hung it from the hook overhead. Then, she tugged the curtains closed and dove back into reading.

The entries stretched over years, sporadic. Alinore wrote when she was upset or impassioned. She rarely took the time to make note of day-to-day affairs. She skimmed through several pages on the scolding her mother received for skipping lessons. Then, on the next page, after a brief, shaky mention of the official declaration of war, Alinore wrote:

Mother and Father and the army departed for the border today with as much fanfare as the city could muster. They'll be cleaning up the flower petals for weeks – probably until the army returns in a month, victorious. Our warriors will crush those wild horsemen in their sleep. If such an act wasn't barbaric and beneath us, that is. I hope there are some flowers left in Mariana to shower them with when they come home.

But they didn't return, not in victory, and for many, not at all. With a lurch, Ari Ara realized that Alinore was about to lose her parents. The next year, Queen Elsinore and her husband would die on the battlefield.

Ari Ara bit her lower lip, shaken. The night-shadowed ship creaked and moaned. Anchored in the shallows, the wind shoved the hull like a violin's bow over the taut strings of the river's surface. The sailors called it the Old Lament and claimed the vessel sang to the Black Ancestor River, where the spirits of the dead dwelled. Ari Ara heard the hiss of wind over the mast and decks of the Fair Defiance and wondered if they knew that the Harraken – their mortal enemies – believed the spirits dwelled in the restless air. The Old Lament might be more ancient than they thought.

If you looked far enough back in history, all the ancestors had once been friends, not foes. In the time of the Three Brothers, they were family, three siblings in a single nation that stretched from the western expanse to the Mari River. Then Marin and Shirar split the world in two . . . and their descendants had been fighting ever since. The third brother, Alaren, had chosen the Way Between and spent his life working for peace.

If only more people had joined him.

Ari Ara bent back over the journal, steeling herself for the entries on the war. Month after anxious month, Alinore wrote down her fears and frustrations as her parents fought the Harraken riders and horses - the finest in the world. On their terrifying warhorses, the desert fighters picked off the Marianan Army one by one, circling like wolves, culling the edges, harassing the supply lines, assassinating commanders and strategists, crippling the strongest regiments, decimating the new recruits. When the drumroll of skirmishes built to the crescendo of battle, the Marianans floundered in disarray.

Ari Ara remembered only vague mentions of this conflict. Her lessons with the monks hadn't lingered on the nation's failures. This period was only taught because the deaths of Alinore's parents forced her to ascend the throne. She was young, scarcely eighteen. Back when Ari Ara had studied this bit of history, it had been mere names in a dull recitation of battles.

But, in her mother's handwriting, she read of the deaths of her grandparents, flesh-and-blood people with habits and quirks, hopes and humor. Just like the thousands of others who died in that conflict. The true cost of war was masked in numbers; the loss should be calculated by measures of the heart. A father's lullaby silenced forever. A grandfather's secret recipe lost. An uncle's jokes buried with him in a mass grave. Ari Ara read page after tearstained page of her mother's grief, and imagined it echoing through thousands of other homes.

Many of Alinore's early journal entries reflected her rage, her desire for vengeance. She vowed to destroy the Harraken for killing her parents, to sack their cities and raze their villages to the ground. Then, unexpectedly, in an abrupt skip over six months, Alinore wrote:

I could battle the Harraken for ten thousand lifetimes and never end this grief that weighs upon my heart. More violence does nothing but thrust it on another person. But this pain of loss, like the love that sharpens it, does not shrink by division. It multiplies and strikes again ... and again ... and again. If the Ordeal of Queens taught me anything, it's to choose my enemies wisely.

Ari Ara halted at the mention of the ordeal, but Alinore said nothing more about it. Something earth-shattering had clearly occurred, however. Alinore had entered the ritual burning with vengeance and exited as an anointed queen harboring a deep yearning to break the cycles of war. Ari Ara didn't know what had transpired, but it boded well for her. Perhaps the ancestor spirits, in all their wisdom, were not as bloodthirsty as their mortal descendants. Alinore's startling about-face hinted at this hope.

It is not the Harraken who are my enemy, but the wars we have fought for centuries. And since a war to end all wars is an impossibility – more absurd than barking cats or talking pigs – then I am left with one conclusion: if I want to stop this pain, for myself and for my country, I will have to learn to make peace instead of war. Ancestors give me strength.

Here, in the cradle of her mother's conviction, rocked by the subtle rise and fall of the ship on the ceaseless river current, Ari Ara drifted into sleep. For the first time in weeks, no nightmares haunted her. Instead, she dreamt that Alinore sat beside her, stroking her hair and reading her words aloud in a voice her daughter had only ever heard in dreams.

The next day, as the ship sailed down the swift-paced river, Ari Ara dove into her mother's love story. She curled up in the bright sunlight on the foredeck, settling into a pile of thick rope coiled on the prow. Clouds grazed the brilliant blue sky like mountain sheep. At her invitation, Finn joined her, leaning his arms over the rail and watching the river in companionable silence. Finn did not pry. He knew her mother's story would stir up hard-to-express emotions. He was Paika. He was good at watching and waiting. He had the patience to hold still until a wild creature tiptoed out of hiding. When Ari Ara wanted to talk about it, she would. And she did.

"It didn't start like I thought," she commented at last, looking up from the book with a furrow creasing her brows. "They didn't meet until long after her parents' deaths, and then they detested each other."

"It wasn't love at first sight? A thunderclap from above?" Finn asked her, remembering the ballads he'd heard in the mountain taverns.

She shook her head. Far from it. Alinore had not been thrilled at the prospect of Tahkan's first visit to Mariana.

Blast my royal duties back to the ancestors! Why does the Desert King have to come to Mariana this year? Couldn't he wait? Brinelle tells me I can't send him a polite refusal. Apparently, a Desert King hasn't requested a formal meeting in a century. Usually, they just invade. Or we do.

They'd met when Alinore was twenty-five, old for an unmarried queen, but so caught up in her duties that seven years on the throne passed faster than the spring floodwaters. She had led the nation even before she passed the age of maturity at twenty-four. Her honorary regent had officially retired that year, leaving Alinore to bear the full weight of the throne on her slender shoulders. Her advisors had pressured her to marry swiftly and bear an heir, but she had no time for courting. From daybreak to midnight, her days were crammed with trade negotiations, border disputes, and nobles' quarrels. She had only just managed to carve out a brief respite in her relentless schedule when the arrival of the Desert King forced her to cancel her plans.

In the golden glow of hindsight, Alinore was known for her open-mindedness, her tolerance and her respect for her former enemy's culture – but that was not how the story started. Even with her passionate determination to break the cycles of war, the young Marianan queen held as much prejudice toward the Harraken as her subjects did. She knew little of the Harraken beyond the ambassador's family and the battle tales she'd heard. Ari Ara wouldn't have believed it, but it was all there on the page, written in her mother's own hand.

I can scarcely breathe for laughing. Or write. But I promised Brinny I'd set this down so in six months' time, we can see who was right about this Tahkan Shirar, the Desert King.

Me: Grey-haired and grizzled, skinny as an old lizard, half-stooped and crafty-eyed.

Brinny: Red gleaming eyes, pointed ears, fangs. (She thinks he's literally a demon.)

Shulen says we're both wrong. He met Tahkan Shirar and he was a scrawny little boy. But that was years ago, of course.

Ari Ara didn't know whether to smile at their misperceptions, or be disappointed in her mother's prejudice. She tried to remember what she and Minli had thought about the Harraken, back before they'd known any. She supposed that she'd thought of them as vaguely demonic. Shulen had even chastised her about it once, saying: *You live on the Marianan side of the story. Be careful about believing everything you've been told.*

"I just thought she'd have been more accepting," Ari Ara sighed to Finn, squinting up at him as the bright sunlight poured through the ship's rigging.

Finn held his tongue, the sting of Brinelle's scorn still harsh in his memory. Unlike Ari Ara, he had no trouble imagining the prejudices of the royal house of Mariana. He tucked his knees to his chest and slid down to sit next to her. Stretching his legs out long across the weathered deck, he offered his hand to Ari Ara.

"She changed her mind about him and his people, though. Right?" A hopeful note crept into his tone. Maybe he and Ari Ara stood a chance, too. "Did the journal say anything about how that happened?"

"I'm just getting there."

He waited patiently as she read. Finn loved the way concentration made the crease between her brows scrunch up into a little furrow. When she blinked up at him, sensing his gaze, he swiftly studied the slow stampede of clouds overhead.

Ari Ara crawled through three more entries on the preparations for the Desert King's visit. Then Alinore jotted down a quick scrawl of a note, too busy to write more.

He's here. Not old. Not a monster. Not a boy. Oh bother, not enough time to explain! More later.

When Alinore found a moment to breathe, reflect, and write, she wrestled with the ways Tahkan Shirar defied her expectations.

What a week! I haven't had a minute to myself from dawn until midnight. Meetings. Functions. Balls. Escorting Shirar around the capital. Biting back sharp retorts to his arrogant comments. Suppressing the urge to slap that little smirk off his handsome face – well, he is handsome, I'll give him that. We were all wrong in our guesses. Tahkan Shirar is only a few years older than me. His father just died and he's taken up the throne – though, apparently that's not quite right? He's not a head of state, but a keeper of honor? I don't really understand. He just said 'king' was a terrible translation, though he 'expected no better from river dogs'. Honestly. The man is insufferable.

Ari Ara read breathlessly, wondering what happened to change her mother's mind. She cringed over how misinformed the Queen of Mariana was about the Harraken. No wonder the two nations were always fighting. Ignorance and insults were lit matches in the drought-cracked centuries of animosity.

Tahkan is tall – our gazes fall level – dark bronze as if the sun dwelled within him. His eyes are green and his teeth sharp white against his face. His nose is hawk-like. His gestures bold and dramatic, but containing that economy of purpose so typical to his people, sparse as the desert itself. He is tuned like an instrument. It's as if song could be evoked from him with a mere brush of life's hand. (He has yet to sing, though I've been told his people hardly draw breath without singing. Odd. I shall have to discretely inquire about it. Is it a slight to Mariana that he remains silent? An indication of their distrust?) Of all his characteristics, the one that burns in my memory is his hair. A shocking copper – brighter than Shulen's.

Ari Ara paused, remembering with surprise that Shulen's hair had once been red. It was hard to imagine. All she could picture was the iron-grey of the old warrior. Not like her father's blazing red.

It's like a torch, burning. He wears it tied back. I wonder what it's like unbound. Oh, for ancestors' sake! Now my cheeks are a matching color! Enough of that. I can scarcely go fantasizing about him. *Of all people.*

Alinore wrote copiously about the struggles for diplomacy and the countless incidents in which the tenuous peace could have blown up over trivial slights. Ari Ara saw where her mother's reputation as a peacebuilder began, and noticed, for the first time, a streak of stubborn grit in the queen that felt all too familiar to her daughter. Yet, for all Alinore's determination, Tahkan Shirar did not warm to her, or to the Marianans. He remained prickly as a cactus and more likely to fall in love with a pig than the riverlands queen.

Then came the single line entry where everything began to change.

I have heard Tahkan Shirar sing. Nothing will ever be the same again.

Ari Ara's grin burst wide across her face. She stifled a squeal of anticipation. No one sang like her father. His was a voice of his people. His songs bore the dust of his land and the wide skies that crackled with dryness. His music carried his culture, ancient and proud. You could not understand the Harraken until you heard them sing. And up until this point, the silence of the delegation had been their strongest statement of distrust.

"Here it is," she told Finn, jostling his hand, "the turning point."

His black lashes fluttered open – he'd been dozing in the sun's warmth. Craning over her shoulder, he saw a solid block of handwriting filling every scrap of the page. Ari Ara was already absorbed; she didn't even look up when he rose to stretch. He asked her what it said. No answer. Fidgeting from foot to foot, Finn finally wandered off. Ari Ara would tell him the story when she was ready.

Her eyes were tethered to the page.

My ministers and spies produced no satisfying explanation as to the silence of the Harraken dignitaries. So, I asked Shirar directly: why do you not sing? I have heard it is a gift of your people. "One does not pour wine at the feet of cattle," he answered, with that twitch of his cheek that substitutes for the scoff he does not wish me to see.

"I am sorry you think of me that way," I replied, and sincerely, too.

"Do you like music, then?" he asked, polite, arrogant, trying to deflect my question about singing.

I stopped – we were walking to dinner – and the guards swung a few paces around us like a full skirt halted midstride. In the eddy, I said quietly, truthfully:

"I have no skill but for listening."

Ari Ara followed the words hungrily. Her father had told her about this. Her mother's turn-of-phrase had unexpectedly won his trust. In his language, in his culture, that sentence was the refrain of his position as *Harrak-Mettahl*, the honor-keeper of the desert people. In his training, Tahkan Shirar has been asked over and over:

"Do you have the skills to be the next Harrak-Mettahl?"

He had answered in a thousand ways: listing his capacities, bursting into song, recounting a story of his great deeds, quoting what others said of him. Not until he had lived a little and grown a lot did he gain the wisdom to answer the question adequately. At last, he realized that it was not his singing that made him a good leader, nor his words or actions. It was his ability to listen deeply that made him worthy of the honor of his role.

When I inadvertently echoed this significant turn-of-phrase, it was as if a key had slipped into the lock of the door that lay between us. What was his pride but bravado among his enemies? What was my scorn but a shield to his disdain?

Alinore took him to her garden courtyard and told the guards to stand at a distance. Here, he sang and she listened. The world outside churned onward and the dinner went on without them, but in that twilight-suffused garden, time hung suspended. Alinore wrote that she felt like she was meeting him for the very first time, not as Desert King, but as a man, Tahkan Shirar, with as many hopes and dreams and hidden longings, worries and insecurities as she. Even the silence before he began to sing revealed another layer of his humanness. For he did not launch into song, not at once. They were too raw in this newfound honesty, too uncertain in the tenuousness of their unexpected connection.

So, Alinore just sat and waited and watched the last bands of evening sunlight carve golden sculptures in the garden. At last, Tahkan spoke.

"I do not know how to start."

There were so many songs, he confessed, too many, and each with many meanings veiled by language and culture. How could a foreigner understand?

"There are songs we understand no matter the words," Alinore replied. "A lullaby speaks in every language."

He sang, then, the melody with which his mother had rocked him to sleep.

His voice. I have no words for it. It's not operatic, or that of a concert singer. But it doesn't matter. It is the timbre, the nuance. When he sings

. . . the aliveness holds you under its spell. He sang to me his mother's song. In that dry and rasping language of his people, I recognized only a word here and there – wind and dust, a taste of water on the tongue, the scent of a certain plant. Everything is metaphor, of course. Beyond the literal translation, I could sense the comfort particular to the desert: the way dusk breaks the blazing heat of day, or how the sound of running water is a symphony of survival, or how the mothers stand with backs to the wind, cradling their babies in the dust-shelter of their arms.

I learned more about the Harraken in that one song than I have from all my tutors. More true and meaningful things, that is. I've memorized war maneuvers and battle strategies from both sides of our conflicts. I've studied their language so I can parlay directly for their surrender on the battlefield. I've learned the stiff honor code of their warriors in order to use insults to break their discipline.

But I never knew how their mothers rocked their babes to sleep.

Then, of course, he asked me for the song my mother sang to me as a child. I am not a singer! Not by any standard or stretch of the imagination. Certainly not compared to him. Yet, he did not relent when I demurred. Everyone has a voice, he claims, everyone has something to offer to the Song – the great song of the world. I am not convinced of this. Can all his people sing? Are none of them tone deaf?

"Everyone sings," he told me with this little shrug that hinted that will and skill do not always go hand-in-hand. "Besides," he said, "one gift of song deserves another."

"That is hardly practical," I replied. "How does the singing ever stop?"

He smiled at some inner humor.

"I will tell you afterward. Sing."

So Alinore did, feeling strange and uncertain, like a little frog croaking out her first springtime song, her voice scarcely more than a shy whisper with a hum of melody, dredging up a tune from distant memory and words she thought she had forgotten until they tumbled from her mouth.

At the end, Alinore fell silent, tears trembling in her eyes, unnerved, unmasked before this man, her once-enemy. When she dared to look up at him, Tahkan seemed like he had seen a ghost, shaken to his core. He refused to say what rattled him, only:

"Any child would be fortunate to have you as a mother. Your nation is lucky to have you as their queen."

He rose to leave, and Alinore, not wishing to end this evening on such an odd note, called out.

"So, how do your people stop singing? If one song must be returned with another?"

He stilled in the moonlight, his smile unfurling his whole body like a fern. He turned over his shoulder.

"Ah, that is the beauty, see? The Song never stops, only pauses to let the silence have a turn."

CHAPTER SEVEN

. . . . .

The Gateway Abbey

The last leg of the journey south raced by faster than the river's undertow. The journal, her studies, and her dreams all blurred together along with the days and nights. Ari Ara scarcely remembered where dreams left off and waking life began. She read the days away, absorbed in her mother's story. Finn left her to it, hanging out with Minli as the ship sped down the river. Ari Ara scarcely looked up from the journal, shifting to her quarters when dusk's chill settled, taking meals in her cabin, ignoring everything and everyone as her parents' respect forged an unexpected friendship and then blossomed into love.

One evening, as dusk fell, Ari Ara read Alinore's confessions of tender love written in the privacy of her journal. The next night, as the stars climbed the bridge of the dark sky, Ari Ara waded through her mother's plaintive anguish over the impossibility of loving the Harraken honor keeper. The third day, Ari Ara read in snatches between her lessons with Brinelle, breathlessly following how the rumors and whispers of her parents' affair spread through

Mariana. Late that night, she fought yawns, struggling to stay awake while Alinore poured out her heartache over Tahkan's return home. As the silver moon crested the eastern horizon, Ari Ara flipped through the pages on her mother's state visit to the desert city of Turim, heart fluttering with the hope of seeing Tahkan again. As dawn broke, Ari Ara dozed off despite herself. Her head rested on her mother's elaborate descriptions of the desert. She paid for those sleepless hours during her studies of *The Book of Queens*, stumbling bleary-eyed through her lessons, doubting any of it would lodge in her tired mind.

And now, the Ordeal of Queens was beginning.

They had reached the Gateway of the Sisterlands. Steep mountains banked the river, carved smooth at their feet from the endless erosion. Under their shadows, two mighty waterways converged. Rolling over each other like joyful dragons, the Mari and Sister Rivers reunited, laughing, arguing, gossiping, singing. The sailors swore they traded the stories of the entire country. Ari Ara watched the seething crosscurrents and wondered what they chattered about her.

The confluence of the Mari River and the Sister River roiled with such ferocity that the captain ordered all passengers to remain in their berths, out of her crew's way. Ari Ara, Finn, and Minli watched from the doorway of her quarters, braced against the frame. The three clung to each other with white-knuckled fingers as the ship reared and plunged, tilted precipitously then righted itself before plummeting to the other side. A manic gleam shone in the river-loving captain's dark eyes. The challenge of the navigation teased a bared-tooth smile from her lips. Attuned to her whistles and hollers, the sailors whipped from stern to bow, mast to deck, hauling oar against the water's pull, dropping sail into the shove of the easterly wind, heaving an anchor rope across a rocky outcropping and pivoting around and over the thundering collision of rivers.

The hull groaned with the strain of fighting current and the anchor point. The captain muttered a quick prayer to the ancestors. She counted five heart-thundering seconds, then blew her whistle, sharp and exultant. The crew released one end of the rope. It snapped free and coiled out with a hiss of friction. The Fair Defiance leapt over the last tug of the rapids into the far eddy.

They'd made it.

In the calm of the shallower waters, the captain issued the all-clear. Ari Ara rushed to the starboard rail to peer out at the town tucked into the backside of the cliffs. Long ago, the Sister River had swung in a wide crescent. As her path straightened, her ancient footprint left a circle-shaped cove of still water. In its curve, docks jutted from shore to shallows like the spokes of a wheel. Stone buildings crowded up against each other, slate-tiled roofs jumbled and overlapping. In zigzags, carved staircases threaded up five tiers of dwellings. Above the tallest buildings, the crest of the cliffs was etched in silhouette against the eastern sun.

From the peaks, a set of Great Horns bellowed, heralding their arrival. The reverberations thundered around the amplifying bowl of the harbor. People poured out of the buildings, scurrying down the steps, jostling against each other to catch a glimpse of the Lost Heir. The Fair Defiance glided into dock. Two sailors tossed the heavy mooring ropes across the gap. A pair of blue-robed novices looped them over the pilings, cinching the knots efficiently.

In the deafened silence, the horns' rumble resounded in Ari Ara's limbs. She tried to still the trembling in her knees as she looked around. The Gateway Abbey took in orphans from every region. Solemn children lined the terraces of the crescent cove's streets. Ari Ara studied them curiously. At eleven, she had almost been brought here, scooped up with the other young girls at Monk's Hand Monastery and sent to study under the strict tutelage of the Sisters. But Shulen's intervention had saved her. She had won the coveted spot as his apprentice in the Way Between. If not for that, she might have wound up living in one of the Orphans Halls at the Gateway Abbey. Some of the girls were trained in skills and trades. Others would join the ranks of the Sisters. Among them, small boys craned for a glimpse of the heir. The Sisters took them in, too. One day, when they were taller and stronger, if not much older or wiser, the boys would be sent up the Sister River to the Citadel of the Sisterlands to be drilled into soldiers and warriors. The old saying rang in Ari Ara's mind:

Orphans make good soldiers . . . and good soldiers make more orphans.

Her lips tightened into a thin line, hating the cynicism of the adage. Ari Ara shook her head. She would end that cycle, someday. It was a vow she had made years ago.

The orphans wore brown and cream robes, belted at the waist. Ari Ara watched their unsmiling faces; the older girls were orphans of war, like Minli. What did they think of the Lost Heir? The younger boys, however, had been born after the end of the War of Retribution. Their parents would have died of plague or accident. A few might have been sent to the Sisters when their families fell into hardship and they had too many hungry mouths to feed. It was one thing to know such sorrows existed, Ari Ara thought, it was another to look into the eyes of an orphaned child and know your society has failed them.

"Remember," the Great Lady murmured to her as the gangplank slid out, connecting ship to dock.

"I know," Ari Ara hissed through gritted teeth, "everything from this moment forward could be part of the Ordeal of Queens."

"Everything."

Ari Ara straightened her spine and fixed a smile on her face, thinking of a line in *The Book of Queens: a queen must be friendly and welcoming.* Then she dropped her smile, remembering another line. A *queen must be genuine and honest.*

"Your first official test will take place tomorrow morning," Brinelle informed her, "but I suggest you watch your every action, every word, every tiniest gesture, even the expression on your face. You will never know what will - or will not - be weighed and measured, not only by the Sisters, but by the ancestors spirits."

Ari Ara glanced around nervously.

"Of course," Brinelle went on, "your mother, too, will be watching over you, guiding you. All of your ancestors back to Marin himself will help you succeed."

Her aunt sounded so certain, so confident. Ari Ara tried to take heart from that. She'd met Marin once, dreamwalking in the Fanten style, where dreams ran truer than true. He hadn't said much to her then . . . and she wondered how he felt about her vow to follow his brother Alaren's Way Between. When he was alive, Marin hadn't been very happy with his little brother's peacemaking. Many of his descendants had persecuted the followers of the Way Between through the centuries. The kings and queens who led the Great Persecution, and all the wars in history, were her blood relatives. What would their ancestor spirits make of her?

She sent a silent prayer to her friendly ancestors, especially Alinore, to help her out. Across the invisible realms, she suspected a struggle of epic scale was unfolding, a mirror to the everyday world. As the blue-robed sisters lined the shores to scrutinize her, a similar assembly of spirits gathered beyond the veil of the visible. The air turned thick with watchful eyes. Ari Ara resisted the urge to hunch her shoulders under the weight of the gazes. There was no way out but through. From here forward, all eyes would stay fixed upon her.

The Twins of the Sisterlands met them on the wharf. Their smaller, faster ship had overtaken the Fair Defiance days ago, sliding past silently and without hailing. Ari Ara exchanged the words of the formal, ritual greeting and laid an offering at the Twins' feet. The Mother Sister, Sorra Maro, smiled kindly at her, brown eyes crinkling into half-moons that echoed the shape of the cove. Strange how the same features on one face shifted under the animosity of the other. The Warrior Sister's eyes narrowed into tight sickle blades, cutting at her without mercy. Roka Maro had none of the soft edges of her sister. Her muscled arms held threat, not comfort. A thin white scar marred her chestnut face from temple to jawline. Where the Mother Sister's hips curved from her childbearing years, the Warrior Sister's hard body hit angular in her robe. The sword belted to her waist was not merely ceremonial.

In the broad sunshine, their moonlight enshrouded mystique surrendered to the ordinary wrinkles of day. Sorra had a brown mole on her cheek; each of its fine hairs caught the light like a spiderweb. Roka had a permanent furrow creased in her brow from her perpetual scowl. The frightened awe they had invoked on the dock at the capital faded to a measured wariness in Ari Ara. She followed the strange pair up the wharf to a receiving line of the highest-ranked sisters. Anticipating this reception, Brinelle had drilled her on the proper degree of the bows she must make to each one and the quality of her dignified respect.

"You are an heir apparent, not yet a queen. Humility before their wisdom is more becoming than entitled haughtiness," the Great Lady had told her, first demonstrating the proper way to bow, then gesturing for her to try.

Ari Ara had bent awkwardly over the fitted petticoat the dressiers had made. Brinelle insisted she practice in her gown, but the seamstresses gasped over the thought of wrinkles and tears. They'd spent weeks working on the intricate and exquisite, curling river dragon design of this dress.

"If she makes her bows properly," Brinelle argued, "there will be no wrinkles."

Dubious looks flashed across the dressiers' faces before they politely hid them. Ari Ara scoffed, insulted. How hard could it be to bow properly?

Her first attempt was a complete failure.

"No, no!" Brinelle halted her mid-bend. "You cannot fawn like a gawking village girl. You are the royal heir to two thrones!"

She tried again . . . and again . . . and again. Dizzy, short of breath, the petticoat creasing with wrinkles under her ribs, Ari Ara had wrestled with the baffling contradictions for an hour before she gave up. Days later, standing before the row of blue-robed sisters at the Gateway Abbey, Ari Ara crossed her fingers inside her hand, folded her other palm over them, and made her bows with dignity. Tahkan had once taught her that a degree of self-respect in one's bow increased the honor offered to another. So, she strove for a balance of respect for the elders and respect for herself. She just hoped they wouldn't object to the echoes of Harraken culture running through her heart. Ari Ara breathed a sigh of relief when she reached the end of the greetings. The last, wizened elder beamed a toothless smile at her and patted Ari Ara's head with a wrinkled and quivering hand.

Beyond, the older girls and younger orphans watched with burning interest, whispering behind their hands until an elder sister hissed at them to stop. Ari Ara found it all eerie, the stillness, the silence, the staring. When she was ushered into the main hall of the abbey, however, a river's rush of murmuring voices erupted as the inevitable gossiping broke out.

Since the official trial would not start until the next morning, the Twins and the Abbess led her on a tour of the Gateway Abbey's workshops and libraries, sleeping quarters and offices. Ari Ara asked many questions – or as many as she dared. A queen was not nosy, after all. She watched the twelve-year-old girls learning soap making, sewing, candle dipping, and thought how fortunate she had been that Shulen took her under his wing and trained her in the Way Between.

All through the city streets, up the steep staircases, over the jumble of walkways and through the verdant rooftop gardens, Ari Ara could sense the hard glare of the Warrior Sister drilling into the spot between her shoulders where the Mark of Peace was inked, indelibly, onto her skin. The Mother Sister offered a friendly counterpoint, falling into step beside her, showing her interesting statues or sharing tidbits of the city's history. Ari Ara never forgot that this could be a test. She held the door into the workshops, gesturing for the Twins to precede her. She marveled appreciatively at the book-lined walls of the study halls. She spoke kindly to the young orphans in the sleeping halls, asking where they had been born.

A queen cares for her people.

A queen takes interest in the workings of her nation.

A queen listens attentively.

She spoke with girls her own age who were nearing the completion of their apprenticeships. Shyly or boldly, they shared their dreams for their futures, responding to her interest in what they wanted to do when they got a little older.

"I'm going to marry a warrior," said one with a small giggle as she batted her black lashes flirtatiously at Emir Miresh, ignoring the reproving cough of the Abbess. Roka Maro, however, nodded approvingly.

"Those who marry warriors end up widows," Ari Ara muttered under her breath, quoting from Alaren's book of stories on waging peace.

Brinelle coughed and elbowed her. Then she distracted the

group by asking the next girl about her future plans.

"I'm going to be a battlefield healer," she answered with a determined set of her chin. "I'll save and heal our nation's greatest defenders."

Ari Ara almost made a face, but didn't. There were plenty of people to heal without a war. She held her tongue, though, and simply replied with a careful compliment on her dedication to the healer's profession. She admired the vibrancy of the herbal salves the girl was making and told her she'd make a welcome addition to any healer's hall.

"I am training in records so I can serve our army," said a third girl when they visited the abbey's thousand-year-old records hall. "I will make sure the warriors receive their pay, food, equipment, and so forth. You can depend on me to keep your army functioning!"

Ari Ara didn't quite know what to say to that, so she said nothing, swallowing her unease. Every aspect of life at the Gateway Abbey seemed to circle - subtly or obviously - around war and warriors. The girls weren't fighting the enemy with swords, but they were part of the vast machinery of industry that kept the warriors fighting. From the workshops to the kitchens, Ari Ara heard the same things: the girls' dreams revolved around war, battle, and warriors.

Lifting a wriggling orphaned boy onto her hip, a girl scarcely older than Ari Ara cooed to the toddler that he'd grow up to be a great warrior. Ari Ara held the child for a moment and silently prayed that he'd grow up to be whatever he wanted - a dancer, a scholar, a follower of the Way Between, a farmer - in a time of peace. In the smithy, the muscular, red-faced girls at the forge brought out their knives, swords, and helmets for the Lost Heir to admire. Ari Ara asked if they'd made any farm implements or jewelry and they started blankly at her, wondering why they'd waste time and steel on such things. They crafted weapons, not rakes or plows.

"What if we have peace?" Ari Ara finally asked the girls. "What will you make then?"

"Peace is but an eye in the storm of war," recited one. "It is a lull in which to prepare for the next battle."

The Warrior Sister nodded approvingly at that response.

"My mother maintained peace for a decade," Ari Ara pointed out.

"And look what happened to her – " the girl blurted out thoughtlessly.

"Mind your tongue!" the Mother Sister scolded.

The girl blushed and stammered out an apology. The Twins hustled Ari Ara onward, leading her through the Shrine of Fallen Warriors, the Armory of Unusual Weapons, and a healer's research hall – the pride of the Gateway Abbey, funded by the nobles of the Westlands whose son had died of an untreatable wound during the War of Retribution.

Ari Ara was dismayed by how much of the abbey's focus was oriented toward war. She'd expected it at Monk's Hand Monastery – they were famous for training warriors – but she'd assumed the Sisterlands would be different. Of course, the Warrior Sister ran the training grounds at the Citadel, but Ari Ara thought the Mother Sister's work with the orphans would stand in sharp contrast with her twin's.

Instead, the pair worked in tandem, two sides of the same bloody coin.

"It was so strange to hear those girls," Ari Ara complained to Finn and Minli later, stretching like a cat on the woven rug by the hearth in her quarters. Moonlight pressed against the windows. She should go to bed – the first test of the ordeal would start at dawn – but she was too wound up to sleep. Snippets of conversation twanged like taut bowstrings through her memory. The words of the young girls kept snapping back into her thoughts.

"It was as if they couldn't dream beyond war," she went on, "as if the rest of the world of possibilities didn't exist."

Minli nodded in agreement, rubbing his stomach and sipping mint tea after the rich and sumptuous feast held in their honor. Ari Ara had been so busy minding her manners that she hadn't eaten more than two bites. She had been insistently warned by the dressiers not to spill sauce on the soft gold of her layered robes. Sitting stiff as a stone statue, she had stayed on her best behavior while the feast dragged long into the night. She'd been patient with the orphans, attentive to the Sisters, generous with her smile and careful with her words. When she finally shut the door to her sleeping quarters behind her, she flopped onto the bed with an exhausted groan. She'd endured hours of sweat-dripping drills that were easier than this!

And the official trial wouldn't even begin until tomorrow.

She had been glad when Minli knocked on the door and let her vent her pent-up steam with a long-winded tirade. By the time Finn showed up with some bread and cheese he'd charmed out of the kitchen girls, she had changed into her favorite set of patched-up practice clothes and was in a much better mood. The three sat on the mats and cushions next to the hearth. The furnishings were finely-made, but sparse; until she passed her ordeal, she was an aspirant, not a royal leader. Minli and Finn's room was larger than hers. Brinelle's was an entire house. Ari Ara didn't mind - she slept better on a simple cot in her Fanten cloak than on a springy mattress buried under featherdown.

"If we'd grown up here," Ari Ara mused, nudging Minli, "do you think we would have wanted to serve war and warriors, too?"

"I grew up at Monk's Hand Monastery," Minli reminded her, "and yeah, I might not have known I could have a different future if you hadn't come along."

"That's your task though, isn't it?" Finn told Ari Ara as she munched on the bread he'd brought. "To make space for other dreams?"

"It's our task," Ari Ara countered, gesturing to him and Minli. "All of us who follow the Way Between."

Since ancient times, against unspeakable odds, amidst bloodshed and terror, these dreams had refused to surrender: a time of peace, a world beyond war, a generation who could do more than survive. In Alaren's time, a world without battles dwelled within living memory. Their parents and grandparents remembered it, clung to it, and worked with Alaren to restore it. One brutal battle after another, this hope faded from humanity's memory. But the dream never vanished, not entirely. The longing for peace wove into the language of myth and the beauty of vision. And some people continued to work for it. Even when Alaren's followers had been hunted down, imprisoned, and executed, the warmongers could never rid the world of those who still kindled the dreams of peace. Blood cannot wash off blood, after all.

Every person who sees the light fade in a wounded friend's eyes will one day long for an end to violence. Every child who loses their parents will wish for a world where peace could have kept them alive. Every terror-struck youth on the eve of battle, every war-weary fighter soldiering on, every haunted veteran wracked by the past yearns for peace to come sooner, last longer, and hold faster. Under their heartache, despair, fear, and bitterness lies the hunger for what could have been: lives beyond the sharp edges of violence, loved ones growing to old age; vocations of healing, building, and creating; communities that can live and rejoice.

"Imagine," Ari Ara murmured, her eyes distant with the stories of both ancient times and future hopes, "if Alaren had succeeded in reuniting his brothers. Imagine if our world had known peace this whole time."

Thousands of years. Millions of lives. Libraries of stories.

By the crackle of the hearth, they murmured out glimpses of how the world might have been - still could be - without the vast nightmare of war. The muscular strength of warriors poured into dance, or barn-raising, or stone carving. The steel of swords forged into crafts halls and tools. The marching armies transformed into people working for peace in every village, town, and city. Historians and storytellers spinning epics of how war was averted, how conflicts were solved, how peace was won for a little while longer.

Who might they be in a world such as this?

How many bright futures had been lost to war?

If their societies - Marianan and Harraken - stopped wasting even a single breath, droplet of sweat, or moment of time longer on preparing to kill each other . . . what sort of lives could they live?

Even a day of this possibility loomed unfathomable. It quickened Ari Ara's pulse. It shone in Minli's eyes. It caught Finn's breath in his chest. And a year of such a world would change everything. A century of peace stretched beyond even a lifetime of wild imagination. A thousand years entered the star stuff of legends.

Still, they could dream. If ever the dreams of peace had a chance to take root in the fertile ground of reality . . . this was it. It started with them, with three friends committed to change. With the resurgence of the Way Between. With the Mark of Peace printed on their tunics and inked between Ari Ara's shoulders. With the potential of the heir to two thrones, coming closer to wearing the crown.

CHAPTER EIGHT

. . . . .

The Orphans Hall

Two blue-robed novices woke her just after dawn, shushing her questions and handing her a plain-woven tunic and pants. *A queen is humble and unpretentious,* Ari Ara thought happily as she dressed. She'd much rather wear these clothes than a fancy dress in the high styles of the capital. If the Sisters thought she'd balk at such common clothing, they were wrong.

She followed the novices to breakfast, enjoying the porridge and fruit despite her nerves over the impending ordeal. A buzz of tension hissed through the dining hall. Whispers chased her like a swarm of bees. After she'd washed her bowl - all the while sensing the watching eyes of the Sisters - the Mother Sister summoned her.

"Now we will begin."

She took Ari Ara by the arm and led her to one of the Orphans Halls. Her first test - the first official one, anyway - would be a Trial of Service.

"A queen is the servant of her people," the Mother Sister intoned.

"She works for them without complaint," Ari Ara finished, reciting the line from *The Book of Queens.*

The gentle woman smiled and nodded approvingly.

"Your task is simple: tidy the Orphans Hall."

Ari Ara grinned. That sounded easy enough.

Then the doors swung apart and her mouth dropped open.

The Orphans Hall looked like a tornado had struck. Beds stood on end, their mattresses sprawling like honey-drunk bears, the blankets flung in every direction. Robes and tunics carpeted the floor like autumn leaves. Plates of half-eaten dinners rotted on the windowsill. A thick streak of mud marred the wooden floor and bore telltale signs of small feet sliding through it repeatedly. A pair of pigeons had been let loose in the rafters, leaving white splats everywhere. Cobwebs draped the high corners. Sawdust piled up by the foundation. They must have spent weeks preparing this challenge.

"May the ancestors smile upon you," the Mother Sister murmured as she shut the double doors behind her.

Ari Ara rolled up her sleeves and got to work. If they expected her to be too proud to scrub mud on her hands and knees, they didn't know her at all. She hadn't grown up as a pampered noble – she doubted her cousin Korin had even wielded a broom except as a pretend sword. Ari Ara had tended sheep and mucked stables, washed linens and emptied stinking chamber pots. All the Monk's Hand Monastery orphans, the village children, and the Fanten younglings did chores. It was part of life and must be done. Expecting parents or adults to do all the work was the kind of foolishness that only the very entitled could afford.

Ari Ara scrubbed and mopped, folded and sorted, swept and tidied for hours. At last, she stood back and surveyed her handiwork. Rows of remade beds, clothes stacked on the foot, plates by the door gleaming with dripping wash water. She'd chased the pigeons out the window and scaled the rafters to sweep out the cobwebs. The sawdust had been cleaned from the corners right down to the last woodchips. She'd emptied and refilled her bucket of soap and water more times than she could count, but the Orphans Hall shone.

Just as she turned to tell the Sisters that she had finished, the doors burst open. A mob of shrieking and laughing orphans rushed in. By the mischief in their eyes, Ari Ara could tell they intended trouble.

The smallest ones jumped on the beds and flung the carefully folded clothes on the floor. The bigger ones upended buckets of kitchen scraps. A pair hauled a crate of piglets in and set them loose. A trio of giggling girls tossed baskets of cornhusks into the air. With a cry of dismay, Ari Ara spotted two scruffy little boys grinning like their birthdays had come early as they dipped their hands into jam jars and smeared sticky streaks across the length of the walls.

In minutes, it was over. The orphans emptied from the room, leaving Ari Ara alone in the wreckage, all her hard work ruined.

Ari Ara stubbornly lifted her chin. If they thought she'd give up or shout or break down in tears, then they were wrong. She'd been through far greater challenges. She pushed back her hair and went to work.

The second time the orphans returned, she was ready for them. As the doors flung open and the laughing horde churned toward her perfectly polished hall, Ari Ara unleashed the Way Between on them. She caught the little ones by the waist and gently turned them back into the surprised arms of the older girls. She blocked the boys who tried to burst through and redirected their momentum back into the corridor. Jostling and bumping, the orphans tangled in each other's limbs and wound up on the floor, staring up at her.

"That's more like it," she muttered under her breath.

Then a creaking groan moaned from the ceiling above her. She peered up . . . an attic door opened and a cascade of feathers emptied onto her head.

The orphans burst out laughing.

Ari Ara spat out a feather and wrestled with her temper. Queens did not yell at little children . . . especially if they were only following the instructions of the Sisters.

The group of orphans watched her curiously, waiting for her to react. Ari Ara's mind raced, thinking back to her days at the monastery, scouring her trainings in the Way Between, looking for something, anything, that could help her out of this impasse. For it was clear that she could clean this hall a hundred times and the orphans would simply wreck it in a new way. Ari Ara supposed the trial of service was intended to test her fortitude, her control of her temper, and her commitment to helping others. At some point, the Sisters would call off this game.

But she didn't have the patience for that.

Far better to solve this problem another way.

"Who wants to play a game?" she asked, eyeing them.

No one answered, but they shot looks at each other, wondering if this was allowed. Ari Ara plucked a feather from her hair and twirled it.

"Let's race. All of you against me. I'm going to try to put these feathers in a pillowcase. You try to throw them out the window first. If I get more than fifty in the sack, I win. If not . . . then you do. Deal?"

"What do we get if we win?" said a scrunch-faced little boy.

Ari Ara thought a moment.

"I'll show you the Way Between."

A hushed conference broke out among the huddled children. Then, they stepped apart and nodded. She had a deal.

Just as the trick had once worked on her, it worked on them. Scrambling to their feet, the orphans erupted into a squeal of motion, grabbing fistfuls of feathers and tossing them out the window. Ari Ara didn't hold back either, leaping and whirling, plucking feathers from the air, laughing as she dove for one just as another orphan snatched it.

In minutes, there wasn't a feather to be found – the cheekiest little boy had snatched her pillowcase and emptied it out the window. When the Sisters came to check on her progress, they found Ari Ara and the children practicing the tap-and-evade training of the Way Between, the room spotless, and the orphans unwilling to interrupt their fun to make more messes for her to clean.

"Well done, Ari Ara de Marin en Shirar," the Mother Sister said with a smile. "True leadership does not consist of doing everything for everyone, but in inspiring them to undertake the effort together."

CHAPTER NINE

. . . . .

Triumph & Suspicion

The trials at the Gateway Abbey lasted a week. Ari Ara was tested on her sense of duty by lugging a storehouse of sacred scrolls up to a temple - one at a time. She proved that she had the dignity of a queen by maintaining her composure while a group of mischievous orphans threw dung at her. She demonstrated discipline by gritting her teeth through an interminably long ritual to honor the warriors of bygone times.

There were tests of patience and decisiveness. Tests for endurance and swift response. Tests for tact and diplomacy. Tests for gracefulness and poise. The hardest part was not knowing *which* virtue she was being tested on . . . or that an ordeal was even underway. Ari Ara spent an entire evening chatting with the three girls from the workshops before realizing that the curved walls of the hall slid their whispers along the pale stones straight into the ears of the Twins of the Sisterlands.

Ari Ara and Minli spent the rest of the night sleeplessly reviewing every word that had passed her lips. Urged on by the girls, she'd told stories of her time in the capital, the desert, the

Border Mountains. Their eyes widened with each tale. Ari Ara remembered how small her world had been, once, when it could be contained in the single sweep of the High Mountains. She saw the girls' curiosity overpower their prejudices as she spoke of the ceaseless songs of the Harraken, their magnificent horses, their sweeping lands of dust and sun. They peppered her with questions about the Peace Force and all the border towns she'd visited. They begged for every last detail she could remember about Mariana Capital from the fashions to the architecture to the street urchins.

"I want to see all those places," declared the girl who had wanted nothing more than to marry a warrior.

"Even the desert?" squeaked her friend, the one who dreamed of becoming a healer.

"Yes. And if there's peace then maybe I'll get to go, someday. You should be a healer for the Peace Force – imagine the places *you'd* go!"

The third girl didn't say much to Ari Ara. But later, she sought out Minli of Monk's Hand and asked how one applied to the Capital University.

"What will you study?" Minli asked her after explaining the process.

"Anything," she answered. Then she paused and amended her statement. "Everything."

Her voice grew taut with fierce longing. The boundaries of her world had been breached by story. As the walls toppled, she peered over the hints of the known and longed to see what lay beyond the horizon. Her old dream of keeping records for the army felt as constricting as a too-small pair of shoes. She could walk no further in them.

Each morning, the dawn trainings in the Way Between swelled with new participants. A crowd of children jostled to watch along the sidelines. At first, only a few wide-eyed girls had paused as they crept about their early chores. The next day, they were back, dragging friends along with them. After Ari Ara's first trial, so many children crammed into the courtyard that there was hardly room to turn around. Shulen moved the practices to the docks, standing on the central wharf while the orphans spread out across the other docks and up the rising crescents of the tiered streets.

Ari Ara poured the fierce heat of her passion into the demonstration against Emir Miresh, the youngest champion warrior in Marianan history. Hair flying in a flame-red blur, she whipped past his attacks in *attar*, the Warrior's Way. She spun and lunged as she turned aside the unavoidable blows. Fine wisps of harbor mist prickled her skin. The boards of the dock creaked and turned slick underfoot. A hush fell as Emir nearly forced her off the side, into the water. She tottered and used her last degree of balance to shove her momentum back to firmer footing. Flinging her hands out, she gripped the metal post that moored the boats. With a wrench she suspected she'd regret the next day, she swung her body around and tapped Emir with her feet – not enough to bruise, just enough to tip him into the water.

The cheer that rang out brought every sister in the abbey running. Shulen met the Twins at the head of the wharf to explain. Ari Ara leaned over the water to offer Emir a hand up. Instead, he tugged her in. She came up bursting with startled laughter. Her sense of humor set off the suddenly quiet orphans. Before long, she and Emir were not the only ones in the water.

Later, as Ari Ara wrung out her sopping tunic and shook the water out of her curls, she felt the slam of the Warrior Sister's stare hit her. The hot anger in Roka Maro's eyes could have dried out her clothes. But Ari Ara didn't flinch. It had been worth risking the ire of the Warrior Sister to dispel the barrier of reserve between her and the orphans. For the rest of the week, clusters of children trailed in Ari Ara's wake. A rotating flock gathered at her table for meals. Clusters accompanied her as she walked along the halls. Small crowds skipped their chores to watch her undergo the rest of her tests in the Ordeal of Queens.

"She's a distraction to them all," Roka Maro grumbled.

"She should be," Brinelle countered. "This is a once-in-a-generation moment. Let them make the most of it. They will speak of these days to their children, and their children's children."

"That's what I'm afraid of," Roka muttered in a voice so low, the Great Lady almost missed the words.

By the time they prepared to board the Fair Defiance to sail upriver for the next set of trials, Ari Ara was ready to fall into her berth and sleep for a month. She was such a quivering bundle of exhausted nerves and exhilarated triumph that she bungled the ritual words of farewell on the dock, calling Roka Maro a "spirit-infested blister" instead of a "spirit-blessed sister".

Not that the Warrior Sister could hear her.

The crescent harbor of the Gateway Abbey throbbed with noise. Orphans and sisters lined the cove's walkway and leaned out the windows of the tiered buildings. Great Horns trumpeted on the cliffs, the thunderous cascade of echoes rolling around the harbor. Children cheered and waved blue handkerchiefs wildly overhead, hoping to catch the Lost Heir's eye one last time. A set of older girls stood on the rooftops, heaving handfuls of primrose petals into the breeze. A pack of boys leapt into the harbor, striving for the biggest, sparkling spray of water.

Ari Ara waved in gratitude and the chant dissolved into a wordless roar. She staggered back a step. The Great Lady hid her satisfied smirk and put a hand on the girl's back to steady her. Whatever motivated the Sisters in calling for this Ordeal, the young people clearly supported the Lost Heir.

"What are they saying?" Ari Ara asked, trying to pick out the words that hopped from one mouth to the next, growing into a half-drowned chant slowly rising through the din.

River Dragon! River Dragon!

"They are calling you the River Dragon," her aunt explained, a smile broadening across her stern face.

Ari Ara's hairs prickled up her arms and down her back. The river dragon was the symbol of the royal house, the emblem of the nation. Vast and powerful, she did not simply live *in* the Mari River. She *was* the Mari River. Angered, she rose up in coils of water, massive and unstoppable, ready to battle those she deemed foes. Harraken armies throughout history had claimed to see her, often as a river of blood. Kings fell to her justice. Queen rose on the back of her grace. She could nourish the crops, or drown them. Turn the mill wheels, or smash them. Carry the boats, or sink them.

"The greatest leaders in our history were called *River Dragon*," Brinelle told Ari Ara. "They were seen as the human embodiment of the river's majesty and power. She is the force that unites us all, constant, ever-changing, unstoppable."

Dangerous. Nurturing. Life-giving. Life-taking. Flowing through the heart of the country, connecting all the people, collecting the waters of their world in her currents. By calling Ari Ara by the honorific of *River Dragon*, the young people were voicing their unequivocal support.

With a satisfied nod, the Great Lady signaled to the captain to cast off. The Fair Defiance slid through the harbor and surged out of the eddied calm into the writhing Sister River. Pointing her prow upstream, the sails opened wide, using the billow of wind to counter the current. Ari Ara cast one last look over her shoulder, smiling at the cheers of the orphans until the sound faded.

"Remember this," Brinelle urged the girl, placing a hand on Ari Ara's shoulder. "When the ordeal pushes you to the breaking point, when you feel all alone, or in the moments when it seems no one is on your side. Your people love and support you, Ari Ara. Just as they did your mother."

"And you," Ari Ara added graciously.

Brinelle's mouth drew into a thin line. She shook her head.

"The people respect me - as well they should - but I am not foolish enough to pretend that they love me. It is enough to have their respect. Love is a temperamental creature, fickle and flighty. A fact which your mother found out the hard way when she announced her betrothal to your father."

That night, Ari Ara grabbed the journal and read long into the darkness, unable to tear her eyes away from the story. In Turim, under the expansive skies, Tahkan proposed and Alinore accepted. Then she returned home and fought the fiercest political battle of her life to secure her right to marry him. *This* was the part Brinelle had been remembering - when the nobles turned against Alinore and her people protested her treacherous choice in the streets.

Some days, Alinore wrote, *I feel I haven't a friend left on this side of the Border Mountains. Who knew love – and peace – could be so reviled? I almost think some people would rather keep dying on the battlefield than live in peace with their enemies. Rannor Thornmar even offered to lead the charge to 'reclaim my honor'. I asked him what on earth he was talking about and he said the Desert King had obviously worked song magic on me. I could barely think of an answer, I was so dismayed.*

It was a testimony to Alinore's tireless peacebuilding that she succeeded in marrying Tahkan Shirar. That her people accepted Ari Ara at all was a tribute to the persistence with which the young queen had persuaded them to open their hearts and minds. Person by person, Alinore brought them all around . . . mostly. A week before her marriage, she complained about a young novice sister who waylaid her at the temple.

There I was, deep in trance, the long night of fasting and vigiling aching in my bones, and this sister – hardly more than a girl – sneaks into the temple and starts warning me about the Prophecy of the Lost Heir. As if I hadn't known about it for years.

The Prophecy of the Lost Heir. Ari Ara frowned. It had been hidden after Alinore's death, and forgotten before then. How had Alinore learned of it? And how dare the novice sister threaten her with it! The words rushed out from her memory, along with the scent of dust and crumbling parchment. Four years ago, in the chill of the stone-carved archives of Monk's Hand Monastery, she and Minli had read the forbidden text, the one that warned of her coming.

One will come, a child born of two lineages, mother dead, father distant. Lost at birth, appearing half-grown, this child shall inherit two thrones, one in the desert, the other on the water. Uniter, Divider, Liberator, Destroyer; floods follow in this one's footsteps, famine stalks the heels of the heir. Upheaval and conflict surround this child, a war breaker, change maker. By the Mark of Peace, the lost one is found. Then the once broken becomes whole; the once wounded, healed; and the once forgotten remembered again.

Shulen had caught them bent over the secret scroll, guilty expressions on their faces. Even then, Ari Ara couldn't see what the fuss was about. The prophecy wasn't *all* gloom and doom. But, as the stern old warrior had cautioned them, there were some people who would rather control a piece of a broken world than share the whole world with everyone. Ari Ara scowled at the curve of the low ceiling over her bunk, thinking about the eggs hurled by the chanting sisters in Stoneport. Their twisted version of the prophecy sowed nothing but fear and discord. The sect that spread rumors of her doomed reign through Mariana Capital had turned people against each other and triggered brawls and fights. Had they been working to thwart the prophecy since before she was born? Maybe even since before her parents married? Alinore hadn't given into their threats . . . and Ari Ara wouldn't either.

I told that sister I knew all about the Prophecy of the Lost Heir and dismissed her. Her face seemed familiar. I've seen her in the training yards – she's a warrior. Shulen suggested her for the Royal Guard a few years ago, but much as we need more female guards, I didn't like her. Nor do I trust her now.

Alinore said nothing more. Ari Ara's eyes burned in their sockets as she flipped forward a few pages, hoping for another entry on the young novice. She had a sneaking suspicion it was Roka Maro – and if so, Ari Ara didn't trust her either.

CHAPTER TEN

. . . . .

When I Am Queen

The success at the Gateway Abbey buoyed Ari Ara's spirits and although everyone warned her against overconfidence, excitement verged on cockiness in the young heir. For the first time since the fire ritual in the capital, Ari Ara considered that she might actually pass this ordeal. A tingling thrill flooded through her at the thought of being queen. There was so much that could be done! So much *she* wanted to do! Teach people how to wage peace. Retrain the soldiers and warriors. Lift up the forgotten stories of the Way Between. Forge friendship and understanding among both cultures.

As the Fair Defiance followed the serpentine coils of the Sister River toward their next stop, Ari Ara returned to her neglected studies of *The Book of Queens* with renewed purpose. Bottling herself up in her quarters, she hefted the thick book onto the desk and sat straight-spined in the chair. She intended to memorize several chapters each day until they arrived at Marin's Mountain, the home of a shrine to the ancestor spirits and the site of her next test. She was determined to pass this ordeal. It wasn't just her future at stake, but everyone's. Peace depended on her getting to the throne. The words on the page however, hit her like a brick wall.

A queen rides into battle against her enemies.

A queen honors her warriors.

A queen raises the funds necessary for victory.

Ari Ara's heart sank at the rest of the verses on the page; each detailed the expectation that she would battle, vanquish, subdue, and destroy her father's people. Slouching in disappointment, she flipped through the chapter. It only grew worse. As queen, she'd be expected to cheer the army on, ride at the head of military parades, wear the uniform of a commander, make proclamations on the anniversaries of historic victories, hand out medals to valiant warriors, fund pensions for war widows and education for their children. But that wasn't all. The role went beyond mere ceremony. The monarch of Mariana served as a military leader in times of war. Heirs to the throne were expected to study battle history and war maneuvers. They drilled alongside the warriors and trained in military strategy.

Ari Ara buried her head in her hands and quit reading. She could never do those things. It curdled her stomach to think of charging onto a battlefield and swinging a sword at someone's neck. She'd been thrown out of the Nobles Academy for refusing to play war games or accept the limited rules of battle strategy.

Where was the section on how a queen ensured peace?

Ari Ara lifted her head and scanned the next chapter. Nothing. Desperately, she flipped the pages, trying to find the words *peace, negotiation, diplomacy*. Why didn't *The Book of Queens* list out all the actions a queen could take to stop a war, not just win one? She refused to accept that a queen had to support war. If she passed the ordeal - no, *when*, she corrected sternly - she was going to rewrite the book.

Maybe: A *queen defends her people by befriending her enemies.*

Or: A *queen rides into danger to seek peace.*

Perhaps: A *queen honors the peacemakers and invests in the Way Between.*

She spent the rest of the day revising the expectations of a queen. It took force of will – and a strict, horrified admonishment from Minli – not to scribble her thoughts down in the margins of *The Book of Queens.*

"For ancestors' sake, Ari Ara!" her tousled-haired friend gasped when she asked if he'd make the notes in his perfect handwriting. "This is a rare, priceless book that's been studied by hundreds of monarchs. You can't *change* it."

"Why not?" she countered, hands on her hips. "Maybe we wouldn't have so many wars if our rulers weren't told it was their duty to wage them."

Minli shoved a blank piece of parchment at her and told her to write her thoughts down as an addendum to stick in the back of the book. She pushed it back across the desk and tried to cajole him into scribing for her.

Minli refused.

"I share your ideas," he assured her hastily, lifting his hands up in a helpless shrug, "but aren't you getting distracted from your ordeal? Instead of daydreaming about what you'll do *when* you're queen, maybe you should focus on getting there. The Sisters will definitely test you on this."

He left her to it. Ari Ara stared balefully at *The Book of Queens.* What was the point of studying it if she was just going to change it?

"When I am queen," Ari Ara declared the next morning during *azar* training, "I'm going to get rid of all the warriors."

A thick mist trailed across the deck of the Fair Defiance. Shulen paced the floorboards, instructing several groups. Ari Ara had been matched two-to-one with Finn and Minli. She whipped out of reach as Finn lunged wildly. She spun around Minli as he nearly caught her. A beam of sunlight cut the mist and stung her eyes. Partially-blinded, she reacted by instinct as they shifted closer. Ari Ara dropped down and rolled across the creaking floorboards of the ship, narrowly evading them.

A pair of the Great Lady's guards stood three paces away, scanning the shores for any sign of threat, listening to the three youth's chatter with studied disinterest. On the other side, a sailor watched openly as he sanded down a stack of long oars. A stench of fish oil skimmed the air as another crewmember reapplied the waterproofing to a canvas covering for the dory. Like the rest of the crew, they didn't hide their interest in the Way Between. With several days of sailing before their next stop, Shulen had opened up the daily trainings to the sailors, guards, and servants. The Way Between welcomed everyone. It bolstered morale and started the days on a lively note. It built trust between the crew and the heir. Slowly, the practices won over the skeptics and showed them that Ari Ara de Marin en Shirar's dedication to the Way Between was rooted in strength, not weakness; courage, not cowardice; and vision, not wishful thinking.

"I think my mother would have abolished the army," Ari Ara added, leaping to her feet and pivoting to meet the boys' next feint, "if she had lived long enough."

Minli frowned.

"You said she wanted to gradually shift some of the war budget to other projects as lasting peace was established."

Ari Ara shrugged.

"Same thing."

"No, not really," Minli argued.

A statement like *I'm going to get rid of the warriors* wouldn't go over well anywhere in Mariana, least of all the war-obsessed

Sisterlands. For thousands of years, they'd been blessing the army and praying for victory on the battlefield. The nobles funded their orphanages to assuage their guilt over making so many orphans. Taxes on Mariana's industries paid for the upkeep and training of thousands of warriors in the Sisterlands. War was nearly inseparable from the spirituality of the nation. Even as Ari Ara and Minli spoke, the ship sailed through river-eroded cliffsides that bore carvings of battle scenes. Towering warrior figures loomed above them, forming a wall of ferocious statues. At their feet, just above the waterline, alcoves of offerings held hundreds of tokens, candles, and gifts to warriors of old. Each living fighter had a patron ancestor spirit among these legendary war heroes. Ari Ara's bold declarations would be viewed as an affront to the living and the dead. The past and present would strongly object to being excluded from the future.

Minli drew breath to tell her all of this, but Ari Ara wasn't in the mood to listen. She ducked and dodged, using speed and sweat to blow off the steam of her restless excitement. She felt like a leaf hurled high in hope's wind. Alinore had written in her journal about her plan to reduce the army as she forged peace with the Harraken through her marriage to Tahkan.

If I could cut the costs of maintaining such a large army, just think of the good I could do for my people! Schools. Arts. Research funding for the healers halls. Investments in new inventions for other industries. Finally repairing the roads.

"It could be done. It *should* be done. And I'll be the one to do it," Ari Ara declared, her confident tone flirting with the edge of arrogance. "When I am queen - "

"Less talk, more focus," Finn interrupted, red-faced with exertion and irritated by the offhand ease with which she ran circles around him and Minli. He'd rather not think about the day Ari Ara would be queen. Secretly, he hoped she would fail the ordeal. Not fatally . . . just enough to disqualify her so they could go back to the way things were. But she'd done well at the Gateway Abbey, as he expected she would. He knew Ari Ara would make a great queen . . . and it broke his heart. Finn had dreams for his future, too, and it didn't involve formal dinners. The more she succeeded, the closer he came to the day he'd have to leave her side.

"When I'm queen," she repeated dreamily, "we'll launch an effort to get young girls like the ones we met to learn the Way Between. And the trainees can study *azar* instead of *attar*. We'll have an army without weapons, a thousands-strong Peace Force."

Each word tore Finn in opposite directions. He wanted that vision, too. He'd lived through enough war to know the value of peace . . . but he wished she didn't have to ascend the throne to do it. In a churning whirlpool of conflicted emotions, Finn circled the training area, sliding between her and the midship mast.

"Just you wait," she stated boldly, feinting around Finn and whipping past Minli's attempt to catch her. "I'll change everything: the culture, our education system, even *The Book of Queens*."

"One step at a time, Ari Ara," Minli broke off his warning as she grabbed his arm and tugged him off-balance. Carefully, she levered his weight to the ground so he didn't take a bruising fall.

Minli's glint of a smile was her only warning.

On his back, he kicked out his good leg and swept her knees out from under her. Startled, she sprang backward, arching onto her hands and flinging her feet out to the side. She would have broken free, but she forgot about Finn. Straightening out of her crouch, he caught her in a two-armed embrace.

Ari Ara hid a grin. She knew the secret to getting loose if she wished. But she didn't. The light hit Finn's eyes like a lightning flash and his black curls blazed, awash with gold. The curve of his wiry muscles against her back sent a delighted shiver up her spine.

Heat flushed under her skin. The moment lingered and lengthened. A guard shifted. A sailor whistled. Threading her hands up to hold Finn's acorn-shaped face, she leaned in –

Shulen coughed.

Finn's look darkened like a storm cloud, sensing a warning. He pushed away. Ari Ara's confused expression hurt his heart. His simmering unease boiled over. He wished – longed with every fiber of his body – that she was just some girl he'd met at a village festival, that their paths could entwine as simply as joining hands in a dance. But she wasn't. Ari Ara was going to be queen of a world that had no place for him. Each time she declared *when I am queen*, she flung a hammer at the fragile illusion that this would somehow all work out. Each look from Brinelle cracked another hairline fracture through his hope. Shulen's cough struck a hard blow through his wishful thinking. The sky of Finn's heart fell down on him. To his horror, tears pricked his eyes. He whirled hastily away from her worried look.

"Finn!" she called after him.

He flung a hand back behind him to stop her from following and leapt down the ladder to his berth. Ari Ara's heart plummeted in her chest. Her wild excitement smashed onto the hard rocks of reality. Her hopeful mood cracked like a fragile robin's egg. Baffled and hurt, Ari Ara spun on Shulen.

"Look," she hissed at him, "what you've done."

CHAPTER ELEVEN

. . . . .

For Love's Sake

Ari Ara stomped back to her quarters in a seething temper, flung herself into her chair, and pulled out her mother's journal. Dimly, she registered her aunt's voice fading along the ship's length and a sour gratitude hit her for this moment of privacy. Brinelle didn't understand her love for Finn. No one did. She wished that her father was here. Or that her mother was still alive. Alinore would understand how she felt – no one had liked her choice in love, either.

Marrying Tahkan Shirar takes more courage than riding into battle against him. If I wanted to defeat him, my people would cheer me on. But, ironically, since I wish to love him, my people must be convinced and reassured that I am acting in the best interests of the nation, not just my silly heart. How can I help them see that peace is possible – and preferable? I am marrying for the good of this nation . . . and for me.

Ari Ara sat back in her chair, kicking the leg of the desk softly with her toe. *Marrying for the nation . . .* Alinore's dedication to her position and thoughtful consideration of how her choices influenced her people made Ari Ara squirm a little. She slouched lower, pensively wrestling with notions she hadn't considered before.

Finn was right for *her*, but would he be right for the country?

And more importantly: would marrying the heir to two thrones be right for *Finn*? Ari Ara tried to laugh – it was far too soon to even think about marrying anyone. She shifted uneasily. If she truly loved Finn, she should think this through. Stuffing Finn Paikason into a double-breasted doublet and making him preside over ceremonial functions as a royal consort wasn't fair to him. It was like putting a bear in trousers and ordering it to serve tea. Something magnificent and wild in him would either rebel . . . or vanish.

In the innermost chamber of her heart, a tiny voice whispered: *and what about the wildness in me? What do I have to give up because of my parentage?* Ari Ara slammed the door of her mind shut hard against that line of thinking. She couldn't consider that question. She had no choice. Finn did.

Besides, there was always a Way Between. Didn't her parents' marriage prove that?

A soft tap on the door pulled her from her musings.

"Come in."

Shulen entered looking uncharacteristically uncomfortable.

"I have to speak with you about Finn."

Ari Ara groaned and buried her face in her hands.

"Must you?" she grumbled.

The grey-haired warrior let out a sigh.

"I think you read more into my cough than intended," he mentioned. "I do not hold the same views of Finn as your Lady Aunt – "

"Thank the ancestors," she muttered.

The intensity of relief in her voice made him pause. Shulen considered his next words carefully. He had been about to say: *and your father.* Another letter from Tahkan had arrived.

As soon as the thudding drumbeats of the warriors in the capital had faded, Shulen had sent a messenger hawk to Tahkan, urging him to come at once and travel unseen. The Great Lady had issued the formal invitation, of course, but protests over the Desert King's inclusion in the Ordeal of Queens had erupted throughout the country. To many, it was unthinkable that a Harraken would bear witness to this sacred ritual. If Tahkan rode in with a contingent of Harraken riders, there'd be trouble. And delays. Nobles would block his path. Warriors would challenge him. The Sisters - some of them - would try to thwart him from arriving. But Ari Ara had a right to have her father at her side. Her mother was not here to offer wisdom and advice, nor solace and support when the grinding pressure intensified. The girl deserved to have the strength of her father to draw upon.

The Sisterhood is neither foe nor friend, he had written to Tahkan, *but perhaps a little of both. The animosity of the Warrior Sister is a concern to me. If she means harm to Ari Ara, she will have plenty of opportunity to hurt her during these grueling tests. She will, at the very least, try to sabotage Ari Ara's chances of passing the ordeal. Come at once.*

But Tahkan - headstrong as his daughter - replied with a stubbornly shortsighted note.

The Sisters present little danger. Ari Ara is my daughter. She will pass their ridiculous tests as her mother did before her. Have you gotten rid of that boy yet?

Shulen had crumpled the note into a tight ball, irritated. Tahkan Shirar was worrying over nothing when it came to Finn. If he truly cared about his daughter, he'd drop everything and come to her side.

Not for the first time, the thin wire of jealousy twanged through the grey-haired man's heart. If *his* daughter were still alive,

Shulen would move mountains to stand beside her. He would not waste a precious minute of her life tracking down old ghosts. Tahkan had squandered weeks trying to find the identity of his wife's assailants. No one wanted to know that secret more than Shulen – those attackers had also brutally murdered his wife and child – but every day spent in the past was a day lost to the present. Tahkan was forfeiting irreplaceable time in his daughter's life. He'd already missed eleven years. Shulen could not understand his friend's actions. Tahkan had snuck into Mariana in disguise to meet Ari Ara. Was the unsolved mystery so much of a threat that he'd sacrifice this time together now?

And the man's fatherly dislike of his daughter's boyfriend was just ridiculous. Tahkan was wrong about Finn. If he saw how much Ari Ara smiled in the boy's presence, the desert man would not have written this letter. The brash sixteen-year-old may not be Shulen's first choice for Ari Ara's affections, but he had a number of commendable qualities. Courage. Intelligence. Pride. Shulen saw little point in fretting over the pair.

The first chance he found, he threw Tahkan's message overboard. The fish could eat the man's foolishness. It was beyond hypocritical for Tahkan Shirar to try to control his daughter's heart – the man who had navigated the most star-crossed love in the history of the world.

Shulen took one look at the lost and confused expression on Ari Ara's face and knew he was right to ignore Tahkan's warning. Nothing would be gained by acting on it, or even mentioning it to the girl. The man was a fool and he was too far away to understand. Resolving to send another messenger hawk urging Tahkan to come, Shulen turned his attention to the redheaded girl caught in an emotional tempest. He pulled up a chair as Ari Ara glared moodily at him.

"I am not your enemy, Ari Ara," he began.

"Are you Finn's?" she challenged him sharply.

He blinked.

"Not at all."

"Everyone wants to get rid of him."

"Not everyone."

"Brinelle."

"Well, I don't share her views," he said simply, quietly. How could he? "It is not easy to love across cultures. It takes courage and determination. When I first met Rhianne – "

He broke off. Ari Ara held her breath, still as a deer when a twig cracks, hoping he would go on. Shulen rarely spoke of the Fanten woman he had fallen in love with. Ari Ara had once broached the subject with Rhianne's mother, the secretive matriarch of the Fanten of the High Mountains, but the Fanten Grandmother brusquely changed the subject. She surpassed even her customary tight-lipped habits in her refusal to say anything about her daughter's life, love, and death. The silver-haired old woman dwelled in shadows and mist; no one could pry her secrets from her. But Ari Ara knew the Fanten Grandmother blamed Shulen – a blood-dripping warrior – for leading her daughter into danger. Seething animosity still burned between them. Ari Ara didn't expect to learn much about Rhianne from either of them.

Alinore, however, had written copiously about Rhianne's startling arrival in the Mariana Capital. It was unheard of for a Fanten to come to the city. Ordinarily, they dwelled, aloof and remote, in the immense forest that flanked the eastern boundary of the nation. Reclusive and disdainful of lowlanders – as they called the river valley inhabitants – the Fanten kept to themselves. By twist of fate, Ari Ara had been raised among them in the High Mountains, but when Rhianne arrived in Mariana Capital, few city-dwellers had even *seen* one of her kind. Twenty-three year old Alinore had only heard the legends about them.

You'd think a unicorn had walked down the cobblestones for all the stir it caused, Alinore wrote in her journal. *Tiny, scarcely bigger than a child, wearing this lovely dress with a dark black cloak, her hair braided and coiled in a crown. Brinny whispered to me to take notes on regal demeanor. I rolled my eyes, but my cousin has a point. Rhianne walked straight into the House of Marin and somehow secured an audience with me. All the guards just let her through, like they were half-dreaming. So peculiar. She announced in this strange accent that she has come as the emissary of her people. When someone pointed out that we've never had a Fanten ambassador before, she looked him dead in the eye and said: "We have dreamed it." Mouths literally fell open. She said it completely straight-faced. As if just because it had been dreamed, it would be so.*

Ari Ara had grinned, reading that last line. Fanten dreams defied belief. They ran truer than true. While lowlanders churned through rehashes of their days or mottled mashups of their hopes and fears, Fanten walked through dreams like an extension of their forest. They could deliver messages faster than hawks, read the future, and commune with the ancestors. And that was just scratching the surface. Ari Ara had stumbled into dreamwalking more times than she could count; her years with the Fanten had gifted her with the ability. But although she had once spoken to her mother's spirit and sent messages through the Fanten Grandmother, Ari Ara sensed that she merely skimmed in the shallows of the fathomless ocean of the dreamrealm. She didn't have the proper training to navigate the depths.

Since most lowlanders scoffed at tales of Fanten dreamwalking and the Fanten Grandmother had made Ari Ara promise not to reveal the nature of her dreams. She wished she could tell Shulen. He might understand. His love for Rhianne had taught him to respect the Fanten.

"We were so different," he told Ari Ara, eyes distant with memory. "I was the Great Warrior of Mariana, Head of the Royal

Guard. She was Fanten, with all her people's abhorrence of violence."

Ari Ara knew from her mother's journal that although Shulen was lovestruck at the first glimpse of the Fanten woman, it took years of slow courtship for him to reveal to her that there was more to him than his fighting skills. Throngs of capital women came to the training yards, hoping to catch the eye of Nshoka Shulen, but Rhianne refused to go anywhere near the sweaty field of drilling fighters. Like her clans, she felt physically sick at the clash of swords and the dull thud of punches.

"Your mother made our love possible," Shulen told Ari Ara. "She and Rhianne were great friends, and since I served as the queen's guard, the two of us were often together with Alinore."

Lovestruck at first sight, Shulen had gone to the queen immediately. Alinore's writing captured the startling confession.

I can scarcely think of the words to say! Shulen requested an audience – so strangely formal of him – knelt before me and held his sword out, flat across both palms. "I must resign my post in the Guard," he stated, solemn and stoic as always. I asked him why and he said:

"For my whole life, I have served queens, first your mother, then you. But my heart has been captured by another. My loyalties are split. If an assassin's arrow flies, I may not leap in front of you to take its death blow."

So Shulen. So dramatic in that quietly serious way. I wanted to shake him. Instead, I asked if I might know the name of the person to whom I was losing him. (I figured it was a woman, but one must never assume.) Oooh, he did not wish to tell me, but I pried it out of him at last.

Nshoka Shulen has fallen in love with Rhianne of the Fanten! Of all the unlikely warriors to be smitten in a single glance . . . and she hasn't a clue, of course, she's only just arrived in the capital. How do you know? I asked Shulen. I mean, he was ready to resign from the post he's held my whole life and a decade before that.

"You just know."

I must have given him a skeptical look at that answer, because he eased up a little and nearly smiled.

"You'll know, too, when it happens."

It hasn't yet, but I thanked him for his optimism. I told him he couldn't quit, I would not accept his resignation, and if he leaves, I'll ban him from the capital and then he'll never be able to court Rhianne.

"As my Fanten emissary, she's going to be at my side . . . where you should be, too."

I doubt he believed I'd kick him out, but at least he agreed to stay. Which means I'll have a front row seat for this love story!

"But Ari Ara," Shulen said, coming at last to his point, "having loved and lost, having withstood the scorn and disbelief others felt at my marriage to Rhianne, having navigated the ravine of our differences around *attar*, I can tell you this . . . "

He caught her eyes and held it.

"It was worth it. All of it. If Rhianne of the High Mountains walked through the door of this cabin, I would do it all over again in a heartbeat."

"All of it?" Ari Ara whispered in a wide-eyed hush. "Even knowing how it would end?"

Shulen's chin trembled. A shine of tears hit his slate-grey eyes. He swallowed hard. He would try to avoid his mistakes, of course. What man wouldn't? But if fate offered him only the love and the loss, he would brave the pain for the sake of the love.

"Yes, Ari Ara," he said, rising to leave, "I would do it all over again."

He paused at the door.

"And I hope you and Finn would, too."

CHAPTER TWELVE

. . . . .

Marin's Mountain

Ari Ara's lungs burned. Her legs screamed. Thousands of stone-chiseled steps lay behind her. Three hundred more awaited. The second test of her Ordeal of Queens had begun at dawn at the river's edge. The steep, shadowed forest of Marin's Mountain loomed over her. The morning mist beaded on her face as she set out on the winding trail toward the shrine at the summit. She had been climbing all afternoon, the sound of her breath growing ever more ragged in her ears. Thirst scraped her throat raw. A dark stain of sweat dampened her back. The coarse fabric of the simple shift clung to her skin. Moss capped the heads of boulders and curled between their huddled shoulders. A dense canopy of trees cloaked the sun. The forest throbbed with birdsong and frog chants.

Then it all went silent.

The hair on Ari Ara's arms lifted. She paused, one foot suspended above the next step. In the shadows of the tree trunks, her eyes picked out the ancestor pillars. Ancient, half-buried in leaves, they crowded the slope with watchful presences, the names of her forebearers carved onto them. Marin's Mountain held stone pillars for each of the bloodline relatives of King Marin, all the way back through history to his one hundredth great-grandparents and down through time to Queen Alinore. Ari Ara's mother's stone greeted her at the bend, its carvings smooth and clean, and a marking that indicated one child. Brinelle's pillar had been placed near Alinore's. Her son Korin's stood slightly to the east. Should Ari Ara fail her ordeal or die childless, the lineage of Marin would shift onto his line. But if Ari Ara passed her ordeal, her pillar would be placed beside her mother's, her child's next to that, and so on into the infinite future, the Sister River carving out more hillside for the generations yet to come.

The monuments spanned thousands of years. Somewhere on the mountain, even Shirar and Alaren were named, though their descendants were not. There were stones to the Three Brothers' mother and father, though, and their grandparents, back and back through time. A great-great-granddaughter of Marin had begun the carvings, transforming a crumbling record of the royal house to enduring stone. The shrine at the top of the mountain honored the pillar of the oldest-known ancestor. A hermit sister tended the shrine. Others guarded the pillars, watchful for erosion or desecrators. Ari Ara had been warned not to stray off the footpath. If she was lucky, she would never see the Guardian Sisters.

Ari Ara cautiously took her next step. She could hear the whispering of ancestor spirits. Quiet at first, they swelled from a sough of wind into a buzz of swarming insects. Ari Ara couldn't decipher the hissed words, but her skin crawled with the sense that they had been angered over something. Was this a test? Or a sign? Was she not welcome? Shouldn't her ancestors support her?

In the boughs overhead, shades of silvered figures gathered. Among the darkest shadows, rows of spirits hovered. Ari Ara held her breath. The ancestors were mysterious and powerful. They could speak, if they chose, or remain silent. They could clear the path for the living, or they could bar their descendant's progress. They knew secrets that mere mortals could only guess at . . . and how they'd act upon this knowledge was anyone's guess. The ways of the unliving rarely made sense in the logic of flesh and blood.

"Please let me pass," Ari Ara whispered.

Be careful.

The words sighed in the wind, a single voice made of thousands. At first, she thought the spirits were warning her to tread carefully. But the ancestors turned silently and stared balefully into the forest. Without rustling a leaf, two Guardian Sisters stepped out of the trees, heads shaved in honor of their renewing vows. One held a water flask. The other, a chalice.

"Drink," she offered, "you must be thirsty."

The ancestor spirits shivered in the air, a thousand heads shaking at once.

Their warning was the only thing that kept her from accepting the Guardian Sisters' water. Ari Ara swallowed her temptation. The sound of the water pouring into the chalice pulled a groan of longing toward her throat. She caught it in her chest and hastily turned it into a cough.

"Thank you, gracious sisters, but I will endure," she told them, regretfully.

They tried again . . . and again. Their voice rose insistently. Each time, Ari Ara refused. At last, she took off at a run, the sisters' cries shouting after her. The ancestor spirits hummed in her ears. In gossip or warning or disapproval, she couldn't tell. She glanced nervously into the woods, wondering if the Guardian Sisters also heard the mutters of the spirits.

She stiffened her resolve. Her instructions had been clear: *go to the shrine at the top of the mountain. Tend the altar through the night.* Ari Ara recited lines from *The Book of Queens* to take her mind off her thirst.

A queen acts with confidence.

A queen confronts her fears.

A queen braves the opinions of others.

Ari Ara silently whispered one verse for every six steps, matching the litany to motion, the chant pushing back the sound of the spirits.

She crested the peak. The voices fell silent.

A small temple of wood and slate crouched in the shelter of a towering boulder. An ancient, twisted juniper curved over the lichen-encrusted roof. Inside the propped-open door, a single incense stick curled in the thin beams of westward sunlight.

Ari Ara glanced around. Whoever had lit it had seen her coming and vanished. This was it, then. Her vigil had begun. Across the yawning expanse of night, all the way to daybreak, Ari Ara would keep the incense burning, one stick after another. She would ensure the candles continued gleaming, lighting one from the flickering wick of the last. She could see the incense boxes from here. Were there enough to last until morning, even in a windstorm?

Ari Ara's anxious concern nearly propelled her over the threshold, but she caught herself in time. At the corner of the shrine's entry, a rock-encircled spring bubbled. It was the wonder of Marin's Mountain – a spring on a mountaintop - and the reason this peak had been chosen.

Ari Ara knelt, cupped her hands and drank. Carefully, she performed her ablutions, Fanten-style, washing the sweat and dust of the hike off her skin. No one, let alone a future queen, enters an ancestor shrine filthy. *The Book of Queens* had been clear about that.

A queen honors the ancestors.

A queen respects tradition.

A queen learns from the past.

A touch of evening's coolness shivered down her damp skin as she entered the building. She lit a fresh incense stick and eyed the shrinking candle. Gaging its pace, she counted the remaining candles and calculated how long they would last.

It would be close, she realized uneasily. Each candle would need to be lit from the very last flickering moments of the previous. She would need to be vigilant all night long, not only for this, but to prevent a draft from snuffing out the sole flame. She knew without searching that there would be no matches or flint in the temple.

Ari Ara used the remaining daylight to pull the shutters across the narrow, slit window in the western side of the shrine to keep out the drafts. She filled the gaps in the wood door with moss and repaired the mud plaster on the corner of the building. As dusk surrendered to darkness, Ari Ara steeled her resolve, preparing for a long, uncomfortable night. The chill would help her stay awake, as would the hunger in her belly.

Besides, she would need the long hours of thought to figure out her offering.

Tend the altar through the night, the Twins of the Sisterlands had instructed her. *At dawn, make an offering to your ancestors.*

She was not permitted to carry anything up the mountain. The plain-woven shift had no pockets. She could carry no coins, no food, no precious oils or silken cloth. Nothing but herself.

"What am I supposed to offer?" Ari Ara had hissed to Minli, eyes a bit wild.

Minli rattled off a litany of historic offerings - promises to erect shrines, pledges to give away one's wealth, even a vow of one's firstborn child given to the sisterhood. Ari Ara scowled at that - no one asked the child, after all.

"It has to be significant to you," Minli informed her, "and it ought to be a sacrifice, not something you'd do anyway – like practicing the Way Between for the rest of your life."

Ari Ara grimaced sheepishly. That was exactly the pledge she'd been thinking of making.

Darkness fell with suffocating closeness. The still, moonless night hung heavy and secretive. Wild animals rustled out of sight, foraging and hunting in the blackness. The altar candle's light danced an erratic waltz with the shadows. Ari Ara was no stranger to sleepless nights and long vigils. She had taken her turn in the watch rotation, guarding over her friends as they traveled. She'd protected newborn lambs in the High Mountains. She'd stayed up watchful and awake at the temple in the capital.

But the hours dragged slowly with only her thoughts to keep her company. Her muscles stiffened from the day's exertion and weariness overpowered hunger's gnawing alertness. Twice, she nearly dozed off, snapping upright just in time to light a fresh taper from the old wick flickering in a pool of beeswax. Ari Ara could feel the dreamrealm tugging at her like an undertow. At last, in the utter stillness partway between midnight and dawn, she drifted.

She didn't realize she was dreaming, not at first. She knelt by the altar, watching the candles gutter and spit. She reached out to light the fresh taper – but paused in surprise.

That was not her hand.

She turned the palm over, then back. Her callouses had vanished. Her fingers had lengthened. The indents of removed rings encircled them. She glanced down. Her body was larger, older, a braid of dark hair fell over her shoulder.

Ari Ara spun in shock . . . and stepped out of the vessel of her mother's body.

Alinore de Marin regarded her steadily, hand still extended toward the candle, a slight smile of bemusement on her lips. She was eighteen years old.

"Who are you?"

Ari Ara licked her dry lips and swallowed, stalling for time, searching for a response.

"I am your daughter," she said at last.

The dream shuddered and shifted. Alinore grew older, her dark hair lengthening, lines of weariness touching her eyes, until she began to fade silver-grey into an ancestor spirit. The sound of rushing water rose in Ari Ara's ears.

"Where is my daughter?" Alinore's spirit asked plaintively, rising and casting about, searching for something.

"Here!" Ari Ara cried out. "I'm right here!"

"Who are you?"

"It's me. Your daughter," Ari Ara repeated.

"You are not my daughter."

Ari Ara froze as the words slapped her across the face. She bit her lip to stop its trembling. The dream quavered under the shine of tears in her eyes. She blinked rapidly, swallowed down the hard lump that choked her throat, and thrust the moisture from her lashes with an impatient palm. This was surely a test.

"I am Ari Ara de Marin en Shirar," she said slowly, fiercely. "Heir to Two Thrones."

Alinore shook her head mournfully. Wisps of her spirit form slid into nothingness like mist rising from a river. The sound of growling water grew louder, hissing with the voices of the ancestors. Ari Ara glanced at her feet. The ghost river surged around her ankles. Black-grey fingers of spirits slipped around her crawling skin.

"Don't you recognize me?" Ari Ara pleaded desperately, her heart aching at the baffled expression on Queen Alinore's face. "I was raised by the Fanten in the High Mountains. The Mark of Peace is inked between my shoulders. *You* asked the Fanten

Grandmother to put it there."

A surprised frown crossed Alinore's face, almost recognizing her. Then she tilted her head, listening to unseen council. Her brows creased.

"I have a message for you."

"From who?"

But Alinore did not answer the question. Instead, she drew herself up, tall and towering, eyes blazed, looming over Ari Ara.

"Do not complete this Ordeal," she thundered in a warning tone. "Withdraw now and live."

"What?!" Ari Ara yelped, staggering back in shock.

"Step down," she hissed sharply. "Back out and survive. There are forces at work, schemes at play. Your life should not be sacrificed to their fears."

"Whose fears?"

Ari Ara shouted over the roar of the water. The Black Ancestor River groaned as the currents swelled around her knees. Alinore faded into mists, leaving Ari Ara alone. Silver-edged spirits threaded into the flooding waters. The river tugged, insistent, climbing higher and higher, its clutching swells gripping Ari Ara's thighs, hips, waist. She craned around, seeking the river's bank, hoping to climb out. But the Ancestor River snatched at her ribs, yanked at her body, tried to pull her legs out from under her, and drag her down into its depths.

"Help!" Ari Ara cried.

The dream shivered in a silver-sheen flip of fish scales. Her shout rippled through the murky depths of the dream's edges. A mist sighed and settled, drawing apart like curtains. In the shallows of the river, a thin figure waded up the swirling black waters, picking her steps as cautiously as a stalking heron. Silver hair, long and loose, hung down her back. One braided strand swayed from her temple, weighted by three blue beads. Her unadorned robe of soft white wool fell to her ankles, belted at the waist with a cord of shining black yarn. Even at a distance, Ari Ara recognized the Fanten Grandmother dreamwalking with a dancer's grace. With a snap of her fingers, she could part the floodwaters – if she chose.

"Help me!" Ari Ara called out, stretching her hand toward the woman. Aloof as the Fanten Grandmother was, she would not leave Ari Ara to drown in dreams. At least, she hoped not.

"What are you doing here?" the woman snapped, whirling and hitching up her robes.

She took a running leap onto the surface of the currents. The water held her weight. Her bare feet alighted with scarcely a ripple as she bounded over. She gripped Ari Ara's hands and heaved her out of the Black Ancestor River. Grabbing the girl by the scruff of her tunic, the Fanten Grandmother hustled her out of the water. The edges of the dreamrealm blurred and shifted as they moved. The woman's wiry strength propelled her swiftly, dizzyingly. Ari Ara scrambled to get her feet under her, arms flailing, damp hair plastered over her face.

"You should not walk through dreams like this!"

A note of alarm tinged the old woman's scold. She hurled Ari Ara's dreambody to the ground. Ari Ara recognized the forest outside the shrine, but they had not crossed into the waking realm yet. Overhead, the dream's wind still brushed the dark slick of leaves. Dappled moonlight fluttered in the understory. A hush hung on the mountain, the frogs and crickets silent, the birds huddled in their nests, the furred beasts hunkered under shrubs or curled in burrows. Spirits walked the woods tonight. The living stayed out of their way.

The Fanten Grandmother leaned her hands on her knees, winded. She was too old to go chasing wandering dreamwalkers. Thank the ancestors that Ari Ara had only drifted this far. The barrier between worlds stretched thin at this shrine. The girl could have passed through centuries and continents, too far for even a skilled dreamwalker like herself to haul her back to waking. Where were the Guardian Sisters who usually sat in trance, prepared to guide the potential heir from vision to body to waking once again?

The Fanten Grandmother scowled into the silver fog wisps. There was no sign of the vigilant sisters. She tightened her gaze, piercing the depths of the forest, bending distance to her will.

Ah! There they were.

Clutching Ari Ara's wrist and towing her along, the thin woman strode through the shadowed trunks of moon-blued trees. The stone ancestor pillars watched their passage, silent sentinels lining each slope. The Fanten Grandmother crossed impossible distances with each footstep. The steep forest blurred and shifted uncannily. Ari Ara recognized the split oak that stood midway down the mountain, right around the bend from where the two sisters had offered her the water.

There, at their usual sentry posts, the Guardian Sisters slumped sideways, sound asleep beyond the lighter realms of dreaming.

"I thought lowlanders couldn't dreamwalk," Ari Ara commented.

"Do they look like they're walking?" the Fanten Grandmother snapped, gesturing to the unmoving forms. "Even when in trance, the best they can do is bar the royal heir from straying too far - as they should have done for you."

She bent over the prone figures, sniffing once above each set of lips. Then she picked up the water flask and took a whiff.

"Strange," the Fanten Grandmother muttered, "I would not have suspected longal."

"What's longal?"

"Fanten herb," the silver haired woman informed her brusquely. "We use it for deep dreaming."

She looked sharply at Ari Ara, then whirled and sniffed her breath, ignoring the girl's affronted squawk.

"Stranger still."

She peeled open the eyelids of the sisters, touched their pulse, and straightened up shaking her head.

"These two will not wake again. Watch your back, Ari Ara. It seems someone is trying to kill you."

Before Ari Ara's question could lift from lungs to lips, the Fanten Grandmother gave her sternum a firm nudge. She toppled backwards. The forest spun. The canopy of stars and branches flipped. Ari Ara fell into the shrine and woke . . . just in time to stop the candleflame from spluttering out.

CHAPTER THIRTEEN

. . . . .

Two Dead Sisters

Before the dawning light fully pierced the rustling leaves, Ari Ara hurtled down the eroded footpath from the shrine. She paused only to check the pulse of the two sisters slumped at their posts. She had dreamed true with the Fanten Grandmother. Ari Ara felt no signs of life in either. They looked eerily peaceful, as if simply slumbering. She shivered. The longal-tainted water flask had vanished, though she searched the underbrush carefully for it. Would anyone believe that she'd seen it in a dream-vision? Probably not.

At breakneck speed, Ari Ara ran the last miles to the riverbank. Her churning stride devoured the steep trail. The trees blurred. The leaves turned into green-grey streaks punctuated by somber brown trunks.

The Twins of the Sisterlands waited at the age-blackened archway at the foot of the trail. Brinelle, Shulen, Minli, Emir, and Finn had all gathered behind them, anxious to hear how the vigil had gone. A huddle of blue-cloaked sisters chanted in a low rumble, invoking the presence of the spirits, their voices calling the ancestors closer. Cobwebs of the unseen clung to Ari Ara as she neared. She shuddered and shook free. The chants died off as she crashed through the archway and skidded to a halt. In the hush, Ari Ara heard the angry whispering of ancestor spirits. Roka Maro and Sorra Maro caught the hint of voices, too. They exchanged looks, their eyes flicking into the murky depths of the woods.

"Well? Does the flame still burn in the shrine?" Roka demanded.

"Does the incense still carry your prayers to the ancestors?" Sorra added more gently.

Ari Ara nodded curtly, quickly. She faltered for a moment, unsure how to break the news of the poisoned sisters. She'd forgotten about the ordeal and the ritual required upon her return. Formal phrases should be spoken, the story of her night recounted, her efforts weighed by the Twins, and her trial judged. Ari Ara had no patience for all that.

"There are two dead sisters on the trailside," Ari Ara blurted out, abandoning etiquette.

Shock struck like lightning. Horrified gasps. Hissed in-drawn breaths. A short yelp of a scream. Roka Maro dispatched her warrior sisters at once. Shulen quietly ordered Emir to accompany them. Sorra peppered her with concerned questions. Brinelle spat out a command and silenced the babble of voices that drowned out Ari Ara's words.

"The vigil was fine. I saw the sisters as I returned and came as quickly as I could."

"What happened?" Roka Maro demanded, fury tightening her jaw.

"I don't know."

"Did you kill them?" the steel-hard woman asked, her tone accusatory.

"What?! No!" Ari Ara gasped, horrified. "How could you even think that?"

The Mother Sister caught her counterpart's arm.

"Let us wait for answers before leaping to conclusions," she murmured.

But no answers came.

No dead sisters were ever found. The search party saw nothing unusual. No bodies. No flask. Nothing.

"How can that be?" Ari Ara cried, still feeling the sensation of their lifeless skin under her fingertips.

The Warrior Sister and the Mother Sister exchanged somber looks and suggested it had been a vision – a bad omen from the ancestor spirits.

"They are angered for some reason," Sorra Maro hazarded. Her pity was almost as painful as Roka's scorn. They denied the very existence of the sisters on the trailside, insisting that offering water was not part of the ritual test. They chalked it up to a vision sent by the spirits, and waded into divining its meaning. None of their interpretations boded well for Ari Ara. She was either rejecting the life-giving sustenance of the Sisters or stubbornly plowing on without accepting aid.

Sitting on a stone bench on the edge of the river dock, Ari Ara endured an excruciating hour of questioning under the hard glare of the Warrior Sister. Ari Ara slumped as exhaustion slammed her and straightened her spine as pride stiffened through her. She repeated the same answers in a fog of sleeplessness and worry:

No, she'd heard nothing in the night.

No, she hadn't recognized the two sisters when she saw them.

No, she hadn't seen them again until she found them dead.

Some questions were trickier than others, though: Was it a dream? Did she nod off?

Ari Ara struggled to answer. She couldn't tell them about

dreamwalking with the Fanten Grandmother. No one would believe that, anyway.

"I felt their necks for a pulse. Their flesh was cold, human, dead, and real," she answered.

Was it a vision? What could it mean? Did she receive other visions from the ancestors that night?

Ari Ara did not want to tell them about Alinore's plaintive voice failing to recognize her own daughter. Fortunately, the Warrior Sister took her silent pause for a negative and barreled on to the next question.

At last, the Great Lady intervened, saying all other inquires could wait until Ari Ara slept.

She crashed into dreamless slumber and woke to the soft rocking of the ship catching a gust of wind and gliding along the river. Minli sat in the wooden chair by the desk, nose in a book, waiting for her to wake up. Finn broke off his brooding by the window.

"Are we moving?" she asked groggily, rubbing sleep from her eyes and stretching.

"Yes," Minli replied, shutting his book with a thump. "You slept all day."

After spinning in endless circles of arguments with the Twins, Brinelle had ordered the Fair Defiance to set sail. Nothing could salvage this disaster. It was better to move onto the next challenge in the Ordeal of Queens than dawdle in the wreckage of this vigil. The Twins stalked off. The Great Lady headed upriver.

"What really happened up there?" Finn asked, perching on the side of the bed and twining his fingers into hers. "You looked like you've seen a ghost."

"Maybe I did," she murmured, though not softly enough to avoid Minli's sharp look.

A breathless tumble of questions burst from him.

"What do you mean? The two sisters? The ancestor spirits? Was it a vision?"

Ari Ara shook her head.

"It was a – " she hesitated. She'd sworn not to tell anyone that her dreams were more than the regular lowlander dreaming. Fanten dreams were more potent, more accurate. A truth learned in such dreaming held true in waking. But she couldn't tell Minli that. She wrestled with the secret. This was important, after all.

"Never mind," she finished awkwardly. "You know I can't talk about the ordeal."

"Does it have anything to do with forgetting your offering?" Minli guessed. "The Twins were fuming about that once they realized they hadn't grilled you about it."

Ari Ara stared at him in horror. It had completely slipped her mind. She'd been so flummoxed by tripping over poisoned sisters while dreamwalking that she'd raced from the temple shrine at dawn without a backwards glance. She hadn't made an offering, hadn't even figured out what offering to make.

All in all, it was clear that she hadn't done well in this part of the Ordeal of Queens. She'd kept the candles and incense going, but forgotten the other important tasks. Vision, dream, or real, if anyone believed her about the dead sisters – which few did – it was still a bad omen.

"I believe you," Finn assured her quietly, a perturbed look on his face. "I don't think we can trust the Sisters."

He couldn't say why, only that he had a feeling.

"There's something else," she mentioned.

Taking a deep breath, she told them about her vision of Queen Alinore.

"It can't be a good sign, though," she sighed, "any of it. Not recognizing me as her daughter, delivering a warning, telling me to quit."

"She didn't," Minli interrupted.

At Ari Ara's baffled look, he explained.

"She didn't tell you to quit. Alinore didn't say that."

"Yes, she did," Ari Ara protested. "I heard her."

"But wasn't she delivering a message?" Minli argued. "It could be someone else who wants you to quit. Not your mother."

"But who?" Ari Ara wondered, relieved and concerned at the same time. "It could have come from anyone, living or spirit."

"The Sisters," Finn cut in. "They can talk to the spirits. Maybe they sent a message through Alinore."

"But why?"

"To test you," Finn argued. It was the Ordeal of Queens, after all.

"If so, it's a rotten thing to do," Ari Ara growled furiously. "Using my mother that way."

The Great Lady reacted to the setback by doubling down on *The Book of Queens*, drilling Ari Ara on the passages for hours each day. The river widened and turned shallower as Ari Ara memorized and recited the lines on a queen's duties to her people and ancestors. The steep mountains peeled back to an open marsh as Ari Ara came up with examples of how she would embody the sayings in the book.

"As a virtuous queen . . . " Brinelle prompted.

"I will respect the monks and sisters, fund the orphanages and university, and, uh, listen to my elders."

Ari Ara wasn't sure if the last line was part of the traditional response, but she eyed her aunt's scowling and figured it couldn't hurt.

One hour of recitations blurred into the next. On the third day of endless study, the Fair Defiance glided into the Brackenmarsh. Here, the Sister River thinned and widened, siphoning off into a thousand cross-channels that curled through rushes and reeds. Bog mounds swelled like half-drowned islands. The salt-sour scent of mud and rot clung to the air. The bracken of the marsh seeped purplish, the reddish stalks decaying into water tinted by blue roots. The murky channels made navigation difficult. They traveled slowly over shifting sandbars that snaked beneath the rippling current.

Tiny skiffs dotted the snake-coiled waterways on either side of the main channel. Fisherfolk built elaborate weirs along the migration paths of the spawning fish that returned each year to their birthplaces. Dye gatherers collected the roots of the bracken to make the iconic Marianan blue. Vast flocks of birds winged from one watery corridor to the next. Long-legged herons stalked frogs in solitary silence.

At dusk, fog rose thick as a wall and cut off all sight. These banks of hard grey could settle for days at a time. After a half day sailing blind, the fog put everyone on edge. Brinelle blustered at the delay. The captain chaffed under the regent's distemper, but held firm to the slow pace necessary to avoid running aground. The crew nervously crept about their tasks, whispering about river ghosts and monsters lurking in the gloom. A hushed fear clung to the ship. Without the horizon's landmarks, they could only creep forward one boat length at a time, plumbing the depths cautiously and fighting the current's pull with constant work at the oars.

Ari Ara and Finn squabbled over nothing. He huffed off to hang out with Minli. She holed up in her lonely quarters, ignoring her studies with a pessimistic come-what-may attitude toward the ordeal. Either she'd pass or she wouldn't. No amount of memorization would help her now.

Ari Ara returned to her mother's journal. In this section, Alinore was busy with her wedding; the entries skipped months at a time as the preparations swept up each minute of her day. Each piece was short and sparse, leaving Ari Ara with the empty hunger of an unfinished meal. Alinore's first lengthy scrawl arose just after she learned she was pregnant. But instead of the blissful, delighted anticipation of a child, Alinore's words revealed how she fumed against the cruel warnings of the Sisters.

How dare they! I can't believe they requested a private audience and demanded that I get rid of the child?! The gall! The heartlessness. There cannot be a child of two nations, they said. The sky will fall, the Mari River will drown us all. Famine and plague will break out. They recited that cursed prophecy and urged me to remain childless for the good of the nation. Or divorce Tahkan. Neither of which I intend to do.

Ari Ara frowned. She had never heard this about the Sisters. It made her dislike them even more. It was strange to read these entries and realize that *she* was in them, a tiny child in her mother's womb. Ari Ara scanned the next lines. Maybe not so tiny. To the chagrin of her people, Alinore decided to spend the second and third trimester of her pregnancy in Tahkan's home village of Orrak.

I cannot think for this child's kicking! Rhianne told me she could not sleep due to Tianne's motions – and that little girl is a born dancer, always moving – her daughter turns and rolls now as well as then. Once born, Tianne didn't just crawl and toddle. She wriggled as if movement were a river and she a little fish. Rhianne made a terrible face at that metaphor. Apparently the Fanten don't share my lowlander love of fish. We riverfolk delight in them, minnows are embroidered in children's clothes and sturgeon are sculpted for décor in our great halls. I call Tianne a little minnow as a term of endearment. Rhianne shakes her head at that. Fanten call their babies lambs, or inni, *which is their word for the sapling of a Great Tree.*

Ari Ara's smile was tinged with sadness. Reading about the early days of the two families - Alinore and Tahkan, Shulen and Rhianne - always brought the sting of tears to her eyes. So much love. So little time. The two families had been shattered by the assailants who attacked the queen. The journal entries on their happiness and friendship evoked an inescapable foreboding of the tragic future that loomed.

Ari Ara tore her eyes from the page only when it grew too dark to read. She fumbled for a match to light the oil lantern then cupped her hands around the crosshatch windowpanes and peered out. From the gloom, she'd thought the hour late, but dusk had not fallen yet. Instead, a thick fog plastered the glass. She heard the river sailors sounding the depths in advance of the bow. They relayed the measurements in a muted call-and-response with the first mate. Interspersed with the reports were bellowed commands to the oarsmen to hold or stroke against the current. The first mate's low baritone merged with the higher alto of the depth-sounder's voice. Punctuated by the creak-clunk of oars, the sounds composed a cautious song in the blinding fog. They crept slowly forward, tracking the narrow channel through the shallower sections. The river shifted here, continuously carving new paths and mounding up sandbars in its shuffle.

Ari Ara returned to Alinore's journal, hanging the oil lantern on the hook above her berth. Her mother, seven months pregnant, wrote about the decision to leave the desert city of Orrak.

Shulen and Tahkan are agreed: we must go. It is no longer safe here, not until Tahkan tracks down the person who tried to poison me. He has bound the entire city in song magic searching for the truth, but to no avail. It was not the Harraken who did this – or not a Harraken who remained in the city.

I am too big to travel comfortably, not on horseback or in a wagon. Everything hurts, every bump in the road jars, every sway aches, every step twinges. Rhianne boils endless teas and spreads salves on my womb and lower back. I can tell she is worried for me. Shulen tried to order her to take little Tianne and leave, but she refused. I must confess to crying with relief. All of this would be unbearable without her.

Last year, Ari Ara's father had sung all the songs he knew about her mother. As Tahkan had shared the stories and memories, Ari Ara had learned how Alinore had been poisoned while she stayed in Orrak, a small city in the southern region of the desert. Only Rhianne's knowledge of Fanten herbs and remedies had prevented a miscarriage. The blow left Alinore weakened and thrust her pregnancy into jeopardy. Seeking safety, she left the desert. Tahkan, swept up in the investigation and his duties, reluctantly stayed behind. Alinore's short entries revealed the depths of her fear, stress, and exhaustion as they fled eastward, crossed the border into Mariana, and sought shelter in the south. Her terse, jotted notes reflected the escalating dangers they faced.

The Riderlands protect us. Thank the ancestors for their loyalty to me and respect for the Harraken. I am so exhausted, every bone in my body is weary.

*

I am frightened. We have ridden for days. Rhianne forced Shulen to stop, fearing the pangs in my womb will worsen. I should not be riding, not so hard, not so late in my pregnancy. But we have no choice.

*

Rhianne and Shulen are arguing. I cannot bear it. Shulen wants us to go to the Southlands for help. Lady Ilsa would welcome us with open arms. Rhianne argues for her people in the High Mountains, at least until the child is born. No one hides like a Fanten, she says. We will be safe and protected among them.

*

We must go. They are near.

It ended there. Abrupt. Unsatisfying. Aching in silence. Galvanized by a second attack, Alinore, Rhianne, Tianne, and Shulen fled east into the High Mountains. They never made it to the Fanten. The journal revealed nothing of the tenor of that flight through the shadowed woods, nor how those early pangs worsened into premature labor as assassins chased their heels. They were attacked in the Riderlands, but that was now thought to be a ruse, a foray meant only to draw the queen out into the open, away from the protection of the fierce horse riders. They left in the dead of night, traveling incognito, riding hard even with Alinore round as the moon with child. They were watched - or betrayed - and ambushed in the forest just west of Monk's Hand Monastery. So close to safety. But not close enough.

Horses killed, Rhianne and Alinore fled on foot, little Tianne clinging to her mother. Behind them, Shulen took his famous stand, holding off the attackers. Labor pains gripped Alinore as they scrambled up the steep slopes. Rhianne hid the queen in a Fanten cave beneath a Great Tree. Later, it was thought that she ran back for Shulen. One of the mercenaries must have waited, hidden, but this part of the saga was shrouded in mystery. The accounts said only that Rhianne and her child were murdered. Was she tortured to reveal the queen? Was her child murdered before her eyes?

No one would ever know. And Shulen, haunted by his losses, walked the world scarred with both visible and invisible wounds from that day.

Ari Ara set the journal down with a disappointed sigh. What had she expected? If the truth of her mother's attackers were in the journal, Brinelle would have discovered it long ago. Still, she had harbored hope of finding some clue that had been overlooked, some hint that spoke across time to her and her alone.

Fingers tapped on the door. Finn's head popped in. She waved him over and scooted sideways on the edge of the berth so he could sit next to her.

"Finished it, then?" he asked, seeing the journal opened to the blank pages in the back.

"I just . . . it's silly, but I thought there'd be *something* about her death, you know?" Ari Ara sighed.

Finn rubbed her shoulders. Ari Ara smiled with delight and let her emotional knots unravel. Finn listened as she rattled on about what she'd read, asking a question here and there. At last, she swiveled to face him. Dusk had truly fallen and the ship's motion stilled as it had anchored in the shallows for the night.

"It must be hard, not knowing who did it," Finn said in a small voice, his expression veiled by the shadows.

"I can't decide if it's worse to know or to not know."

"There's no way to tell that ahead of time," Finn agreed, his tone uneasy, as if the dark, the fog, and the topic spooked him. "Once you know, you can't ever un-know it, right?"

Ari Ara nodded.

"Still," she said slowly, "I want to know."

Finn sat in silence. There was nothing to say. The truth would probably never come to light. It couldn't.

CHAPTER FOURTEEN

. . . . .

The Brackenmarsh

"Who's there? Name yourself!"

Ari Ara heard the boatswain call out in a sharp voice. She could hear the sound of a boat poling closer. Thick fog hemmed them in, dense as the night before, only slightly lightened by the pressure of the rising sun. According to the captain's charts, they were nearly out of the Brackenmarsh. The Border Mountains should be pushing their crowns up over the tangle of knolls that bounded the western edge of the swamp. Not that anyone could see further than their noses.

Out of the gloom, a boatman neared. He stood in the stern of a small skiff, propelling the vessel through the reeds with a long pole. As the prow nudged into the Mari River channel, he nimbly tucked the pole into the boat and took up a paddle as a tiller, steering crossways to the current to reach the Fair Defiance.

The first mate growled a warning to state his purpose. His low voice boomed loud and muffled in the dense fog.

"Passenger for you," came the curt and taciturn reply.

"We're not taking passengers."

A new voice spoke.

"This one, you will."

Ari Ara recognized those ringing tones - and the dry rasp of desert wind in the accent.

"Father!"

She spun so fast her boots slipped on the slick deck. Shulen caught her midfall and hauled her upright. With breathless thanks, Ari Ara skidded to the railing. The fog thinned around Tahkan Shirar as if sucked into the inexhaustible dryness of his land. The thick greyness gave way under the force of the Desert King's glad laughter. He bore the stamp of the hard sun in his bronze, leather-lined face. His presence invoked dust and dunes and spines of cacti. He vaulted from skiff to ship as smoothly as he leapt onto a horse's back.

Tahkan swept his daughter into a hug, counting her limbs and fingers, relieved that she was still in one piece, surprised to find she'd added an inch to her height.

"You've grown," he said, struggling to mask his wistful sorrow under pride.

Since he'd last seen her, the Marianans had molded her in their image, accentuating the traits of their people, subtly masking the traces of the desert. In the swirl of Marianan blue robes, his daughter bore the unmistakable stamp of the riverlands. The long trousers lengthened her legs, bestowing a maturity beyond her years. The stiff fabric of the belt hugged her hips and straightened her spine, granting her the dignified posture of queens. The copper curls of her Harraken heritage had been slicked back and darkened in the damp mist to a chestnut brown. She reminded him of her mother, which was bittersweet. As always, the Marianans spoke in the language of style . . . and Tahkan did not like the statement they made: *she is ours, not yours. Marianan, not Harraken.* They would erase all signs of her desert blood if they could.

They would fail. Tahkan Shirar had heard the songs of his people in her voice, seen Ari Ara ride without reins, watched her skin darken to bronze under the harsh sun. He had seen *harrak* - honor, integrity, dignity - shining in her eyes. His daughter was a force of nature, strong of limb and sharp of mind, not beautiful by the conventions of either of her parents' cultures, but dazzling in an irreplicable way. Tahkan regretted the time he'd been away from her. It was unavoidable, though. Ari Ara's life, her future, depended on understanding the past. The dangers remained, lurking in shadow unless he exposed them to the withering light of day.

"I've missed you," Ari Ara whispered fiercely.

"Not nearly as much as I have," Tahkan assured her, looping an arm around her shoulders as he turned to greet the startled crew.

The captain eyed him warily, her face contorted as if she couldn't tell whether to be honored or insulted that the infamous Desert King stood on her ship. From the moist fog-beads clinging to his burning red hair to the oiled boots of his Marianan riverman's garb, her narrowed gaze took in every inch of him, assessing for threats, calculating whether he was friend or foe. From his choice in clothing, she assumed he had traveled discretely through the lands of his enemies. He would have had no trouble finding them - every croaking frog and nosy fisherman knew where the Fair Defiance was.

"So, Tahkan Shirar, you've come for your daughter's ordeal after all," Brinelle's tone was clipped with a touch of annoyance. Her boots drummed against the deck as she drew close. Shulen's soft, swift stride followed.

"I was already in the area," Tahkan answered, waving vaguely in the fog-covered direction of the Border Mountains.

Shulen looked sharply at him, wondering what he'd discovered so close to the Sisterlands.

"Dare I ask why?" Brinelle said archly, her spine stiffening in reflexive distrust.

"It is not a story for so many ears."

New footsteps clunked across the wooden deck as Minli, Emir, and Finn arrived, mouths agape at the unexpected appearance of the Desert King. Tahkan's smile widened at the first two – he had respect for Emir's loyalty and Minli's friendship – but for Finn, he had only a murderous scowl.

"What is he doing here?" Tahkan's accusatory tone shot at Shulen like an arrow. "I told you to get rid of him."

"What?!" yelped Ari Ara and Finn on the same, horrified breath.

"Perhaps you should get to know him before rejecting him outright," Shulen suggested diplomatically.

"It has nothing to do with that," Tahkan roared. He released Ari Ara's shoulders and strode across the deck to the startled Paika youth. Swift as a snake's strike, his hands gripped Finn's shirt and nearly lifted him off his feet.

The ship burst into motion at the assault. Emir and Shulen grabbed Tahkan by the arms. Someone called out for him to leave the boy alone. The Great Lady barked out commands over the clamor.

"Tahkan Shirar!" Brinelle shouted. "What is the meaning of this?"

"Are you going to tell them or should I?" the ferocious Desert King snarled at the youth.

"T-tell them what?" Finn stammered, but his eyes flicked sideways, not at the Great Lady, but at Ari Ara.

Her stomach suddenly dropped. He knew something, she could tell.

"Don't pretend ignorance, you little weasel," Tahkan growled in a threatening tone. "I will sing the truth out of you if I must."

"Stop, *affa*," Ari Ara cut in, using the Harraken word for father, feeling chilled to her bones. "Give Finn a chance to tell us whatever it is."

"He's had chances - plenty of them - hasn't he? Nine long months you've wormed your way into my daughter's heart, fooling her guardians and companions, securing a spot at her side. Such treachery!"

"Tahkan!" the Great Lady barked. "What are you so riled about? What does the boy know?"

In sudden, furious disgust, Tahkan flung Finn away from him so hard the youth stumbled to the ground. From a half-kneeling position, Finn looked up at them, eyes pleading with them to understand. Ari Ara saw the flash of guilt and secrets in his face.

"He knows who attacked Alinore," Tahkan said flatly.

The world shattered under Ari Ara's feet. She swayed as everything reeled at the force of such betrayal.

"How could you? How could you know and say nothing?"

Ari Ara's voice cracked at the edges. Her anger cut through Finn's blustering like a knife. Her eyes stabbed accusingly into his. Finn drew breath to lie, to cover his tracks, to conceal the truth: he had known who killed her mother since before they met.

"Ari Ara, I can explain - " Finn protested, holding his hands out in a plea.

"Who was it?" she cut him off, unwilling to hear explanations or excuses.

"It was - "

"*Gitten.*"

The Desert King sang out the Harraken word, silencing the youth as a streak of lucidity cut through his anger. "This is not a story for so many ears," he repeated, giving Brinelle a pointed look.

She nodded and snapped out a series of orders, sending the crew scurrying to their posts, telling someone to pay the boatman and send him on his way.

Tahkan countered that.

"He's been paid to stay," he informed her, stiff with insult over the insinuation that a Harraken would not pay his debts, "and he will be needed after we hear the boy speak. Either he goes, or *we* go."

He jerked his head at Ari Ara, indicating that he would not allow her to travel any further on the same ship as Finn Paikason. Brinelle nodded curtly over Ari Ara's protests. The boatman was invited aboard, a rope flung out to tether his vessel. Brinelle led the others to her quarters and shut the door behind them.

"Speak," she commanded.

Finn looked miserable. He wished a hole would open up in the floor and swallow him.

"It was Paika," he muttered, almost inaudibly. "Not my family, but the Southern Clans. They were hired to do it. We - *The Paika* - our leader - had those clans dealt with. No one could have known. How did you find out?"

He stared at Tahkan in confusion.

"I have heard their spirits speak," the honor-keeper of the desert said, his eyes never leaving Finn's face.

With the cadence of a born storyteller, Tahkan Shirar told the others of his journey. After storming off in annoyance at the affrontery of the Marianan nobles, he'd done what the Harrak-Mettahl always did: he traveled among his people, listening, singing, serving them. In a village along the southern range of the Border Mountains, he'd heard a snatch of song, a shepherd's ditty from the southern range. Haunting tones in minor chords caught his ear, almost dissonant. The singer-shepherd sung it to him, the Harrak-Mettahl, the honor-keeper of her people. The tune spoke of how she had stumbled onto the ruins of a Paika village while chasing a stray lamb. The Ancestor Wind stirred ceaselessly there and, in its hissing, wove the howls of the Wild Hunt.

Ari Ara gasped at the mention of the Paika's trance-like ritual that meted out a brutal justice between humans, fate, and spirits. The hairs on the back of her neck rose as she recalled the eerie horns and frantically racing fiddles of the music that whipped the Paika into the froth of the chase. She had seen them turn like wolves on a man who had betrayed the clans. They chased him out of town, over the mountains and into the hands of fate. Whether he was slain by his pursuers, or struck by lightning, or perished over a cliff, the Paika considered it the will of the spirits. Even escape was seen as the justice of the Wild Hunt.

That the Harraken had run across the lingering hints of one hinted at serious crimes. It had been years since the hunt, but the punishment still echoed through the ceaseless winds. Curious, suspicious, half-guessing the answer, Tahkan asked the shepherd what had prompted Paika justice.

The shepherd shifted uneasily and avoided his eyes. It might be nothing but imagination, she hedged. The Ancestor Wind speaks in riddles. Nights stretched long and lonely up there. The Paika couldn't be trusted and their shifty spirits even less. *Tell me*, Tahkan had urged and he sung a spark of song magic into the words to give courage to the fire of her story. Three images repeated in the spirits' howls, the shepherd said.

"A queen. A babe. A chase."

It was not much to go on, but it was something. Tahkan quietly pulled aside the shepherd's aunts and uncles, elders and relatives, neighbors and friends from the region. They all shared the same fragments of knowledge: sixteen years ago, a band of Paika hunters left in the dead of night and never returned. Then, a few months after Queen Alinore had died and the child had been lost and war was crashing down upon the Harraken, a second band of Paika warriors had come to the village, this time to hunt down every last member of the first clan.

Tahkan traveled to the ruined village. He sat vigil in the rubble of the abandoned houses, singing to the Ancestor Wind until it turned and returned the lost spirits to their birthplace. On the eve of the long-ago Wild Hunt, ghosts howled in the chill storm. One by one, Tahkan Shirar caught them with his song magic. One by one, he heard their tales. One by one, he released them back to their torment. The clan leader who accepted the gold. The fathers of the men who had chased Alinore. The sisters of the fighting women who had gone. The younger brother of a hunter killed at Shulen's Stand. The aunts who had urged the clan to accept the mission.

Next, Tahkan sang the thread lines of the assailants' spirits, tugging the wandering ghosts of the Paika band back across the distances, trying to wrench their stories from them. But he could not pry a word from those who had led the chase. They came to him with mouths sewn shut. He would get no answers from the culprits.

But someone among the living knew.

"The ghosts were bound in life and death for all eternity. They could not reveal the binders' name . . . but when I asked them who knew that person and still lived to tell the tale, all silvered hands slid north. North along the Border Mountains, north to where *The Paika*, leader of all the clans, holds her spider's secrets tight to her chest, north to where my daughter dwelled so close to this unseen danger."

Tahkan's voice turned deadly, song magic infusing his every word, fury burning hot in his eyes. He had longed to travel to *The Paika*'s home in the Spires and wring the truth from the old woman. But he did not have time. His daughter had been called to the Ordeal of Queens. He turned his horse east and rode faster than the floodwaters in the spring. He sent his hawk with the message:

Keep your eyes on that Paika boy. Don't leave the two of them alone together.

"Why did you not heed my warning?" Tahkan growled to Shulen, throwing a sharp glower of dislike at Finn Paikason, great-grandson of the treacherous old woman.

"I thought - I merely thought you meant . . . er, the usual warning about young couples," Shulen stammered out, discomfited. It would have been funny had his error not been so perilous.

Finn Paikason could not be trusted.

The truth hit Ari Ara like a flight of arrows, one stab for each part of the sentence. She staggered. Shulen's grip kept her standing as her knees weakened and buckled with the aftershock of a betrayal's stab.

"But - how - I stayed at the Spires for months - you said nothing."

She could only stammer out incoherent phrases as the questions collided in her throat. She had trusted *The Paika,* come to the old woman for wisdom and advice, sat at her feet and listened to her stories, combed the elder's hair in the evenings by the fire. Ari Ara's stomach lurched. Her heart lodged in her throat.

"Who else knew?" she choked out.

"We all did," Finn confessed, a hint of anguish in his otherwise stoic face.

All this time. He had known. They all had known. As they broke bread. As they laughed over the children's antics. As he kissed her -

There are too many secrets between us, he had told her once, back when they stood on the precipice of allowing their hearts to tumble into love.

A roar, a ripping scream of anger, boiled up inside her. She clenched her teeth over it and breathed hard. All of them had known who attacked her mother. She had likely seen the haunting truth in their eyes as she passed them. Dread. Shame. Awkwardness. Pity. Fear. Guilt.

"Why?" she cried. "Why wouldn't you tell me?"

"It just – the moment never seemed right," Finn exclaimed. "It is too big a secret to tell lightly. Then, the longer we said nothing, the harder it became to say anything."

Now that he blurted it out, the words flooded from him, the weight of secrets bursting the dam of silence.

"My great-grandmother had a plan. *The Paika* hoped we could atone for the past actions of our kin. But it required time. And trust."

They had punished the Southern Clans, unleashed the Wild Hunt, held their own people accountable. But their silence had a price and the war had been a heavy toll to bear. When Ari Ara and her Peace Force came to the Border Mountains, *The Paika* saw her chance. The time of reckoning for the Paika had come. They had gambled for safety by holding this secret for fifteen years as the two nations hurled accusations across the border, as Mariana launched the War of Retribution and slaughtered the Harraken for attacking their queen. *The Paika* had tried to buy her people a chance of survival by bringing – kidnapping! – Ari Ara, drawing her into their lives and homes, letting the girl's crush on her great-grandson flourish, teaching her to understand and respect the difficult choices her people had been forced to make. The elder had hoped to tell the girl this secret in a gentler way, to help her understand what had happened, to explain the circumstances so her clans would be protected from the inevitable backlash the knowledge would provoke.

"Who?" Shulen growled, breaking out of the tangled web of *why*. "The Paika hunters lifted the sword, but who commanded it? Who hired them to attack Queen Alinore?"

Finn shook his head.

"We don't know. Not exactly."

Tahkan strode across the deck. Here was the crux of the secrets, the most essential piece of the entire puzzle, the information he'd been searching for over the long years and recent months.

"Stop these games, boy. Tell us the truth."

"All I know is that the Southern Paika were supposed to apprehend Queen Alinore and bring her to a place where she would be held until her child was born. The *queen* wasn't supposed to die."

At the emphasis, a short, sharp breath caught in Brinelle's throat. A look of shocked understanding whipped across her face, as if fifteen years of confusing history suddenly clicked into focus.

"Alinore was not supposed to die," the Great Lady repeated, slowly pivoting to gesture to Ari Ara, "but she was. The prophesized heir to two thrones."

Finn swallowed, miserable at the appalling weight of the truth. His people had caused so much damage.

"How could they!" Ari Ara railed at Finn. "They chased a pregnant woman, my mother, hoping to kill her unborn child, all to stop a stupid prophecy?!"

Ari Ara spun from one person to the next, desperate for answers, but no one had any. She rounded on Minli, her best friend, a boy who had read libraries. Yet even he wore a puzzled look.

"He knows more." Tahkan's voice was deadly quiet. "What are you still hiding, Finn Paikason?"

"Nothing, I – "

But the honor-keeper of the desert knew the look of a lie. Song magic ripped from his throat sharp as a lightning crack, binding as iron chains. His chant rumbled, low and ominous, and Finn's features fell lax in trance. The singer lifted the truth from him like a fisherman reeling in a catch.

"*The Paika* suspects the involvement of the Sisters," Finn confessed.

"The Sisters?!" Brinelle cried.

"Shhh."

"Who else could have bound the spirits of the Southern Clan to silence?" he continued. "We cannot. Someone did. My great-grandmother instructed me to find out, to search as our trackers do, to hunt as our most skilled hunters do. My quarry is their names, those among the Sisters who were involved, and to find proof of their connection to the attack. Then, we Paika will deal with them. Or, if our culpability was revealed, we would at least know who passed the gold and whose orders the southern hunters followed."

Tahkan released him from the song, his face ashen from the strain of binding another against his will. Finn was strong. He had not wished to give up this secret.

Ari Ara was livid.

"You . . . were . . . never . . . going to tell me," she ground out through gritted teeth. "This whole journey, this trip with me, pretending to support me through the ordeal – it was all a ruse for covering up the tracks of your people?"

"No," he interjected, "we are making amends – "

"You're making things worse!" Ari Ara roared. "By lying all the time! At every turn! Did you ever even love me? Or was that just a lie, too?"

"Of course, I do!" he cried. "Don't you see? All this hate. All these lies. It's a cycle that never ends . . . unless we end it. Tahkan and Alinore tried. Why can't we?"

His eyes implored her to understand. Silence was her only reply. His gaze narrowed, hurt.

"You know what, Ari Ara de Marin en Shirar?" he spat out. "You talk big about peace and forgiveness, but it's all hollow words when it's your turn. What happened to your mother is not my fault! I couldn't even walk!"

"Your lies are on you, Finn Paikason," she hissed between clenched teeth.

"Ari Ara – "

"No." She couldn't stand the sound of his voice right now. "Don't talk to me. Don't look at me. Don't even think about me."

She shoved him backwards and pointed to the boatman's skiff.

"Get out of my sight, Finn Paikason," she snarled. "I never want to see your lying face again."

CHAPTER FIFTEEN

. . . . .

The Water Maze

A fat drop of rain smacked her nose. Ari Ara jerked out of her clouded thoughts. Her hands ached with chill. The rain, at least, concealed the tears that brimmed in her eyes. Her heart had a crack down the middle. At the slightest relenting of her fury, she was horrified to find herself missing Finn – his laughter, his rule-breaking, his smile – then her anger flared up again at her foolishness for missing such a lying backstabber. Ari Ara couldn't concentrate, couldn't read, couldn't even sit still.

She dreamed of Finn, restlessly, relentlessly, searching for him, demanding answers, even dancing with him before recalling how he'd lied to her all this time. She fell - for him, from him - through stone, through darkness, through rivers of time and continents of distance. In slumber, her longings took shape and tugged her into his arms. She and Finn spun in dances of their own invention, but just as the sweetness drew them together, just as she folded herself into the trust of his embrace, just as their lips brushed . . . he stabbed her in the back. Pain exploded between her shoulder blades, the dagger driven straight into the black-inked Mark of

Peace. Ari Ara woke gasping for breath, her spine arched and her heart racing.

But the dream that hurt the most was the time they sang the Atta Song. The words of the Harraken ritual of apology and forgiveness had no language in the dream, only meaning and understanding. All the things that burned like hot coals in her belly in the waking world were spoken, heard, and answered. The sharp needles of her broken heart melted. She understood the weight he'd carried, trying to protect his family and his people. She learned how much it bothered him to conceal the truth from her. When they reconciled, their love had deepened. Their shattered trust began to heal. A thin hope blossomed.

Then she woke. And it was just a dream.

Finn had lied. She had sent him away.

He had fought against leaving, professing his loyalty every step of the way as the sailors and Tahkan hauled him across the deck and tossed him in the skiff. He'd begged for a chance to prove his good intentions, sacrificing his stiff pride and hurling himself to his knees before them. He was here to set things right, he claimed; he was trying to atone for the past, to find the truth.

Ari Ara stopped listening. She couldn't bear any more words. Brinelle had wanted to lock Finn in the brig. Tahkan had wanted to hurl him into the river. Shulen kept his own counsel, but his jaw worked over the strong emotions he held clenched within. Minli quietly assessed the situation and turned to Finn.

"Perhaps it's best to go until things cool off," he murmured.

He worried for Finn's safety on a boatful of furious warriors and rulers. Minli thought the others were judging his friend unfairly. Finn's only crime was concealing the knowledge that he - and all his clan - had been bound to hold in secrecy. Who among them had no secrets? Whose hands were clean? Whose actions faultless?

But no one wanted to listen to reason. Finn left with the boatman, hunched in a miserable bundle in the bow, rain hissing down in thick veils that swallowed him faster than fog. The Fair Defiance crept out of the Brackenmarsh into a tangle of river channels dubbed the Water Maze. While the crew carefully marked and charted their passage through the snarls of tributaries, Ari Ara endured endless rehashes of the same conversation they'd had every night since her father had pried the truth out of Finn. With suspicions pointing at the Sisters, the Desert King wanted Ari Ara to withdraw from the ordeal and return to the desert.

Brinelle would hear none of it.

"That's preposterous. She can't quit over a wild accusation. It would throw the country into turmoil."

"She can't go through with it," Tahkan argued. He didn't care if Mariana rolled in political somersaults, he intended to keep his daughter safe. "If the Sisters are involved, they will try to kill her."

The argument crashed around Ari Ara's ears like a swarm of agitated bees. She couldn't think, couldn't breathe.

"We don't even know for certain that it is the Sisters," Brinelle pointed out. "We have only a lying Paika's suspicions to go on."

"The Great Lady could launch a formal investigation into the Sisterhood" Shulen suggested.

"On what grounds?" Brinelle objected, shaking her head. "A Paika's claim and desert song magic? We'll need more than that."

"Tahkan could sing to the ghosts at Shulen's Stand," Minli tentatively put forward.

"What would that prove?" Brinelle scoffed. "Only that the mad Desert King is delusional."

Tahkan started to object, but Shulen interrupted with a shake of his grizzled head.

"The Great Lady is right. Paika suspicions, desert song magic, and spirit-murmurings aren't evidence. Not in the eyes of the

Marianans."

"They are to my people," Tahkan reminded them, his pride stung, his temper short. "Our word is truth. A Harrak-Mettahl does not lie."

"For ancestors' sake, Tahkan, stop bristling like a cactus," Brinelle snapped. "I'm having enough trouble with the Sisters already. I cannot accuse them without hard evidence."

Minli stifled a sigh and refrained from pointing out – again – that they shouldn't have sent Finn Paikason away. Finn was good at slipping in and out of places, searching for proof, going about unnoticed, and ferreting out secrets. Everyone was taking out decades of fury on a boy who couldn't even talk when this all happened. But, Minli reminded himself, it was not his mother, child, wife, or cousin who had died on that day. Forgiveness is easy when you haven't been hurt. Scars are harder to heal.

"Ari Ara, what do you think?"

Minli's quiet question cut through the clamor. His friend sat slumped in a chair, the weight of the world pressing down on her. She blinked slowly, clawing her way out of the tangle of her thoughts only to land in the snarl of everyone else's.

"Nothing has changed," she declared bitterly, "not really. I still have to pass this ordeal."

"No," Tahkan objected. "I will not risk your life on a ridiculous riverlands ritual."

Protestations erupted all over again. Ari Ara cut them off. She couldn't stand another hour of this.

"There's only one option," she held up her hands to forestall objections. "We proceed with caution."

They would keep their ears to the wind and their eyes alert for signs of trouble. And they would pray for the ancestors spirits to watch over them.

Ari Ara spent a week pacing the deck restlessly, rain or shine, dawn or dusk, even in the depths of night. Underfoot and in the way, the river sailors navigated her like a boulder in the currents. The splintering labyrinth of the Water Maze required their full attention. Channels and tributaries wove through floodplains and falls. Sandbars and underwater springs dotted the river. The captain posted the second mate in the bow to carefully mark their passage on a chart, counting each stream cautiously to determine their next turn.

Steep cliffs lined this part of the Water Maze, thick with trees and creeping vines. The sky narrowed to a sliver, a mirror of the river below. Shrines and hermitages dotted each bend. Some hung at the water's edge; simple, rough-cut shelters with a tiny mooring for a carved trunk boat. Others clung to the cliffside, nigh impossible to reach. Once, they watched a hermit-sister ascend a bare stone rockface and salute them from her temple at the top. In these huts, sisters purified their hearts, emptied the chatter of their minds, chanted the ancient prayers, and communed with the ancestor spirits. A noble woman might pay a hermitess to keep constant vigil for her son during battles. A childless mother might seek out a sister to ask for the Mother's divine aid. Devotees of each branch of the Sisterhood built hermitages in these hills. On one slope, an armed woman drilled in sword work. On another, a robed sister collected fertility herbs. On a third, an elder stood in deep meditative trance, far from the clatter of the river.

The twisted branches of the Water Maze held secrets and strange sights around each bend. A masked figure perched in a tree's limbs, tilting a bird's beak at the ship as it passed. Eerie chants and drumming slipped through the gloaming at dusk, disembodied and dislocated. A trio of black-robed sisters with ash-covered faces stood on the stone pilings of a ruined bridge and croaked out curses upon the enemies of Mariana. Tahkan stared back at them unflinching, muttering counter spells in song under his breath. The river sailors shuddered and made hex warding gestures against both.

It was no wonder that they lost their way. Distracted by odd sights, crossed curses, and having the infamous Desert King aboard their ship, the watch sailor miscounted the channels. The helmsman took a wrong left turn and found their passage blocked by a roaring falls. The captain lambasted her crewman, apologized to the Great Lady, and backtracked down the river. Pushing twilight to make up for lost time, they veered right at the wrong fork and nearly ran aground on a sandbar. The captain was forced to anchor for the night before returning to the proper route.

In the morning, it began to rain.

Ari Ara sniveled and suppressed a shiver. The downpour dampened everyone's spirits. Visibility poor, they lost their way again, then again, until the captain worried they'd never get out of the Water Maze. Even the hardiest sailors were muttering about inns and waystations, hot fires and warm baths. The cook churned out pot after pot of hearty soup, and kettle after kettle of hot tea, but the bursts of heat faded quickly in the deluge.

When the gleam of dock lights emerged from the veils of rain, more than one river sailor paused to stare longingly at the glow. Ari Ara stood alongside them, huddled under the impenetrable warmth of her Fanten cloak, hoping her aunt would call a halt. A blue-robed sister hailed them from the shore.

"Come!" she called, gesturing from beneath her woven umbrella. "You must be bone-weary and chilled. Come rest in the Ancient Springs."

A collective groan of yearning swept through the crew. Like all Marianans, they knew the legend of the Ancient Springs. The grandson of their founding king, dying from a festering battle wound, had sought healing in the warm water. Soaking for three days and three nights in the mineral-scented hot spring, he rose on the fourth day fully healed, rode into battle, and vanquished the enemy.

Tales abounded of the Ancient Spring's miraculous cures. Great Warriors made pilgrimages to the sacred well. Visions of victory came to commanders here. Young kings sought wisdom and prophecies in the steam. Aging queens came to atone for the mistakes of their reigns. The Ancient Springs purified the spirit, cleansed past misdeeds, and washed one free of transgressions.

The sharp pinch of minerals hung in the misty air. At the edge of the river, a rest house of blackened, oiled wood breathed steam and promised the comforts of its natural hot springs. Moss carpeted the grey tiles of the roof. Centuries-old pines towered above the buildings. A footpath curved through their wide trunks, up a steep slope to a smaller temple that sheltered the original well.

A swift council was held by the mainsail mast.

"We need to stop for the evening soon, anyway," the captain stated, her yearning for the hot springs matched by the crew's. Her sailors stood by the port rail in a line, every sinew of their cold, damp bodies longing to soak away the weary grime of their journey.

"It could be a trap," murmured Tahkan, thinking of Finn's suspicions, seeing dangers in the twitching of each shadowed leaf.

"Or a test," Minli chimed in, reminding them that the Ordeal of Queens never ceased.

"I doubt it. This is an unscheduled stop," Brinelle pointed out, one finger tapping her lips pensively. "Should we detour or proceed onward?"

She pivoted to Ari Ara, placing the decision in the girl's hands. The trial was hers alone, after all.

Ari Ara shivered as a cold raindrop ran down her collar. This could be a test of fortitude or a test of compassion for the ship's crew. It could be a test of accepting hospitality or a test of resisting easy distractions. Maybe Ari Ara was supposed to pay her respects to this legendary place of healing. Or maybe she was supposed to honor her commitment to reach the Citadel in time for the start of the Summer Trials. Raindrops gathered on her limp curls and plopped onto her eyelashes as she wrestled with the decision. She glanced at Minli. He just shook his head and shrugged silently, as uncertain as she. At last, Ari Ara peered into the darkening gloom. Every bone in her body ached. If that wasn't a sign, what was?

"Let's stop," she said. "For the crew's sake."

The sailors cheered and leapt to row them to port. Shulen, Emir, and Tahkan held a hasty conference on security measures. Minli watched the sister on the dock warily. Although this wasn't a planned stop in the Ordeal of Queens, the heir's every action would still be reported on when the Sisters convened at the Citadel. Minli wondered if he should remind Ari Ara about that.

Tied to the mooring, the crew and passengers followed the soft footsteps of the blue-robed sister to a cluster of stone buildings. She ushered them into a hall, pausing to shake out and fold her woven umbrella. More sisters hastened to welcome them, offering warmed towels and dry blankets.

All but one sister, that is.

She wore the black and blue overtunic that signified one who had not yet chosen which Twin to serve - the Warrior or the Mother. Her shaved head already bore the inked markings of a young healer, but a sword hung from the belt at her hips. Her eyes landed on the Desert King.

"You."

Low and ominous, the single word struck like a blow. In a swift burst of motion, the iron blade hissed out of the sheath as she drew her sword. The air quivered with the force of sudden gasps. The young woman took a defensive stance between Tahkan Shirar and the steps to the Ancient Springs' original well.

"He cannot set foot in our sacred springs," she declared.

"Novice!" Brinelle exclaimed. "Sheath your blade. Immediately."

The girl did not budge. Tahkan Shirar was the mortal enemy she had sworn against for all eternity. The ancestors had heard her vows. She had made many sacrifices to prove her worthiness. Desert demons like this man had killed her father and brother in the War of Retribution. She would not back down.

"Like it or not, Tahkan Shirar is the father of our heir," Brinelle reminded the novice curtly. "The previous Twins of the Sisterlands officiated his marriage to our queen. It is sanctioned by the ancestors . . . and tradition accepts that he may accompany his daughter through the Ordeal of Queens."

"Tradition also demands that I kill him here and now," the young woman retorted.

"Novice," Ari Ara interjected, taking one step toward the woman. "Please. War has robbed too many of us of loved ones. One way to avenge them is to end the cycle of violence that led to their deaths."

Her voice sounded calmer than she felt. Under her tightly-controlled expression, a howl of fear-tinged anger bashed at her grip on her inner *azar*. The sight of that blade so close to her father sent a stampede of horses galloping through her heartbeat. It snatched the air from her lungs, threatening to cut off her voice. Only her hours of training kept her from lunging forward, knocking the sword from that girl's grasp and flinging her to the side.

But she knew the foolhardiness of that impulse. If you leapt at a snarling sand lion, it would rip you to shreds with its claws. Even if you carried a sword, only one of you would walk away from that fight. Ari Ara needed both this novice and her father to survive. So, she spoke to the young woman in a tone meant to disarm, to ease the tension, to get her to lower her weapon.

"Please," she repeated, opening her empty palms slowly. "If my mother, Queen Alinore, were here, she would ask you to think this through. What good will more bloodshed serve?"

The young woman said nothing. But neither did she move to strike. Ari Ara kept talking.

"You do not need to forgive him. Or like him. Or even accept him. But let us address the past in a way that gives us a chance of a future. Put the sword away. Receive the Harrak-Mettahl as he comes . . . in peace."

The novice's face twitched. She shuddered with heavy breath.

"Sister," Tahkan said, his hands spread wide to show he was unarmed, "this I vow before your ancestors and mine: I will not harm a hair on anyone here. Your peace is my peace."

Ari Ara could sense his tension feinting through his careful words, making no promises he could not keep.

The Head Sister caught the girl's arm.

"Let the man come with his daughter. They have had so little time together. He does not need to see the sacred spring."

The novice's scowl did not recede, but she stepped out of her blocking stance and abruptly sheathed her sword. A sigh of relief flew out of the hall, followed by a wind of whispering. As the novice was escorted out of the room by another sister, the Head Sister begged their forgiveness.

"Her grievance is fair," Tahkan admitted. "Wars leave long scars, not all of which are carried by those who fought in them."

"Oh, it's more than just her father or brother bothering her," the white-haired woman sighed. "She holds a grudge against the heir. She has been listening to nonsense, I'm afraid."

"What nonsense?" Ari Ara asked, wide-eyed.

"Oh, the usual. That you're a harbinger of doom, a plot by the Harraken to take over Mariana, that sort of thing. It is unfortunately common in these hills. We are a bit isolated. Mistaken rumors fester."

"Are the heir and her father safe among you?" Shulen queried in a growl.

"Oh yes!" the Head Sister assured him. "Few are armed . . . and you may accompany me as I collect their blades tonight."

Mollified, Shulen consented to their stay.

The other sisters welcomed them warmly. Devotees of the Mother, they rejected the ascetism of some sects of the Warrior. Instead, they strove to honor the gift of life by nurturing, healing, and fostering well-being. Their food was simple but savory, the accommodations humble but comfortable. Candlelit altars stood at the end of each corridor. Statues of the many aspects of the Mother gleamed in the gentle light. A pregnant Mother smiled over dozens of small candles, each a prayer for a mother hoping for a child, worried about a difficult pregnancy, or yearning for a smooth delivery. A Healer-Mother cradled an ailing child in her arms, one hand mopping a fevered brow. A Kitchen-Mother, Weaver-Mother, and Carpenter-Mother fed, clothed, and sheltered. Scholar mothers, merchant mothers, inventor mothers, smith mothers - in a series of alcoves along the main hall, the statues honored the trades and crafts the mothers of Mariana engaged in. There was even a crowded shrine of queens with tiny ancestor statues for Alinore, Elsinor, Eliane, and their mothers back through time. In the center was a special figurine for Brinelle, regent of the nation, and honorary mother to her people. Ari Ara paused to light a stick of incense to the queens of history, praying for their blessing during the ordeal.

In the covered walkway to the Spring House, a shrine of alcoves had been built into the pillars. These shadowed niches held aspects of the mother that yearned for healing. Here, seekers came to scrawl a chalk note upon the stones, words that the steam and mists of the healing springs would erode and erase over time, carrying the request of the seeker to the Black Ancestor River. Missing mothers, neglectful mothers, grief-wracked, drunken, broken-hearted, despairing . . . the Ancient Springs acknowledged that some mothers carried shadows and some yearned for healing. The crew of the Fair Defiance trod uneasily past these shrines, following the sister toward the comfort of the Spring House. She did not hurry, however. Deep healing requires us to face the pain, hurt, and illness inside us and the world.

Once inside the bathhouse, they were free to relax in the hot water. Sighs of relief and relaxation wound through the hiss of steam and splash of water as the crew eased into the warm pools. Small, private rooms were offered to their illustrious guests. Outside of another askance glance from a second novice, the Desert King was treated with the same deference as the Great Lady.

"We are honored to welcome the first Harrak-Mettahl to ever visit our sacred waters," the Head Sister said graciously. She even cracked the *k* properly in his title.

For his part, Tahkan Shirar withheld his scornful disbelief at the notion of immersing himself into a pool of yet more water after being rained on for days. He longed for the dry heat of his desert home. He could almost feel the mold growing behind his ears. But he returned courtesy for courtesy and thanked the Head Sister for her hospitality.

"As for you, young heir," she said to Ari Ara with a warm smile, "only one pool will do."

She gestured for the girl to follow and lifted an umbrella from the collection beside the door.

Shulen reached for another and gestured for Emir to do the same. At the sister's glance, he spoke.

"Where she goes, we go."

"Of course, Nshoka Shulen," the woman acknowledged with

a small bow. "This way."

The Head Sister led them up a stone-and-moss path, her high-soled sandals lifting her feet out of the puddles, her oil-waxed umbrella carving a gap through the downpour. A small building sheltered the wellspring. Two stone statues dwelled in the back corners of the modest room, each as tall as a person, one representing the lineage of the Mother Sister, the other depicting the Warrior Sister. There were no windows except for the narrow one in the single door. While the rest of Ari Ara's companions relaxed down the hill, the hairs on her arms stiffened with uneasy awareness of the presence of ancestor spirits.

"Emir and I will be right by the door," Shulen promised, reading her clouded countenance. "A shout, a word, even a whisper, and we'll come."

"I know. Thank you."

Ari Ara rolled up her cuffs and sat on the edge of the stone basin that contained the pool. She refused to undress and immerse herself entirely – not with prickles running up and down her spine and the hairs on her neck rising. She peered into the well. It was small and square. Though the water brimmed at the top, she could not fathom the bottom. Some said it was bottomless. The waters were startlingly clear. She saw no end to how far it extended.

After ten minutes, the warmth and steam calmed her jangled nerves. The quiet trickle of the spring's overflow spilled into a stone channel that flowed through a slot drain under the outside wall. The hairs on her arms eased flat again and the telltale prickle of spirits subsided. After twenty minutes, Ari Ara felt a little silly – maybe she'd overreacted. The Ordeal of Queens had her on edge. No one knew they were here, no trials or tests could have been prepared. Maybe this was just what it appeared to be: a rest house, a healing spring, a sanctuary. She squandered another ten minutes, feeling guilty at the thought of Shulen and Emir enduring the rain while the Lost Heir supposedly luxuriated in a sacred spring.

In a flurry of decisiveness, she tossed off her sodden outer tunic but kept on a short underrobe – if there was a problem, she didn't want Emir Miresh bursting in on her naked! Feet first, she eased into the pool, fingers gripped tightly on the stone edge, nervous at the thought of the endless well stretching deep into the subterranean world beneath her. Some of the sailors claimed that this was the birth canal of the Black Ancestor River, where the spirits came in and out of the world. Ari Ara just wanted to get this over with. Was she supposed to feel healed? Purified? Sanctified? She just felt wet.

With a huff of exasperation, Ari Ara took a breath and ducked her head under the water.

In the corners of the room, the statues came to life. Grey eyelids snapped open. Soundless feet lunged off pedestals. The figures hurtled to the edge of the pool just as Ari Ara surfaced, water in her eyes, gasping for air. Stone-silver hands grabbed her head and shoulders, and shoved her back down. In a panic, Ari Ara struggled against them, beating at their firm grip, eyes wide through the clear water, trying to see their faces through the veil of bubbles. Her feet scrabbled against the slick sides of the well, finding no purchase. She thrashed and tried to use the Way Between. Her twisting arms broke their grip enough to shoot above the surface. She gasped for breath, but couldn't cry out before the statues shoved her under once again.

Ancestors! Help me! She shot her prayer out in a desperate, unvoiced shout. The Black Ancestor River roared in her ears, flooded her eyes as her vision went dark. Her hands dropped, limp, as the breath faded in her lungs. Her head hung, curls floating in a wreath around her face.

In the depths beneath her feet, she saw her mother's spirit.

Alinore surged through the waters toward her, face fierce. Rhianne rose with her, a look of wrath on her Fanten features. The two women grabbed her by the arms and flung her up, out of the river of death, up and out into life.

Ari Ara's eyes snapped open, gasping, choking up water. She lay sprawled on the floor of the well temple.

"Shulen!" she screamed.

He burst through the door in an instant, eyes scanning the room for threats.

"The statues!" she cried, pointing and coughing. "Alive. Tried to . . . drown me."

Shulen barked orders to Emir. They spun to the statues, pounding each with a swift fist. The solid thunk of hard stone disproved her words.

"But - but," she stammered, "I *saw* them."

To his credit, Shulen inspected the statues inch by inch, sending Emir to examine the outside for signs of passageways. They found nothing.

"Perhaps it was a vision?" the old warrior suggested tentatively, wrapping her Fanten cloak around her now shaking shoulders.

Ari Ara protested. Her lungs still burned with the sting of drowning.

"Someone was here," she insisted. "They were real."

"Did you see their faces?"

Ari Ara closed her eyes and tried to recall. The grey paint masked their flesh tones and blurred their features. She hadn't seen much through the thrashing water. Nothing had been clear.

Shulen asked Emir to search the forest. Ari Ara curled her knees to her chest, hugging her arms around them. The statues in the corners terrified her. She kept waiting for their eyes to snap open again.

"Come, let's get you to bed. You must be exhausted," Shulen

sighed, extending a hand and half-heaving her to her feet.

He promised to keep watch all night, never leaving her side, but Ari Ara could see the hint of doubt and uncertainty in his eyes. Visions and spirits haunted this spring. Far stranger things had happened here. Ari Ara was shaken, that much he knew, but it could have been a message from the ancestors, or a test of the spirits. Her babbling story of her mother and Rhianne saving her only lent credence to his theory that she'd been swept away by a vision. Shulen resisted the urge to comment on the symbolism of the statues trying to kill her. It sounded a lot like the nightmares she'd been having for months. Maybe she dozed off in the warmth of the hot spring?

The night stretched interminably long. Ari Ara refused to close her eyes. At last, Tahkan sang her into slumber with Harraken lullabies and a dose of song magic. He stroked her hair and sat beside her bed, waiting for her breath to soften with the signs of deep sleep. When he was certain she would not overhear, he murmured to Shulen.

"What do you make of this?"

The grey-haired warrior shook his head. He did not know.

"We found no signs of intruders, saw no one. The only way in was through the single door I guarded. The statues were solid stone, Tahkan, I bloodied my fists on them."

On the other hand, he had seen Ari Ara cough up water and heard her half-drowned voice call out to him.

"A vision, then? A dream?" Tahkan wondered. "Is it just the suspicion Finn Paikason planted in all of us about the Sisters? Or some deeper message?"

"I do not know what happened," Shulen said carefully, "but I am glad our wives are watching over her."

"Perhaps it was just a dream," Tahkan sighed.

In the morning, though, the truth was not so clear.

Bruises bloomed on Ari Ara's shoulders and arms. Bruises in the shape of human hands.

CHAPTER SIXTEEN

. . . . .

Fanten Dreams

The Fair Defiance creaked through the river channels under a cloud of doom. The ghostly handprints on the Lost Heir lifted the hairs on everyone's necks. Sailors' superstitions ran thick as the swarms of eels in the shallows. The ship's crew pinned wagon-wheel hex wards to the mast, prow, and bulkhead. They remained staunchly loyal to Ari Ara, though. Everyone from the kitchen lad to the captain conspired to bolster Ari Ara's faltering confidence. Off-duty sailors played music on their fiddles and pipes. The crewwoman who served as ship's carpenter carved wooden pins for everyone in the shape of the Mark of Peace. The cook went out of his way to make dishes that would tempt Ari Ara's appetite out of its anxious queasiness.

Their steadfast support was appreciated. A streak of bad luck had chased them from the Ancient Springs. Weevils hatched in the stores, forcing them to toss out their porridge grain and skip breakfast until they reached port. The moment the clouds parted and a lively wind hustled them onward, the mainsail tore, causing delays while the replacement was hauled out of storage in the hold.

Loosened by the heavy rains, a hillside gave way, slamming into the river in an impassable blockade of tree trunks, mud, and boulders. If their lookout hadn't hollered a warning to halt, they would have been buried under the mountainous weight. As it was, the surge spun and battered the Fair Defiance against the rocks, driving a crack into her hull. Two crew members manned the bilge pump night and day to prevent the leak from sinking the ship.

They would have to backtrack to Seeker's Station and stay for several days while the Fair Defiance was hauled into drydock for repairs. The stores would be restocked and the sails sewn. The captain was determined to break the spell of ill fortune with the practical, down-to-earth magic of hard work.

Ari Ara tried not to surrender to the suspicion that she was cursed. As they retreated down the dammed channel and up an alternate route, Ari Ara spent hours each day training in the Way Between on the foredeck, using exertion and motion to silence her gnawing anxiety.

When the Fair Defiance limped into port, the crew and passengers took rooms at a crowded dockside inn. Seeker's Station thronged with travelers. A tangled nest of waystations, temples, and supply shops, the town squatted like a roosting hen at the mouth of the main tributary up the Water Maze. Here, the snarl of side channels reunited briefly with the central flow of the Sister River before unraveling like strands of hair. Whether one was headed for the Citadel of the Sisterlands or for the hidden hermitages in the Water Maze, the town offered a gathering point for rest, restocking, and renewal. With the Summer Trials nearing, every mooring on the docks did brisk business. Ships and skiffs slid in and out. Fees were paid by the hour to the sister who served as harbor master. The prices climbed steeply for overnight stays.

Ari Ara couldn't fathom the expense of a three-day repair in dry dock. There'd been talk of hiring another vessel and crew for the final leg of the journey to the Citadel, but Brinelle, Tahkan, and Shulen were united on one point: they trusted no one in the Sisterlands.

"At the very least, a new ship's crew could try to sabotage the ordeal," Brinelle sighed, resigning herself to the delay.

"At worst, they could conspire to harm Ari Ara," Tahkan growled.

"We followers of the Way Between are not so easily killed," Shulen murmured quietly. But he did not object to the plan to continue with the Fair Defiance. Weeks of traveling with the crew had woven bonds of friendship and familiarity between them all – two of the strongest protections in the world.

But none of his protections could help Ari Ara in the dreamrealm.

Unless she exhausted her body in training and fell into a dreamless sleep, nightmares gripped her the moment her eyes shut. Assassin statues chased her through spirit-whispering forests, drowned her in roiling black waters, embalmed her in dripping candlewax, smothered her with pillows of sand. She woke gasping, screaming, her head spinning over her galloping heartbeat.

That night, while moonlight etched the town in veins of silver, Ari Ara tossed and turned in the drowning softness of her bed. Her eyes burned holes in her skull. Her bones ached with weariness. She resisted sleep, though, dreading the nightmares that lurked on the other side of her anchor-heavy eyelids. She re-read sections of her mother's journal until her yawns engulfed her. The book settled on her chest.

The nightmare started swiftly. A hiss of steam released its serpent-sigh. A trickle of water whispered in the corner of the room. Stone grated over stone. Stealthy footsteps crept closer. Grey hands gripped her shoulders and pressed down hard as rock-heavy statues. Water closed over her head. Ari Ara flailed and tried to throw off the figures, frantically reliving the horrible drowning at the Ancient Springs. She kicked her feet and shoved against the narrow stones of the well, breaking the surface, sucking in air.

"Help!" she cried with her last wisp of breath, her voice so feeble it hardly reached her own ears.

Snap! The dream froze.

At the edge of Ari Ara's vision, the Fanten Grandmother appeared. The hissing steam crackled into soft frost lace. Feathered white patterns etched the air, tracing the walls, figures, stones, even the gleam of lantern light, with intricate creeping tendrils. The elder glanced around with a scowl. Ari Ara gripped the edge of the pool with white-knuckled hands, sopping, close to sobbing. She slouched under the looming figures of the two grey statues. The Fanten Grandmother stalked across the room and studied them with a disdainful - and unsurprised - expression.

Ari Ara hauled her body out of the water, limp hair plastered to her face, gasping in lungfuls of sweet, precious air.

"When this ordeal is over," the Fanten Grandmother commented sourly as Ari Ara coughed, "we are going to have a long chat, you and I."

"Is that supposed to make me feel better?" Ari Ara exclaimed, incredulous. The Fanten were not to be trifled with. The grandmother wasn't going to pat her head and tell her everything was going to be alright.

"No," the silver-haired old woman replied. "It's supposed to make *me* feel better. Your dreams bellow louder than the Great Horns. No one can sleep. The babies howl in the caves."

"Well, at least my mother heard my cry for help when I was actually drowning," Ari Ara grumbled, recalling how the spirits had flung her to safety.

"Oh yes, your mother certainly came to your rescue," the Fanten Grandmother said with a strange twist of tone.

Ari Ara glanced sharply at the silver-haired woman.

"What does that mean?"

The grandmother sniffed and didn't answer. She wasn't going to spill all her secrets.

Not yet.

"You," she informed Ari Ara testily, "are going to learn to control your fears in the dreamrealm. Otherwise, they will control you."

"How am I supposed to do that?" Ari Ara sighed.

"By listening," the Fanten Grandmother told her, "and learning."

With a swipe of her hand, the Fanten Grandmother shifted the dream. The frost feathers shrank back into steam, furling into rising hisses once again. The two statues remained still but now they held a second version of Ari Ara under the water's surface. Ari Ara swallowed hard at the sight of her terrified face.

"Watch. Do not blink. Not for an instant."

Ari Ara stiffened her stomach muscles, set her jaw, and steeled her resolve. The Fanten Grandmother snapped her fingers and everything came horribly alive. Ari Ara saw her frantic thrashing, the silent snarls of the statues, and the gritted teeth shining oddly white against the ashen faces. She felt the moment when Alinore and Rhianne's spirits slammed up from the pool, flinging the statues back, tossing her limp body out of the water. The statues lifted their arms against invisible blows, frightened looks on their faces. One gave a signal and both leapt toward the pedestals in the corners. With a hiss of oiled gears, the bases turned . . . and stone facades slid around, concealing them behind carved, life-sized figures of the Mother and Warrior.

Ari Ara gasped. That's how the attackers had escaped, leaving solid statues behind them.

She stared at the floor, shuddering.

"Did you see their faces clearly?" the old woman demanded.

Ari Ara shook her head. Images of her half-limp body coughing up water had stolen her attention. With an exasperated flick of her fingers, the Fanten Grandmother turned her around and swept the dream back to the beginning. The statues returned to shoving the frantic version of Ari Ara under the water.

"Take a close look at them," the Fanten Grandmother commanded. "Face those . . . statues."

She snarled out the word with scoffing disdain. The old woman recognized them for what they were. So would the girl, if she dared to truly look.

"I – I can't," Ari Ara quaked, shaking her head, too terrified to move. "What if they turn on me?"

"They won't. Not while *I* hold them."

The Fanten Grandmother's haughty confidence jolted a spark of courage into her. Nothing twitched without her permission. When a Fanten Grandmother held a dream, it froze stiller than stone ... or statues.

"Look."

Ari Ara obeyed, lifting her eyes to the two figures that had shoved her brutally under the water, arms outstretched with gripping fingers, grimaces on their grey faces. The Fanten Grandmother waited for the girl's baffled look to clear like storm clouds. When it didn't, she made a grumbling noise in the back of her throat and stepped forward. With her fingertips – and a disgusted grimace – she peeled off the grey mask covering one of the statue's faces.

"Oh," Ari Ara spat out grimly.

It was just as she had suspected. Roka Maro had tried to drown her.

With somber determination, Ari Ara turned away.

"Where are you going?" the Fanten Grandmother called, her

fingers poised over the second statue's mask.

"I'm waking up. I've got to deal with her."

Ari Ara eyed the edge of the dream, trying to figure out how to leap into waking. Roka had undoubtedly roped that novice into helping her.

"But - "

Ari Ara didn't listen. She took a running plunge, twisted in the air, and fell backwards . . . out of the dream.

The Fanten Grandmother watched her vanish. Then she sighed and flicked the mask off the other statue.

It was not the novice who stared back.

CHAPTER SEVENTEEN

. . . . .

Seeker's Station

After breakfast, Ari Ara hitched up the copious folds of her fancy overcoat and dragged Minli up to the rooftop platform above the inn's attic. A jostling throng clogged the street outside, peering in the windows, hoping for a glimpse of the heir. The innkeeper's cook was collecting fees for the chance to crane through the kitchen doors. Even after they realized that Ari Ara wasn't there, people still paid to look in at the Great Lady sipping her morning tea.

Ari Ara took one hasty glance over the rail at the crowd below and ducked back before she was spotted. She shoved the sleeves of her overcoat back and loosened the collar. Shulen had delivered a stern warning to beware of archers' arrows before taking up his post at the bottom of the attic's ladder. He took threats to Ari Ara – dreams, visions, spirits, flesh-and-blood – seriously.

Used by traveling merchants as a lookout for ships, the dock-shaped rooftop platform was long and thin, following the shape of the inn. Upturned wooden crates and a half-broken chair stood around a low barrel table. A melted candle in a lantern and an old mug of beer hinted at midnight card games in the cool night air. Deserted at this early hour, it still offered an impressive view of the curling river and huddled skyline of the town.

Ari Ara pulled Minli over to the western corner, furthest away from the attic steps, and relayed her dream in a hushed whisper.

"It was Roka Maro. I know it," she concluded, chin lifting with stubborn certainty. "She's trying to kill me."

"But . . . it was just a dream, Ari Ara."

Minli hesitated to point out the obvious – it didn't prove anything. Ari Ara bit her lower lip and stared pensively at the rise and fall of the hills across the river. She'd promised not to tell anyone that she could dreamwalk, but how else could she explain the truth of what she'd seen? It tipped the scales of suspicion against the Warrior Sister, adding weight to Alinore's journal entries and the Paika's hunch. Also, Roka Maro had the ability to bind the spirits to silence the way Tahkan had discovered in his search. With the Fanten dream as evidence, the case against the woman seemed clear as day: Roka had tried to murder Queen Alinore's child . . . and was still trying to.

Ari Ara had to speak up. Too much was at stake.

"What do you know about dreamwalking?" she asked Minli.

"Only that the Fanten do it," he answered with a frown, trying to recall more. "I think I read something about it in the Capital Library. It's supposed to be different from regular dreaming."

The book had been full of wildly unbelievable tales – flying on mists, speaking to the spirits, delivering messages across vast distances.

"But that can't all be true," Minli said in a tone of disbelief.

"It is," Ari Ara confirmed.

"How do you know? Lowlanders don't do it."

"I've been dreamwalking since I was eleven."

Minli's mouth fell open in his astonished face. For a moment, her confession rendered him speechless. His eyes widened, reflecting the sharp blue of the morning sky. Below them, a fish merchant's voice sounded over the crowd, hawking fresh catches to passersby. A distant temple bell struck, faded under the babble of voices, and rang again. Minli's mind overcame his surprise.

"Since you were eleven?" he repeated, thinking. "Was that your dream about Alaren and bringing back the Way Between?"

She nodded.

A cascade of questions erupted from him.

"What's it like? How is it different? Do you know when you're dreamwalking versus regular dreaming? When else have you done this?"

Ari Ara leaned her elbows on the rail and shoved her hair back from her face. It was a relief to tell him, to spill the secret she'd been carrying, and join him in wonderment and curiosity. Dreamwalking *was* different. Clearer, more potent, richer in symbol and metaphor. The dream realm became malleable through intention and skill - not that Ari Ara had much of that. She'd only dreamwalked a handful of times. Once in the High Mountains when she met Alaren, once when her moon blood started, again before the confirmation hearing on her claim to the throne, a few times in the Border Mountains, and also when she found Emir wandering in the desert. Every now and then, her experiences with Fanten-style dreaming blurred with waking life, revealing knowledge or passing along messages. But dreamwalking was unpredictable; she never knew when she'd stumble into it . . . or what would happen when she did.

"So, the statues?" Minli asked.

"The Fanten Grandmother showed me who they were. Fanten dreams run truer than true. That's how I *know* it was the Warrior Sister."

"No one will believe you, though," he argued. The Marianans

wouldn't accept dreams as evidence any more than they would Harraken song magic or the Paika's untrustworthy secrets.

Ari Ara kicked the rail in frustration. Minli chewed on their options, but it all boiled down to the same thing: they had to find hard evidence. He fidgeted thoughtfully, tapping the end of his crutch on the floorboards.

"You can't tell anyone about your dream."

"But Minli – "

"*Think* Ari Ara," he urged in a worried tone. "If they hear you can dream like a Fanten, they'll just assume you *are* Fanten."

Ari Ara snorted and tossed him an amused glance.

"I look nothing like the Fanten."

"You *are* short for your age, and darker than the Marianans."

"I have Harraken blood," she retorted, "and the Mark of Peace on my back."

"Don't get all huffy with me!" Minli exclaimed. "I believe you. It's just that lowlanders can't dreamwalk. Marianans will never believe that the heir can. Or that a dreamwalker is the true heir."

Ari Ara had no intention of telling anyone else about her dreaming. She could feel her promise to the Fanten Grandmother twanging a warning inside her. Promises forged in the dreamrealm should not be broken in the waking world.

As for Minli, word of this would never pass his lips. This changed everything. Certain long-buried possibilities now unearthed once again. He told Ari Ara to give him the day to think everything through. Then, cautiously, Minli started digging into the graveyard of the past. Ari Ara saw him speaking with Tahkan, Brinelle, and Shulen, asking each one a careful question. He borrowed a messenger hawk and refused to tell her why. He spent hours staring out at the river, lost in thought. When she pestered him for an explanation, he just shook his head.

"Shhh, I'm thinking."

The next day, Minli slipped off before breakfast. Ari Ara fidgeted through her studies until Brinelle dismissed her with exasperation. She hung out on the rooftop for a while. Then boredom crept in. Curiosity quickened in her blood. Where was Minli? What was he doing?

"Let's go out," she declared, tromping down the attic stairs to where Emir stood guard.

"I'll get Shulen – "

"He's sleeping, getting well deserved rest," Ari Ara pointed out. "Come on, I'm dying of boredom and there's a whole town out there to see. Please?"

She hung on his arm, making pleading faces at him. Emir was like a big brother to her – and like a little sister, she knew how to sway his better judgment. Ari Ara cajoled, reasoned, and finally took off down the hall at a run threatening to go out by herself if he didn't come.

"I'm the heir. Shouldn't you do what I say?" Ari Ara argued.

Emir gave her an annoyed look. Technically, that was true.

They slipped out the back to avoid the throng of people. Ari Ara pulled her Fanten cloak over her distinctive copper hair. Emir stuck closer to her than a shadow. Seeker's Station roared with voices and bustled with trade. In a strange blend of spirituality and commerce, shops and temples crowded together along the waterfront of the Sister River. Behind them, a jumbled labyrinth of alleys and side streets led to inns, taverns, warehouses, and residential houses. Foot bridges arched over wide canals. Small boats moored beside buildings or ferried supplies to larger ships anchored in the river.

Ari Ara gawked and grinned like any first-time seeker. She tarried by a stand of ornately inked prayer scrolls as the vendor extolled their powers, promising that they could summon the ancestor spirit of Marin, himself. She stared through the window of a mapmaker's shop, marveling at the display of Water Maze maps – no two alike. She gaped at a stall of relics – saints' toenails, curling locks of a legendary sister's hair, the finger of a renowned warrior. Emir hustled her along, hissing that it was probably just a shriveled old carrot. On every corner, a blue-robed novice rang a bell and proffered her bowl, raising funds to support the orphans, vowing that charity won the goodwill of the ancestors and turned fate in one's favor.

There were potions for fertility and charms for childbirth, specially-blessed polishing waxes for swords and shields anointed with protective holy water. Each shop held its share of statuettes of the Mother and paintings of the Warrior. River dragon symbols curled everywhere, painted on banners and flags, carved into small pendants, printed on cloaks and tunics. Shopkeepers did brisk trade as travelers headed to the Citadel of the Sisterlands for the conclusion of the Ordeal of Queens. Ari Ara even spotted little figurines of the Lost Heir, though she grumbled that it looked nothing like her. Emir laughed and dug into his pocket, buying one just to tease her.

"Hot item, that," the merchant remarked cheerfully. "I'll be sold out by midday, thanks to the Ordeal and all."

"Do you think she'll pass?" Emir asked, unable to resist making Ari Ara squirm a little under her hood.

"Not up to me, is it?" the merchant answered with a shrug and a nervous glance around, as if he could sense the spirits listening. Then a small grin tugged at the corner of his mouth. "But she is a right little *River Dragon*, isn't she? I'd be proud to have her as our queen."

Emir shifted position as Ari Ara's beaming face snapped up at the man's kind words. From every flag and pennant, the river dragon symbol rippled and curled. Its cheerful blue waved at her from every corner of his stall. A gaggle of passersby overheard his commendation and stopped to buy trinkets emblazoned with the dragon.

Emir nudged her along before she was recognized. River traffic had surged as people journeyed from all quarters of Mariana. Nobles' pleasure boats moored next to the clunking vessels of commoners. Farmers and grocers sailed barges up and down the river with foodstuffs to feed thousands. Merchants brought cloth and garments from the mills in simple shades of blue, black, brown, and white – the appropriate colors for a spiritual visit to the Sisterlands. Even the hermits poled their tiny skiffs down from their quiet hideaways to witness this historic moment. Guides sat on barrels next to the docks, their knowledge of the tangled routes of the Water Maze sought by all.

Emir kept a sharp lookout through the crowds, but Ari Ara was just one black-cloaked girl in the bustling tumult. No one recognized her so long as she covered her hair, lowered her voice, and didn't draw attention to herself. With the discretion of her Fanten upbringing, Ari Ara slipped through Seeker's Station without notice. She had just paused to examine some silly-looking love trinkets when a familiar flash of fox-red caught the corner of her eye. Her heart lurched.

Finn!

CHAPTER EIGHTEEN

. . . . .

The Ruse

Across the square, Finn's unique cap shifted as he bent his head toward another boy. Ari Ara gasped as she recognized the bird's nest of Minli's hair. Why was he talking to Finn? She burst into motion, angling toward them, but a horse shied at the blare of a temple horn and careened in front of her. Emir lunged and hauled her out of harm's way. By the time the chaos settled, the two boys had moved. She danced on tiptoe trying to see over the crowd of heads.

There!

Her eyes caught the flash of Minli's white tunic with the black Mark of Peace as he hurried across the square with Finn. She tugged Emir after her as she wound through crates of squawking chickens, street-side shrines with burning incense curling off them, and pushcart vendors with trays of herbal cure-alls and racks of good luck charms. A gong sounded. A flock of white-robed sisters poured out of the temple into the street. Minli's tunic was lost in the crowd of flapping garments.

There!

Finn's autumn-red fox cap blazed in contrast to the robes. Plunging after him, Ari Ara bumped her hip into a rickety fruit stand. The stacked apricots toppled onto the stones. She blurted out an apology, her feet hopping madly through the rolling fruit. In the scramble of that knees-up jig, she lost Finn for a second.

There!

Minli and Finn crossed a cobbled street, their animated talk buried under the babble of the bustling town. Ari Ara bolted after them, but collided with a procession of a hundred blue-robed pilgrims. They filled the street like a flashflood, chanting and hoisting a saint-statue aloft. A forest of banners with gold emblazoned symbols proclaimed their pledges to the spirits. Ari Ara wheeled in the river of surprised faces and blue cloth, ducking and diving until she emerged out the other side of the stream.

There!

Minli's bird's nest of brown hair bobbed as he climbed a flight of stairs to a wooden walkway along a building. Finn took the steps two at a time after him. Ari Ara edged along the house, shimmying sideways past the pilgrims, dancing from foot to foot impatiently when an immense brown ox barred her forward path. At last, she put her palms on the beast's smooth back and vaulted up and over. He bellowed and bucked, sending her flying. Ari Ara twisted midair and landed on the slick, scale-lined cobblestones near a fishmonger's cart. Her arms windmilled as her feet slid. She flailed, grabbed the banister of the exterior staircase and hauled herself up it. Behind her, Emir hollered at her as he held out his palms, trying to placate both the enraged bull and the cowherd. Ari Ara's hips churned as she bounded up the steps. Her legs burned as she hurtled down the wrap-around porch. Her lungs screamed for air as she rounded the corner –

- and smacked straight into Minli.

They toppled. Instinctively, Ari Ara grabbed him and flung her foot forward as a brace. Lurching to stillness, Minli blinked at her like a bewildered owl.

"What are you doing here?" he exclaimed, exasperated. "Did you follow me?"

"No. Yes. Sort of," she blurted out. "I saw you with Finn."

"Ah."

Minli straightened up and adjusted his tunic. He tucked his crutch under his arm, steadily ignoring her pointed look.

"You should talk to him."

"Who?"

Minli gave her an exasperated look.

"Finn, of course."

Ari Ara scoffed.

"I don't want to talk to him," she huffed.

"Uh-huh," Minli snorted, unconvinced. "That's why you chased us halfway across town? Because you *didn't* want to talk to Finn?"

Ari Ara blushed sheepishly.

"Alright," she agreed.

Emir caught up with them, breathless and glowering.

"I'm not sure that's a good idea," he warned when they told him where they were headed. Then he read Ari Ara's stubborn expression and threw his hands up. She'd had worse ideas - far worse - and lived to tell the tale.

Minli led them around the back porch, down a curling staircase into a secluded seekers' shrine in the courtyard behind the inn where Finn was staying. Used by seekers for dawn and dusk prayers, its garden alcove stood empty at this hour of the day. Under the shelter of the staircase, a row of ancestor statues huddled, all smaller than a cat. Wealthier seekers made their offerings at the temples, but the farmers and craftswomen, orphans and seamstresses left their modest gifts at tiny shrines like this. Unofficial, unsanctioned, and unmonitored by the Sisters, these altars cradled the faith of everyday people. Their locations passed word of mouth from one seeker to the next, their miraculous powers often exaggerated by innkeepers who set up lodgings nearby.

Ari Ara looked around with the strange sense that she'd been here before. Clusters of showering roses bloomed over scraps of seekers' robes tied to the branches as prayers. Star-like flowers hung soft as breath among the pendants strung from the shrubs. Five ancient dwarf oaks embraced the garden in a protective ring of moss-lined arms and rustling greenery. At the far end, Finn stood by a set of iron-curled chairs in a cobblestoned alcove. Minli nudged Ari Ara forward. Then he and Emir withdrew to give them some privacy.

"Ari Ara."

Finn said her name warmly with love and longing.

"Finn."

She clipped his name with coldness.

Ari Ara folded her arms over her chest, as if that could block his heart from reaching hers. She tried to ignore the pounding sensation. The sight of his dark curls and wiry muscles sent tingles up and down her limbs. He looked hollowed out, his lean build tightening over his angular bones. A mix of grief, sleeplessness, and taut determination put shadows under his eyes. Finn looked older. Sorrow and loss had shoved him over the threshold of boyhood, closer to the man he would become. Ari Ara swallowed hard at the sight of him. A long silence hung.

"I dreamed of you, you know," Finn said at last.

She blinked. She hadn't expected that.

He stared at the earth and nudged a pebble with his shoe. Then he lifted his head and grasped her eyes. The gesture took courage.

"In the dream, we were dancing, like in the old days, then you turned away and I – I could see all the pain I'd caused. I'm so sorry, Ari Ara. I should have told you."

Ari Ara scarcely heard his apology, hit by another thought: he'd dreamed *her* dream. The same dream. A Fanten dream. With longing and fury, love and heartbreak, she and Finn had whirled in a dance of invented steps to a tempo that raced faster and faster. Over and under, they'd spiraled around each other's outstretched arms and leaping limbs. He'd caught her waist and pulled her into his spin. She'd anchored her feet to earth and flung him around her. Just as their breath struggled to keep up with the pace, the dream hurtled to a stillness. In the silence, they stood. If it had truly been a Fanten dream, he would know what happened next. Did he stab her in the back like in so many of her dreams? Or not?

"In the dream," Finn said in a hush, "we sang the Atta Song."

Ari Ara's mouth dropped open. She, too, had dreamed that they sang the Harraken song of apology and forgiveness. Foreheads pressed together, breaths entwining, they'd sung with a vividness that had seared into her waking thoughts. Drifting through the day distracted, the melody had hummed in her throat. Her father even overheard her and asked who the song was for.

"You know who," she'd told him.

"You have no need to ask Finn's forgiveness," Tahkan had responded shortly. "Quite the other way around."

"*Atta* flows as one, backwards and forwards," she had quoted from the old saying, "through the apology and the forgiveness, neither complete without the other. I dreamt Finn sung *atta* . . . and I offered *atta* to him in return."

"Well," Tahkan had commented tersely, "that was just a dream."

But it had been more alive than life itself. Finn wouldn't

recognize it as a Fanten dream – lowlanders rarely did - but Ari Ara knew it was . . . and that changed everything. In the streaked shadows of the secluded garden, Ari Ara asked Finn the proving question.

"Where did we sing the Atta Song?"

"Here," he answered with a wide-eyed shiver. "We sang it here."

Ari Ara surrendered. To deny a shared dream was to invite disaster. At least, that's what the Fanten claimed. She sat down on one of the intricate, wrought-iron chairs, arms folded across her chest, tilting back on two legs.

"Very well," she grumbled. "Begin."

"Uh, I don't actually know the song," Finn confessed.

He drew up a chair, the legs scraping the courtyard's age-darkened cobblestones with a raspy groan. Finn leaned his elbows on his knees, hands cupped out toward her. Ari Ara tipped her chair down with a clang. She rattled off the opening refrain of the Atta Song, but even to her ears, the discordant resentment in her voice burned. She stopped.

"How could you, Finn? How could you lie about something like that?" she cried. All her bottled-up words poured out of her at once, glugging in her tongue-tied throat.

They had vowed in a secret passageway through the mountains to tell the truth to each other or acknowledge that there was a truth they could not reveal. By doing neither, Finn had broken her trust along with her heart. Words poured from her. Every thought she'd had in the last two weeks. Each lightning sizzle of anger. Each glass shard of hurt. She'd watched the Atta Song countless times, seen former enemies make amends and reconcile even after unforgiveable horrors. *This* was nothing in comparison, but it felt like everything. She sensed herself losing the Way Between, swept up in a riptide of emotion.

Finn, however, had studied the Way Between alongside her. He'd listened to Shulen and wandered through hours of conversation with Minli. It shattered him to watch Ari Ara hurl the invisible shards of her anger at him, but instead of flinging back verbal barbs, he listened quietly. He turned the pain of her words to one side or the other of his heart. Some accusations he put in the pile that he would take responsibility for. Others he put aside, knowing that it was just her heartbreak that she threw at him. Ari Ara wanted a war between them. He would not let her have it. It took two to fight.

He wanted to make things right. So, instead of flinging back insults and accusations, Finn listened . . . and waited. When the heat of her temper broke into tears like a growling thunderstorm into a downpour, he spoke.

"I am truly sorry. My actions hurt you. I chose loyalty to my clan over truth to you."

Finn did not - could not - say he was wrong to do so. He could accept the consequences and acknowledge how hurt she was, but the secret he'd held represented life and death to his family. Had the Marianans and Harraken known of the Southern Paika's involvement, all of the Paika would have been targeted in retaliation.

"I don't know how to put things right between our people. Or us. But I am sorry for all of it."

Finn rose and stood before Ari Ara. He pulled his fox cap off his curls and held it in his nervous hands. Then he swallowed the last dregs of his pride and knelt in the opening position of the Atta Song, the placing of oneself - vulnerable, sorrowful, willing to make amends - at the feet of the one you've hurt. Cupping one palm in the other, he extended his people's gesture of fealty and service. He spoke in formal language, not merely as friend to friend, or young lover to beloved, but as he might to the queen she would one day become.

Ari Ara wrestled with the lump in her throat, tempted to sing the first lines of the song. But she couldn't. The day of their Atta Song would come. But today was not that day. Not for her. Not with her heart still cracked like a lightning-struck tree, blackened and smoldering. She wasn't ready to forgive.

Finn read her hesitation as skillfully as he followed elk trails in the mountains. He rose to standing and shoved his fox cap on top his black curls. A burn of nerves, shame, and rejection flamed scarlet on his cheeks.

"I see. Well. That's that."

He rushed to leave, ducking under the green boughs of the blossoming shrub, knocking his head and wincing as a shower of petaled stars shook loose. Ari Ara bit back tears – because despite everything, the sight of his star-sprinkled shoulders still made the breath catch in her throat.

At the edge of the garden, Minli blocked Finn's path, dark eyes firm in his round face, one hand lifted. He craned around, eyeing Emir, making sure the older youth was out of earshot before murmuring:

"Did you even tell her what we spoke about?"

Finn sighed, his body tight with defeat.

"What's the use? She'll never agree."

"Want to bet?" Minli muttered under his breath. He nudged Finn back into the grove.

Minli had known Ari Ara longer than any of the companions, longer than her father, longer than Shulen. He knew how wide her stubborn streak was and how to dance around it. He knew how hot her temper flared and how to throw a bucket of cold water on it. He knew when to ignore her foolishness and when to stand up to her pig-headed pride.

"Sit down, both of you," Minli insisted, hooking his crutch

under Ari Ara's legs as she leapt to her feet in protest of whatever he was about to say.

She plunked back down on the chair and glowered up at him. Minli wasn't fooled. Ari Ara desperately wanted to reconcile with Finn . . . she just didn't know how. Fortunately, her best friend had a few ideas. He cut straight to the point.

"What if Finn could prove who was behind the attack on Queen Alinore?"

Ari Ara gaped at him. Then at Finn.

Minli took her surprise as an opening to spit out his plan. He'd been mulling on the scheme all day. Finn had already agreed to try it. It could work – but they needed Ari Ara's help.

"I asked Finn to set a snare for Roka Maro."

"You what?!"

"Shhh," Minli urged, rolling his eyes at her reaction. "We need evidence, right? Well, Finn is the perfect person to draw it out."

"How?" Ari Ara demanded, skeptical. Roka Maro wouldn't just spill her deepest secrets to a Paika boy.

"I'll send her a message," Finn explained. "Arrange a meeting, tell her *The Paika* sent me to finally finish what was started fifteen years ago."

Ari Ara lifted an unconvinced eyebrow. Then what?

"I'll get her to hire my services," Finn said with a bitter note in his voice, "to kill the Lost Heir. That will get us the evidence we need to catch her."

Ari Ara suddenly saw it, the simple, deadly elegance of the boys' scheme.

"No," she whispered in a fearful hush. "You can't. It's too dangerous."

But Finn was already tangled in this up to the tips of his fox cap. When Ari Ara had thrown him off the boat and out of her life, Finn hadn't run away. He wasn't going to slink back to his home in the Spires. *The Paika* had sent him to accomplish a task and he intended to do it. He didn't need to be on the Fair Defiance to find out if Roka Maro was involved with the attack on Queen Alinore. Using all his guile – and a fair amount of Paika charm – he would worm his way into the confidences of the Warrior Sister and find the truth.

"But why would she trust you?" Ari Ara spluttered. "You l-loved me once."

"Still do," he confessed quickly, quietly.

Ari Ara leapt to her feet, striding around the bricks, ducking under the oak trees.

"She'll never believe you."

"I'll convince her my affections for you were all an act," Finn argued. "A ruse to get closer to you. I'll tell her *The Paika* ordered me to do it.

"Did she?"

"No!"

"Enough," Minli cut in, forestalling their argument. "Finn will do what he must to get the proof that the Warrior Sister means you harm. He will persuade Roka Maro that he shares her dislike of Ari Ara. Why else would he still be lingering around after you clearly sent him away?"

"It's a ruse for a ruse," Finn explained. "If she agrees to hire me, I'll send the Warrior Sister a message saying that I've gotten you – Ari Ara – to agree to a secret rendezvous at . . . I don't know, some lovers' spot, and I'll be in a position to do whatever Roka wants. She'll send further instructions – and that's how we'll get our proof."

For a moment, Ari Ara's hope soared . . . then it crashed. She shook her head.

"That would implicate Finn in a plot to kill me," she pointed out. "I can't let him do that."

"Then you should help him," Minli said. "Hire him. Write an official contract for his Paika services, outlining how he entered into this ruse on your orders."

"Since when does Finn follow orders?" she snorted.

"Since he fell out of your good graces and is desperate to prove his loyalty again."

Minli was right. She could write out an official record hiring Finn Paikason to work for her. Minli could witness it and hide it where no one would think to look. Ari Ara bit her bottom lip, considering the scheme. It was dangerous, but it might work.

"Please," Finn pleaded softly, "allow me to take a risk to help all our peoples. Let me seek the source of the secrets that drove us apart, the dangerous truths that threaten us still."

This was the last part of the Atta Song, the offer of how to heal the deeper causes, the actions one would take to prevent the old harm from happening again. Finn waited for her response, feeling as if his whole life depended on her answer. He had other offerings to make to her, personal ones, but he yearned to prove himself worthy, loyal, a true friend. If he got proof, then perhaps they could sing *atta* together, perhaps the shattered trust could be slowly repaired.

Ari Ara drew a shaky breath.

She nodded.

She, too, longed for the day when their Atta Song was finished. And for the day that would come after.

CHAPTER NINETEEN

. . . . .

Two Roads

"May these senseless deaths not be in vain. May we prevent the idiocy of another war."

"Whoa, whoa," Minli interrupted, opening one eye and looking up at her from the deck of the Fair Defiance. "You can't say that."

Ari Ara shifted the wilting wreath from one sweaty palm to another. The heat of the day pounded at her temples. They'd been practicing this speech for hours. Minli lay on his back, arms crossed over his chest like the crypt covers at the Tomb of Young Warriors. Ari Ara stood over him, struggling to find the words to honor a tragedy she considered horrific and the rest of Mariana saw as heroic. She'd tried her hardest, but couldn't look at Minli's prone, lifeless-looking figure without hating a world that made soldiers out of children and then laid flower wreathes on their tombs as they sent more children off to war.

"Why can't I say that?" she shot back, huffing in irritation. "It's the truth. War is idiotic."

"No one wants to be told their death is meaningless," Minli answered.

"They don't care. They're dead," Ari Ara countered.

"Speeches aren't for the dead. They're for the living. Such as the young warriors' relatives," Minli reminded her with a pointed look.

Ari Ara groaned and wiped her dripping forehead with the bottom of her tunic.

Across the deck, Brinelle made a sound of protest. Ari Ara rolled her eyes. She could imagine the line in *The Book of Queens: a queen does not sweat like a horse – but if she does, she uses a handkerchief to mop her brow, not her shirt.*

"Maybe they should hear the truth," she argued. "It might convince them not to be sacrifices for warmongering queens."

Brinelle shot her an aggrieved look. Too late to consider the insensitivity of her words, Ari Ara winced. Her aunt had lost her husband in the War of Retribution – a war she pushed for and led.

"No ruler enters war lightly," Brinelle stated. "Nor leaves it without regrets."

"Hmph," snorted Tahkan Shirar. "You might have considered that *before* you attacked us."

A crackle of temper seethed around him as he leaned against the ship's rail. He glowered at the Great Lady. With sheer force of will, Brinelle refused to be baited into a fight. She compressed her lips shut into a thin white line. All afternoon, the two had been hurling poison-tipped spears of words at one another. The combined diplomatic efforts of Minli and Shulen had barely managed to avert another war from igniting out of the still-smoldering embers of the last.

The hot weather didn't help. High summer threw heat down from a blazing sun. The river sailors dipped their shirts into the water or leapt in to cool off. The slight breeze could scarcely fan the hair off their sticky faces, let alone propel the ship against the tug of the downstream current. The crew heaved at the oars, sweat pouring down their backs. The cabins baked belowdecks. The age-darkened boards of the top deck were hot enough to burn bare skin. Even under the woven awning stung across the foredeck, the passengers sweltered.

As the Fair Defiance traveled up the Sister River from Seeker's Station, Shulen and Minli had been drilling Ari Ara hard. Not in physical *azar* - she'd have preferred that - but in inner *azar*, the emotional discipline of holding one's temper in check and wrestling with strong emotions for the sake of peace. They took turns hurling thinly-veiled insults at her. They lobbed tricky tests of tact at her. They trained her on points of diplomacy in preparation for entering the stronghold of Mariana's war culture.

Tomorrow they would reach the wide floodplain surrounding the Citadel of the Sisterlands where thousands of warriors, sisters, and visitors gathered for the Summer Trials and the conclusion of the Ordeal of Queens. Everyone's scrutiny would fall on the aspiring heir to the throne. The decision of the ancestor spirits would be announced in four days. The pressure was on. Ari Ara felt it like a vise clamped down on her soul.

The waterways crawled with boats, some swifter than the Fair Defiance, some slower. Ari Ara tried to ignore the constant shouts of greeting, the frantic waves, and the small gifts or notes that people lobbed across the water at her. Shulen claimed it was good training for what was to come.

"It will only get worse," he warned. "You must concentrate."

At the Citadel of the Sisterlands, she would be mobbed by people - supporters and detractors, alike. She would be confronted by war culture on all sides. Everything she abhorred would be on display. The Warrior's Way she rejected was not just respected in this place, but it was revered.

"This is a city of warriors and war rituals," Shulen cautioned her, "where they worship battle heroes and dream of slaying their enemies - your relatives on your father's side - and coming home covered in glory and blood."

Ari Ara grimaced in disgust.

"Better not make that face," Minli said, his short laugh shadowed by his worried eyes.

"So, you want me to lie about how I feel?" she retorted, insulted at the notion.

"No," he countered. "But maybe you should control your expression for the sake of achieving your goals."

"Worried my war-disgust will wreck my ordeal?" Ari Ara asked with a grin, though she was only half-joking.

To her surprise, Minli considered it seriously. Then he shrugged. It was possible.

"I think it's not your dislike of war, but your scornful dismissal of warriors that's a problem. It will hinder your efforts to show another way forward. It's probably better to show some respect for their sacrifices."

"The ones buried at the Tomb of Young Warriors already had to sacrifice their lives," Ari Ara pointed out somberly. "Isn't that enough?"

"Yes, and that's why you should show compassion, not disdain."

"Huh," Ari Ara snorted. "The best way to show compassion would be to dismantle the army, retire the warriors, retrain everyone in the Way Between, and make sure we never have another war."

"I agree with you," Minli assured her, "but the best thing would be if the warriors joined you in that massive task. They know better than most how horrific war is."

Minli's brown eyes stared at her, imploringly.

"Wage peace, Ari Ara," he urged her softly, "even in the least expected places."

Breaking the bitter cycle of war required her to disarm her heart and to cease making enemies out of the warriors.

"We may never have an opportunity like this again," Minli pointed out. Thousands of warriors and visitors had gathered in one spot, all curious about the heir to two thrones, all scratching their heads over the rumors flying around the Way Between. Was it a hoax? A trick? Weak and vulnerable? Were the stories they'd heard mere exaggerations?

"Remember your common ground," Minli encouraged her. "Care for people. A desire to protect. A willingness to risk your life to keep people safe."

"Well," Ari Ara huffed, "I've got one thing they haven't."

"What's that?" Minli said, sighing over her stubbornness.

She grinned.

"A wise friend like you."

And she needed all the help she could get. Ari Ara promised to work on her speech and hauled Minli to his feet. Brinelle and Tahkan broke off their latest bout of quarrelling and turned the hawk-eyed weight of their scrutiny back on Ari Ara. She rolled her shoulders and shook out her limbs, trying to ignore them both. Minli had spent days thinking up tests for Ari Ara. Whatever he had up his sleeve next would undoubtedly be harder than the last exercise.

"Why do we honor the warriors?" he boomed, mimicking the ritual questions she might be asked.

Ari Ara jolted, caught by surprise. When had Minli's voice dropped so low? She squinted at him, noticing that he was inching taller than her again. He lifted an eyebrow and Ari Ara scrambled to come up with a response to the ritual question. The proper answer was: *because they are willing to die for their country.* But Ari Ara couldn't forget all the hungry orphans who died of starvation and sickness while war - and warriors - gobbled the grain and demanded the healers on the battlefield. Why should a warrior's sacrifice be honored more than an orphan's? Were either of their deaths unavoidable? And if so, where was the honor in needless death? Why not honor peacemakers who brought justice, fed children, and healed the sick?

None of these musings would fit into the ritual question Minli had posed. His lips curled, mimicking the sneering frown of Roka Maro, reminding her that the Warrior Sister had a vendetta against her. One that could cost her a lot more than the throne if she wasn't careful. Ari Ara's eyes strayed to the heat-hazed sky, scanning for messenger hawks. There'd been no word yet from Finn. Tomorrow, she would face the Warrior Sister, suspicions churning in her gut, no solid evidence in hand, nothing to confirm what three cultures suspected: Roka Maro wanted the Lost Heir dead.

Minli cleared his throat in such a precise mimic of the woman that Ari Ara flinched. She reined in her wandering thoughts and stood up straighter. She shoved her sweat-plastered hair off her face.

"Uh, we honor the warriors because they want their people to be safe," Ari Ara answered finally.

Minli was unimpressed at the lackluster response, but continued on.

"As queen, would you disband the army?" Minli asked, naming the rumor that dogged the heels of the heir, barking up distrust among the warriors.

"Yes."

"Ari Ara! You can't just say that," Minli objected.

"It's the truth."

Minli threw his hands in the air with exasperation. Brinelle rubbed her temples. Shulen hid a smile. Tahkan openly smirked.

"Wipe that smug look off your face, Tahkan Shirar," the Great Lady snapped. "You won't be smiling when she wants to dismantle *your* war-obsessed culture. How well do you think that will go over? How many armed, honor-drunk warriors will try to kill her to preserve their *harrak?*"

"At least my fighters won't slit her throat because she's threatening their war profits," Tahkan retorted, hinting at the number of nobles who made their fortunes through weapons, war training, and supplying the army. The Harraken, on the other hand, rejected greed as a motive for fighting. Protecting their honor was motivation enough.

Still, the Great Lady had a point. His people would be no more enamored of Ari Ara's blunt promises than hers were. Tahkan crossed the deck to the two youths. Placing a hand on Ari Ara's shoulder, he spoke to his daughter.

"Sometimes, truth must bow to the situation and let other concerns go first."

"Where's the *harrak* in that?" Ari Ara grumbled.

Honor, integrity, and dignity were the prized values of Harraken culture. There wasn't much integrity in concealing her dream of getting rid of the armies.

"There is not much *harrak* in throwing stones in a sand lion's face, either," Tahkan pointed out. "If you want to get rid of a sand lion, you need a better plan than that."

Ari Ara pondered this.

"I won't lie," she declared, "but I could speak the truth differently."

Thanks to the Fanten, she had plenty of practice in that distinction. She nodded to Minli to repeat the question.

"As queen, are you going to disband the army?"

"As queen, I will do my best to keep Mariana safe and protected."

And the best way to do that, she added silently, *was by making armies unnecessary.*

"But will you keep the desert demons at bay?" Minli barked in a gruff imitation of a skeptical noble.

"As queen, I will do my best to ensure peace for our country," she replied tactfully. But inside, she thought: *and for the Harraken.*

When it came to peace, the two nations were inseparably entwined.

"Will you rise to vanquish our enemies?"

After resisting the urge to denounce the whole framework of enemies and vanquishing, she finally said:

"I will leave no enemy unaddressed."

Next, they practiced accepting ritual gifts. Minli held out a broom representing the bloodstained sword of Callan Illin, a famous war hero. Shulen, Tahkan, and Brinelle looked on, watching the youths at work.

"May his sword shine one day," Ari Ara said, having rejected and revised several other - less advisable - responses to such a disgusting gift. "May we never have to draw it again."

Then, Minli offered a shriveled head - or rather, a half-rotting cabbage from the ship's galley standing in for the grisly war trophy.

"They wouldn't really give me a head, right?" Ari Ara asked, nauseated at the idea.

Brinelle and Shulen exchanged glances. It was possible.

"Just try not to vomit on it," Minli advised.

It went on . . . and on . . . and on. When Minli finished, Brinelle hit her with a barrage of etiquette tests. Who walked first in precedence: elder sisters, nobles, the heir, or the Great Lady? What honorific should be used for a retired warrior with battlefield distinctions? Which of the war heroes must be greeted at the Summer Trials and which could be politely ignored?

Ari Ara wondered if it were possible to be bored and panicked at the same time. Her thoughts wandered, drifting after Finn, worrying about him, weighing the dangers of double-crossing someone as ruthless as Roka Maro. Maybe's and what if's tugged her focus in ten directions. Maybe they should have gone to the Mother Sister with their suspicions and asked for her help in rooting out the truth. Maybe they should have gotten Brinelle or Tahkan involved. What if Roka got suspicious? What if Finn got caught?

She gnawed on her fingernail as anxiety chewed at her.

"Stop that," Brinelle chided. "This is hardly the time to pick up more bad habits."

And I've got plenty already, Ari Ara thought sheepishly. She whipped her hand away from her mouth and tucked it behind her back. She straightened her spine into the posture Brinelle had been drilling her on for weeks. It still felt odd to Ari Ara, as if she were standing in someone else's body, wearing someone else's polite look of interest.

"Stop nagging her, Brinelle," Tahkan cut in.

"I'm helping her. Preparing her to step into her role as leader. They must *see* the future queen in her. A river dragon must rise in her soul," the Great Lady concluded poetically.

"The river dragon that drowns my people in blood?" the Desert King muttered.

Tahkan touched his damp fingers together and spread them apart with a grimace. Trust the riverlands to ruin the gift of heat. The humidity was so thick he could slice it with a sword. In the desert, a burning warmth like this crackled with dry vigor, snapping the limbs awake. This moisture sapped the strength from his body, drowned the fire of the heart's courage, and smothered the last vestiges of patience.

"When you are shown the Hall of Heroes," Brinelle continued, "what should you do?"

Ari Ara tried to remember.

"Ask to pay my respects at the shrines of Ellesan the Brave and Girresh the Glorious."

Tahkan choked and strode over.

"She can't . . . she won't. What respect could she - a half-Harraken - pay to those brutal monsters? They burned Turim to the ground two centuries ago. They *hunted down* women and children, and cut their throats. They beat pregnant mothers and broke the legs of our elders."

Ari Ara turned pale.

"Lies," Brinelle growled. "Ellesan and Girresh liberated our people from *your* ancestors' occupation. Burning Turim was a response to the scorched cities and towns of the Westlands, the siege of our capital, and the beheading of our king. You speak of brutality? Look in the mirror, Tahkan Shirar."

"Enough. Please." Ari Ara pleaded, lifting her hands and stepping between them. "Rehashing the past won't help us find peace in the present, let alone in the future."

Tahkan set his chin, proud and defiant. She winced, knowing the look. She'd worn it often enough.

"By taking you to these tombs, they're already stirring up the past. You cannot *pay your respects* to those brutes without losing *harrak.*"

The word rippled over the r's and cracked the consonant at the end.

"Isn't this another stone-in-the-sand-lion's-eye moment?" Ari Ara asked, sighing with confusion.

"This is different," Tahkan insisted stubbornly.

"It is not," Brinelle countered, crossing her arms over her chest. "If she does not do this, she will fail the Ordeal of Queens.

Everything at the Citadel is about honoring *our* warriors. Swallow your pride, Tahkan. You'll just have to endure this for her sake."

"Some things cannot be swallowed. Swords, for instance. Truth, for another," the fierce desert man squared off with the formidable riverlands regent. "If she does this, she will not be worthy of being our next harrak-mettahl. How can she keep our people's honor when she has none? What good is a river dragon to us?"

The heat thickened like a blacksmith's forge as Tahkan and Brinelle fought. Ari Ara's head throbbed. Her splitting headache brewed like a lightning-laced thunderstorm. Every word, disagreement, drill and question pounded her against the anvil of time. Tomorrow she would face all this for real, not in practice. She gnawed at her fingernails again, nervous. Then stopped, more nervous.

Ari Ara sensed the iron core of her spirit melting. The scorching pressure fizzled white, softening her edges, weakening her resolve, eroding her confidence. There was ringing in her ears. The ship heaved. Her legs buckled.

She woke flat on her back, laid out on the Great Lady's deck chair. Shulen perched on the edge, patting her forehead with a cool cloth. Everyone else had been sent away. Shulen had summarily told the two leaders to go cool their heads - advice he suspected he should follow, too. His fury at their bickering crackled sharper than the heat. They should be supporting Ari Ara, not confusing her and putting impossible burdens on her young shoulders. Thousands of years of monarchs had not been able to resolve the questions they demanded a fifteen-year-old recite the perfect answer to. Shulen had watched the strain and worry build in Ari Ara until she buckled. It was bad enough that the Ordeal of Queens tried to break the aspiring heir's will. Her aunt and father should not do the work of the Sisters for them.

"What happened?" Ari Ara asked, groggily.

"It appears you fainted from heat stroke," Shulen told her gently. His eyes scrutinized her closely, though. "But, I'm guessing it was more than just the heat?"

Ari Ara's lips trembled. She glanced around to see if anyone was nearby. Then, in a very small voice, she murmured.

"Shulen? What if I can't do it? What if I mess up and fail?"

He studied the shimmering heat waves roiling off the boulders along the riverbank, his scarred face still as stone. He took her question seriously, not because he doubted her abilities - he knew them better than most - but because her fear deserved more than a glib reply.

"Then you won't be queen," he said softly, as if it were nothing. "So? You'll still be Ari Ara. That alone is plenty to offer this world."

Her face scrunched up in a quiver of relieved tears. In a burst of sobs and motion, she flung her arms around his neck. He patted her back, surprised, remembering when she'd been small enough to carry, treasuring the gift embodied in a child's trust. He'd lost that when his tiny daughter was murdered. He'd found it when he had taught his red-headed apprentice how to find the Way Between the flowing water of the river. As he'd carried her back, tired and happy, he'd committed his heart to doing everything he could to help this girl find her way in the world. If that meant the throne, so be it. If it did not, so be that, too.

He let her cry herself out, then handed her a handkerchief to blow her nose on. Queens were not the only ones who shouldn't smear snot on their sleeves.

"Do you remember how Alaren felt about the throne?" he asked her.

She sniffled and nodded. The Third Brother had a claim to the throne just like his brothers, Marin and Shirar. On the day they split the world, Alaren had vowed to restore it. Not through claiming kingship, but through building peace. Minli and Ari Ara had spent hours wondering what their world might have been like had Alaren succeeded . . . and trying to understand Alaren's decision to *not* claim the throne, even when he could have, even when the majority of the people on both sides of the border would have supported him.

The Stories of the Third Brother, a book of ancient tales about the Way Between, related how Alaren sought to restore the Whole World, the reunited nation that had existed before his brothers tore the map in half. Many urged Alaren to declare himself king and put a stop to his brothers wars.

But Alaren refused. He feared a third king, a third claim, would only make things worse. Either the people and the two feuding kings would bring the nations together, or it would never happen. No decree by a self-proclaimed ruler would make it so.

"It was tried," Shulen told Ari Ara. "Not in Alaren's day, but centuries later. One of his descendants tried to claim both nations."

"What happened?" she asked, sensing a tone of doom in his voice.

It had been a disaster. Too much blood had spilled by then. Too much hate had spread. Too many lies had burrowed into people's hearts. The Marianans and the Shirarans - they would not call themselves the Harraken for another century - turned on Alaren's descendant. A three-way war erupted. Armies massacred villagers on every side. Hundreds of years later, the conflict still haunted historians. One of them cited it as the reason to launch the Great Persecution of the followers of the Way Between. After that, Alaren's lineage was thought to have been eradicated, taking with it the threat - or hope - of a reunited world.

"Until now."

Shulen's final words startled Ari Ara. The grey-haired, scar-lined man straightened his tunic to display the black-inked Mark of Peace, the symbol of the Way Between. It was the sign inked between Ari Ara's shoulder blades, the mark that declared her the child of Alinore and Tahkan, the direct descendant of Kings Marin and Shirar. Ari Ara's existence dredged up the blood-soaked sediment of the past. It heralded a future once unimaginable. To some, it was exhilarating. To others, it was chilling. To everyone, it was life-changing. For better or for worse, their world would never be the same.

And no one could predict just what it would become.

"There are two roads to the world you dream of," Shulen told her. "One leads through the queenship. The other follows another way. Both routes may succeed. Both may fail."

"Then which should I take?" Ari Ara asked, her blue-grey eyes wide, her voice scarcely a whisper.

Nshoka Shulen studied his young apprentice, her strong, muscled form so capable of rising to the greatest challenges. Her bronze face with a smattering of freckles across the nose, so unlined by time and disappointment. Her slight, yet sturdy shoulders that carried so much of the world's burden at such a young age. He could not answer her question.

"I can say this," he promised, vowing with all of his heart, "whichever road you choose, I will walk it with you."

CHAPTER TWENTY

. . . . .

The Citadel of the Sisterlands

Like a gasp of breath, the river opened onto a wide, flat floodplain. The mountains peeled away into a distant ring of jagged teeth. Caught by the slam of morning sunlight, the Border Mountains reared above the toothy foothills in the west. Beyond the farmlands, the white granite of the high city walls of the Citadel of the Sisterlands gleamed in the early sun. Two statues crowned the highest towers, honoring the divine figures of the Mother and Warrior. Defended by terrain and warriors, the city feared no invasions from the desert. Marshes and river gorges barred the passages of horses – and the Harraken would rather charge into battle without armor than fight without their horses.

Ari Ara strode down the gangplank of the Fair Defiance onto the wharf. Her boots clipped with a precise stride. The stiff leather of her vest creaked. The metal links of her silvermail gleamed in the sun, bared across her chest in a warning to would-be attackers. The high collar protected her neck, stiff gloves guarded her arms. Ari Ara hated all of it: the scent of fear, the presage of violence, and worst of all, the way her wardrobe echoed the warriors' garb.

It was a calculated move, designed to win allegiance from the warriors, bearing hints of a queen-commander's uniform. Ari Ara's skin crawled beneath it. But even she could see the shift in the warriors' gazes, the subtle gleam of recognition, the surprised respect with which they snapped to attention. She was the heir apparent, their next leader shining in the morning sun, a young queen on the cusp of victory.

An honor guard had turned out to greet them. Standing at strict attention, they lined the raised causeway between the farm fields and training yards. The double flanks of armed figures saluted in unison as the aspiring queen approached the city gates.

All of them were children.

Ari Ara's stomach curdled. She'd known, of course. Everyone knew the Twins of the Sisterlands took in orphans and trained them into warriors and soldiers. The youngest trainees were eleven; the oldest, twenty. Each stood in the brilliant blue uniform of the Marianan Army, the gold river dragon of the House of Marin emblazoned on the front. As Ari Ara passed by with a weak smile plastered on her face, they lifted their hands to their foreheads and radiated their fingers out in a sunburst gesture of respect. Then they snapped their arms to the side, boots clipping together, before easing into a wider stance and folding one arm behind their backs.

As the old saying went: *orphans make good soldiers . . . and good soldiers make more orphans.*

They had no relatives to hate the monarch who sent them off to war. They burned with anger for the enemy that had killed their parents, and families.

The cycle of horror would never end. Not until Ari Ara ended it.

A hum of energy hissed through her limbs. Danger and challenge twanged in the air. The focus of her last trial in the

Ordeal of Queens was no mystery. She would be judged on one thing only: respect for the warriors. As Queen of Mariana, she would command an army of thousands. She could not rule unless the warriors accepted her as their leader.

"And for that," Brinelle had informed her in an unflinching tone, "you will have to treat them with respect."

"I respect them," Ari Ara muttered. "I'd just respect them *more* if they put down their swords and followed the Way Between."

"That," her aunt told her sharply, "is exactly the sort of remark that could cost you the throne."

It was a precisely planned test, Brinelle conceded. The Sisters had designed it well. Presiding over the ceremonies of the Summer Trials would challenge the girl like nothing else. Tact, discretion, diplomacy, leadership – Ari Ara would need all of those virtues to pull this off. One headstrong misstep or thoughtless comment could sink her chances of passing the ordeal.

Over the last days of their journey to the Citadel, Brinelle had resumed Ari Ara's studies with ferocity driving the girl to memorize protocols, ritual sayings, and the ceremonial expectations of her role. Had she been raised from birth in the House of Marin, Ari Ara would already be able to glide through these sorts of royal functions. But she had grown up wild with the Fanten, tending sheep, doing chores with monastery orphans, traveling the desert and the Border Mountains. She had many skills – just not the ones she needed for this.

But she did have the Way Between.

As she walked down the long causeway toward the city, Ari Ara dug deep into her spirit and brought a sense of inner *azar* singing into her veins. She greeted the young honor guards with composure, neither bursting out in hot-tempered disdain, nor flinching from meeting their eyes. In the faces of the youth, she caught glimpses of curiosity, trepidation, and an occasional sharp flash of dislike.

What had they heard about the Lost Heir? Ari Ara was no stranger to the rumors that swirled around her. Undoubtedly, they'd been told that she was in league with the desert demons, heralded doom for Mariana, and intended to get rid of all the warriors. On top of that, she'd thrust the nation into economic chaos a few years ago by ending the Water Exchange that exploited the Harraken. Some Marianans loved her for it – the families of factory workers and seamstresses who had secured their livelihoods once more - but others resented her for it - particularly the noble families and the factory owners who lost the free labor that had generated their vast fortunes. If she put herself in their shoes, she could understand why some people might dislike and distrust her. She would simply have to prove that she was not a threat – and that the change she embodied heralded peace and prosperity, not collapse and calamity.

Ari Ara couldn't wait for the honor salute to end . . . but it was a long way to the city.

The Citadel Training Yards stretched in a ring outside the city walls, all the way to the edge of the farmlands and wet grain fields. The farmers were also warriors, alternating their efforts between growing food and drilling in the deadly arts. They lived in thatched cottages on the circular road that bounded the yards. Over five hundred families dwelled in the floodplain, and more resided in the foothills beyond the mist-hazy horizon. In skiffs and boats, they floated and poled through the canals to converge in a festive spirit for the annual tradition of the Summer Trials. Only Mariana Capital's tests of warriors could match these for ceremony and skill.

Tents and awnings lined the roads that splayed out from the city in spokes. Benches and tiers of viewing stands rose along each section. Archers' targets tested waves of competitors in one area.

Horses and riders galloped and clashed in another. In one wedge, strategists competed in war games, mapping out sequences of battles until one team prevailed over the other in the simulated wars on a large board.

Ari Ara's face ached from masking her reactions. Violence had always triggered nausea in her, a Fanten-instilled reaction that had only worsened as she grew older. To see it on such a scale, among so many assembled warriors, sent shockwaves of disgust through her body. It took every ounce of her discipline to not lurch around and vomit.

You can do this, she told herself sternly.

Because of their delays on the river, the Summer Trials were already well underway. In the fields outside the city, the youngest hopefuls among the trainees had already been sent sprawling in the dust. The cream of this year's crop was rising through the matches to the finals. Ari Ara merely had to hold it together for three days, long enough to watch the last competitions, hand out a few awards, and make a congratulatory speech.

At sunset on the third day, the Sisters would announce the decision of the ancestor spirits. People had converged from the farthest reaches of Mariana to hear whether or not the notorious girl from the High Mountains would pass the Ordeal of Queens. Summoned by the Great Lady, and drawn by curiosity, nobles had packed up their whole families and journeyed south from the capital. Merchants had delayed shipments in order to attend. Craftsmen and women closed workshops and brought their households. The population of the Citadel doubled, then tripled. Every bunkhouse was packed to the rafters. Every inn put up six to a room. The residents housed guests in attics and storage rooms. Latecomers resorted to setting up tents along the road. Boats clogged the waterways, packed with visitors sleeping aboard.

At the towering gates of the city, the Peace Force awaited.

Ari Ara's heavy heart leapt, falcon-fierce, at the sight of them. Their white tunics gleamed in the throng of war-leather and polished armor. The simplicity of the black-inked Mark of Peace stood out against the splashing colors of the rest of the crowd. One member carried a banner pinned to a tall pole, lifting the symbol of peace high above the tumult of the streets. The twenty friends who had accompanied her return to Mariana had come south to join her for the end of the Ordeal of Queens.

To keep her heart strong.

To keep her safe.

To show the world of warriors that another world was possible.

Like Ari Ara, they had spent the voyage to the Citadel drilling and training, preparing for the challenge that awaited. They could not pick a fight or rise to the inevitable baits of warriors who neither trusted nor understood the Way Between. They had to keep their tempers and remain disciplined. They had agreed not to show off, nor give into the urge to spar with the warriors to prove the power of their unconventional non-martial art.

They would, however, share their stories and welcome any and all to their dawn practices. Humility and focus would serve them better than arrogance or putting a heckling disbeliever in their place. From the youngest to the oldest, the Peace Force members were no strangers to this approach. No community in their war-torn world trusted that peace could be won without weapons. Not until they saw a grandmother break up a fight. Or watched a pair of young girls talk sense into two brawling hotheads. Or witnessed how the gentle words of a man could go further than a show of his muscles. Or heard someone persuade a monarch to step away from the brink of war.

Each Peace Force member knew: if Ari Ara was being tested, so were they. So was the Way Between. And so was the hope for peace.

Here at the Citadel, in the final days of her ordeal, the friends who had journeyed across borders and mountains together would do what they could to ease the warriors' wariness over their prospective queen's commitment to peace.

As she passed through the massive city gates, Ari Ara met each person's eyes, giving and receiving support and gratitude. Her tensed jaw softened into a smile. Her narrowed eyes curved into half-moons of joy. By the time the last Peace Force member fell into step alongside her, her heart no longer pounded in the dull drumbeat of dread, but rather soared with pride and hope in her friends.

The Peace Force helped to clear a path through the teeming crowd. The procession followed the arc of one of the wider curved streets. On the other side of the road, orderly rows of barracks and bunkhouses splayed out in a snail shell spiral. Ari Ara could see how the design would baffle any attackers, leading them through countless ambush points before they reached the towers. There were sections for orphan schools and craft halls; areas full of armories and smithies. They passed bathhouses, kitchens, healers' halls, weaving workshops, and all the necessary sundries that churned the gearworks of daily life in this isolated city of thousands.

The Mother Sister murmured at Ari Ara's elbow, pointing out landmarks as they passed. The Altar of Great Warriors, where Shulen's name was displayed. The Baths of Purification, where one washed the blood of battle away. The Wall of Honor, in which the names of war heroes were inscribed. Ari Ara kept her face blank and tuned out most of the words.

Then a phrase caught her attention.

" . . . this is the Three Kings Temple."

Only discipline kept her from jerking around – and a good thing, too, because the Warrior Sister's gaze impaled her like a sword, trying to see her flinch or squirm, or show even a glimmer of excessive interest. With force of will, Ari Ara contained her reaction, trusting that Minli would note the temple's location and map the route back to it.

This is where Finn had said to meet.

The messenger hawk had winged in last evening, its speckled feathers catching the traces of sunset. Low and silent, it sought out Minli. Battered-chested and missing tail feathers, the bird looked like it had run into trouble on the way. The hawk held out the message on its leg, let the boy untie it, and took off without waiting for a reply. Peering over Minli's shoulder as he unrolled the tiny scroll, Ari Ara read Finn's message.

Come to the Three Kings Temple. I have what you need. Be careful.

Nothing more could be trusted to writing. Messenger hawks could be shot down, intercepted, caught in nets. Ari Ara's heartbeat quickened with hope that Finn had the letter from the Warrior Sister. His last line, a warning, hinted that their suspicions were correct. Ari Ara tried to talk Minli into letting her come with him to Three Kings Temple – he might need her as back up in case of an attack – but her friend refused. It was too risky, she was too recognizable, and besides she couldn't slip away from the Summer Trials and the Ordeal of Queens. Even Minli might have trouble finding a spare moment to meet Finn.

For three days, Ari Ara danced on a tightrope, fell into exhausted and dreamless sleep, rose at dawn and did it all over again. Though her duties consisted of presiding over the sparring matches and ceremonies of the Summer Trials, she never lost sight of the hard fact that she was being tested for the Ordeal of Queens. Not just by the Warrior Sister, who dogged her elbow hoping she'd slip up, but also by the flocks of blue-robed sisters who whispered incessantly at every gesture she made. Wherever she went, a wind of gossip trailed behind her, infecting not only the sisters, but the warriors, too.

Three years ago, she and Shulen had worked hard to win over the warriors in Mariana Capital, sharing the Way Between, opening trainings to all, and reassuring the concerns of the fighters. But back then, Nshoka Shulen was the Great Warrior, Captain of the Royal Guard, and revered throughout the nation. Now, they had neither the time nor the social standing to coax the reluctant to their side. Shulen had been exiled as a traitor for losing the Champion's Challenge over the water workers. Then he threw salt in the wound by making a vow to the Harraken to give up *attar,* the Warrior's Way. The muscled fighters of the Sisterlands held him in contempt and disdain. Their scowling looks shot not only at Ari Ara, but also at him for making such a pitiful promise to their mortal enemies.

Ari Ara could sense the skepticism and distrust behind their carefully blank expressions. The martial flair of her garments could only do so much in the face of the growing rumors that she would bring about the downfall of the warriors. And, secretly, Ari Ara hoped she would prove those rumors true. Perhaps they could sense that. As the days went on, the attitude of the warriors shifted subtly. Nothing blatant, nothing you could put your finger on, nothing mutinous . . . just a sly faltering of respect and duty.

Their salutes snapped perfunctorily. Their words to the heir sounded hollow. They moved woodenly through the ritual motions of the ceremonies. Ari Ara suspected they were under orders to behave - otherwise, more than one might not have accepted the medals from her hand, or bent their heads so she could slip the winner's sashes around their chests and shoulders.

"Just let me into the sparring matches," Ari Ara fumed to Shulen on the second night. "Let me trounce them with the Way Between and cut their arrogance in half."

Shulen regarded her steadily, his hands calmly continuing to polish his boots to a gleaming shine.

"Are you sure it's *their* arrogance that needs to be cut down?"

His gentle reproval halted her furious pacing midstride. She gave him a sheepish look.

"I just mean that maybe they wouldn't be so dismissive if they saw what the Way Between can do!"

"Show them your inner *azar*: treat them with respect, ignore their petty slights, and don't let them bait you into anything foolish."

Ari Ara sighed and redoubled her efforts. Inner *azar* had never been her strong suit. She composed her expression as she watched the painful, senseless bouts of swordplay. She weathered the hours of flinch-worthy hand-to-hand combat by envisioning how she would have met each attack with the Way Between. She dug deep into her fortitude to enact her ceremonial role and clap at the end of each match. Secretly, she was just applauding that it was over, but she made sure that the spectators were none the wiser.

She could not afford any mistakes.

Ari Ara hadn't felt this intensity of adrenaline-infused alertness since she faced Shulen in the Champion's Challenge, battling for life and death and the freedom of thousands. Her heart pounded in her chest as she presided over the orphan-trainees' awards ceremony, handing out medals for highest scores. With the Sisters evaluating every word that crossed her lips, she congratulated the children on their achievements with cautiously-constructed phrases.

"I wish our Peace Force members all had speed and reflexes such as yours."

And I wish you would put aside attar *and work with us,* Ari Ara added silently.

"Your courageous spirit will have many uses in our troubled world."

Like knowing when to sheath your sword – not swing it, she thought.

"Your ferocity is astonishing," she told a third youth.

May I never see it on a battlefield.

Each ceremony, ritual, and exchange tightened the corkscrew of discomfort in her heart. Polite words. Half-truths. Qualifiers. When did diplomacy and tact veer too far into silence and implied approval? She had no wish to insult, disrespect, or alarm the young warriors, but neither did she want to send them into war as their queen. She wanted to retrain them all in the Way Between or other skills. Their nation needed healers, scholars, craftspeople, farmers, artists, and inventors. Instead of dying for the glory of their country, she wanted them to *live* . . . to raise children and grandchildren, make masterpieces of art, invent tools and discover better ways to grow grain or channel water into millworks. She endured the endless sparring matches by imagining new futures for them all.

But it took a toll.

She had no focus to spare for her companions. Each waged a near-constant battle on her behalf. The Great Lady lifted the shield of her position as regent to deflect crippling blows from reaching Ari Ara. She warded off subtle schemes to entrap the girl in an inadvertent snub. She blocked the attempts to trick Ari Ara into paying her respect to the tombs of traitors. She parried the thrusts of insinuation that could turn rumors into ruinous lies in the ears of the elder sisters. Over and over, the Warrior Sister tried to maneuver Ari Ara into losing her temper or stumbling into a social slight. Brinelle matched the steely woman move for move. Roka Maro was a worthy adversary. She wielded politics as skillfully as her sword, and twice she nearly tripped Ari Ara up in a snare of protocol, only for her aunt to smooth the incident over. Brinelle had no qualms about helping the heir in this manner. After all: *A queen inspires loyalty. A queen trusts her deputies and ministers. A queen wins the support of her nobles and people.* Brinelle's choices would influence the decision as much as Ari Ara's.

As would Tahkan Shirar's.

The Desert King caused a stir everywhere he went. Here was the Marianan's fearsome enemy in the flesh. Here was a target for their hatred. Here was Tahkan Shirar, leader of the warriors who had spilled the blood of countless relatives and brothers-in-arms. From the fiery red of the Desert King's blazing hair to the deep bronze of his skin, every inch of the man triggered the Marianan warriors' animosity. The sound of his dry, song-tinged voice unleashed a furious rage in the army. All their lives, they had been trained to kill him. Now, here he was, the father of their royal heir, standing at her side during the prestigious rituals of their Summer Trials. The hate roiled off them like heat waves.

Tahkan Shirar did not flinch. He was no stranger to this reaction. It took a certain stoic courage to walk unarmed through thousands of his enemies. Older warriors had fought him on the battlefield during the War of Retribution. Younger ones had lost parents to his warriors. A hot band of tension ran through every muscle of his body as Tahkan invoked *harrak*, sharpening the power of his honor, integrity, and dignity, wielding it as skillfully as the warriors lifted their swords.

Shulen assigned Emir Miresh to keep the Desert King from harm. Then, after the first day, he added Minli and a rotating set of Peace Force members to the detail.

"Use every degree of skill you possess in *azar* to keep Tahkan Shirar safe," the older man instructed them. "De-escalate hot tempers. Move people away from the brink of violence. Ease us out of range of an international incident."

This was the best protection he could offer. When a novice refused to hold the door for the Desert King, Minli caught it with the end of his crutch, preventing the snub from erupting into a scandal. When a young warrior shouted threats at the enemy leader, Emir Miresh crossed the street and listened to the youth's grievances while Tahkan continued onward. Minli changed the subject when a sister insulted the 'desert demon'. Another Peace Force member blocked the path of a trainee with a knife in his hand. They even spoke quietly to Tahkan when his strained will hit the breaking point.

The Peace Force members understood how strange their approach must seem to warriors and armies, how naïve and idealistic. Some people they encountered even believed the wild rumors about how Ari Ara Shirar was building her own army to take over Mariana. These they patiently countered with the truth: the Peace Force existed as a cooperative effort between Mariana and the Harraken to prevent violence and war. That was all. They did not debate. They did not argue. They conversed . . . and performed their duties. Time and time again, the Peace Force demonstrated their worth. They met the skeptical looks with quiet dignity. They responded to outright derision with patience and a touch of humor. They deflected attempts to rile them into fights. They endured and persevered.

On the third day of the Summer Trials, Shulen had Emir offer a demonstration of *azar* versus *attar*, turning aside attackers' blows with easeful confidence. The young man still possessed the admiration of his fellow warriors, for all that he associated with such dubious company. Shulen had intended to send Minli to the field next to show that the Way Between offered strength to one-legged boys as much as to muscled warriors. But Minli was nowhere to be found.

"Uh, perhaps his leg's bothering him? Maybe he went to fetch his salve?" Ari Ara suggested, trying not to lie – Shulen could always tell – but also covering for her friend as he made his way across the city to meet Finn at Three Kings Temple.

It was the only moment they'd found for him to slip away. Tahkan would be seated next to Brinelle all day, watching his enemies spar with stony-faced endurance, his mind's eye seeing each blow leveled at the hearts of his people. Nothing could spare him that pain, but Minli had swapped places with other Peace Force members and the Desert King should be safe enough for a few hours.

Minli's absence added another set of jitters to Ari Ara's already jangled nerves. The Sisters could not have devised a harder test in the Ordeal of Queens. Ari Ara could not afford to get distracted thinking of Finn, worrying about Minli, or wondering if they would succeed in trapping Roka Maro. Even now, as she gritted her teeth over each clang of sword and clash of shield, Ari Ara could not forget that the convocation of the sisters and ancestors spirits had begun.

She could sense the feathery touches of the spirits in the long shadows of the afternoon sun. Inside the high walls that encircled the Citadel, behind the closed doors of the meeting chambers, the sisters she had met along her journey were ruminating on her fate. Each step she'd taken, every false move she'd made, any mistaken turns were being reviewed under the intense double-scrutiny of sisters and spirits.

Even now, she could feel the eyes of the blue-robed women watching her. Any one of the throng of novices and older women could be the one to report to the convocation on how she'd handled her duties at the Summer Trials. Ari Ara sat up straighter and tried to pay attention to the sparring matches. She burned with longing to take the field instead of sitting on the sidelines with a polite smile on her face. Brinelle had tried to tell her that discretion *was* a form of the Way Between, but Ari Ara wasn't sure. Biting her tongue over the ways of warriors and war culture felt more like *anar*, the Way of Shadows. She was just avoiding a scandal, running away from things and concealing how she really felt in order to pass her ordeal. It grated on her like grit in the eye.

A fierce yearning burned in her to do the work of the Peace Force, easing tensions, stopping fights, keeping people from harm. She envied her friends in their white tunics. The Mark of Peace emblazoned on the front and back boldly and proudly declared them to be followers of the Way Between. Her half-truths sat as uncomfortably as the stiff fit of her clothes. The garments reeked of the military's uniforms, sharing similar neck collars, colors, and gold-trimmed shoulders. The martial style was only temporary, intended to evoke a sense of loyalty and patriotism in the warriors, but Ari Ara's skin itched with unease over it. She sensed her father's discomfort, too. Shadows of past battles haunted him as he saw his daughter stuffed into an echo of his enemies' uniforms.

Shulen struggled, too. His mind understood that the martial styles were just a tactic to get her through the ordeal and shore up the support of the warriors. His *mind* knew all that. But his heart broke a little. He wondered, for the first time, if the throne was worth the cost of getting there.

As the sun sank low over the western mountains, images of her early apprenticeship flashed in Shulen's memory. While Ari Ara handed out medals to the winners of the various trials in archery, riding, and swordsmanship, Shulen remembered her at eleven, leaping over the heads of warrior monks to avoid being sent here, to the Sisters. He saw her standing on one foot on a pillar long into the starry night to prove she was more than a match for the rigors of the Way Between. He recalled her red hair blazing as she danced through the autumn leaves.

Shulen somberly listened as she mouthed respectful platitudes to the victors of the battle axe competitions and wondered if some indescribable spark of Ari Ara was being snuffed out in her effort to be a good queen. He watched the tense clench of her jaw hold back her cry of horror at the dripping wounds on the competitors and felt a sense of shame. No one should have to suppress that reaction, least of all her. As Ari Ara clapped politely for the winners, he stared at her gloved hands as if they belonged to a stranger. This was not the Ari Ara he'd come to love as deeply as a daughter. The girl who fell off a roof, landed on her feet, and beat Emir Miresh at *azar*. The girl who risked death to confront the injustice of the Water Exchange. The girl who had snuck out to celebrate with the street urchins and danced the Way Between the falling snow.

Impetuous. Headstrong. Impassioned. Courageous.

Utterly Ari Ara. Not this, not that, but everything possible in between.

As the Sisters led a prayer for the warriors, Shulen leaned close to her and drew breath to speak.

"Ari Ara – "

Her head inclined toward him, eyes still lowered in prayer as she'd been taught.

"Yes, Shulen?" she murmured – and he could hear the echoes of Alinore in her along with the hints of the queen she would become. He ought to feel proud of her. Instead, a surge of sorrow swept over him.

"Remember that you are enough, just as you are."

But the prayer ended and the rumble of the Great Horns drowned out his words. Ari Ara rose to her feet. Words hung on the tip of Shulen's tongue, but he had no chance to speak again. The Sisters led Ari Ara out of the stands into the jubilant procession through the city streets, sweeping her toward the Sanctuary of the Citadel and the looming decision on the Ordeal of Queens. Following at her side, Shulen shoved his thoughts away. There was no time for his worries now. Dusk fell on the shadowed streets. The high towers blazed gold and scarlet, high above their heads. The air rippled with the passage of the ancestors spirits. A few more steps, a last breath of waiting for the announcement about the ordeal, and then it would all be over, one way or another.

CHAPTER TWENTY-ONE

. . . . .

The Pledge

The city's dusk-shrouded streets relinquished their grip as Ari Ara climbed the steps up to the sunset-suffused threshold of the Sanctuary of the Citadel. Nestled between the tall double towers on the highest knoll inside the city walls, the temple sheltered the sacred rituals of the Sisterhood. Seven immense statues, legendary ancestors of old, formed the pillars of the Sanctuary's entrance, holding the roof aloft. Behind Ari Ara, the wide plaza filled with people: warriors, nobles, sisters, commoners. Thousands had come to witness this moment of history.

As Ari Ara burst into the lingering streaks of sunset, a hush settled over the crowd. The light cast an otherworldly glow on everything. The gold threads of the river dragons embroidered on her sleeves blazed. The silvermail gleamed. The ribbons running through her braided hair shone like a crown. Ari Ara sensed, rather than saw, the Peace Force assembling behind her and Shulen stilling at her side. Tahkan and Brinelle drew close, larger than life, glowing with a hint of the mythic.

The newest warriors who had just passed their initiation tests in the Summer Trials ascended the flight of steps and halted in a line just behind them. All of them were young, ranging from Ari Ara's age to the Marianan age of maturity at twenty-four. Through their skills in the deadly arts, they had won the position of honor at the ceremony. Their ears would be the first to receive the verdict of the ancestor spirits, the fate of the aspiring queen and future.

Sisters filed out of the temple, two lines veering apart to flank the steps. Armored devotees of the Warrior formed a line of steel and sword on the left. Blue-robed initiates of the Mother glided into position on the right. The convocation members slid out of the double doors to stand in a curve between them. Ari Ara recognized them all: the Abbess of the Gateway Abbey, the caretaker of Marin's Mountain, the Head Sister of the Ancient Springs. With a lurch, she spotted the novice who had challenged Tahkan. A hermit from the Water Maze, a street vendor from Seeker's Station, the prayer leader at the Summer Trials, and the smiling elder from the Gateway Abbey completed the convocation.

From the doors of the Sanctuary, the Twins stepped forward, strides matching as they halted on the landing in front of Ari Ara. She fixed her gaze firmly on the statue in front of her, resisting the urge to try to read the verdict in their expressions. The Great Horns rumbled from the heights, echoing over the rooftops of the city and rattling in the bones of the people. Ancestor spirits gathered in the reverberations. Ari Ara's breath quickened in her chest as their silvery figures glinted in the twilight.

Silence fell. The wind flapped through the tall blue banners. Someone coughed. The Twins drew breath. Before they could speak, though, a different voice boomed out from behind Ari Ara.

"Ancestors be with you!"

Ari Ara spun around. The young champion stepped forward and lifted his sword.

"If the spirits accept you," he declared, "it will be my honor to pledge my sword to you!"

A rustle of surprise shot through the crowd. But the Mother Sister did not seem perturbed – she was even smiling slightly – and Roka Maro's disapproving horseshoe of a scowl remained unruffled by the cry. Passion shone in the young warrior's face, a fervent loyalty gleamed in his eyes. Beside him, this year's runner-up, not to be outdone, stepped forward and drew his blade.

"Ancestors be with you, Ari Ara de Marin! It will be my honor to pledge my sword to you."

"Ancestors be with you, Daughter of Queen Alinore!" said the next youth, joining in. "It will be my honor to pledge my sword to you."

One by one, the other initiates joined in.

"Lost Heir . . . "

"Descendant of Marin . . . "

"River Dragon . . . "

Each invoked another part of her Marianan lineage. No one mentioned Tahkan Shirar. No one spoke of her Harraken blood. No one brought up the Way Between. Everyone ended with the same phrase:

"It will be my honor to pledge my sword to you."

Just who was this person they were making pledges to? Ari Ara wondered, resisting the urge to snort and shake her head at the flowery honorifics. She scarcely recognized the person they spoke about . . . the defender of the riverlands, shield of her people.

"Ari Ara de Marin, leader of warriors . . . "

She jolted. What had that last youth just said?

"Commander of armies . . . "

"Destroyer of enemies . . . "

The gold light of sunset burned in her eyes as she studied their faces. Sincere. Loyal. Devoted. Ari Ara fought the urge to cry. They did not know her at all. She would never, *ever* lead them into battle against her father's people. Or vice versa. She would not - could not - send any of her people to spill the blood of the other. She was not a 'battle queen of future glory' as the most recent young warrior had just called her.

She was Ari Ara of the High Mountains, follower of the Way Between.

Suddenly, every word she'd swallowed for the past six weeks surged up from her heart and lodged in her throat. She felt the burning stings of each of the thousand cuts to the soul she'd silently endured during the Ordeal of Queens. It all came flooding back, every war speech, every battle statue, every ritual of death and destruction. The pointless, painful devotion to war. The horrifying worship of killers. The armor of military clothing. The neglected ancestor pillars to those who stood for peace. The way the young people's dreams conformed to the expectations of war culture. The children shiny-eyed with visions of glory, ready to march off to battlefields strewn with bodies.

Ari Ara choked on it all, her spirit flailing against the bonds of duty. She'd been drawn into this world of violence despite her convictions. She had handed out awards at the Summer Trials to this year's most skillful killers. She had sat in the stands with a smile plastered over her gritted teeth, reciting tactful phrases as thousands of people practiced massacring other people.

Was it worth it?

How many years of this would she have to endure before she could start changing everything? She glanced at Brinelle. Even if the Great Lady trusted her, the nobles would not let her make decisions until her age of maturity at twenty-four. Nine years of polite agony? If she had to bite her tongue that long, there'd be nothing left to speak with.

Ari Ara shut her eyes. She reached down deep within her soul. *Ancestors be with me*, she prayed. She called upon her mother, Tahkan's parents, and everyone back through time to the generation who had started it all with three feuding brothers. She kindled the spark of her inner *azar*, fanning it into a fire inside her heart, considering her next words. She released the impulse to run out of the ceremony – that was *anar's* way. She dropped her urge to yell at them over the idiotic nightmare of war – that was *attar's* way. She called out to Alaren's ancestor spirit and sought the Way Between. Her answer thundered through her like the rumble of the Great Horns across the bowl of the mountains.

She could not accept their swords, their words, their weapons and wars. Not today. Not ever. Not to be polite. Not to pass her ordeal. Not even to win the throne.

She opened her eyes. A hush hung like held breath. Thousands of faces turned in her direction, waiting for her to speak. Backlit by the amber sun, the row of youths traded uneasy glances, worried by her silence. The Twins bent close, conferring in whispers. The Warrior Sister straightened and spoke, bringing the stirring unease to a head.

"They offer their swords to you," Roka Maro reminded her, a cruel curl of a smile on her face. "Will you accept them?"

All at once, Ari Ara spotted the hungry gleam in Roka's eyes. Her focus snapped to sharp attention. This was it - this was the last test of the Ordeal of Queens. It wasn't presiding over sparring matches, nor enduring war ceremonies under the pressure of polite behavior. It was this pledging of swords. Her heart sank. It was an impossible test, one she couldn't win. If she silently accepted their swords, she'd be lying. If she rejected them, she'd be unfit to be queen and commander of the army.

She scrambled to dredge up a useful line from *The Book of*

Queens, searching for guidance through this quandary. To her surprise, three verses echoed through her, some of the few she agreed with and committed to heart from her studies:

A queen is truthful and honest.

A queen cares for the future of her people.

A queen stands tall with integrity.

Ari Ara knew what she had to say next.

She glanced at her aunt. The Great Lady Brinelle shook her head imperceptibly – a signal to say nothing. Ari Ara caught her father's eyes. His stony expression implored her to just get through this ordeal. She looked to Shulen. His steady regard held her unwaveringly, reading the conflicted thoughts running through her. He trusted her, supported her. He knew what weighed on her heart. He understood the choice of sacrifices before her. He gave her a small smile.

Ari Ara lifted her chin. She would not take another step surrounded by polite lies. In a moment, the Twins would announce her fate. As soon as it was read, her words would hold less weight. No matter the outcome, she could not accept it based on the silences that had brought her to it. The warriors thought she could lead them. Ari Ara knew she could not. She would not. Except toward peace . . . toward the practices of the Way Between . . . toward the eventual demise of the violence they glorified and worshipped.

"No."

Her voice broke at the edges, tight with pent-up emotion. Her fingers flew to her collar, tugging the clasps of her outer robe apart and loosening its chokehold around her throat. She unhooked the clasps of the silvermail on her chest. The links fell to the ground at her feet, leaving her vulnerable to assassins' arrows, guarded only by the Way Between. Ari Ara was not afraid. There were words she had to speak . . . and she could not say them bound in the trappings of war.

The youth looked around uncertainly, eyes appealing to the Twins to help smooth over this bewildering moment. Roka Maro's mean smile twitched, but she did nothing. Sorra Maro stood beside her, eyes kind, yet unwilling to intervene.

"No," Ari Ara repeated, shaking her head. "I cannot accept your swords."

Murmurs rose like a swarm of angry bees.

"What use do I have for your weapons?" Ari Ara explained, raising her voice to be heard. "I am not a *destroyer of enemies* or a *battle queen*. I will not command the army to wage war. I am the Heir to Two Thrones, the descendant of Marin *and* Shirar, the child of Queen Alinore *and* Tahkan Shirar of the Harraken. I will not go into battle against either of my families. I am a follower of the Way Between."

Ari Ara could see the consternation in their eyes, the confusion and discomfort at her rejection of the words they spoke to honor her. She softened the blow as she continued.

"I *will* promise to defend the riverlands – but I will also defend the desert lands, too. I will protect us all with the Way Between. I will be a shield of my people – both my peoples – and keep everyone safe through the practices of *azar*. I can lead the army . . . but only if you let me lead you toward peace."

She stepped toward the row of young warriors, searching for a particular boy.

"You called me the River Dragon," Ari Ara said to him, remembering how he'd shouted it out with fervor shining in his eyes. "You honor me with that title. The River Dragon is the embodiment of the river that connects us all, the current that carries us toward our future."

Ari Ara paused and took a deep breath.

"But what if I am not the River Dragon?"

The crowd stirred in shock. A rumble of protest broke out. Ari Ara lifted her hands and raised her voice over the clamor. She drew closer to the young people and grasped the shoulder of one, then the outstretched hand of the next, followed by the eyes of a third. Through the youth, the future of the nation flowed. Through them, the watercourse of their world would be shaped.

"What if *we* are the River Dragon?"

She lifted her gaze to the crowd beyond them, stretching her meaning to include all of them – the warriors, nobles, merchants and farmers, sisters and orphans.

"Alone, we are each just one drop in the river, but together? Together, we make the river dragon rise."

A ragged cheer broke out, half-surprised at the audacity of its own sound. Those who lifted it peered over the heads of the silent to see who else had dared to give voice to hope.

"Each of us chooses," Ari Ara went on. "We choose whether we push our future toward war . . . or whether we will bend it toward peace. We choose whether we will smash our enemies or water the fields that feed our children and theirs. We choose whether we will destroy the bridges between us or strengthen them to connect us. At war, the River Dragon drowns the world in blood. But at peace? At peace, the River Dragon carries us all forward, together."

This time, when the bold few lifted their cheers, more voices joined them. Not everyone. Not everywhere. Not all at once. But enough to kindle the courage of the crowd.

Ari Ara smiled at them, hopeful and defiant. Inner *azar* burned in the hearth of her heart, warmth radiating through her limbs. She felt it rippling in her veins like water moving around stones, inexorable, unstoppable. She heard it singing in her bones like the songs of the desert wind. It rumbled underfoot like the heartbeat of the world.

"If you want to make pledges to me," she told the young warriors, "then offer me your courage, not your sword. Pledge your willingness to risk your life in pursuit of peace, not to die in glory on the battlefield."

Gleaming golden in the last tendrils of sunset, she paused before the champion of the Summer Trials.

"Pledge your compassion, perhaps, or your dedication. Pledge your love or hope or determination."

The shadows of the city crept closer as she paced the length of the line.

"In the trials," she told a lithe boy with brown hair, "you moved so fast your motions blurred. Pledge that speed to the Way Between."

A touch of rose seeped into the evening as she turned to a burly young man with a hint of a beard.

"And you! I saw you stop your friends from fighting. Pledge *those* skills to Mariana. We need you."

She took a deep breath and studied them, each as strong as she, muscled and straight-spined, eyes bright with the future. Beyond the youth, the older warriors, scarred by the battles they'd survived, watched with guarded expressions.

"If you must pledge your swords to me, give them wholly, utterly, once and for all. Let's build a world where we can put aside our weapons and live together in peace. Isn't that worth fighting for? Not with violence, but with vision?"

In a few moments, the ancestor spirits would speak through the Sisters, announcing the results of her ordeal. The will of the past would determine the fate of her future, the direction of the nation, and the shape of the world to come. But here, now, in this instant, the generation who would live in that future should have a voice. They would be the ones to kill or be killed; they would be the ones sacrificed to war. If they harbored a secret longing for peace, now was the chance to speak up for it.

One by one, the young warriors swallowed and looked at each other. Then the champion – who had risen to victory through his courage, speed, intelligence, and fierce determination – stepped forward. He lifted his sword and did the unthinkable.

He knelt and laid his blade down at her feet.

The crowd's astonished applause erupted like a rain shower surging into a downpour. Out of the corner of her eye, Ari Ara saw the Great Lady's gloved hand fly to her trembling lips, emotion sweeping through her. Tahkan's look could not be translated, an inexpressible blend of wary hope and shining pride in his daughter. Shulen's rare smile blossomed, unfurling wider as - one after another - the most decorated young warriors of this year's competitions knelt and laid their swords at the feet of the Lost Heir. Under the clamor of the crowd, only Ari Ara heard the words spoken by the young champion kneeling before her.

"I want the future you will bring."

Ari Ara reached for his arm and clasped it in the handshake of warriors, lifting him to his feet. Her words, too, were swallowed by the sound of the crowd. But he heard them and smiled.

"The future *we* will bring, together."

A strange contentment fell over Ari Ara as she moved to the others, gripping their forearms and raising them to stand with her. Perhaps she had thrown the queenship into jeopardy, but she knew her future was assured. If she could not work for peace on the throne, she would do so in the streets. Alaren had no crown. Even if she had no royal powers, she still had the Way Between. Whatever the ancestor spirits decided about her Ordeal of Queens, she knew she had done what was right.

Like a gasp, the light faded into the grays of dusk. A rumbling blast of the horns demanded silence from the people. A chill of anticipation rose. The end of the ordeal had arrived. At the edges of the unseen, the ancestor spirits stilled. Their presence sent shivers through the twilight and tingled on Ari Ara's skin like river mist. The crowd stood riveted. Thousands of breaths hung suspended. The fate of the nation poised on the sword's edge of the present. The crossroads of history converged on this night. The lives of their children and their children's children would be shaped by what happened next.

Thud-Thud. Thud-Thud.

Flat. Metallic. Wooden. Hard. The sword and shield drumbeat broke out as the warrior sisters initiated the ritual invocation of the Ordeal of Queens, heralding the announcement of the decision.

Thud-Thud. Thud-Thud.

They hammered the heartbeat of life with the weapons of death. Then, in strict precision, they paused. All the air left Ari Ara's lungs.

The Mother Sister spoke.

"In the sanctity of the Sanctuary, here under the protection of the Citadel, the Sisters and the Ancestor Spirits gathered to weigh this girl's failures and achievements during her Ordeal of Queens. She showed leadership at the Gateway Abbey, along with persistence and determination."

Thud-Thud. Thud-Thud.

The sound punctuated the night, this time joined by the young warriors. Once again, they halted as one.

"But," the Warrior Sister took over, her voice ominous, "at the Ancestor Shrine, visions of death and disgrace marred her vigil. No offering to the spirits was made. An augury of murder haunted her."

Ari Ara opened her mouth to protest then snapped it shut again. Now was not the time to argue over unprovable details.

Thud-Thud. Thud-Thud.

The older warriors picked up the drumbeat, a seething mass of muscle, armor, leather, and steel. A chill shivered down Ari Ara's spine.

"Here at the Citadel, she has performed her duties in the Summer Trials admirably," Sorra Maro pointed out.

"Yet she defies the traditional pledge," Roka Maro snarled, "and refuses to lead the warriors into battle."

Thud-Thud. Thud-Thud.

The Twins of the Sisterlands lifted their arms to the assembled and spoke in one voice.

"Sisters!" they cried, pivoting to the robed women. "Darkness falls. Light our way. Reveal the will of the ancestors!"

A rustle of motion.

A snap of flint.

A spark of light.

Fires rose and spun. Seven sisters lifted circles of light, the same symbol that had barred Ari Ara from the capital, the throne, and the queenship. The ancestor spirits hissed in the wind-rush of flames and whispered through the chants of the sisters. Ari Ara strained to hear, but could not make out the words. The fire circles spoke plainly, though: the path to the throne was still closed to her.

As darkness clutched the city, Ari Ara's heart pounded louder than a thousand shields. She had failed. Breath shuddered in her chest. She fixed her gaze firmly on the ground in front of her. Any other landing place – the sisters, the warriors, her father, her aunt – would sting the press of tears loose in her eyes. Their disappointment, she knew, would hit her harder than a punch. Ari Ara bit her bottom lip, miserable, muscles clenching in anticipation of the final words.

"Look!"

A youth's voice broke out, cracking with emotion, choking

with awe. A gasp ran through the crowd. Ari Ara wrenched her eyes up. The Twins whipped back toward the crescent of fire-spinning sisters.

A lone woman had broken formation. The ancestor spirits called through her voice, her hands, her muscles, her body. The flames altered course, leapt sideways, over, around, and back.

A river dragon rose in the air.

Gasps erupted in the crowd.

A second circle shifted, matching the pattern of the River Dragon.

A third fire curled and coiled over itself. Then a fourth. And a fifth.

One by one, the symbol rose.

The Twins lifted their hands high in the air and turned.

"Ari Ara de Marin en Shirar," they declared, "the ancestor spirits have spoken. The Sisters have heard and agreed."

The next words hit Ari Ara like a lightning strike. She staggered. Her mouth fell open.

"You have passed the Ordeal of Queens."

CHAPTER TWENTY-TWO

. . . . .

The Sanctuary

The roar deafened the city. It rattled the peaks of the mountains. It shook the rivers like ribbons. Torches flared throughout the plaza, igniting one from another in a crown of light.

Ari Ara scarcely noticed. Cheers pummeled her. Her aunt and father embraced her. Emir pounded her back in congratulations. The Peace Force threw their arms high in the air, repeating a single phrase in a breathless chant: *She did it! She did it!* The row of warrior youths behind her jumped up and down in unbridled thrill. Here and there, torchlight caught a shocked scowl marring the face of a warrior, but most exploded in awed applause, accepting the will of the ancestors. The sisters tossed decorum to the wind and cheered madly.

Ari Ara couldn't believe it. She'd passed?

It was true. She could see it in the smile that split her father's face. Her aunt was crying tears of joy. The Twins pushed their way over to her and held out their hands, gesturing for her to come with them. The ritual of the blood oath would happen inside the

Sanctuary of the Citadel, sacred home to spirits and sisters. Under the eyes of the ancestors, the Twins would receive her vow to be a good queen to her people, to be loyal, just, and compassionate. Only they and the spirits would be present for this most sacred of ceremonies. Ari Ara trailed after the Twins in a daze, hardly able to believe this moment had truly come.

At the threshold of the Sanctuary, Ari Ara cast a glance over her shoulder, looking back at everyone who had brought her to this moment. In the torchlight, the faces of her friends and relatives shone. Her eyes searched further, though, for someone who stood close to her heart. She just needed to see him once before she stepped through those doors and truly became queen.

There.

Shulen stood quietly to one side, unabashed tears streaming down his cheeks. Pride, joy, and sorrow tumbled in his eyes; love and loss comingled in celebration, colliding as she crossed another threshold in her life. He saw her gaze and smiled. In a silent message, he lifted his hands and brought his fingers together in the triangular shape of the meditation they shared each morning.

We may never know what the day might bring, but we can always rise to greet it.

Ari Ara grinned back and turned to step through the doors. She straightened her spine and held her head high. She strode into her future, determined to make everyone proud.

She did not see Minli run up to Shulen, frantic.

She did not see him hand over a letter.

She did not see Shulen's face fall slack in shock as he read it.

The heavy oak doors swung shut just as the old warrior whipped his head toward her in alarm.

Once the doors closed, the roar of the crowd hushed to a faint whisper, muffled and distant. Under the cavernous, vaulted rafters of the Sanctuary, all was still and quiet. A sense of calm suffused everything, sweet and delicious after all she had endured. The Twins halted in the center. A stone slab lay between their feet, black with age, mottled with the blood oaths every monarch of Mariana throughout time. Her mother's blood. Her grandmother's blood. Ari Ara stepped closer and glanced curiously around the chamber.

"No one watches, child," the Mother Sister told her, a gentle smile of understanding creasing her face.

"This is between you and the ancestors," the Warrior Sister informed her less kindly.

Ari Ara's ribs expanded as she breathed, deep and achingly, sensing her life teetering on a precipice of irreversible change.

"Hold out your palm."

The Mother Sister pulled out the ceremonial knife, a sickle blade curved like the waxing and waning moon that tugged the wombs of women and brought life into the world. Like a horse's skin taut with alertness, a quiver rippled through Ari Ara. Finn's warning echoed in her ears: *be careful.*

If the Warrior Sister had held the knife, Ari Ara would not have dared put her hand out. But the Mother Sister smiled as warmly as ever, her gentle eyes brimming with emotion, her cozy patience softening the silence. So, Ari Ara lifted her palm. Her arm muscles twitched, ready to pull back if the cut plunged too deep.

But the slice was quick and light, breaking the surface of the skin with a shallow wound that scarcely hurt. As blood welled scarlet, the Mother Sister turned her palm over. Three drops hit the stone floor.

Ari Ara's smile illuminated her face. She had done it! She had passed the Ordeal of Queens. Tears leapt to her eyes. She whispered her thanks to her mother's spirit for guiding and aiding her. She moved to wipe them away.

The Mother Sister's grip tightened. Her kind face hardened.

"We hoped it would not come to this," she murmured, her gentle voice suddenly steely.

Ari Ara's heart began to race, thundering beyond thrill, nerves, and excitement; galloping through alarm, skidding into panic, slamming to a stop. There, it wheeled about and hammered into an ever-slowing drumbeat that filled her bones with dread.

The chamber spun.

Ari Ara reeled, dizzy.

Something was terribly wrong.

CHAPTER TWENTY-THREE

. . . . .

Prophecy's Daughter

The stone floor stung cold against her sweaty back. Overhead, the candlelight reeled and splintered. The faces of the Twins of the Sisterlands bent unnaturally in her burning eyes.

"You did not think we would let you live, did you?"

The voice of Roka Maro throbbed in her pounding head, ringing with triumph, with treachery, with tones impossible to translate. Each beat of Ari Ara's pulse slammed against her heart. The edges of her sight blurred. Her cut hand screamed with pain. Her arm burned as if fire crawled slowly up her veins.

They had poisoned the knife blade.

"We are so sorry," the Mother Sister murmured in a façade of tenderness, lips close to her ear, hand stroking her hair. "If you had failed the Ordeal of Queens, it would not have come to this. We - I - hoped you were not truly the Heir to Two Thrones. I wish you could have lived."

Ari Ara parted her lips, but only one word croaked out.

"Why?"

"Well, the prophecy, of course," Sorra Maro replied. "There

have always been a few of us willing to do whatever it takes to thwart its warnings of doom. For five hundred years, we've worked in secret, in shadows. Our sect nearly died out, but then the signs of the prophecy began to appear."

"Yes," Roka Maro agreed, a nasty smile curling on her lips. "Our ranks swelled considerably when that fool Alinore fell in love with Tahkan Shirar."

Ari Ara struggled for breath as the two women threw salt in the wounds of her panicked heart. They'd tried to kill her mother numerous times, they admitted. When they were mere novices, Roka had threatened Alinore during her pregnancy. Later, Sorra had tried to cause a miscarriage. Their secret sect hired the Southern Paika to chase her down, capture her, and kill the prophesized heir as soon as it was born. But Shulen fought off the fighters. Fate took the child . . . or so they thought.

"For eleven years," the Mother Sister said, her voice hardening, "the Fanten Grandmother managed to deceive us. Then you reappeared, the Mark of Peace inked on your back, daughter of that cursed prophecy."

Ari Ara's eyes darted left, right, above her head, desperate for help, escape. Why couldn't she move? She had to warn everyone – it wasn't just Roka Maro. Sorra Maro was involved, and others, too. These fanatics could be hiding in the ranks of the warriors, the noble houses, anywhere.

Ari Ara shuddered as the Mother Sister stroked her hair, soothing her with deadly malice. Her twin crouched on the opposite side, relishing the chance to tell Ari Ara all the ways they'd nearly stopped the fabled Lost Heir from ascending the throne – an assassin's dagger, a split confirmation vote, prolonging her exile, resisting her return. Then, at last, invoking the Ordeal of Queens with all its opportunity to do her harm.

"Someone at Marin's Mountain must have warned you not to

drink the longal-laced water," Roka grumbled. "Pity that message didn't reach the two sisters who died."

Then I did see them, Ari Ara tried to say over lips as immovable as stone. The poisoned Guardian Sisters had been real. Someone had removed the bodies.

"We tried again at the Ancient Springs," Sorra admitted, her kindness sinister in its bald confession of murderous intent.

She was the second statue, Ari Ara realized with a silent gasp. *Not the novice. The Mother Sister!*

"I still don't understand what threw you off," Sorra sighed to her sister.

My mother and Rhianne's spirits, thought Ari Ara, a surge of gratitude giving her a brief reprieve from the burning, tingling sensation crawling through her limbs.

"If it is any consolation," the Warrior Sister stated callously, her flat tone indicating that she did not really care, "your death – your sacrifice – will save thousands from the floods, famines, and wars of the prophecy. You will be a legend."

I'd rather be alive, Ari Ara thought wildly. *Legends are overrated.*

Shivers ran up and down her limbs. Suddenly, she was so, so cold.

"You truly are the Heir To Two Thrones," the Mother Sister told her, a note of awe in her frighteningly tender voice. "Your mother would be so proud of you."

My mother is dead, Ari Ara snarled back wordlessly, *because of you.*

And much as she longed to see Alinore, she would not surrender to the Black Ancestor River. Not yet. Not now.

She struggled to rise, but couldn't. Her limbs hung heavy as iron. Her eyes darted through the dimness clouding them. She squinted against the sharp swords of light spiking out from the pinpricks of candleflame. A slow thud pounded in her ears. As the sound boomed and echoed beyond Ari Ara's reeling mind, the Twins of the Sisterlands snapped their heads toward the heavy double doors. Someone was trying to break in.

"They suspect," Roka muttered. She snatched the ritual knife from Sorra's hand and brought it to Ari Ara's throat. "This is taking too long. Why isn't she dead?"

"Don't," the Mother Sister ordered, gripping her sister's wrist. "It will all be over soon. We can still blame her death on the will of the ancestors. Longal works swiftly and leaves little trace to those who do not know its scent."

Ari Ara twitched at the mention of the herb. The Fanten Grandmother had identified it on the lips of the two dead sisters on the mountain. She shut her eyes.

"Don't struggle," the Mother Sister cooed. "Sleep."

"Sleep," the Warrior Sister echoed. "Rest in the long slumber of the ancestors."

But Ari Ara had no intention of joining the ancestor spirits. As the Black Ancestor River roared around her, she dove into the dreamrealms in search of the Fanten Grandmother.

CHAPTER TWENTY-FOUR

. . . . .

The Fanten Grandmother's Secrets

Ari Ara snapped upright, her heart in her throat. The dreamrealm pooled around her, black as night. The edges rustled, astir with prowling dream creatures. The whisper of sleek fur, the pad of pawed feet, the click of claws and heaviness of hot breath. This was a dream poised to pounce. The unshaped potential of the dreamrealm churned in a circle, an eddy of endless possibility ready to fold itself into the forms of her fears.

But the Fanten Grandmother held it at bay. She hovered above her, one hand on her hip, half bent over. She scowled as she peered down. Her other hand lifted to ward off whatever circled them. Her fingers twitched slightly as if shoving back the bristling snout of a wild boar. Annoyance clung to the old woman's wrinkles; the force of Ari Ara's will had yanked her out of a distant dream ceremony.

"Help me!" Ari Ara pleaded, relief bursting through her at the sight of the old woman. "I'm dying."

"Don't be ridiculous," the Fanten Grandmother scoffed, a short laugh bursting out. The dream creatures slunk further away at its sound. "You're not dying. Just sleeping."

"The Twins poisoned me," Ari Ara insisted. "They're both involved."

"I tried to tell you," the silver-haired woman agreed sourly. "What did they do?"

"They cut me with a longal-laced knife."

"Bet that hurt," the old woman snorted. "Longal isn't meant to be put in the blood. Fanten drink it to open the gateway to deep dreaming. Whether or not you'll wake up, now that's another matter."

"What do you mean?" Ari Ara asked in alarm.

"I doubt those lowlander idiots know you'll need *perchan* – the antidote herb - to awaken."

"So, I'll die?"

The Fanten Grandmother shot her an irritable look.

"Eventually, of old age, having slept through your life."

"But you said there's a cure?"

"Must I repeat everything twice?" the Fanten Grandmother sighed. "Yes. Longal doesn't kill Fanten, only lowlanders."

Lowlander was the Fanten term for anyone who lived in the valleys below the Fanten's mountainous forests, Marianans and Harraken alike.

"I'm not Fanten," she muttered bitterly, remembering how the Fanten girls had tormented her by calling her *lowlander*.

The grandmother's smile curled, secretive with hidden delight.

"Are you sure? You can dreamwalk, after all."

"Of course, I'm sure," Ari Ara snorted. "I'm the heir to – "

She broke off. The dreamrealm shivered slightly through its inky blackness. The Fanten Grandmother stared steadily at her, motionless save for the wisps of her silver hair that floated in the windless air. The words of Ari Ara's next question dammed up in her throat. A shudder rumbled overhead like a brewing storm. The half-veiled beasts in the dream's margins whined and howled. The tempo of their restless pacing ratcheted faster. They loped and lumbered in a maelstrom of a circle as objections stammered out of Ari Ara.

"But I dream because I'm Fanten-raised."

"Fanten born," the grandmother corrected.

"Because of Fanten custom."

"Fanten birth."

"Because of Fanten herbs."

"Blood."

The truth hit the girl like an earthquake. Her body shook. The churning dreambeasts roared and flung themselves into nothing, disintegrating into splintered teeth and cracked claws and showers of fur that fell like inky snow. The dreamworld lurched in the shudder-rumble of continents shifting. The groundless ground heaved. The Fanten Grandmother flung out her hands to hold it in place. Cracks snapped through the blackness beneath their feet, split the edges, and broke across the canopy of starless sky overhead.

"You," the Fanten Grandmother told her, "are the daughter of my daughter, child of Rhianne . . . and Shulen."

The dreamworld shattered with the sound of smashing glass. Silver and black shards wheeled like falling ice, reflecting a thousand moments of her life. Each time she'd slipped into Fanten dreaming. Her days as a shepherdess in the High Mountains. The sly smile on the Fanten Grandmother's face, hinting at secrets. Bullies teasing her about her desert demon hair . . . which was also as copper red as Shulen's had been. Noble girls scoffing at her desert-dark skin . . . which also resembled the earth and shadow tones of the Fanten. Her winter exhaustion as Rhianne's relatives slept the deep sleep of their people. Her restless wakefulness as Shulen's lowlander blood prevented her from joining them. Veiled hints from Rhianne's ancestor spirit. The strange looks Shulen gave her, wondering.

Ari Ara slammed her foot down in the reeling dreamworld. The shattering halted. Immense shards suspended briefly then settled into new positions. Up and down realigned. The dream settled into the shape of the Fanten Forest.

"It's true?" Ari Ara's shocked voice boomed through the somber trunks, shoving the Fanten Grandmother backwards with its force.

The old woman hid a smirk. The girl proved her bloodlines with that bellow. Alinore's child would *not* be able to push a Fanten Grandmother around in the dreamworld. Rhianne would be pleased to see her daughter's strength. The old woman braced her limbs against the ripple shocks of Ari Ara's heated outbursts.

"You lied," Ari Ara accused wildly, eyes narrowing in suspicion. The boughs of the Great Trees thrashed overhead, storm winds lashed the upper canopies. The Fanten Grandmother stilled them with a calming flick of her hand.

"Fanten do not lie. Especially not in dreams."

"You did, though. You told the world that I was Alinore and Tahkan's daughter!"

"No," the old woman's age-rasped voice scoffed. "They believed what they wanted to believe. I never said you were Alinore's daughter. Typical lowlanders, they asked all the wrong questions and didn't listen carefully to the answers."

Ari Ara's head spun. The giant trunks reeled in a towering carousel above her. She sank to her heels on the thick carpet of needles. Memories from that night, four years ago when the Mark of Peace was discovered on her back, bled out of her thoughts and into the shadowed vaults of the trees. A dream-image of herself danced the Way Between wearing Alinore's white dress. With a lurch, Ari Ara realized that the Fanten Grandmother had never specifically said that it was *her mother's*, only that it was *once the dead queen's*. The open back of the dress revealed the black-inked Mark of Peace between her shoulders. The throbbing drumbeats of that evening's rhythm pulsed in her ears. She remembered the Fanten Grandmother gripping her hand tight and lifting it high in the air. She heard the old woman's voice declare to the stunned faces of all who had gathered:

"Allow me to present Ari Ara of Monk's Hand . . . the Lost Heir of two lineages, next to inherit the thrones of King Tahkan of the Desert and Queen Alinore of Mariana."

She hadn't said *daughter*. Nor *child*. But she did call Ari Ara the heir.

"You told everyone I was the heir to two thrones," Ari Ara prompted when silence stretched too long. "Was that a lie?"

"Not exactly."

The wiry wrinkled woman smirked, amused by something she did not deign to share.

"How could it be the truth?" Ari Ara huffed, indignant, tired of veiled words.

"Not all secrets are mine to tell," the Fanten Grandmother retorted, aloof as ever.

"Fine. Tell me what you can," Ari Ara demanded. "Better still, show me the truth. Dream the past with me. What really happened in the cave with Alinore's child?"

"What good will that do?" the Fanten Grandmother sighed.

No one would believe the girl even if she woke up and told them. They'd call her dreams delusional and dismiss her claims. But Ari Ara insisted. *She* would know the truth. A dream shared with another person bound them to that knowledge. The memories the Fanten Grandmother dreamed with her could be trusted, far more so than the old woman's waking words. Ari Ara did not intend to slumber forever. She'd find a way to break out of longal sleep and wake up. And when she did, Shulen would believe the veracity of a Fanten dream.

"Show me."

"No."

"Now."

Opposing wills slammed together with the force of a lightning crack. The Great Trees shook and swayed as Ari Ara tried to wrench the dreamrealm out of the Fanten Grandmother's control. The old woman placed a hand on the bark of the nearest trees and steadied them. The thin tightening of her papery lips hinted at the effort that trembled beneath her implacable surface.

"A fox kit can't trick a vixen," she told the girl sternly. "Stop this or I'll pick you up by the scruff of the neck and carry you home with your tail between your legs."

"And where is home, exactly?" Ari Ara snarled, taking a running charge at the tree and hurling her shoulder into it, hoping it would budge, or buckle, or bend out of her way.

The blow knocked her to the ground. The Fanten Grandmother had breathed the force of her determination into its wooden hardness. Ari Ara groaned and clutched her shoulder. The old woman looked on, unsympathetic.

"Done?"

Ari Ara glared up at her and scrambled to her feet. She was just getting started. She had all the time in the world to pry the truth out of the old woman . . . or find it in the unfathomable corners of the dreamworld. Determined, Ari Ara started walking in the direction of the Queen's Cave where Alinore had died. Just as she passed through the edge of the grove, however, the elder made a twisting gesture. The dream warped.

Ari Ara returned to where she'd started.

She took off. Again . . . and again . . . and again. Each time, the Fanten Grandmother sighed, tugged the dream, and brought her back. Ari Ara felt like a wayward lamb hooked at the end of a shepherd's crook. Chest heaving, hands on her hips, she eyed this woman of wrinkles and power, secrets and truth.

"What if we made a bargain?" Ari Ara offered.

The Fanten Grandmother's eyes widened. Then narrowed. A cat-like smile curled over a toothy grin.

"Are you sure?"

Perilous and unpredictable, Fanten bargains were tricky at best. At the worst? They were tragic. Barter for a love potion and you'd get an herb of passion that erased the memory of your lover. Ask for the location of ancient treasure and the Fanten would tell you – then move it before you got there. Offer your weight in gold and they'd take payment in golden wheat, stripping your farm of decades of harvests. The Fanten lived for the trick of the bargain, the cleverly-crafted words, the secret twists. Ari Ara had grown up hearing these stories recounted over and over. She herself had struck a bargain to prevent war. She asked the Fanten Grandmother to reveal the heir. The Fanten Grandmother demanded one thing in return, a simple thing, it had seemed: join the Fanten in their dances that evening. Little had Ari Ara known that the low-backed dress would uncover the Mark of Peace and reveal her to be the Lost Heir.

Fanten bargains were not to be entered lightly.

"What do you want from me?" Ari Ara asked, blurting out the words before she lost her nerve. "In exchange for showing me what happened fifteen years ago at the Battle of Shulen's Stand, what must I promise you?"

Specificity was crucial. Give a Fanten a loophole and they'd knit a sweater out of it. Or unravel the world.

The Fanten Grandmother's deep, dark eyes regarded her steadily, a touch of mournfulness in their depths, along with regret at the past, uncertainty for the future, and concern for her people.

"When you wake up," she said in a gentle tone that Ari Ara had never heard from the woman, "come to me in the High Mountains. I will show you the Fanten Ways – the rituals, customs, stories, drumming, dancing, and dreaming - all that I should have shown you long ago."

Ari Ara blinked in surprise. Like the bellow of the Great Horns, an old, hollow ache from her childhood moaned in her chest. The Fanten Grandmother had demanded – no, offered – the one thing Ari Ara had longed for as a small child: to be welcomed, to belong, to be included in the Fanten rituals. Wariness crept in like hoarfrost. What was the catch? This was not how these bargains worked. The Fanten Grandmother would not give her something she longed for in trade for something else she wanted.

The old woman sensed her suspicion and sighed. There was no trick to this. After fifteen years of casting her grandchild away, the time had come to bring her home. The consequences of misleading the world would soon come to roost on the Fanten like a murder of crows screaming in the boughs of the Great Trees. The Fanten had endured thousands of years of danger . . . and the next year would be the most perilous of all. Marianans and Harraken would be united in their fury at her deception, outraged at the swapping of her granddaughter for their leaders' heir. Ari Ara had to come – for her sake and the Fanten's.

With hope and unease churning inside her, Ari Ara agreed.

The Fanten Grandmother began to dance, slowly at first, then quicker and quicker. In the pace of her footsteps, the mountains trembled. Her outstretched hands churned the air like cream into butter. The stars spun and shifted in the sky. She brushed the trees with her fingertips. Gracefully, they lifted their roots and lumbered into new locations. Ari Ara flung her arms out as the slope tilted under her feet, climbing steeply uphill.

An arrow whizzed past her ear. She ducked. Ari Ara heard the distant shouts, the clash of swords, the stinging whip and thunk of arrows, horses whinnying in alarm.

The Fanten Grandmother gestured toward the mouth of a cave. Ari Ara approached warily. Inside, Rhianne's petite frame bent over Alinore as the queen panted and pushed in labor pains, her face ashen grey. Rhianne cast a wild-eyed glance over her shoulder as a battle roar sounded through the woods. Her black hair flung about her worried face as she whirled and pressed her finger to her lips. Tucked into a black cloak, a small child with a shock of red hair sat with her face scrunched-up, holding back her terrified wail. Ari Ara met her own blue-grey eyes and knew it was her. She shivered.

"Rhianne tried to summon me," the old woman said softly, pointing.

Ari Ara watched the younger Fanten woman close her eyes, enter trance, and send a message to her mother to *hurry, come.* Then Rhianne rose, kissed her daughter, whispered for her to stay silent, and tucked her deeper into the cavern, out of sight. She urged Alinore to stay strong, then ran out of the cave, searching for help.

She would not return.

"I found her not far from here," the Fanten Grandmother murmured in a voice so small, Ari Ara could hardly hear it. "An arrow in her chest, gasping her last breath, drenched in blood."

There was something more, something the Fanten Grandmother kept hidden. Ari Ara wrestled with the dreamrealm, but the old woman would not be budged. The Fanten Grandmother sensed the girl's yanks and thwarted her attempts to shift the scene. Ari Ara was strong, but her skill was as raw as a newborn babe. She was no match for the elder's ability to hold and shape this world.

"No. I will not show you. No child should see her mother die. Not like that."

Instead, the elder tugged time along like a wayward sheep, hooking it with her hands and pulling it to the moment when she arrived at the cave. Ari Ara blinked as the Fanten Grandmother stepped into the scene, shedding wrinkles and age. Silver hair slipped back to black. Her muscles rounded with strength. Then as now, the Fanten Grandmother was not to be trifled with. She went straight to the laboring woman and helped guide the infant into the world. Alinore's exhausted eyes burned with love for her newborn. Her smile trembled. The iron-tainted scent of blood stung the mineral air of the cave. The queen shuddered. Her eyelids fluttered shut. The Fanten Grandmother grabbed the child as the woman's grasp faltered. The Black Ancestor River roared in Alinore's ears. Feebly, she drew the Fanten elder to her weak lips.

"Put the Mark of Peace on her. The heir to two thrones must be identifiable, must be dedicated to peace. Keep her hidden and safe. Promise me! The pro-prophecy – "

Ari Ara wept then, tears welling and tumbling down her cheeks. It shook her soul - the queen's courage, her determination right down to her last breath to ensure peace in her world. Alinore gazed at her daughter for a lingering moment, then the river's blackness flooded into her eyes and she left this world.

"No, no, no," the Fanten Grandmother whispered, her attention focusing on the infant. "Do not follow your mother. Stay here, little one. Wait!"

But it was no use. The child yearned for her mother; spirit chased spirit into the river of ancestors. The Fanten Grandmother's keening flooded the cave. Still holding the lifeless infant, she stepped toward the entrance of the cave. Then an eerie wail echoed through the cavern. The Fanten Grandmother paused, pivoted, and strode back into the shadowy depths. She crouched by the alcove where Tianne was hidden.

"You."

The word trembled with emotion - anger, loss, yearning, surprise, resignation, sorrow. She loved the daughter of her daughter. She loathed the daughter of Shulen, the blood-soaked warrior who brought her child to her death. In grief, she hurled blame upon him for Rhianne's murder and heaped her hatred upon his child. The words of the prophecy echoed in her mind, the Old Tongue words, so close to Fanten speech. The Fanten Grandmother knew them well; it had been her ancestor who first spoke the prophecy that foretold of a peacemaker who would unite the world and bear the Mark of Peace. Everyone assumed that the heir would be Tahkan and Alinore's child, born of double royal blood. But that infant was dead.

And prophecies have a strange way of flipping around to fulfill themselves.

The Fanten delighted in little tricks of language. They wielded power through the unexpected meanings hidden in turns of phrases and twists of words. To them, the prophecy did not promise that the child of two lineages bore royal blood. There were countless children with Marianan mothers and Harraken fathers, or the other way around, who could wind up sitting on the thrones by circumstance, intrigue, or fate. Children of two lineages abounded, born of love, of war, of hope or despair. Children raised by merchant parents from both sides of the border. Children born in the mountains where the dividing line between nations shifted with every war. A Fanten who had a child with a lowlander could fulfill the prophecy . . . like Rhianne and Shulen's daughter.

Perhaps, the Fanten Grandmother mused, it was time to grasp hold of that prophecy and nudge it in a sensible direction. She stared at the redheaded daughter of her daughter, *born of two lineages, mother dead, father distant,* and recognized the signs of the prophecy in her. In a fit of anger, in a burst of hope, in a madness of vision or delusion, she made her choice.

She put the Mark of Peace on her granddaughter.

The dream dissolved, shifted, and reformed in the underground homes of the Fanten. Ari Ara saw Tianne – herself – lying limp on a blanket. The dregs of a sleeping draught sat in a small wooden child's cup beside her. The Fanten Grandmother bent over the girl, carefully inking the Mark of Peace between her shoulders. A swirl of a circle, a waving line through the middle, waves of sand dunes on one half, ripples of river currents on the other. The sign of the Way Between, the symbol that identified the Lost Heir.

"So, you put the Mark of Peace on my back," Ari Ara sighed, "and hid me for eleven years."

"I tried to give you back," the old woman retorted with a snort. "But all those lowlanders thought the Desert King had you. No one bothered to listen to me. It was easier to keep you hidden until fate took hold of you."

And it had. The old woman felt a rumbling chuckle stirring in her chest. Fate had taken the girl as the Great Horns reverberated through autumn's edge, sending her to Monk's Hand Monastery, delivering her to her real father, leaving Shulen unaware. Although he had suspected the truth. Once, the Fanten Grandmother had almost confessed her secret.

Almost.

She could have changed her mind four years ago. She'd nearly spilled the weight of her secret to Nshoka Shulen on the night that the Mark of Peace had been revealed on Ari Ara's back. But the ferocity of his resentment had scorched her courage. He called her cruel, vicious, vengeful – and perhaps she was all these things – so she had vowed to carry the secret of Ari Ara's parentage to her grave, to deny Shulen the gift of his own daughter, to inflict upon him the pain she felt at the loss of her daughter.

But in the end, it didn't matter. Shulen had vowed that no matter whose bloodlines gave rise to Ari Ara, no matter whose womb had carried her, she would be the daughter of his heart, and nothing - not the Fanten, not the thrones, not the Desert King, not time, not even death - could take that away.

Against the vast tragedy of truth, the heat of Ari Ara's fury dissipated into a poignant ache in the center of her chest. She paced the grove, galvanized toward action, but bound by confusion. What should she do? What *could* she do? Somewhere, her body lay sprawled on a cold floor, longal-laced, breath shallow with poison, heartbeat slow with slumber, the pulse stretching long between throbs.

"How do I wake up?" she demanded suddenly. "You said there was a way, an herb."

"Yes, *perchen*."

The Fanten Grandmother twisted the empty air and a small, spear-leafed plant appeared. Jagged teeth rimmed its edges. Yellow veins threaded through the furry hairs of its green surface. Ari Ara examined it carefully, then frowned in concentration. She grasped at the nothingness of dreams and yanked a second cluster of *perchen* into view.

"Well done," the Fanten Grandmother conceded, arching an eyebrow. Like mother, like daughter, it seemed. "What do you plan to do with that? You need the real herb, not the dream version."

"I know," Ari Ara grumbled. "How is the remedy prepared? Pound the leaves? Grind the roots? Tea or tincture?"

"Steep the leaves for ten minutes and drink it. Someone is going to have to bring that herb to you."

"*You* could," Ari Ara said pointedly.

"I am a month's journey from you in the waking world," the Fanten Grandmother reminded her.

"You could dream to Shulen. He'd believe you."

"He won't sleep for days, knowing you're in danger. And even then, he might not listen to me," the old woman admitted with a wry and bitter note.

Ari Ara snorted. She didn't blame him.

She screwed her face up in thought, seeking a solution, searching for a Way Between dreams and waking, trust and suspicion. It must be night by now, lots of people could be slipping into dreaming.

"In a Fanten dream, we can talk to anyone who is sleeping, even if they don't know it's a true dream, right?" Ari Ara asked.

The elder nodded, tilting her head like an owl, curious and watchful.

"So, I could find someone, a specific person?" Ari Ara mused, an idea stirring a faint hope in her chest. "I could cross the dreamrealms and ask for their help."

"I wouldn't advise it," the Fanten Grandmother replied cryptically, scoffing ever so slightly and chuckling as if bemused by the notion.

"Why not?"

The elder sighed. Youth bleated that question as often as lambs.

"You have neither the training nor the focus to go wandering through dreams," the old woman told her scornfully. "Even if you had the skill to make such a journey, who would believe a dream? And then, if a lowlander did trust the message, who among them could *find* the rare herb in the marsh? Who could get it to you through the dozens of guards and warriors? Who could convince Shulen to let you drink it?"

Ari Ara knew one person who could help her, a finder of ways, a walker of hidden paths, a guide along secret roads. Someone who loved her enough to try. Someone mad enough to take the risk. Someone strong enough to make the journey.

If she could reach him, she knew Finn Paikason would listen to his dreams and come.

CHAPTER TWENTY-FIVE

. . . . .

River Dragon

Before the Fanten Grandmother could stop her, Ari Ara spun toward the edge of the Fanten Forest. She ran between the trees to the starry field of unbound dreaming. Grasping a fistful of nothing, she twisted it, gripping her intention firmly in her mind. She sensed the Fanten Grandmother trying to stop her. But this time, Ari Ara was one step ahead of the older woman. With her free hand, she tugged the dream out from under them like a rug.

Ari Ara dove, spreading her arms until falling veered into flying. The inky darkness shimmered, shivered, and gave way to silvered clouds and pinprick stars in an endless night sky. A crescent moon, sickle-thin, hung as a landmark on her right shoulder.

How would she find Finn? This was the dreamrealm. Distance folded at will. Time stretched or scrunched in a heartbeat. In dreaming, intention mattered more than logic. Imagination mapped more accurately than direction. There was no east or west, north or south. Which way should she go when up and down had no meaning?

Confronted by the overwhelming expanse of an infinite sky, Ari Ara faltered. Flight toppled into falling. She dropped like a stone, curling heels over head. She flailed. Who was she to think she could traverse the dreamrealm? No experience. No training.

No!

If she was Fanten-born, she could walk the dreamrealms.

Like a dog, Ari Ara shook all over, flinging off doubt. Confusion evaporated, replaced by determination. She dug her heels into the air and halted her mindless plummet.

Finn Paikason. She shut her eyes and invoked him in her mind, in her heart, remembering his black curls and crooked smile, his pointy dog teeth and folded dimples. She thought of the storms that brewed in his eyes and how the lanky strength of a mountain goat ran in his limbs. She recalled his courage and wild spirit, his determination to make right the wrongs of the past.

Bound by her resolve, the dreamrealm shifted, one image sliding into another in an endless stream without beginning or end. She glimpsed moments of her past and strange places she'd never been. She passed under the somber, towering trunks of the Fanten Forest and slid through the streets of Mariana Capital. The scent of dust thrust her out into the dry dunes of the desert. A rumble of horns called her into the mountains.

A trickle of water tugged at her ears. It surged into a rivulet that pulled her toward it. The water toppled into an ice-cold stream, quickened into a brook, grew into a creek, and tumbled through valleys and hills until it fell into the great body of the Mari River.

The River Dragon rose with a roar.

Towering over her, the great beast's coils seethed with ceaseless motion. Brackish shallows and green depths stirred beneath the sharper blues and grays of ripple-shaped scales. Flecks of foam flung off the River Dragon's roiling mass and turned into stars overhead. A hundred horns moaned in the creature's roar. The brush of her scales sawed in the tones of dissonant fiddles. She hissed in the shiver of whispering gongs.

Ari Ara trembled. Betrayed and deceived by an imposter child, the River Dragon was furious with her.

Ari Ara's hope turned to dread. Inside the beast's murky body, figures spun into shape and stalked out of the dark depths: Marianan nobles. Common folk. Detractors. Supporters. Friends. Foes. Monks. Sisters. Orphans. Warriors. Townspeople. All knew the truth: she was an imposter, she was not the heir to two thrones, never had been. In her blood pulsed the ancient rhythms of the Fanten and the mystery of Shulen. She could see the rage in their eyes. They would tear her limb from limb. She tensed to run.

"Stay."

The voice was a whisper that slipped through the screaming violins of the River Dragon's roars. A delicate hand settled on Ari Ara's shoulder. A slight woman, shorter than the girl, silvered at the edges, stilled silently beside her.

Rhianne.

Slender as a reed, strong as a stone-cracking root, her ancestor spirit gleamed. Her dark hair had been braided into a crown. A black wool cloak faded into the edges of the dreamrealm. Like Fanten mothers throughout time, she had come to guide her dreaming daughter past her fears. In this place where dreams shifted into nightmares at the tiniest hint of anxiety, fear was more dangerous than poison.

Rhianne took her daughter's face in her hands. She kissed her brow and bent their heads together. The Fanten woman set aside fifteen years of unspoken words. Right now, there was only one message Ari Ara needed to hear.

"You are my daughter and the daughter of Nshoka Shulen," she said in a soft voice that brought tears to Ari Ara's eyes.

Rhianne moved her hand and placed her fingertips under Ari Ara's chin, lifting it to meet her gaze.

"You are more than a match for a river dragon."

Rhianne laughed then, the sound of a hundred small, tiny bells breaking through fear, through nightmares, through darkness. She stepped back with a smile that brimmed with mother's love. The River Dragon flinched in the face of it. The creature tightened her coils and hissed at Ari Ara. With a snarl, the vast beast – a seething, roiling creature of judgments, expectations, dislikes, hatred, scorn, and disappointment – leapt.

Instinct took over. Ari Ara launched into the Way Between.

The River Dragon was fluid, shapeshifting in a flash, flinging figures from her past at her. With each slash of her tail and slam of her coils, another threat emerged. Ari Ara evaded nobles, rolled past desert riders, narrowly missed the knives of would-be assassins. A bully and his gang took swings at her. She dodged them, grasping each blow and turning the boys away gently as snowflakes. A war-obsessed military commander lunged at her. She flung him back. A noble girl hurled a dagger toward her heart. Ari Ara twisted out of harm's way and knocked it to the ground. A band of warrior women tried to seize her. She spun to evade their clutches. Honor-mad fighters challenged her. Blue-robed sisters tried to drown her. She rose to face each one, refusing to run and refusing to retaliate with violence. Friends, foes, strangers, Ari Ara met them all, as resolute in the dreamrealm as in the waking world. She held fast to the Way Between, following her vow to neither fight nor flee, and to cause no further harm as she ended an attack.

All at once, a surge of fierce joy sung through her. Her mother was right.

She was more than a match for a river dragon.

Long ago, Ari Ara had been tossed in the river and told to find the Way Between its currents. Instead of dodging the creature's attacks, Ari Ara took a deep breath . . .

. . . and dove.

Under, over, around, through, she danced the Way Between the river's rage, hurt, confusion, and fear. She looked and listened, wheeling and leaping. *Azar* meant *the way water flows between obstacles without giving up*. Old as the River Dragon was, *azar* was equally ancient, immortal as the river, eternal as time. Without a foe to fight, the dragon faltered, slowed, and stilled. Her coils unraveled from their tossing. The River Dragon shifted form, splintering into three strands, twisting into figures.

Ari Ara swallowed hard, recognizing the Three Brothers - Marin, Shirar, and Alaren. Two drew swords and barred her way. The third lifted his hand.

"Ancestors," she said respectfully, "I must pass."

"Why?" asked Shirar in a voice that sang like the wind over vast desert sands.

"Because I need to reach my friend," she answered.

"Why?" Marin roared in a voice that growled like water over falls.

"Because I need to wake from the endless sleep."

"Why?" Alaren spoke in a soft voice, human and gentle. With his hands, he parted his brothers' swords and stood before her. His smile reminded her of Shulen.

"Because the world needs me," she answered, humbly, truthfully, because it did. Not as queen, not as heir to two thrones. Just to be a part of it. To show up in this time, in this moment, and give all that she could, however small or vast, to the turning of another day. She wanted to wake, to live, to love, to leap headlong - and maybe headstrong - into adventure, to laugh with friends, to brave the dangers, to face the odds, to stare down the madness of it all and come out soaring.

She was not the heir to two thrones, nor the Lost Heir, nor the prophecy's child. She was not the daughter of Alinore, nor the child of Tahkan. She didn't feel like a Fanten, not truly. She did not feel like a lowlander, not entirely. She was neither dead nor alive, neither sleeping nor waking, neither here nor there. Not this, not that. She was Ari Ara, *everything possible in between.*

And that was enough for now.

Alaren's eyes crinkled as he saw the fire of passion burning in her gaze. He stepped to the side, opening the way for her.

"You may pass."

Ari Ara thanked him and his brothers, bowing, breathless with hope. The three ancestors spun with a whirl and curled back into the vast shape of the River Dragon. The mythic creature retreated like an ebbing flood, settling back into the banks of the river valley. The dream shifted, twisting into another time and place.

Ari Ara recognized it at once. Luminous algae glowed green and silver on the walls of the underground cavern. A teal and midnight pool of water rippled at her feet. Stalactites slowly dripped from the ceiling. Her first kiss had happened here . . . and there was the wiry youth in a fox-red cap who had shared it with her.

"Finn!" she called out, leaping forward.

His head whipped up. A shock of a smile hit him, lighting up his eyes. Finn bounded to his feet. Ari Ara flung her arms around him. He lifted her up and spun, staggering over the uneven ground of longing, loss, and love. Their lips met in a kiss as if no time had passed, no trust had been betrayed, no hearts had been broken.

It defied belief, even in dreams. Finn froze and pulled back.

"This must be a dream," he whispered. "You're still mad at me, aren't you?"

Ari Ara laughed and cried at the same time. She had so much to say to him – too much. Her entire life had been tangled up in a web of lies that made his silence seem small by comparison. The Fanten Grandmother and *The Paika* had to bear the weight of their choices; Finn had carried them long enough. He had apologized and risked everything to make amends. When they woke, she'd sing the Atta Song with him. She was ready now.

"No," she told him hastily, "I'm not mad at you. Not anymore."

"Did you get the letter in time?" Finn blurted out, anxious. "Minli brought it to Shulen. It has the evidence. The Twins are going to poison you."

"They already did," she answered sourly.

His body tensed in shock and alarm. He clutched her.

"Oh ancestors! You're dead. This is a spirit-dream, isn't it?"

"No, no, no!" Ari Ara cut in, rushing to reassure him. "I'm still alive. I'm just stuck in dreams."

His breath shuddered raggedly in his chest. She caught his eyes and held them, shaken by how worried he looked. She flashed a grin, swift as a sparrow.

"Come on, Finn. We followers of the Way Between are not so easily killed."

A shine of relief hit Finn's dark eyes. Ari Ara basked in the sight of him, loving the feel of his warm arms around her, wishing she could linger all night. But dreams wriggled, slippery. At any moment, the connection could dissolve under the sweep of a stray thought. There was no time to waste.

"I need your help, Finn."

"Yes, of course," he answered swiftly, "anything."

"It won't be easy."

"I don't care."

"It could be dangerous."

"No matter."

"I need an herb called *perchen*, from the marsh."

She cupped her hands and opened them before him. A cluster of *perchen* bloomed in her palms. Finn studied it, examining the leaves, yellow veins, and roots. He questioned her about how it grew, and where, and what to do with it once he found it.

"You have to bring it to the Citadel," she told him. "Get them to steep the leaves into a tea and give it to me."

"I'll go to Minli. He'll convince the others," Finn assured her.

"Remember this," she pleaded. "When you wake up, remember me."

Finn's storm-tossed eyes softened. His smile curled. He kissed her gently, sweetly.

"Ari Ara," he sighed with a hint of a laugh, "how could I possibly forget you?"

CHAPTER TWENTY-SIX

. . . . .

Nshoka Shulen

Shulen was too late. As soon as the doors swung shut, he knew it. Minli clutched his arm, shouting out panic-stricken warnings. The boy's garbled story scarcely made sense. Something about Finn setting a trap for the Warrior Sister? Shulen read the letters in a daze, their significance sinking in too slowly.

A note signed by Ari Ara, hiring Finn's services.

A message in Roka Maro's handwriting: *Arrange to meet her. We'll take care of the rest.*

Then a second note: *If the ritual succeeds, your services will no longer be required.*

"Don't you see?" Minli hollered, red-faced with desperation. "She's going to try to kill Ari Ara during the blood oath! The ritual in the Sanctuary!"

With sinking horror, Shulen saw the trap as it sprung, barbed and deadly. It was sinister. It was ingenious. It was the only way the Twins of the Sisterlands would ever get a blade into Ari Ara. Armed with the Way Between, the red-headed girl could run circles around warriors. She could protect herself against any threat . . . as long as she recognized it. But, having passed the Ordeal of Queens, Ari Ara would step willingly into the clutches of the Twins. Cut off from the protection of her friends, bound by a sense of duty and ritual, she would hold out her hand to their knife.

The earth broke open beneath Shulen. He spun with the terror of nightmares, shouting warnings lost in the noise of the crowd, sprinting forward in slow motion. He slammed his shoulder into the heavy oak doors of the Sanctuary. His bones nearly broke. The wood did not budge.

Dimly, he saw Minli speak to Brinelle. The regent of Mariana did not hesitate. Shulen's alarm was evidence enough for her. She snapped into motion and ordered the doors to be opened. Then she spoke swiftly to the crowd, urging calm, quelling the uneasy stirring. Shulen hurled his body at the doors, again and again. Emir threw his weight into rhythm with his. Tahkan Shirar joined them with a roar. It was hopeless, the desperate flailing of the doomed. The Citadel had been built to withstand sieges. Mere mortals could not open those doors.

But someone did. Or something.

Shulen had no time to search for the sister or spirit who had lifted the metal latches from the inside. He hurtled into the candlelit Sanctuary without a glance for anything but the three figures in the center of the room.

Ari Ara sprawled on the ground, unmoving. The Mother Sister spun toward him, alarmed. The Warrior Sister snapped her head up with a snarl, the knife in her hand at Ari Ara's throat.

Time stopped.

Shulen crossed the room faster than sound. He dove at Roka Maro, hurling her aside, twisting the knife from her grip. Emir was at his heels, gripping Sorra Maro.

"What have you done?"

The words of Tahkan Shirar caught up with the speed of the attack. The desert man flung himself down to the stone floor, shaking his daughter, lifting her limp figure with a keening cry. Brinelle ran up, breathing hard, a look of horror on her face.

Burning laughter rang out, sharp as a sword blow, echoing off the curved ceiling of the chamber. Roka struggled against Shulen's hold, eyes wild, triumph twisting through her sneer. Shulen looked for the blood, the slice across the throat, the stab to the heart. But he saw no death wound. He repeated Tahkan's question, shaking Roka hard.

"What have you done?"

Her steely gaze froze him.

"What was necessary."

Then the scent hit him. Longal. Shulen would know that herb anywhere. It was etched into his memories of the long winter nights when Rhianne held her Fanten need for the season's deep sleep at bay through two-day bouts of longal-aided dreaming. He knew the shape of the plant's velvet leaves and the gold liquid of its tea. He still felt the sting of her hand knocking the cup from his grip when his curiosity brought it to his lips.

Lowlander, she had hissed, fear making her words ferocious, *you will die if you drink that. It is poison to your people. Only Fanten can survive it.*

Then she threw her arms around him as if the strength of her embrace could ward off such a fate.

"Longal. Poison. Deadly," he stammered to the others.

The blood drained from Brinelle's face. Longal had assassinated several of her ancestors. Tahkan's nostrils widened, sniffing. His outbreath keened in mourning. He clutched his daughter tight and rocked back and forth. Shulen saw Minli sink to the ground near his best friend, a deep frown furrowing his face as he reached for Ari Ara's hand. He tested her pulse, felt for her breath, and slid his hand to her heart. His head snapped up.

"She's still alive!"

Tahkan loosened his hold just enough to feel for her heartbeat. Hope flared like a torch across the shadowed lines of his face. Brinelle gasped in a small cry of tentative relief.

"She should be dead by now," Roka growled, furious and baffled. "Why isn't she dead?"

Shulen's heart rose like a hawk . . . and then sank like a stone.

He knew the answer to that question.

Tianne.

The scar-lined warrior looked at the prone figure of the red-headed girl from the High Mountains and knew that she was his daughter. Not Alinore's. Not Tahkan's. His. His and Rhianne's. A half-Fanten child. In her still-pulsing blood beat the ancient drums of the forest-dwelling clans. In her slow-dreaming breath sighed their secretive ways. How many hours had he and Rhianne argued about longal during her pregnancy? Shulen had feared their baby would die from her mother drinking it, but Rhianne could not carry a child to term without it.

"She will survive and be stronger for it," the Fanten woman promised. "Someday, our child may need to sleep the deep sleep with my people. Longal will prepare her to dreamwalk with us."

Rhianne never doubted she would have a daughter. She had dreamed it.

Shulen handed the Warrior Sister into Emir's keeping, calling for the Peace Force to aid him in preventing the Twins from escaping. With memory stalking in his bones, he stepped close to the daughter he thought he had lost. In a trembling voice, he murmured a few words to Tahkan and Brinelle – who did not yet know what they had just lost.

"She will live," he told them. "Probably. Possibly."

He swallowed at the uncertainty. Rhianne had navigated the

dreamrealm with the skill of her people. She'd known how to awaken on her own. She had mentioned an herb, once, that was used for weak elders who struggled to wake. Shulen did not know what it was, but they could find out. They must.

"She'll live?" Tahkan repeated, his voice cracking on hope and worry. "It is a miracle."

Shulen shook his head.

"There is an explanation," he stated with a sigh. "You will not like it."

Brinelle stiffened. A sharp breath flared in her nostrils as she guessed his meaning.

"No," she breathed, stunned.

"Yes," Shulen affirmed. "It is the only possible reason she still lives."

"What?" Tahkan cried, looking from one to the other. "What is?"

But Brinelle shook her head brusquely. Not here. Not now. They could not tell Tahkan Shirar what they suspected, not with all these eyes and ears watching. The shockwaves would topple the tenuous stability of their world. The warriors would revolt. The sisters would mutiny.

With the political astuteness born of years of regency, the Great Lady Brinelle whipped out commands and brought order into the chaos of the night. She told people only as much as they needed to know: Ari Ara had made the blood oath of queens. The Twins of the Sisterlands had attempted to poison her.

Then Brinelle sent everyone home or to the temples to pray for the girl's recovery. She put Emir Miresh in charge of guarding the Twins in the prison cells and moved Ari Ara to a bedchamber in one of the high towers of the Citadel.

The next two days seemed like an eternity. Shulen did not – could not – sleep. He and Brinelle broke the truth to Tahkan as gently as possible, knowing that there was no solace for a man who finds a long-lost daughter only to lose her forever. Shulen, the one person who could possibility understand the grief and fury that crashed through Tahkan Shirar, could offer him little comfort in the face of the sharp, seething envy that erupted in the desert man. Tahkan ran a trembling hand down the haggard lines of his face and gritted out a promise that it would pass. He knew it was not Shulen's fault.

"I – I am glad for you, Nshoka Shulen," he forced out. "She is a daughter to make any father proud."

Then he strode away before he wept in front of the Great Lady – or flung a lightning bolt at someone. Brinelle slept in fits and bursts between interrogating the Twins, maintaining order, and praying for Ari Ara to wake up safely. She would say nothing about Ari Ara's parentage until then.

"Only a few people know the truth," she cautioned Shulen on the second day. "It should stay that way until we are absolutely certain. She passed the Ordeal of Queens, Shulen. If she wants to be queen, I will back her, blood kin or not. But until Ari Ara awakens and I speak with her, I don't want the whole country up in arms over this."

In a high tower flooded with sunlight and held by stone, Shulen watched Ari Ara dream. The sweep of wind circled, hawk-like. Clouds sailed across the mountains on the western horizon. The hard wooden chair bit into his shoulders. His stillness poised, absolute, resolute, as if by motionless vigil, he could will Ari Ara's eyes to open.

The sight of Ari Ara sprawled lifeless on the floor would haunt him forever. Even now, his eyes clung to the subtle rise and fall of her breath, unable to glance away for fear it would stop. Shulen prayed ceaselessly to the ancestors, begging them to help Ari Ara wake up. All he wanted, longed for with every fiber of his being, was for her to know how much her father loved her.

He dozed off once on the second day, drifting briefly into dreaming. Rhianne came to him then, stroking his hair, placing a hand on his aching heart.

"Help is on its way," she assured him.

Then his wife tipped him back into the waking world to watch over their daughter. As he had done since the day he met her in the High Mountains.

On the third day, in the darkness before dawn, Finn Paikason hurtled into the bedchamber with a bundle of herbs in his hand, babbling about seeing Ari Ara in his dreams. Minli charged in on his heels. Forewarned by the Fanten dream, Shulen believed the youths' wild tale. He caught Finn Paikason as his legs trembled and gave out, listening as the boy wearily relayed the instructions on how to prepare the *perchen*. The old warrior crushed the leaves and steeped the greenish-yellow tea. Together, they spooned the remedy into Ari Ara's lips.

And waited.

An hour crept past.

Just outside the door, Finn sprawled across a bench, exhausted, fox cap askew, three days of racing at breakneck speed demanding its toll of rest. Minli waited next to him, reading quietly to pass the time and calm his nerves. In the bedchamber, Shulen sat still as stone, looking on as Ari Ara's breath rose and fell in slow waves and her eyes twitched beneath the lids. Whatever she dreamed now, it was not nightmares. A small smile curled on her lips and once, she startled Shulen with a breath of laughter.

Two thoughts tore at him: a ferocious yearning for her to wake up . . . and a strange, contradictory reluctance to face her as a father. Her father. He'd had so little practice. She had lost so much, so swiftly: royal blood, a lion of a father, an identity she'd worked so hard to grow into, the queenship, the lineage of the harrak-mettahl, three aunts, a cousin. What comfort could one man offer in the midst of such loss? Even if he was her father by blood and birth?

Nothing but what he'd always offered. His presence. His support. His love. Shulen hoped it would be enough.

Ari Ara made a small sound. He bolted over to the bedside. Her eyes twitched. The lashes fluttered. Shulen held his breath. She licked her dry lips. Her unfocused gaze blinked . . . then sharpened into waking.

"There you are," Shulen murmured, squeezing her hand gently, his voice constricting with emotion. He swallowed hard and composed his face, not wishing her to see his naked relief. "You had us worried there, kitten."

He hadn't used the nickname in years. Ari Ara smiled weakly, pleased to hear it. She pushed herself up to sitting, wincing at the sting of her bandaged hand. Every muscle in her body ached. Outside the open window, a faint breeze carried the scent of summer's heat over the fields of ripening grain.

"Finn came?" she asked, her voice a rasping whisper, scarcely daring to believe it true, that the dream message had worked, that he had found the herb and delivered it, that Shulen had believed and trusted him.

"Yes, he rushed day and night to get the *perchen* to you, Ari Ara. He nearly collapsed as he handed it to me."

"He got through the warriors and the guards around the Citadel?"

"As only a Paika could," Shulen acknowledged with a chuckle. "He's outside the door, snoring on a bench. Shall I call him?"

"No! Uh, let him sleep."

Ari Ara's heart tripped over its feet. She needed time, a breath of a moment at least, before she spoke with Finn. She wanted to thank him, fling her arms around him, laugh and sing the Atta

Song – both ways, for she had much to apologize to him for, too – but before she did any of that, she wanted to let her head stop spinning and her thoughts cease reeling. Everything had been turned upside down and inside out. Let Finn rest and sleep and dream for a spell while she wrestled, awake and alert, with the truth of her bloodlines . . . and the uncertainty of the looming terrain of her future.

Shulen brought her a cup of water, then hastily helped her drink it as her grip slipped. Shyness swept through her. Her courage nearly failed her, but curiosity lifted her eyes to the scarred man. Her mentor. Her teacher. Her father.

"You know, then," she murmured.

Shulen's answer took a moment.

"I think," he told her gently, "I've known since the day we met."

He just couldn't believe it. He didn't dare to hope so boldly that this fierce, strong, wild, impetuous girl was the daughter he had loved and lost once. But from the moment the eleven-year-old shepherdess in a black Fanten cloak had leapt free of everyone's grasp, twisted out of reach, and whirled with an instinctive use of the Way Between, an uncertain hope had struck a spark in his heart. That copper hair, so like his was once. Those Fanten gestures, so like Rhianne's.

And yet . . . and yet . . . there had always been another explanation. Raised by the Fanten, not born of them. The copper hair of Tahkan Shirar. The blue eyes of Alinore de Marin. The Mark of Peace on her back. The claims of the Fanten Grandmother. That midnight conversation, four years ago, in which the old woman could have told him . . . and didn't.

Ari Ara bit her bottom lip, thoughtful. Resurging energy rushed into her limbs, tingling like river water over the dry sandbar's edge. The sunlit chamber sharpened into focus as her sleep-groggy head cleared. Realizations swept through her, one after another, too swift to explain. Then one stopped all other thoughts in her head.

"Minli knew, didn't he? Who I really was?" Ari Ara realized, thinking back. "The moment I told him about my Fanten dreams."

Shulen nodded. The clever youth had figured it out before anyone else, putting the uncertainties and logic together like pieces of an intricate puzzle. Minli had come to him during their stopover in Seeker's Station, gingerly asking a disquieting question.

Had Nshoka Shulen seen the dead body of his daughter?

The old warrior had nearly barked the boy's head off with his shocked response. How dare Minli ask him such a thing!

"I . . . I just wondered if . . ." Minli tripped over his tongue as his ears burned red.

"No," Shulen growled. "No, I did not see Tianne's lifeless form, though I did in nightmares for years after her death. No, I did not dig up her bones from the tomb under the Great Tree where the Fanten Grandmother said she was buried, cradled in the arms of her mother."

And, he thought silently, *there has not been a day since the moment I first saw Ari Ara when I have not wished that she was my child and not another's.*

Minli slunk away, ashamed of causing the old warrior such pain. But the man's answer meant there was another possibility for how Ari Ara could dreamwalk.

His friend was not the double royal heir.

"It took the rest of us longer, much longer, than Minli to figure it out," Shulen said with a tired laugh that creased the age-lines by his eyes. "In the end, the Twins' longal poison proved that you were not – could not be – Alinore and Tahkan's daughter."

At the name of the desert man, Ari Ara's heart broke. The fierce and proud, hawk-nosed singer had lost his child twice over. She scarcely dared to imagine the burning storm of grief and fury Tahkan felt. She had grown to love him. He had guided her well, if not smoothly, celebrated her daring and her boldness, laughed with joy at the impetuousness that everyone else scolded her over. Tahkan Shirar may not be her father by blood, but the kinship of spirit they shared was undeniable. She could not fathom what he was feeling. Ari Ara only hoped their connection would survive, that not all would be lost on the other side of this excruciating crucible.

"Where is he?" she murmured, her eyes darting toward the window.

"Tahkan is probably pacing the halls, calling down lightning bolts on the heads of the Sisters or cursing the Fanten to the furthest reaches of the earth," Shulen relayed. He'd sent three Harraken members of the Peace Force after the man, just to keep him out of trouble. Seeing Ari Ara's stricken look, he added, "None of this is your fault."

Then it hit her.

Her mouth went dry and her lips trembled. A dam of tears broke loose. Her face scrunched up. She rolled over and buried her head in the pillow.

"What? What's wrong?" Shulen leapt to his feet, anxious. "I'll call a healer."

"No! No," she cried. "I've just – it's just that I've let everyone down. I am an imposter, like so many people said. There is no heir."

Shulen fell so silent that she knew the situation was worse than she thought.

"Well," he began, "technically, you *did* pass the Ordeal of Queens. You could claim the throne, at least the Marianan one, if you wish."

"I don't want the stupid throne!" Ari Ara burst out, frustration and worry twisting her insides in opposite corkscrews.

"You don't?"

Shulen's exhale of relief caught her by surprise. She shook her head vigorously then moaned as the room spun.

"Whoa, breathe. That's it, deep and slow."

Shulen spoke quietly. His voice anchored her like a boat in a flood surge, steadying her as he explained. Ari Ara was under no obligation to rule. She had undergone the Ordeal of Queens in good faith and sincere belief in her royal blood. And she had passed. The scar of the monarch's blood oath lay across her palm. But, Shulen told her - his voice carefully level as he tried not to impose his opinions - the choice was still hers. If she wished, she could take the throne. But when the truth came out, many people, perhaps most, would expect her to renounce her claim. If Ari Ara was innocent of this Fanten plot, they would argue, she should graciously step aside.

"Remember those two paths we spoke about?" he asked her. "We are at that crossroads. You can choose which way to go, but once you decide, there can be no turning back."

Ari Ara didn't hesitate. She'd learned a costly lesson through the Ordeal of Queens. The power that clung to the throne came with a price. She was not willing to pay it. She wanted to be like Alaren, free to work for peace in the cities and farms, mountains and valleys, riverlands and desertlands. Images of the ancient founder of the Way Between swept through her. Lanky, tall, and stork-like, he strode across mountains in pursuit of peace, rallying people across borders, stalling wars, blockading armies, building friendships, and restoring trust. She'd read his stories, studied his practices, followed *azar* with all of her heart. She wanted to walk in his footsteps with her head held high, her heart clear as the blue sky, her friends at her side.

And her father. Nshoka Shulen had promised to walk with her, no matter where the road took them. With a flood of emotion, Ari Ara realized that she'd rather be his daughter than claim any of the crowns in the world.

"I don't want the throne," she told him, the clarity of ice-cold mountain streams in her voice.

"You're sure?" he asked gently, sensing the weight of this choice with more gravity than she could imagine.

Long sweeps of history curved through this moment, ancient lineages and hidden stories, prophecies and fate. The course of time's river would bend around this decision. And there was one last secret he knew that she didn't. It was something. It was nothing. It was irrelevant in the end. Shulen considered telling her, but caught back the words before his breath carried them past his lips. Ari Ara did not need to be burdened with this. Let her choose her life's path without the pressure of thousands of years and countless generations weighing on her. She was scarcely more than a child, one who had endured and survived so much and given so generously to the world. Shulen shoved back the pinprickle presence of spirits so Ari Ara could make one choice for herself.

"Yes," she said decisively. "I'm sure. I want to be like Alaren."

Tear sprang to Shulen's eyes. She was so much like the ancient ancestor. In heart, in spirit, in thought and deed, she was an honor to the man. Alaren, too, had refused to claim the throne. Instead, he embraced the whole world as his home. The Third Brother had always insisted that his lineage would be passed through knowledge, not parentage.

A tired smile flitted across Shulen's face. He would tell her this last secret someday, just not today when her head still spun from poison and her heart still reeled. They would have time now, the two of them. Shulen rubbed his weary eyes. He felt like he could sleep for days . . . but he didn't want to miss a single minute of Ari Ara's life.

And what a life it would be.

A sunlit silence fell as father and daughter sensed horizons opening in all directions, vast as river marshes and desert skies. She could rejoin the Peace Force and travel the world, working for peace. She could learn about the Fanten, study with Shulen, live in the east or the west, in the mountains or in between. Like a hawk on the wind, Ari Ara's life could soar to the heights of the clouds or dive deep into forested valleys. Anything was possible. Anything could happen.

Shulen saw his daughter glimpse the wide expanse of her potential. A small laugh touched her heart, lifted by relief over having been released from the pressures of being the royal heir. His weathered gaze caught the spark of wild thrill surging in Ari Ara's eyes. Suddenly he saw her – the Ari Ara he'd missed over these long months, the girl from the High Mountains, the shepherdess who ran full tilt into adventure, who stood brazenly on one foot on an ancestor pillar all day, who leapt like a cat through matches and trainings. He saw the rulebreaker who climbed out the window and clambered over rooftops, who danced with street urchins and played with orphans, who sang with desert women and called the ancestor spirits from the wind. He saw the peacemaker who stood between armies and rose up for change.

He and Rhianne had called her by one name, but fate had given her another, a perfect name, a challenge, a mystery, a vision, a destiny. A name like none other for a girl like no other.

Ari Ara, not this, not that, but everything possible in between.

With a determined set of her chin, she pushed her tangle of red curls off her face and flung back the covers. The Great Lady

Brinelle had held back the earthquake of the truth long enough. The people deserved to know. The world was racing in unknown directions. The fate of nations had been turned upside down. The echoes of prophecies rumbled thunderously around them. The course of history hung poised in uncertainty.

Ari Ara couldn't wait to see what came next.

"Help me up," she asked Shulen when the strength of her will out-stripped the abilities of her trembling limbs.

Shulen gripped her hand. She swung her feet to the floor.

"We may never know what the day will bring," she murmured, the old saying stirring in her heart like a prayer, a promise, and a prophecy.

Shulen's voice threaded with hers, finishing the words together.

"But we can always rise to greet it."

Her knees shook, but she straightened to standing. With her father at her side, Ari Ara took the first steps toward the door.

She was alive.

She was awake.

And it was time to let the world know who she was.

AUTHOR'S NOTE

I remember lying on my stomach by the fireplace during a snowstorm in the high-altitude desert of New Mexico, scribbling down notes on a fantasy series with a main character named Ari Ara. According to the notes in that dog-eared journal, that magical blizzard of winter weather and story inspiration occurred twelve years ago. In the margin, tucked inside a red-inked box, were the notes on the plot twist that would grow into *River Dragon's* central story.

So much about the series has shifted and grown as I've written each book. Plot lines have twisted and unraveled. Peace practices have demanded inclusion. Nonviolent actions have eagerly crowded into unexpected places. Names have changed (Korin was named Jym in one version; Nshoka Shulen only received a first name last year). New characters swaggered into scenes and stole the show (ahem, Tala, Rill, Moragh). Even *River Dragon* went through countless changes of scenery (in the first draft, it took place in Mariana Capital) and cycled through several titles (some unbelievably cheesy).

But two things stayed consistent through it all:

Ari Ara was going to learn who she was.

And she was going to collide with Mariana's war culture.

The two are entwined, of course. Beyond blood or birth, Ari Ara's essential character is committed to peace. A confrontation with Mariana's war culture was inevitable. The collision of worldviews loomed like a brewing storm all through her exile in *Desert Song*. It rumbled on the horizon of her journeys with the Peace Force in *The Crown of Light*. I knew she'd someday return to the riverlands and run smack into conflict with the nation's warmongers. From the nobles to the warriors, Marianans can't help but scratch their heads over the fact that their next queen – who is supposed to be the political leader of the military – is a follower the Way Between, and outspokenly anti-war.

As soon as she returns, Ari Ara is thrust into a series of tests to see if she's ready to ascend the throne. Although the Ordeal of Queens is an elaborate spiritual and political ritual, there are plenty of echoes of this kind of grueling test in our real world. Disguised in ordinariness, they're things like final exams, college applications, job interviews, relationship troubles, moral quandaries in our workplaces, problems with friends. Each one tests us on the content of our character and the depth of our souls. We rise to each challenge, sometimes stumblingly, sometimes magnificently.

But then comes a situation in which the world (or society or your boss) expects you to sacrifice a little bit of your integrity in order to get ahead. Cheat on a test. Pad your resume. Tell a little lie. Mislead someone. Say nothing in the face of wrongdoing. Look away from injustice.

Dr. Martin Luther King, Jr. once said, "Our lives begin to end the day we become silent about things that matter."

This kind of silence slowly suffocates our souls and extinguishes our humanity. To reignite it, we must do something very brave. We have to take a risk and make a stand.

For Ari Ara, the troubling situation unfolds amidst Mariana's war culture. In order to move her two countries toward peace, she feels she must take up her duties as queen. But in order to become queen, she has to honor the very war culture she dislikes. Little by little, Ari Ara finds herself sacrificing the qualities that would make her worthy of being queen: honesty, integrity, and her commitment to peace.

River Dragon is a story of how she finds the deep courage to risk everything to be true to what she believes. It's not about battling the enemy on the border. It's about confronting the dangers that lurk within it, even within ourselves. When your culture, nation, and people become obsessed with war, it takes fierce inner strength to say that's not okay. It's not okay that religious figures bless the fighters, not the peacemakers. It's not okay when violence is seen as 'entertainment'. It's not okay when children are recruited into militaries because they have no other options for their futures. It's not okay that some people get rich making weapons while others die in unjust wars. It's not okay that so much money is spent on war and hardly anything is spent on peace.

But when these things become 'normal', it's also not okay that our friends, families, teachers, and political leaders say nothing. We will never have peace if we stay silent about the ways our culture is becoming obsessed, even addicted, to violence and war.

Ari Ara knows that another way is possible - the Way Between. And because she knows that her two peoples can solve their problems without killing each other, she also knows that she has to help them learn the skills and practices of waging peace.

It takes courage to change a culture. Ari Ara finds this courage through her connection to the Way Between, the stories she's learned, her mother's journal, her mentorship with Shulen, and the support of her friends.

What will you draw courage from?

I hope these books, and their growing circle of readers, can give you this courage. So many stories - in print and on screens - make it seem like violence is necessary (it isn't), that it's the only option (it's not), and that it's exciting (it's terrifying and painful). War is not noble or heroic. It's tragic. It's a sign of failure when war breaks out. It means that we failed to resolve our differences with creativity, compassion, inventiveness, and a sense of justice for all, not just for some.

But when we do what is right, when we speak what is true, I believe it sets in motion the great gearworks of the universe. And, no matter how winding the path, how long the journey, and how twisting the road, it takes the world in the direction of peace and justice.

If Ari Ara can stand up to war culture, so can we. If she can speak up for a culture of peace, so can we. If she can build a world beyond war, so can we.

River Dragon is a story that shows, ultimately, that all of us have power, from an orphan shepherdess to a young queen to everyday people.

Including you. Use your power to wage peace.

Rivera Sun

ACKNOWLEDGMENTS

Ari Ara has good friends on her great adventures . . . and so do I. *River Dragon* is a vastly better book because of the loving support showered on me over this lengthy writing journey. Midway through writing the rough draft, I moved from New Mexico to my family's home in Northern Maine. The land of Skylandia Farm cradled me kindly as I stalked the meadows and forests in search of the perfect plot twist or the secret to unsnarling my literary tangles. Thank you.

Cindy Reinhardt, Jenny Bird, Brooke Storry, and Marada Cook gave me invaluable feedback, both enthusiastic and constructive. From titles to tangled plot lines, they strengthened the novel immeasurably. David L. re-energized my creativity by inventing languages with me, nudging me to give characters first and last names, and dreaming into this world together. Seth Fishman pushed me to make precision edits like a surgeon, a skill I've used over and over again. Thank you to all of you for helping the craft of my writing deepen.

To my peace-waging friends and colleagues: you have my admiration, respect, and gratitude for your courage in opposing war, embodying nonviolence, and persistently making peace a little more possible in our world. This book is inspired by you. Keep going.

My life partner, Dariel Garner, has been integral to this book at every stage, from listening to rants and rambles to reading eight drafts. He cooked food when I came up for air from a writing session, ravenous, and reminded me that I always think I'll never finish . . . just before I do. You have my deepest gratitude for all the ways you make these stories possible and my life more interesting along the way.

Lastly, I want to thank the readers. You've been magnificently patient - and enthusiastically impatient - as you waited for this book. Thank you for sending me Ari Ara drawings and notes about how much you love these novels. Thank you for organizing book groups and virtual author talks, for adding the Ari Ara Series to library shelves and school curriculums, and for raving about the novels to friends, grandkids, and random strangers. Your enthusiasm is the fuel that keeps my pencil scribbling across the page.

With gratitude for you all,
Rivera Sun

ABOUT THE AUTHOR

Rivera Sun is the author of the award-winning Ari Ara Series, *The Dandelion Trilogy,* and several other novels, as well as theatrical plays, poetry, a study guide to nonviolent action, and numerous articles. She went to Bennington College to study writing as a Harcourt Scholar and graduated with a degree in dance. She is a trainer in strategy for nonviolent movements and an activist. Rivera has been an aerial dancer, a bike messenger, and a blacksmith's apprentice. She lives on her family's organic farm in Maine and weeds the vegetable garden while working out her plot lines.

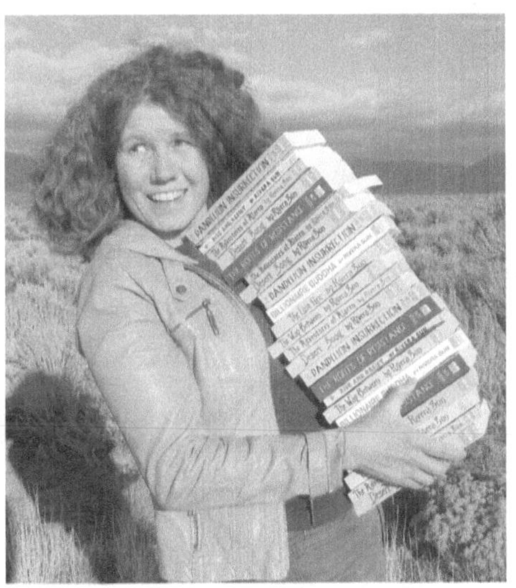

Rivera Sun also loves hearing from her readers:

Email: info@riverasun.com

Facebook: Rivera Sun

Twitter: @RiveraSunAuthor

Read all of the adventures in the Ari Ara Series!

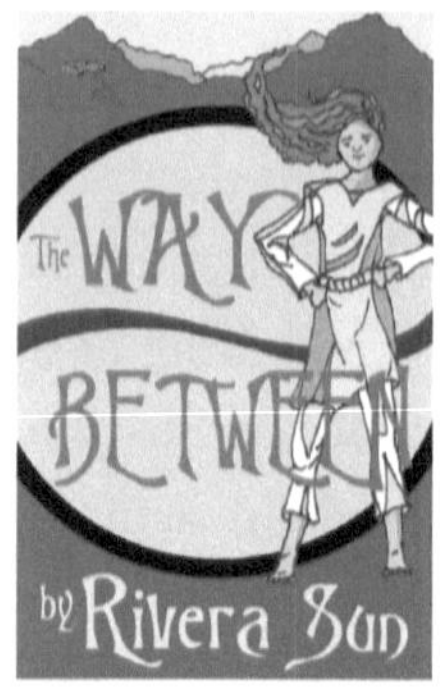

The Way Between

Between flight and fight lies a mysterious third path called *The Way Between,* and young shepherdess and orphan Ari Ara must master it . . . before war destroys everything she loves! She begins training as the apprentice of the great warrior Shulen, and enters a world of warriors and secrets, swords and magic, friendship and mystery.

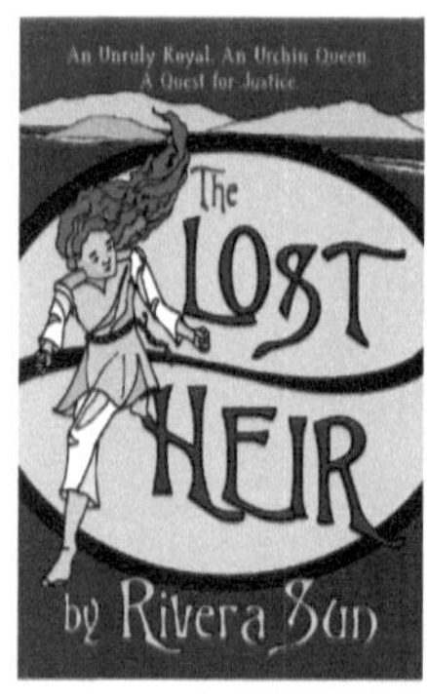

The Lost Heir

Going beyond dragon-slayers and sword-swingers, *The Lost Heir* blends fantasy and adventure with social justice issues in an unstoppable story that will make you cheer! Mariana Capital is in an uproar. The splendor of the city dazzles Ari Ara until she makes a shocking discovery . . . the luxury of the nobles is built by the forced labor of the desert people.

Desert Song

Exiled to the desert, Ari Ara is thrust between the warriors trying to grab power . . . and the women rising up to stop them! Every step she takes propels her deeper into trouble: her trickster horse bolts, her friend is left for dead, and Ari Ara has to run away to save him. But time is running out - can she find him before it's too late?

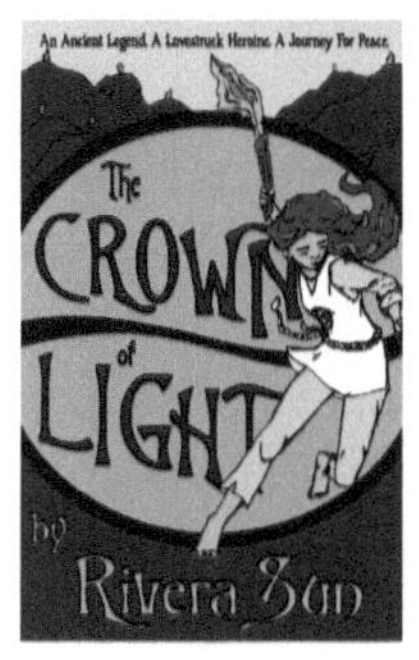

The Crown of Light

In the jagged peaks of the Border Mountains, Ari Ara revives the ancient legend of the Peace Force, gathering friends and strangers to stop violence and prevent war. When the Lost Heir is taken hostage, the Peace Force races to solve the mystery before the sparks of violence erupt into a raging inferno of war.

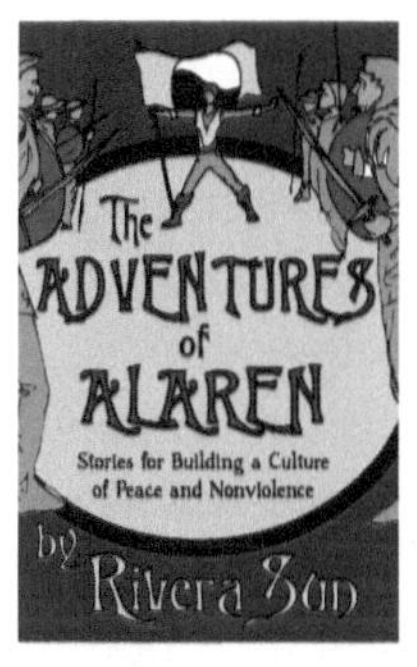

The Adventures of Alaren

In a series of clever and creative escapades, Alaren, the legendary folkhero of Ari Ara's world, rallies thousands of people to take bold and courageous action for peace. Each fictional folktale includes a footnote on the real-life inspiration and discussion questions for classrooms and small groups. For readers of all ages, *The Adventures of Alaren* opens minds and gives us ideas for waging peace!

"The entire Ari Ara Series offers students a warm, exciting, and hopeful adventure, full of problem-solving, love of life, and worthy models of personal growth and peacemaking."
– Scott Springer, teacher at The Bay School

"To read the tales of Alaren is to be opened to a world of creative solutions to seemingly insurmountable challenges. Each tale is inspired by a successful nonviolent action in real life, reminding us of what's possible when we are committed to nonviolence and willing to be bold and brave in our actions." **– Leah Boyd**

More Praise For the Award–Winning Ari Ara Series

"In this book, Rivera Sun pulls off an impressive feat, creating an original exciting story that deftly teaches ways to create a world that works for all. Thank you, Rivera Sun, for another outstanding contribution to the field of nonviolence through this series!" **–Kit Miller, former Executive Director, M.K. Gandhi Institute for Nonviolence**

"I can think of no better source of inspiration for (the topics of peace and social justice) than the Ari Ara series by Rivera Sun."
– Dr. Seán P. Duffy, Executive Director, Albert Schweitzer Institute, Quinnipiac University

"This series contains everything ... a heroic female protagonist, colorful supporting characters, adventure, suspense, and most importantly, nonviolence used as a means to solve conflicts. I highly recommend the Ari Ara Series to educators and students!"
– Robin Wildman, Nonviolent Schools Rhode Island

"I have been in youth work forty-five years, and I have never encountered a more important work than the Ari Ara series to share with young people and their advocates."
– Reverend Michael Harrington

"Ari Ara is the bedtime reading adventure for younger generations that completes my circle of peace literature."
– Patrick Hiller, father, bed-time story reader, Peace and Conflict Studies scholar

"An amazing family read, and one that we will return to again and again. Thank you for bringing these characters and stories into our lives and imaginations!" **– the Palatucci Family**

"Rivera Sun has done it again. She just keeps getting better and better at weaving powerful stories to remind us that courage, determination, vision, and a taste for high adventure, are all essential elements for waging real peace." – **Rosa Zubizarreta, DiaPraxis founder and Co-intelligence Institute Senior Advisor**

"Rivera Sun is an amazing author. The way she threads the principles of nonviolence into the fabric of her novels is a beautiful experience. It is an education that everyone in the world needs – now more than ever." **–Heart Phoenix, River Phoenix Center for Peacebuilding**

"Rivera Sun's creativity, wisdom, insight and joyful nonviolent activism for all ages fills me with awe and hope. If we were all to read her books the way we have read Harry Potter's, we would be well on our way to sending a different message to our children."

– Veronica Pelicaric,

Pace e Bene/Campaign Nonviolence

"A beautiful story that expands the imagination into the possibilities of peace and active nonviolence ... this book will prepare our children and ourselves for the real-life world we so desperately need." – **David Hartsough, Co–founder of Nonviolent Peaceforce, author of Waging Peace**

"Generations of young adults will be helped to find this way in the adventures of Ari Ara ... and we will all be so greatly in Rivera's debt." – **Michael Nagler, Founder of Metta Center, author of Search for a Nonviolent Future**

Discover more at:
www.riverasun.com

Find your next great book.
Read essays and excerpts.
Check out behind-the-scenes stories.
Hear about new releases.
Join an upcoming book club.
Sign up for Rivera Sun's fun and personal newsletter.

Love this book? Tell a friend!

Most readers discover the Ari Ara Series when a friend tells them about it. Spread the word among your family, friends, and fellow readers, in-person or on social media. Ask the librarians at your school and public libraries to put the series on the shelves.

www.ingramcontent.com/pod-product-compliance
Lightning Source LLC
Chambersburg PA
CBHW032242010726
47494CB00002B/589

* 9 7 8 1 9 4 8 0 1 6 2 3 0 *